KATHERINE STONE
THIEF of HEARTS

WARNER
VISION
BOOKS

A Time Warner Company

WARNER BOOKS EDITION

Copyright © 1999 by Katherine Stone

Cover design by Andrew Newman
Cover art by Franco Accornero

Warner Books, Inc.
1271 Avenue of the Americas
New York, NY 10020

Visit our Web site at
www.twbookmark.com

W A Time Warner Company

Printed in the United States of America

First Paperback Printing: July 2000

10 9 8 7 6 5 4 3 2 1

CAITLIN WAS IN THE PRESENCE
OF AN ALARMINGLY SEXUAL CREATURE. . . .

He was moving toward her now, a powerful gait of predatory grace, and at last she saw his eyes. They blazed with a dark green fire, a glittering inferno that sent both warning and promise. Like his own fictional hero, this man was dangerous, and he could be cruel. He was separated from sheer villainy by the most slender of threads.

The stealthy prowl halted a short yet generous distance from her, not crowding her, not invading her space—at least, not physically.

Jesse Falcober did not smile. But he did speak. And his words, low and deep, felt oddly protective.

"Let's get you out of the rain. . . ."

BOOKS BY KATHERINE STONE

Imagine Love

Pearl Moon

Happy Endings

Illusions

Promises

Rainbows

Love Songs

Bel Air

Twins

The Carlton Club

Roommates

Bed of Roses

Home at Last

Island of Dreams

A Midnight Clear

THIEF of
HEARTS

PROLOGUE

LOS ANGELES
APRIL TWENTY-FOURTH
EIGHTEEN YEARS AGO

My darling Caitlin,

Today is your sixteenth birthday. How grown-up you are. How *mature*. And yet, sweet girl, in matters of love—romantic love, that is—you are quite innocent. Which is lovely, the way it should be.

It is your lovely innocence that compels me to write rather than speak my confession of romantic love. Someday, I pray, I will speak these words to you. When you are forty-six perhaps, and I am eighty? What a splendid dream to have had all those years together. But I won't live to be eighty. We both know that. My heart grows weaker with each passing day.

*And tonight I feel such urgency about writing this confession, as if—*Margaret Taylor halted the anguished thought, drew a difficult breath, and willed her trembling fingers to be calm as she wrote anew.

My will to live is not fading, despite the weakness of my heart. If determination were enough, if love were enough, I would be with you always. I *will* be with you, Caitie-love. *Always.*

My confession is about your father. I have told you, quite truthfully, that we knew each other only briefly and that he never knew about you. But I have misled you greatly about our feelings for one another. I have said that there wasn't enough love for the three of us to be a family. And that, my darling, could not be farther from the truth.

You have accepted the truth, and the lie, without distress, and I wonder if I should just let it go. But as my heart grows weaker it becomes oddly stronger as well. You need to know this, Caitlin. You need to know about the love.

Your father and I met aboard the *Queen Elizabeth* during the transatlantic crossing from Southampton to New York. He was younger than I, and so handsome. And although it was of no consequence to me (but of consequence nonetheless) he was infinitely wealthy as well.

That sounds like a fairy tale, doesn't it? The dashing aristocrat and the thirty-four-year-old spinster. Cinderella and her prince. I wasn't truly Cinderella, of course. No wicked stepsisters had tormented me. There had been no wickedness at all, only love, and my own fairy godmother, your great-aunt Caitlin.

Your father's life, too, had been filled with love. But for him, a child of privilege, there was the heavy mantle of responsibility, of choices that were not his. He was a musician, Caitlin, so *gifted*. At dawn in the Grand Ballroom, he played the piano and sang to me. He would have shared his wondrous talent with the world had not fate intervened.

It was an extraordinary fate, for at the same time my life was shattered by the passing of your great-aunt, his world was shattered by his brother's death. He had to soldier on, supporting his parents emotionally even as he assumed the weighty obligations of their wealth. *He* was the heir now. *He* had to carry on the family name. He did all that and something else, yet another filial duty. He married his brother's fiancée.

Yes, he was married. (And prepare yourself, my darling, for there is even more.) The fact of his marriage will upset you whether you are sixteen or forty-six. You are so principled, my sweeting. But so am I. *And so was he.* What we did was wrong. But it was also terribly right. After all, my love, it gave me you.

Shall I tell you that the rules change at sea? That it is a magical world unto itself? Yes, I shall—and more. Love changes the rules, Caitlin. Right or wrong, love changes everything.

And we did love each other.

I was traveling to America to begin my new life, and he was journeying to New York on business. But his parents, quite aware of the toll the past six months had taken, gave him the leisurely ocean voyage as a belated honeymoon. Needless to say, his wife did not make the trip. Even the most gently rolling waves would have been too much to bear in her condition.

Yes, my love, she was pregnant.

There was so much to explain, to reveal: the betrothed's solemn decision, made even before they were wed, to postpone starting their family; the husband's fury at his wife's betrayal of that pledge; his quiet apology to her just before setting sail. The explanations fluttered in

Margaret's mind as her heart beat frantically in her chest. *I haven't the strength for such revelations now. They will come later, when I am eighty. . . .*

Your father was sailing first-class and I was "transatlantic"—a grand euphemism for steerage. Transatlantic passengers were permitted only in certain areas and were expressly prohibited from ascending to the decks reserved for the monied elite. Similarly, first-class passengers were discouraged from descending to our humble depths. No one dared stop *him,* however, when he made his way through the barriers.

He was seeking privacy, I suppose, or wandering in a trance. Or maybe, Caitlin, it was destiny that we meet beneath the moon on the deck near my tiny closet.

He was spectacular, and I was quite plain. Just me. Or perhaps I was beautiful then. Perhaps the moonbeams sprinkled me with a magical golden dust. I felt beautiful, and his eyes, my only mirror during that enchanted time, told me I was the most fascinating creature he had ever seen.

I was his Maggie. Can you imagine such a nickname for me?

We knew from the first that our time at sea was all we were meant to have. His affection for his wife would blossom into a certain kind of love, and they would remain married, and he would be faithful. Faithful? I hear your astonished echo. How is such a prediction possible when he was *un*faithful within months of his wedding and within days of learning that his wife—his bride—was pregnant?

Because, my sweet Caitlin, your father is an honorable man. A *wonderful* man.

The rules change at sea, my darling. But they are not forgotten. He felt great guilt about our illicit love. But he could not resist. Nor could I. Indeed I was quite shameless. If I could love him again, I would. Again and again. Without a whisper of remorse.

You are so like him, my Caitie. Your seriousness of purpose, your quiet dignity, your lovely heart. And, of course, you look like him. I know you believe that you and I look alike. There is *some* resemblance, and I cherish it. But you are so striking, so elegant, an inheritance that comes entirely from him. You've inherited his eyes, that rare, dark, ocean blue; and his aristocratic bones, delicate in you, strong in him, yet oddly the same; and his hair, as black as the midnight sky.

We have neither seen nor spoken to each other since our ship of love docked in New York. Such finality was not what he wanted. Even though our affair had ended, must end, he wanted to know about my life, my welfare. I wouldn't permit it.

I wouldn't, Caitlin. As a result, he never knew about you.

What torment it would have been for him had he known. Torment and joy. Margaret closed her eyes, needing rest, needing remembrance, needing to believe she was right never to have told him the truth. Images flooded her mind, a potpourri of happiness, her love—with him—at sea, her life—on land—with their daughter. It had been a modest life, but rich with love. *Yet there is that other richness I have always wished for my Caitie: a brother, to love, to admire, to trust.* It was an impossible wish, Margaret knew, for she could never love another man. As she opened her eyes, a soft smile touched her lips. Her own girlhood had been devoid of men, far more sheltered even than Caitlin's. *And still I found him.*

My heart, damaged since childhood, faltered slightly before your birth. But a rope of pearls, a gift from your father, came to the rescue. Purchased at the Castille boutique aboard ship, the necklace was a symbol of our love, priceless in a way that had nothing to do with its true value—which was immense I discovered when I sold it to the Castille jeweler on Rodeo Drive.

The money stood us in good stead long after you were born. Indeed it was so bountiful that I permitted myself one small indulgence, a strand of costume pearls. I bought the shortest length that would encircle my neck, a far cry from the rope your father had given me. But those painted glass beads became the flawless pearls, a treasured symbol of his love.

Today I gave you those false but priceless beads, a birthday gift from me to you, from *him* to you. You love them, don't you, Caitie? You sense how special they are.

You are the daughter of a glorious love. That splendor is your legacy, Caitlin, a fortune more valuable than all the riches on earth. You will find passion, my darling, and when you are transported by its magic you will understand what I have written, that love changes all the rules—and that, for love, all risks are worth taking.

I have not told you your father's name. It's not a mistake, an oversight caused by the fatigue that overwhelms me despite the wishes of my heart. You have no need to know his name. You need only to know that he would have loved you as I have.

You can't find him, Caitie-love. Please don't try. Even you, my bright little scientist, cannot solve this mystery. Our ship of love exists no more. She burned to the sea in Hong Kong.

Only the love lives still. You, my precious girl, are its treasure and its proof.

What's happening? The frantic query came with ice-cold fright. Margaret's heart fluttered wildly, and there wasn't nearly enough air. Her trembling hand flew to her throat, seeking solace, the familiar comfort of her beloved pearls. But her neck was naked, save for icy dampness and a racing pulse.

But then, oh then, she felt warmth, a strong and tender hand upon her own, and by magic, the magic of him, her heartbeats became steady and sure. And she could breathe, easily, effortlessly. She inhaled the fragrance of lilacs, the perfume of her scented candle, and now that fragrant column was filling the air with its pastel hue . . . and in the shimmering lavender mist she saw him.

Him. His ocean blue eyes glistened with happiness, for he knew about his daughter at last. Happiness and love.

Dance with me, my Maggie, he whispered. And she whispered in reply, Yes. *Yes.* We shall dance beneath the moon, a waltz as gentle as the waves in a slumbering sea. But first, and together, we must finish this letter to our precious girl.

Never forget, my Caitlin, that I am with you, that *we* are with you, loving you always. *Alw—*

ONE

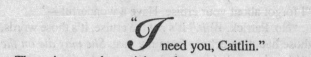 need you, Caitlin."

The voice was deep, rich, male.

An astonishing voice speaking astonishing words.

"Caitlin?" An edge of worry sharpened the voice before a whisper of apology softened it anew. "It's Patrick."

The gossamer web of dreams vanished and—despite the ambient darkness—reality became crystal clear. She was alone in her bed. The clock on her nightstand glowed 12:15. And pressed to her ear was her telephone, answered even from the deepest of sleep.

"Patrick," she echoed. "I was asleep."

"Really asleep."

It was permissible to sleep, really sleep, especially when one was not on call. Still . . .

"I guess so," she murmured. "You have a patient for me?"

"I do. A young woman stabbed by her lover. She may die on the table, Caitlin. She probably will. But it's an absolute certainty she'll die if we don't operate."

Patrick paused for the expected reply: I'm on my way. In fact he was surprised Caitlin hadn't interrupted his succinct recounting of the case.

But Caitlin had not interrupted, and she was silent still.

Had she drifted back to sleep? Had her body—chronically deprived of sleep, starved of it—finally rebelled?

No, Patrick realized with a jolt. It was something else, something he had known, something so important that the surgeon who had always been there when Patrick needed her, when a patient needed her, was silent now. Conflicted. Thanks to him. Apology returned to his voice. "I forgot about your cruise. Have a wonderful—"

"No, Patrick. *Wait.*" It's not the cruise, it's those words, those haunting echoes from my past. *She may die on the table, she probably will, but it's an absolute certainty she'll die if we don't operate.* Then as now the words had been spoken doctor to doctor. The girl who had been clutching her mother's ice-cold hand was not supposed to have heard. But she *had,* and now she was hearing the words again.

The solemn assertion that death was inevitable without surgery was hardly unique. Dr. Caitlin Taylor had made such grave pronouncements herself, many times. But on this night, when her thoughts, and perhaps her dreams, had already begun the emotional journey into her past . . .

"I'll be right there, Patrick."

"Caitlin—"

"I'm on my way."

*E*ven in the middle of the night pertinent information was recorded on the operating-room chalkboard. The data appeared in a prelabeled grid, in spaces allocated for the patient's name, age, and sex, the surgeons, the anesthesiologist, and the pre-op diagnosis.

MSWs, the board read. Multiple Stab Wounds, transcribed in aquamarine chalk. And also in aquamarine, *?Hepatic Lac?*

The patient in question, the only one listed on the board, was a twenty-six-year-old female. And the surgeons, whose names appeared in crimson, were Falconer and Taylor.

"Caitlin. Good. You're here. Patrick's scrubbing."

Caitlin turned toward the OR charge nurse. "And the patient, Jonathan?"

"She's hanging in there. Barely."

"Is she on bypass yet?"

"Bypass? Why?"

"I . . . doesn't she have a heart wound?"

"No. Believe me, Caitlin, she has enough problems without that."

Had Patrick been wrong? Not likely. A knife wound to the heart was far from subtle—and definitely memorable. Hollywood horror films notwithstanding, such wounds were vanishingly rare. The heart was, after all, encased within a wall of muscle and bone, easily penetrable by a bullet but an unusual venue for a knife.

Not that knives didn't kill. They did. All the time. They were the weapon of choice when intimacy was desired, when a murderous rage could be sated only by the gush of blood and the shredding of flesh—vulnerable flesh, yielding flesh . . . the startlingly fragile expanse of a throat or the flimsy armor of the belly.

It was not surprising that a stabbing victim would have as her most worrisome pre-op diagnosis the one offered in aquamarine chalk: *hepatic lac,* a laceration of the liver. But surely Patrick had known that when he called.

So why call *her?* Caitlin Michaela Taylor was a heart surgeon. Period.

Patrick knew that, too.

Patrick . . . Dr. Patrick Falconer. The sable-haired, blue-eyed trauma surgeon was the stuff of dreams, of other women's dreams. Caitlin and Patrick were friends, and more—something which filled her with a deep and quiet joy. Then and still. Then . . . that long-ago night in Boston, that snowy evening of secrets and champagne, when Patrick invited her to become the little sister he'd never had. And still . . . now.

Now Caitlin's surrogate older brother stood before an OR sink, scrubbing, a task which he, like all experienced surgeons, could perform virtually in his sleep. The methodical cleansing of fingernails, hands, and forearms did not require sight; which was just as well, for at this moment Patrick's dark blue eyes were focused beyond the sink to the room where the patient—their patient?—was being draped and prepped.

"Hi," Caitlin greeted.

Patrick did not relinquish his watchful gaze. "Hi. I didn't get a chance to thank you, Caitlin, or to assure you that you will make your cruise. Once we're in, if it looks like we're talking hours, I'll have Jonathan call Gregg."

So why didn't you call Gregg in the first place? Caitlin wondered as she, too, began to scrub. Her silent musing might have become an audible one had her thoughts not been abruptly halted by a glimpse of Patrick's arms. Beneath the golden froth of iodine-tinted soap his skin was the color of chalk. Surely the pallor was an illusion, a false impression created by the exuberant bubbles of gold.

But Patrick's face and neck were equally pale, as was the triangle of chest exposed by the scrub shirt's deep V.

"*Patrick.* You're white as a ghost."

"With a tincture of green? Food poisoning, Caitlin. Something très LA. Alfalfa sprouts, maybe."

"Should you be operating?"

Patrick's gaze remained straight ahead, but Caitlin saw the muscles ripple in his strong jaw. "You mean is it safe for the patient? I wouldn't be operating if it weren't. You should know that, Caitlin."

"I *do* know that. Of course I do. I meant *for you.* Should you be operating? Shouldn't you be home in bed?"

"I'm fine." Patrick Falconer smiled a ghost of a smile. A ghost's smile. "Besides, I've stacked the deck in favor of both the patient and myself by calling you."

"Just because *you're* boarded in both hearts and trauma doesn't mean everyone is so versatile. I'm a heart surgeon, Patrick. It's been years—"

"Since we scrubbed on a case like this?"

"Yes." *A case like this.* There *had* been such cases, once. Caitlin still remembered her stunned query the first time she and Patrick had operated on a victim of domestic violence. Her husband did this to her? And Caitlin recalled, still, Patrick's reply, the solemnity of his words, and the utter absence of ridicule for her naïveté. It seems, he had said, that it's the people you love most who can inflict the greatest pain.

"A few years, Caitlin. I'm quite sure you haven't lost your touch."

Her touch? It had always been Patrick's touch, the decisiveness of his agile fingers, their exquisite grace. He had led and she had followed, and when at last they had gone their separate ways, Caitlin had felt quivers of panic.

But the maestro had taught his student well. Caitlin had become a virtuoso in her own right.

Now they were together again, Patrick as trauma chief, she as queen of hearts. And now, on the eve of her personal journey into the past, Patrick was asking her to make such a professional journey as well.

I'm going to need some guidance, Patrick.

But the master was silent, as if his quiet assertion— "I'm quite sure you haven't lost your touch"—had said it all.

"The major concern is her liver?" Caitlin prompted.

Patrick frowned. "It's not my major concern. But, Caitlin, mine's a minority opinion." His frown deepened, coursing his stark white face with night black shadows. "Maybe the food poisoning is affecting my brain."

"I doubt that." *You wouldn't let it.* "So you're worried about . . . ?"

"Her spleen. She has numerous right-upper-quadrant lacs—thus the concern about her liver—but there's a left-sided wound as well. It's more puncture than laceration and could be a taunting wound from the knife. That's what everyone who saw her in the ER believes it to be."

"Everyone but you."

"I wonder if there was a second weapon, an ice pick maybe. And although it's a very soft call, especially in a shocky patient, to my exam she's rigid over the spleen."

"So you think the left-sided wound is the most significant."

"I do."

Then so do I. Was it an irrational conviction? The pupil ever loyal to her teacher? The little sister blinded by admiration for her older, wiser brother—despite his admission that his findings were "soft" and that some food-borne toxin had, quite possibly, rendered him less astute than usual?

Caitlin would not have the luxury of performing her own exam. Already the patient lay beneath a shroud of sterile drapes, intubated, anesthetized, and connected to monitors that gave graphic testimony to the precariousness with which she clung to life. Blood transfusions poured into her veins, as did pressure medications so potent that they were designed to be dripped, not gushed.

The chance for Caitlin to cast an informed vote regarding which quadrant to explore first had long since passed. And, she knew, the correct choice would not be immediately apparent once they got in.

A lake of blood. That was all they would see. And there would be no clue at the lake's surface, no rhythmic rippling from a severed artery in the scarlet depths. The patient's blood pressure was far too low. Even the most distressed signal from the most frantic pulse would be too weak to bubble through the thick layers of blood.

They would have to go by feel not by sight, like rescuers diving into murky waters in the hope of saving a swimmer who was not quite drowned, racing against an invisible clock that relentlessly ticked away the remaining minutes—or perhaps seconds—of that drowning victim's life.

Such divers had no prior knowledge of the watery depths into which they plunged. They merely guessed which way to swim, to grope, to hope. But Caitlin and Patrick were intimately familiar with the structures submerged in their crimson lake. Their guess would be an educated one, based on years of experience.

Patrick's experience told him that the wound that had sent the invisible clock ticking toward death was a laceration of the spleen—a conclusion that was at odds with Westwood Memorial's ER docs.

Could both quadrants be explored? Could their hands swim left *and* right? Would the clock permit such indecision?

No. Because even now, even as they were still scrubbing, there was commotion in the operating room, followed by the anesthesiologist's matter-of-fact pronouncement—"We're losing her"—loud and clear through the intercom beside the sink.

"You go," Caitlin said. "I should scrub a little—"

"No. She'd be lucky as hell to come out of this with just a post-op infection. We both go, Caitlin. Now."

Caitlin acceded to Patrick's command. It wasn't as though any patch of her bare skin would be touching the patient. She would be gowned and gloved, cloaked in layers of sterility. And it was eminently arguable that the final few minutes of the scrubbing ritual were overkill—an assessment which particularly applied to her, as Patrick had pointed out years ago, when he first observed the rigor of her technique. *We're not going for blood loss here, Caitlin. As a matter of fact, it's not even necessary to remove skin.*

Both surgeons were scrubbed enough, cleansed enough.

As one they moved toward their dying patient.

"Patrick? I think the spleen should be checked first."

"Do it then, Caitlin. You do it."

TWO

He was wrong. The realization screamed as Caitlin curled her hands around the spleen, feeling its smooth surface, slick with blood, searching for the gravestone of a phantom ice pick—and finding nothing.

Patrick was wrong. He had been wrong before, surely. It was impossible always to be right. But this time would torment them both. Had the food poisoning affected his judgment after all? Had he harmed the patient, killed her, because some ill-defined toxin had impaired his ability to perceive that he was impaired?

No—because Caitlin was not going to let this woman die. As soon as her hands finished their compulsive search of the blood-slick spleenscape, she would explore the liver. She would find the lethal laceration right away, and the detour to the spleen wouldn't matter, and—

"She's in V tach."

So treat it! Caitlin managed to keep her irritable thought to herself. The anesthesiologist would treat the arrhythmia—assuming the chaotic rhythm wasn't a signal that all was lost, they had guessed wrong, the clock was about to stand still. Forever.

Then she felt it—the divot in the splenic capsule where something sharp and thin had pierced.

"I found it," she whispered. *I found it.*

"*A*ny chance of seducing you away from hearts, Caitlin? I'm looking for another trauma surgeon, you know."

"Not me, thank you. That was *your* case, Patrick. Your miracle. I only provided a little technical support. And I should have found the bleeding site sooner."

"You found it at just the right time."

"Well. Anyway, trauma is not for me, not anymore. Way too much suspense." She waved a dismissive hand, a surgeon's hand, gloveless now, but powdery still from talc. "So, Patrick, how are you? Feeling any better?"

"Much better. Thanks to you."

Caitlin tilted her head and smiled. "I was wondering about your food poisoning."

"Ah. That's better, too. And now, Dr. Taylor, you have a plane to catch."

"Not for hours. And I don't even have to catch *that* plane. All I'm doing today is getting to New York, to spend the night in a Manhattan hotel. Which means I definitely have time to accompany you to the unit to check on her."

"Not necessary, Caitlin."

What was going on? They had left the operating room together, and she had assumed they were en route to the ICU. But their journey was a far shorter one, Patrick had shortened it, to this night-darkened corridor just beyond the surgical changing rooms.

And now he was what? Dismissing her; sending her on her way, having plied her with compliments so intoxicating that she wouldn't notice the dismissal. Bon voyage, Caitlin.

For what purpose? So that he could go to the ICU alone, to revel in the glory without having to share the credit?

That was not the Patrick Falconer she knew . . . had known.

"I want to see her, Patrick. It's been a while since I've operated on a patient who was already draped when I arrived on the scene. I want to know what she looks like."

"Why don't you go on up, then? I think I'll change first. And if we miss upstairs, thanks again, and enjoy your trip."

Now *that* was the Patrick she knew. Caitlin smiled. "Thanks. I will. See you in a week."

See you. See you. Halfway up the three flights of stairs to the ICU the words that had been echoing in her mind summarily halted her ascent.

She was on her way to see their patient. With Patrick's blessing. But the person she really needed to see, really needed to *look at*, was him.

Food poisoning, he had said. Alfalfa sprouts, he had joked.

But Patrick had been pale four weeks ago, when he arrived in LA, more pale than Caitlin had ever seen him. Pale. But healthy. And strong.

Nothing alarming, and easily explained. The East Coast winter had been so harsh that even the most avid of athletes had been forced inside. What better time for the trauma chief who was also boarded in hearts to spend extra hours in the OR, to be certain that both areas of expertise remained scalpel sharp?

But Patrick had not been this pale four weeks ago, or even four days ago, when she had seen him last. Not this translucent white. Not this luminous hue of death.

What could have transformed his skin from alabaster to snow to ice?

Only one thing: blood loss. Lots of it.

"Oh, Patrick," Caitlin whispered as a disturbing memory surfaced from their encounter four days before.

Their paths had crossed in front of the bank of elevators near Radiology and they had ridden up together. Caitlin had joined him on that journey. But it was Patrick who had been waiting for the elevator. *Patrick* who had made the choice to ride not walk.

Ride an elevator three flights? The Patrick she had known, the man with whom she had roamed the hallowed halls of Massachusetts General Hospital—from Bullfinch to Phillips House and all points in between—would not have taken an elevator when his destination was a mere three flights away. Or four. Or five. Or six.

In fact, unless they were transporting a patient, or happened to be on attending rounds, Patrick and Caitlin had always taken the stairs. No matter how many flights.

Both were that fit. They had to be. They were warriors in the fierce battle against death.

Now Caitlin was running down the stairs, toward the darkened corridor where he had stood in the shadows, professing to be better, unwilling to let her see the truth.

But she had seen. His skin had glowed in the darkness. *Glistened.*

And when she announced that she would see him in a

week, his expression had seemed so anguished that it
stilled her heart—and yet so fleeting that, with immense
relief, she dismissed it as a nighttime mirage.

But the anguished expression had not been a mirage.

From the shadows her friend—her older, wiser sib—
had been saying farewell.

The lettering on the door read "Men's Dressing
Room." Once, not so long ago, it might have read "*Doctors'* Dressing Room." In those days the rare female surgeon had changed from her street clothes to her scrubs in
the room designated "Nurses."

Now there were dressing rooms for women and men,
with no reference whatsoever to choice of career. And
now Caitlin was about to enter the one labeled "Men's"
without bothering to knock. The dressing room would be
empty except for Patrick. The only other man in the OR
this evening was Jonathan, the charge nurse, and he was
still on duty.

Patrick would be in the shower, and Caitlin would call
to him from the foyer, and assuming the men's dressing
room was configured like the women's, an expanse of
lockers would separate them, and Patrick would be amply
forewarned.

Not that it mattered. Nothing mattered. Not when all
her mind's eye could see was translucent skin, and a warrior too weak to climb even three flights of stairs, and that
shadowed look of pain, of good-bye.

Patrick was neither in the shower nor the locker room.
He hadn't made it that far. He had collapsed in a chair in
the foyer, head back, eyes closed. Corpse white. And motionless.

Asleep? Yes, *please.*

"Patrick?"

The corpse jerked to life, but not to health. An image came to her, one Caitlin hated but could not shake: a patient to whom defibrillator paddles had been applied in the hope of shocking a heart in chaos into one with a viable rhythm. In response to the electrical jolt the patient snapped alive, violently—yet briefly. In mere moments he sagged to lifelessness once again.

Don't sag, Patrick. Don't you dare.

He obeyed her silent command. He sat up, alert and alive, and a faint smile touched his lips. "Caitlin."

"I want to know what's wrong, Patrick, and I want to know now."

His eyes were so blue against his ghost white face. Blue and unflickering. "Not a damn thing. You just saved a life, and at any moment, I hope, you'll be leaving for a cruise, and very soon I'm going home to sleep off this case of food—"

"It's *not* food poisoning."

"No?"

"No. You've been pale since you got here—not *this* pale but definitely not your usual self—and you're weak, aren't you? Too weak even to climb a flight of stairs?" *And Patrick! You look almost dead.*

"You always were a good observer."

"Not this time. I should have noticed, should have put this together sooner. I mean . . ."

"It's not subtle, is it? But this colorlessness has just happened. Today. This evening, in fact. When I asked you to operate with me I felt all right, not a hundred percent but certainly capable of operating. I called because I decided the patient needed both of us. But she didn't get both of us, because in just those few minutes . . ."

Patrick grimaced at the memory. He'd had no idea he

was so close to the edge. But maybe something deep inside, some brain cell—or heart cell—indelibly engraved with the Hippocratic Oath had known. *Primum non nocere,* that cell had cried: First do no harm. Then, rendering him uncharacteristically forgetful, the cell had blocked his memory of Caitlin's impending cruise and compelled him to call for her help.

Harshly, hoarsely, he whispered, "It's so lucky I called you."

Caitlin waved his words away, unwilling to be distracted from the topic at hand. "You're *bleeding*, Patrick. An ulcer most likely, the symptoms of which you have resolutely ignored."

"It's not that easy, Caitlin. I'm not bleeding."

Oh, Patrick. "Then what?"

"I don't know. You've heard of denial? I just kept hoping it would go away."

It, Caitlin thought, aching for him, afraid for him. Patrick had checked for blood loss, not a trivial finding by any means; but in a man his age most likely due to a treatable disease.

But Patrick had not found evidence of such a bleed, and he had suspended his diagnostic pursuits. Caitlin knew why, of course. Most reasons for significant anemia in the absence of blood loss were profoundly grim.

Patrick had hoped *it* would just go away. He had neglected his symptoms, denied them—a reaction that was entirely normal, completely human. This man, so superhuman in so many ways, was a mere mortal after all.

A mere mortal. Merely mortal. A human being in whom *it* had only gotten worse.

"We need to find out, Patrick. Now. Tonight."

"*I* need to find out, Caitlin. And I will. I have no

choice. First thing in the morning, about the time your plane is lifting off—"

"I'm not going on the cruise!"

"Sure you are."

"Let me draw your blood. Please? Your crit must be—"

"You know my hematocrit, Doctor. Just by looking at me. Low twenties, don't you think? And my platelets. Well." His ice white fingers, like bones without their flesh, raised the pant legs of his surgical scrubs to reveal his lower calves. There was color there, an infinity of tiny purple dots, a galaxy of stars on the translucent sky of muscled flesh. "They're quite low, too, wouldn't you say? So in actual fact the only number that is truly unknown is my white count."

And, oh, what a pertinent number that was. It was the white count that would determine the diagnosis their medically sophisticated minds both feared.

"Let me draw your blood, Patrick," Caitlin reiterated quietly. *Let me be with you when you learn of your fate, of your leukemia.*

Patrick didn't answer at once, and in those moments Caitlin witnessed his silent debate. He did not want to involve her. Neither did he really want to be alone.

"On one condition," he said at last. "You're on that plane, no matter what."

THREE

THE HEART INSTITUTE
WESTWOOD MEMORIAL HOSPITAL
SUNDAY, APRIL TWENTY-FIRST

*T*he dawn seemed oblivious to the pall that had been cast upon the earth, unfolding in vibrant shades of pink and gold. Patrick and Caitlin watched the day awaken over the City of Angels. They had no choice. Its radiant hues glowed through the glass walls of her eighth-floor office, a brightness that taunted not soothed, and cast such brilliance onto her computer monitor that she would have to strain to see the symbols projected there.

There was nothing yet to be seen. Soon, however, answers would begin to emerge from the blood that was being analyzed *stat*. The golden rays would make those all-important numbers difficult to read. But Caitlin would not, could not, pull the blinds. She would not, could not, induce such darkness.

Besides, Patrick stood by one of the glassy walls, staring out, a near-colorless silhouette against the gold-and-mauve sky. His face was white marble, *he* was white marble, the motionless statue of an ancient warrior surveying his ravaged homeland.

What was he thinking? Caitlin wondered. Was he recalling the sunrises of his past, remembering the ones he had seen even as he mourned those he had missed? And was he grieving, in advance, the myriad awakenings he would never see?

Perhaps he was praying, a silent entreaty to a higher power for a minor miracle, a diagnosis other than the one they both feared. Or maybe he had accepted his fate and was merely negotiating for a slowly progressive leukemia, one that would permit him just a few more dawns . . .

The computer monitor came to life, sending its symbols, its pale green dancers, onto a stage so brightly lighted by the sun that the ballet itself was in grave danger of being eclipsed.

I must see these numbers, Caitlin thought. I *will*. She gazed into the glare—and beyond, to the shadowed screen and its ghostly dancers.

The hematocrit appeared first, testimony in faded green to the clinical acumen of the physician from whom it had been drawn. "Low twenties," Patrick had predicted. The symbol that flickered was *22*, embellished by #, an indication that the level was critically abnormal, a strikingly low blood count for any human being and less than half what it should have been for a thirty-eight-year-old male.

Additional red-cell facts and figures danced out, an entire chorus line of data, numbers that revealed the amount of hemoglobin per cell and their size and shape—all of which were entirely normal. Caitlin greeted the revelation with disappointment not joy. She had been hoping, a far-fetched wish, that Patrick's remark about alfalfa sprouts had been prophetic, that sometime during the years they had spent on separate coasts he had altered his diet so dramatically that essential nutrients had fallen by the wayside.

But Patrick's red blood cells were not nutritionally deprived. A rigorous, ascetic diet was not the reason his bone marrow had failed. Which only made leukemia more likely, made it all the more probable that his normal marrow cells had been crowded out—crushed and destroyed—by an aggressive, greedy mass of tumorous ones.

The cursor blinked, a ballerina teetering on pointe as she awaited the next result, the most critical one, the white-cell count. The blinking became more rapid, impatient and frantic, a beat that kept pace with the racing rhythm of Caitlin's heart.

Then the numbers began to appear, one step at a time, one numeral at a time. 7 . . . 2 . . . 4 . . . 0.

The cursor stalled. But it hovered, blinking, trembling, teetering on pale green toes at the very edge of an abyss. Any fifth numeral would be devastating confirmation of what she and Patrick feared. Seventy-two thousand white blood cells were far too many, an order of magnitude too much.

Ten times pathologic.

Ten times deadly.

But then, oh then, the cursor danced downstage, without leaving a fifth numeral, not even a ghostly shadow, no lethal footprint at all.

The sunbeams became softer, infusing her office with a golden mist. And the marble warrior who stood by the window? He was motionless still, his gaze fixed on the splendor of the dawn. But the mist enveloped him, limning his eerie whiteness, wreathing his stark silhouette in a halo of spun gold.

"Seven thousand two hundred," she whispered.

The gilt-edged silhouette did not move, and Caitlin wondered if he had even heard her words.

Finally his voice came, hoarse and parched, as if he were a wanderer in a vast desert, never imagining an oasis, still not imagining it . . . even though it lay just ahead.

"My platelets?"

"No, Patrick. Your white count."

Normal. Normal.

Maybe. Relief had rushed to Caitlin's lips, a pronouncement of pure joy. But the peripheral white count, the absolute number of leukocytes in the bloodstream, could be normal in leukemia.

The individual cells, however, would be wild, bizarre, a renegade gang of thugs marauding a peaceful neighborhood, wreaking havoc on any law-abiding citizen that stood in their way. Such cancerous cells knew no decency. They were criminals, psychopaths. Their genetic codes had been hopelessly scrambled, irrevocably uncivilized, from the moment of their births.

Such aberrant cells could have invaded Patrick's marrow. Caitlin knew it. And so did he.

After several moments, hoarse still, yet husky with hope, his voice drifted to her on the golden mist.

"And the smear, Caitlin? The differential?"

Caitlin stared at the computer screen, at that infuriating, yet ever more friendly, blinking green cursor. When she spoke it was to that tiny ballerina, her tone coaxing and gentle. *Be nice to him. Please.* "Still pending."

Pending.

Pending.

Pending. During those endless minutes Drs. Falconer and Taylor silently shared the same somber thoughts. The cells were so abnormal, the diagnosis so horrific, that the laboratory technician was soliciting opinions from other night-shift techs, wanting to be absolutely certain of the assessment before entering into the computer the verdict of death. And at the advice of his colleagues, the tech had already called Dr. Stephen Sheridan, who was on his way in to personally handle this delicate—and disturbing—situation.

There were other scenarios, of course, ones far less grim. Maybe the tech was simply busy with other *stat* requests. Or maybe, unaware of the anxiety eight floors above, he had decided to read the slide after his scheduled coffee break. Or—

At last the cursor danced anew, and perhaps the tech *had* been on break, and the caffeine had gone straight to his fingers, because the dance now was fast and furious.

A rumba—and a celebration.

"It's okay, Patrick. Everything's okay. Well, all right, there's a marked left shift, but that's to be expected given the adrenaline levels you must have. But there are no abnormal cells. *None.* The only comment on the smear is that the platelets are markedly decreased and that no reticulocytes are seen."

Freshly minted by the marrow, reticulocytes were dispatched into the bloodstream to replace their elders, the senescent red cells that had died their natural deaths. Typically, the robust youngsters comprised one percent of the circulating red-cell population. In a patient with anemia, however, assuming the bone marrow was functioning properly, the percentage of reticulocytes should have been much higher.

But Patrick had no reticulocytes at all.

In response to the revelation, he turned from the dawn to her. Graceful, elegant, ethereal, he seemed to float.

Like a vampire. The image, like that of a patient subjected to an electrical jolt, came to Caitlin unbidden—and most definitely unwanted.

True, of late, Hollywood had cast vampires in an almost romantic light—sensual creatures, conscience-stricken by their evil plight. Indeed, to secure the most savory of images, Tinseltown had assigned its sexiest men to the controversial roles. A stunningly handsome trauma surgeon would enhance the image even further.

But I will not assign such evil to Patrick.

Besides, sunlight was deadly for vampires, and here stood her translucent friend, embraced by the gilded rays of dawn.

"So I'm aplastic," Patrick murmured, unaware of his choice of words.

He was so careful not to describe patients by their diseases, as if patient and disease were one and the same. Dr. Patrick Falconer never said, "This is a forty-year-old alcoholic/paraplegic/schizophrenic/cystic." He always said, "I'm seeing a forty-year-old man who carries the diagnosis of . . ."

But now, in describing himself, Patrick was breaking his own rule. He wasn't a thirty-eight-year-old man with aplastic anemia, a human being whose bone marrow had suddenly failed in its mission to replenish the blood cells that were essential to life. *He* was aplastic.

Still, Patrick's murmured pronouncement came with

great hope. A remote region of his soul had, after all, been rehearsing something far worse: *So I'm leukemic.*

The hopefulness faltered slightly as he embellished, "If I'm lucky, that is. My marrow could be packed with tumor."

It was true, of course. Aplastic anemia could be primary, marrow failure of unknown cause; or it could be secondary, due to such massive marrow invasion—by cancer or infection—that all normal functions necessarily ceased.

Patrick's hopefulness, and hers, had been based on the assumption that the aplasia was primary. Caitlin clung tenaciously to that belief, a conviction which was, in fact, supported by the data at hand. "It *won't* be packed with tumor, Patrick. Your chemistries are all perfectly fine, including every single hepatic enzyme and the alk phos. If your marrow is packed with anything, it's some exotic parasite acquired during your travels." *During your missions of mercy to the neediest outposts of the planet, those faraway places of bloodshed and famine.* "Malaria can do this, can't it? Or what about TB? You remember Case 12-1963, don't you?"

Of course he remembered. Published in the *New England Journal of Medicine* on February 14, 1963, the clinical case, with its autopsy findings, had become required reading in many medical schools. The case itself was illustrative of the underlying disease process. More importantly, it served as an admonition against VIP treatment, especially when such special treatment meant that usual—albeit painful—measures were forsaken.

The patient described in *NEJM* Case 12-1963 was identified as "a seventy-five-year-old widow" who had "traveled extensively abroad." Despite certain discrepancies, there were those who believed that the widow in question was Eleanor Roosevelt.

Like Patrick, the patient—and indeed, the First Lady—had presented with low platelets and hematocrit. And the VIP treatment she received? A bone-marrow aspirate in lieu of the more painful biopsy. The former did not disclose the true reason for her depressed counts—a marrow invaded by TB—whereas the biopsy might well have. As a result the tuberculosis went undiagnosed and untreated . . . and was responsible for her death several months later.

"No VIP treatment for you, Dr. Falconer," Caitlin was saying now. "One bone marrow biopsy coming up."

With that she reached for the phone.

"Caitlin? What are you doing?"

"Calling Stephen Sheridan, of course."

Patrick knew and liked Westwood Memorial's Heme/Onc chief. Beyond Stephen's impressive academic credentials was the man himself: careful, scholarly, thoughtful, honest.

One could not ask for a better doctor.

If one needed a doctor, that is. Which, apparently, he did not. He already had one, a take-charge physician who even now was beginning to dial the four 3s that would connect her to the page operator, who in turn would connect her to Stephen's home.

"Stop."

Caitlin obeyed Patrick's command. Sort of. The receiver remained suspended in midair. "Why?"

"For one thing, it's six A.M."

"Stephen will be awake." She frowned briefly, then smiled. "In fact, now that I think about it, he and Christine are probably already here, on Five North, visiting their three-day-old son."

"A three-day-old infant who's still hospitalized is not a healthy newborn."

"Well, *he* is. He was born a little premature, that's all, and with a slight murmur."

"All the more reason not to bother Stephen."

"It's just a flow murmur, Patrick. Little David Sheridan is perfectly fine. In fact, he's going home today." Caitlin pressed the third of the four 3s. "So—"

This time she was stopped by a hand. Or was it a bony claw sculpted from ice? Whatever, it was curling over her hand, unmelted by her warmth, and now a glacial talon was removing the receiver from her grasp and replacing it in the cradle.

"So," Patrick echoed. "Sometime between eight and nine I will give Stephen a call, and he'll do the bone-marrow biopsy today, or tomorrow, or whenever his schedule permits. In the meantime you have a plane, followed by a ship, to catch."

"I'm not going."

"Yes, you are. We had a deal." His skeletal hand waved away her protest—that she never precisely agreed that if he let her draw his blood she would leave—before she uttered a syllable. "This cruise is important to you. Very. As a matter of fact, I have the distinct impression that you're meeting someone."

"*Moi*, Patrick? A clandestine rendezvous at sea?"

He did not smile. "Yes. You."

"Well, thank you for the romantic thought. But I'm traveling alone and can easily rebook."

"Caitlin, listen to me. I want you to go on your cruise. Call it superstition, *whatever*, but I truly believe that if you go, everything will be fine. Stephen will find good old-fashioned aplasia from which I'll be on the road to recovery by the time you return."

And if I stay? Caitlin wondered—and saw the ominous answer on his ice white face. If I stay his marrow will be so packed with tumor that even the brilliant Stephen Sheridan will have nothing to offer.

"Okay," she said softly. "I'll go. But may I at least be allowed to know what Stephen finds?"

"As long as you promise that under no circumstances will you come back early."

Caitlin frowned, sighed.

"I mean it, Caitlin."

"All right. I promise." Then, because she knew that it would be far too difficult, impossible really, for Patrick to tell her that he was dying, especially by phone, long-distance, ship-to-shore, she asked, "Will you give Stephen permission to tell me what the biopsy shows?"

The vampire limned in sunlight answered with a vague and wistful smile. "Sure. I'll give him permission to tell you everything."

FOUR

UNITED AIRLINES FLIGHT 904
LAX TO JFK
FIVE MILES ALOFT
SUNDAY, APRIL TWENTY-FIRST

*N*ever forget, my Caitlin, that I am with you, that *we* are with you, loving you always. *Alw—*

That was the way her mother's letter ended. Her mother's life ended. The memory of that word—that life, that love—interrupted caused a flood of emotion.

Caitlin's vision blurred. But that long-ago night burned vivid and clear.

What had caused *always* to be severed? Excruciating pain? Breathless panic? The gasping, suffocating certainty that death had arrived?

Caitlin heard the soft thud. She would hear it forever.

Terrified, she had run to her mother's bedroom. The door was ajar, as always; and on another night Caitlin would already have tiptoed down the hallway to peer into the darkness, to listen until she heard the reassuring sounds of sleep within.

But this was the night of her sixteenth birthday. She had been sitting cross-legged on her bed, dressed for sleep but wearing still the pearls her mother had given her and lost in a trance of sorts, a sense of transition, of blossoming, from girl to woman, child to adult. Had she not been in that trance, had she checked on her mother even seconds before the ominous thud and insisted that all letter writing halt then and there . . .

Years later Patrick would remark on Caitlin's remarkable powers of observation. Most human beings, given a mere glimpse of a scene, were capable of limited recall, a finite number of specific details—at least at a conscious level. Further particulars might be retrieved by plumbing the subconscious depths through hypnosis or with certain drugs. No such interventions were required, however, for Caitlin. As if her mind had taken a photograph, and without subconscious probes of any kind, she could recall a scene even fleetingly noted in extraordinary detail.

On that night, when Caitlin rushed into her mother's room, her entire focus was on the beloved form lying crumpled on the floor. And yet her mind recorded the sheets of pale pink paper, the spill of ink, the lilac-scented candle flickering as her rushed movements stirred the perfumed air. Caitlin's mind noticed even more about the candle: how low it had burned when the paramedics arrived, how much wax had melted, how much fragrance had been released.

Thus, when she returned home and saw that the candle glowed no more, she knew that it had not been extinguished by the paramedics. It had burned longer, lower . . . until the instant of her mother's death . . . the moment when Margaret Taylor's heart stood forever still.

The scented column had extinguished itself then. With a flood of fragrant, waxy tears.

When, at last, Caitlin could see beyond her own tears, she read her mother's letter, cherishing the contents yet hating the pages themselves—and hating most of all the man who had compelled the fatal confession. Margaret had known what the effort might cost her. Her emotional words proved that she knew. But she kept writing, an ultimate peril risked for love, for Caitlin, for him.

For years after Margaret's death, too many years, Caitlin's hatred toward her absentee father dwelled within, a gnawing anger, a festering wound. Finally for herself, but mostly for her mother, she forged a reluctant peace. He was contemptible. That was a given. He had preyed on "his Maggie's" innocence, charming her, seducing her, with his lies.

But Margaret had believed him. Indeed the memory of his "love" glowed within her, radiant and bright, the luminous joy of a woman loved deeply and forever. And for that, for giving her mother such happiness, Caitlin was grateful to the man named Michael. That was his name, of course. That was why she was Caitlin Michaela.

Margaret's letter had promised Caitlin a splendid inheritance, her rightful legacy as the love child of a grand and glorious passion. But Michael's Maggie had been destined for love. Everything about her was receptive, feminine, lovely.

And her daughter? Caitlin's face told the whole story. Striking, yes. Elegant and regal, perhaps. But Caitlin was edgy where her mother had been soft, austere where Margaret had been yielding. Intense, focused, dedicated, driven. Those words, scalpel sharp and surgeon precise, best described Caitlin. Without and within.

Even at sixteen Caitlin Michaela Taylor had decided she would never know the breathless surrender of a reckless love. Of any love. Yet there was passion in her life, for the badly damaged hearts she pledged herself to save.

And in its power to demand, to devour, to consume, Caitlin's passion for her work rivaled Margaret's passion for Michael.

In three days Caitlin would be thirty-four, her mother's age when she was conceived. Caitlin would celebrate, a private celebration, aboard the daughter ship, the *Queen Elizabeth 2*. She had considered booking the transatlantic crossing from Southampton to New York, precisely as her parents had done, but opted for the round-trip from New York to Bermuda instead.

By making no attempt to retrace her mother's passionate steps, her own failure to duplicate the shipboard romance would be a faux pas of happenstance, the scheduled ports of call that coincided with her birthday, not further proof of how different she and her mother truly were.

Caitlin booked a different class of accommodation as well—by default. The best was all that remained. The hierarchy of passengers aboard the *QE2* was not nearly as rigid as on the mother ship decades ago. The more one paid, however, the better the stateroom and the more grand the place where one dined.

Caitlin would be dining in the Queens Grill, the ship's premier restaurant, perched a lofty ten decks above the waves. Caviar was a staple, the booking agent told her, as was the juniper sorbet. And Queens Grill desserts were artistic offerings, lavish tableaux painted with syrups of chocolate, raspberry, and plum.

And with whom would Caitlin be sharing gourmet meals in the rarefied atmosphere above the sea? The love of her life? The man of her dreams?

There was no such man.

But what about that other man, the aristocrat named

Michael? He would be in his sixties now, handsome still, lean and fit. The only clue to his age would be the silver threads in his night black hair.

Cruising had, perhaps, become a lifelong pleasure for Maggie's Michael, the one-time diversion a true addiction now. Maybe he escaped often to the sea, that floating place without rules where he could fall in love—for just a few days—and from which, rejuvenated, he could return to the responsibilities anchored firmly to shore.

Maybe Michael's wife would be accompanying him on this trip, a honeymoon delayed by thirty-four years. Perhaps the long-suffering creature needed to see for herself the allure of the sea. Maybe she even fantasized about an oceanic magic for herself, golden moonbeams that did wonders for even the most haggard face.

It might even be a family affair. The child who had created the land sickness in Michael's wife could be aboard, along with his legitimate sibs. And Michael's other children—illegitimate ones, like Caitlin—might be dining in five-star grandeur as well.

There might be a roomful of such children of the sea. Children whose mothers had regaled them with such wondrous stories of cruising that they had been compelled to visit the venue of watery—slippery?—morality where they had been conceived. They would be searching for answers, hoping to understand the enchantment that had left their mothers so bewitched and themselves without fathers.

*T*he DC-10 lurched, startling Caitlin from her reverie, a jolt so foreboding that her right hand traveled reflexively to her throat, where it found instant solace. She was wearing Margaret's pearls, *her* pearls, the necklace of lacquered glass which for daughter, as for mother, was valuable beyond measure.

Caitlin touched the faux pearls, fingering them gently even as the plane gentled in the stratosphere. But her thoughts were far from calm. She shouldn't be taking this journey, not when Patrick was so desperately ill.

I want you to go, Caitlin. . . . As long as you promise that under no circumstances will you come back early.

Promise, promise, promise—which she had, because his death white face had been so deadly serious when he issued the quiet command.

FIVE

"*I* don't have the marrow results, Caitlin. I didn't do the biopsy until today, about an hour ago."

Why not? she wondered, frowning at the pay phone as she strained to hear the nuances in Stephen Sheridan's voice. The connection was good. But in this place where one gathered prior to boarding the ship the air hummed with festivity.

"Could you tell anything from the procedure itself, Stephen? Or from the way the sample looked?"

"No. Nothing."

"But is there *something?* You sound . . ."

"Distracted? I guess I am. Sorry."

"Is there a problem with David? Or with Christine?"

The answer came swiftly, distracted no more. "No. My wife and son are perfectly fine—thanks to you."

"I didn't do anything, Stephen. I was merely the messenger." *Just as you will be merely the messenger when you tell me Patrick is dying.* "You know what? It's crazy for me to get on this ship. I'm catching the next flight back to LA."

"*No,* Caitlin. It turns out I'm really a pretty competent hematologist."

"I know that!" *But you're also an incredibly nice man, and already it feels as if you're protecting me.*

Or maybe she was just imagining the equivocation in Stephen's voice, a false impression created in protest to the pervasive gaiety that surrounded her. Didn't her fellow travelers understand Patrick's plight? How could there be such happiness when her friend might never laugh again?

The ambient merriment was perhaps a conspirator in her grim imaginings. But it was a minor culprit compared to her own fatigue, an exhaustion caused by dreams so tormenting that absolute sleeplessness would have been preferable.

The dreams had transported her aboard a phantom ship, not the love boat of her mother's memories but a ship of ghouls. And ghosts. And vampires—one very special vampire, the supreme creature of the night. Michael himself.

Elegant and urbane, he charmed, he enticed, he seduced. His black hair gleamed, and his blue eyes glowed—especially when he saw his Maggie. Michael *loved* Maggie. He kissed her neck, such a tender caress, even when it became a biting one. Michael looked at Caitlin then and laughed at his daughter's horror, laughed and laughed as Maggie's blood gushed from his gluttonous mouth.

Caitlin's ghoulish father wanted her to see his hands, too, musician's hands, surgeon's hands. Another inheritance from father to child. Michael was a surgeon, and his passion, like Caitlin's, was hearts. Maggie's heart.

And now—no, *no!*—Michael was opening Maggie's

chest *with his bare hands;* and now he was holding Maggie's heart for Caitlin to see; and now he was laughing anew. Maggie's heart fluttered frantically in Michael's hands, and on its shining crimson surface Caitlin saw a tiny flame. With each racing heartbeat the flame flickered, illuminating even more: the pale pink paper, her mother's flowing script, the desperate plea. Save me, Caitlin. *Save* me!

How she tried, chasing Michael along the endless miles of varnished deck. But Caitlin was no match for the vampire prince. He floated beyond her reach, delighted to be playing hide-and-seek with his daughter, a fatherly enterprise at last.

Eventually Michael grew bored with the game, or perhaps he merely knew that soon the sun would rise over the sea. He took a final drink from Maggie's neck and satisfied, *sated,* he threw his beloved into an ocean the color of his eyes.

Then it was Caitlin who was drowning. She awakened gasping, as if she had inhaled the entire sea.

So much for having made peace with her phantom father.

It had been a wary truce at best, and now the ancient emotions had been provoked, haunting her nights and tainting her days—for now she had actually assigned a diabolic deviousness to Stephen.

"Caitlin?" that impeccably honest colleague was saying. "You do not need to return to LA."

"I know, and I won't. When will you have the biopsy results?"

"Tomorrow afternoon. Why don't you call me when you reach Bermuda?"

"That's not until Wednesday. And I want to know. According to the brochures it's possible, in fact easy, to make ship-to-shore phone calls from the staterooms. It's via satellite, so there may be delays, but is there a time tomorrow afternoon when I could call?"

Two o'clock Pacific time, they agreed, after which Stephen gave her a message from Patrick.

"He wants a full report when you return, the most minute details about the ship, your fellow passengers, the food—everything."

"Okay." Forcing the sudden quaver from her voice, Caitlin added brightly, "Tell him aye-aye."

*A*ll right, bossy big brother. Here we are, stepping onto the gangway, the yellow-brick road—well, the dove gray steel—at the end of which is the *Queen Elizabeth 2*.

Already it's elegant, and terribly British. We're being greeted by a small army of fresh-faced women and men. You know, like the staff of a baronial manor, clean, starched, and standing at attention as they welcome their lord and lady home from abroad. Our small army is uniformed, a nautical motif, navy blue with gold trim, and gloves as white as your—

None of that. Besides, the moment is here. We are boarding the grand monarch of the sea. We're entering on Two Deck, one of our greeters explains. This is the Midships Lobby. Its floor-to-ceiling murals illustrate the history of the Cunard Line. The most dramatic, at least to me, is a wooden schooner in full sail in a wild and treacherous sea. Oh, there's music now, vaguely familiar, nautical and British. I'm sure you could name it right away.

Just a few steps from the Midships Lobby is stateroom 2063, my Queens Grill cabin. Even before I open the door a smiling young man is approaching me. Miss Taylor, he says politely, and with a wonderful Scottish brogue. Yes, Patrick, *Miss* Taylor. That's how I booked myself. Like my mother. She's here, too, of course. Even if you hadn't commanded that I notice everything I would have done so—for her.

The man's name is Paul, and he's my steward. Which means, he tells me, that he'll clean my stateroom twice a day; and he'll be available around the clock if there's anything I need.

He seems so positive, so willing to grant every wish.

Oh, Patrick, if only this eager young man could grant every wish.

Queens Grill cabin 2063 was a far cry from Maggie's windowless closet on the mother ship. Located six stories above the sea, Caitlin's stateroom was spacious and bright. Two large portholes provided an expansive vista—at the moment the Manhattan skyline etched against a pewter sky.

With impressive efficiency her two suitcases had already arrived. Caitlin was amazed, still, by the glittering garments she withdrew.

Except for the rare days when no cases were scheduled Dr. Caitlin Taylor wore freshly laundered scrubs, starched and snowy lab coats, and running shoes. A colorful scarf—she had many—subdued her long black hair into a sedate ponytail at the nape of her neck.

The look was sporty, efficient, fastidious, and it sent the clear message to her patients that she was ready to do battle for them, to wage all-out campaigns with her brain, her knives, her skill. Moreover, according to Amanda,

Caitlin's best friend since college—and Westwood Memorial's psychiatry chief—royal blue was a good color for Caitlin; as, for that matter, was the teal green that had recently come into vogue.

But scrub wear was one thing and cruise wear quite another. With Amanda's expert help Caitlin made the sort of sequin-and-satin purchases that were de rigueur for the *QE2*. Amanda had been decisive, and absolutely unyielding, especially when it came to vetoing a royal blue sheath. It was, she maintained, little more than a shamefully pricey scrub dress.

Amanda's eye was impeccable, her sense of style without peer. The new Amanda, that is. But Caitlin couldn't help wondering if the old Amanda hadn't been far more confident, more happy—

"Welcome aboard."

The voice, British and male, interrupted Caitlin's musings about her friend. It was the captain, broadcast through a speaker above a lighted mirror on the stateroom wall. The intrusion felt more familiar than startling, reminiscent of the paging systems in every hospital in which she had ever worked.

Immediate communication between passengers and the bridge was, Caitlin supposed, an absolute necessity. Perhaps it was even required by law in the event of a catastrophe at sea.

At this moment the link was social not sinister. The captain was extending an invitation.

"Very soon we shall be leaving port. So join us, won't you, for the sailaway party on the Upper Deck Aft? Oh, and don't let this drizzle worry you. We're sailing toward clear skies and balmy breezes."

Neither a snowfall of streamers nor a blizzard of confetti floated in the twilight—a modern concession, Caitlin decided, to the health of the waterways. There was celebration, however, which she witnessed from a vantage point a deck above.

A live band entertained and couples danced despite the rain. The soggy but merry celebrants drank gallons of punch and devoured platter upon platter of hors d'oeuvres, and when the band took its break the sound of bagpipes filled the sodden air.

On this damp April evening the Statue of Liberty stood upon a silvery mist. Her majestic green body gleamed against the charcoal sky. Her bright gold torch flamed brightly, a worthy sun on this sunless day.

Caitlin remained on deck until all vestiges of land— the promised land for so many—was swallowed by the misting night. And even the bagpipes ceased to mourn. It was almost nine, but Queens Grill dining was available until ten-thirty. She had ample time to shower and change.

But as she started to reach for the silver-and-fuchsia cocktail dress she had purchased to wear on this first night at sea, her hand veered instead to her tattered flannel robe.

Caviar and juniper sorbet awaited her, as did—perhaps—a roomful of oceanic orphans reunited at last with their vampire father.

I need sleep, not food, dreamless sleep without ghosts or ghouls . . .

*T*he purr of the engine.

The gentle rocking of the waves.

The two should have conspired to make her feel as if in her mother's womb, serenaded by a maternal heartbeat as she floated in the safe, warm, fluid world.

Perhaps the two had conspired to create just that effect. Perhaps that was precisely why sleep came to her only in brief bouts of torment.

The sea rocked her, a swaying cradle, and the ship's purring engine was her mother's heart, its rumble a murmur, an anguished lubb-dupp.

I am diseased, Maggie's heart whispered. I am damaged, it murmured. I am dying.

The engines of the *Queen Elizabeth 2* generated enough power to light the city of Southampton.

At the service speed of 28.5 knots, the grand behemoth of the sea devoured 380 tons of fuel per day, an appetite which translated into a fuel efficiency of 50 feet per gallon.

Engine officers aboard the *QE2* wore gold-and-purple stripes at the behest of King George V, a tribute in perpetuity to the *Titanic* engineers who had gone down with the ship.

Those were just a few of the fascinating bits of *QE2* lore that Caitlin learned between two and four A.M.

There were more:

The floating hotel in which seventeen hundred passengers—and a thousand crew—were journeying was thirteen stories high, three football fields long, and one football field across. It boasted two swimming pools, ten luxury shops, one bank, nine bars, one disc jockey, five restaurants, and, by Caitlin's calculation, more than enough lifeboats.

For a typical five-day voyage, thirty-three pounds of caviar were boarded, and sixteen thousand eggs, and a thousand bottles of champagne, and a quarter of a ton of lobster.

According to the Daily Programme, April twenty-third was St. George's Day, a commemoration of the patron saint of England, martyred on this date in A.D. 303. Today's featured cocktail was "Hawaiian Outrigger," and the special coffee was "Normandy." A professor of astronomy would be lecturing on the wonders of the universe, and a caricaturist would be plying his trade in the Crystal Bar, while a harpist entertained. Aerobics happened hourly; the skeet-shooting tournament began at two; even the uninitiated should feel welcome at "Introduction to Computers"; and, the Programme admonished, "don't forget high tea in the Lido, or the pleasures of shopping on Grand Promenade . . ."

By four A.M., Caitlin had memorized every printed word in her stateroom. She had even learned how to operate the VCR. And should tragedy strike between now and the requisite emergency drill scheduled for ten A.M., she would become a nautical Pied Piper leading her fellow Two Deck passengers to their designated muster station, in the Mauritania, starboard side.

Wakeful still and unwilling to return to the torment of her dreams, Caitlin abandoned her stateroom to stroll the empty wooden decks. She encountered no one on her journey, neither human nor phantom. Nor did she find peace.

The moon glowered, and the wind seethed, and the silver-tipped waves were a battalion of ghosts.

I'm sorry, Mother. The ship is majestic, a worthy successor to the one you knew. And everyone is terribly nice. But my worries about Patrick, coupled with these disturbing nightmares, are casting unwelcome shadows.

Tomorrow, as soon as I know that Patrick is fine, the shadows will disappear and I will see the splendor of the sea, not its eerie crests.

Tomorrow.

SIX

QUEEN ELIZABETH 2
TUESDAY, APRIL TWENTY-THIRD

"There is a bit of a delay, isn't there? But I hear you, Stephen. Loud and clear. Do you hear me?"

"Perfectly."

"Good. So . . . ?"

Caitlin waited, breath held, as Stephen's answer traveled to a satellite orbiting high above earth, an inert metal object that received the news before she.

"So Patrick's marrow is aplastic."

Caitlin's breath released in a rush. "*Good.*"

"And bad, Caitlin."

"Bad?" Was the aplasia secondary after all? Caused by the invasion of cancer cells or a parasite so exotic that no one had yet bothered to find a cure? "You found a cause for the aplasia?"

"No. But I can't support him. That's why I delayed the biopsy. I was hoping to increase his platelet count before the procedure. But every platelet pack was consumed within seconds of infusion—seconds, literally. Red-cell transfusions met a similar fate."

"He must have been transfused before." That was the logical conclusion, an acquired sensitivity due to previous transfusions—massive ones most likely, given emergently.

"He says he hasn't been," Stephen said. "His only hospitalization was at age fifteen, and he has no memory of receiving blood products at that time. The hypersensitivity must be innate. I didn't mention this to you yesterday, Caitlin, because I wasn't certain how serious it was."

But it was very serious. The satellite faithfully transmitted the solemnity of Stephen's voice, and Caitlin's medically expert mind conjured the rest. If Patrick's dangerously low blood counts could not be supported, if they merely continued to plummet, he would die, right there at Westwood Memorial Hospital, before the eyes of one of the world's premier hematologists.

Gallons of blood and liters of platelets could be poured into Patrick's veins, but to no avail, as long as his immune system rejected every foreign offering the instant it was made . . . as if intravenous feeding were not the way the vampire chose to receive his nourishment of blood.

Patrick is not a vampire. He is a human being, a wonderful one, and . . . "He needs a bone-marrow transplant."

"Yes, Caitlin, he does. As soon as possible. Like yesterday. Finding a donor, however, is going to be very difficult."

Caitlin frowned at the understatement. An immune system which swiftly rejected the blood of strangers would go wild—perhaps lethally so—in response to the invasion of a foreign marrow.

Then she smiled. Patrick Falconer did not need to rely

on the blood of strangers. Even as the thought began to soar, Stephen's faraway voice sabotaged it.

"His best chance, of course, would be a related donor. Unfortunately that's not in the cards. His parents are dead, and he has no sibs, no cousins, no living relatives at all."

But that wasn't *true*. Patrick had a brother, a *twin*. Caitlin knew that truth, and with Stephen's grim pronouncement, she learned another: even when it meant the difference between life and death Patrick was not going to ask for help from the twin from whom he was so bitterly estranged.

"What are you going to do, Stephen?" Caitlin posed the question even as she was formulating her own drastic plans.

"I've entered everything I know about Patrick's immunologic profile into the national transplant registry. So far a close—or even close enough—match hasn't come up. I'm going to widen the net, send queries to blood banks, heme departments, wherever."

"And if you don't find a match?"

"Then I'll take whatever I can get. With aggressive immunosuppression maybe I can make something work. I'm sure as hell going to try."

"Patrick's marrow function might come back on its own, mightn't it? Can't that happen with primary aplasia?"

"Sure—assuming one can support the patient's counts until recovery occurs. We don't have that luxury here, Caitlin."

There was a soft hissing as their sudden silence journeyed to the barren blackness of space.

Barren . . . like Patrick's marrow.

And what of Patrick's heart? Was it so barren of hope that it refused even to try to save itself?

Caitlin, Patrick's surrogate sister, felt the hopelessness; and Dr. Taylor, heart surgeon, imagined the damaged organ itself. Undoubtedly, until recently, Patrick's heart had been a brilliant Valentine red. It had pulsed at a leisurely pace, a rate that spoke volumes about its longevity and sent a promise to his powerful body that it could roam the planet for decades hence.

But no more. Patrick's heart was ice white now, a bloodless fist clenched in rage. And it was racing, galloping, toward certain death.

"How is he, Stephen?" How is Patrick coping with his perch on the very edge of oblivion? Is he teetering? Are his graceful limbs quavering from weakness, if not from fear? And what of the hands destined to save so many lives—some not yet even in jeopardy, perhaps not even born? Are those gifted hands fists of ice? Are they clenched, too, with transcendent rage?

"He's quiet, Caitlin. Quiet . . . dying."

And silent on the subject of his twin, Caitlin mused after she and Stephen had said good-bye. And if she spoke to Patrick himself? If she demanded that he mend fences with his brother?

Caitlin had no idea what had shattered the bond between Patrick and his twin. She knew only her impression that the damage was irreparable and that Patrick was to blame. *Patrick.* But whatever Patrick had done, surely, *surely,* the punishment should not be the sacrifice of his own life. And yet by failing to tell Stephen that he had a blood relative—a blood *brother*—it was as if Patrick actually believed that his crime had been a capital one.

Caitlin could admonish Patrick to reach out to his twin.

She would—except for the fact that Patrick might reject the idea of rapprochement, not only for himself but for her. It was not a conversation Caitlin wanted to have. And as for the other reason to speak to Patrick? To offer words of comfort? That was not the way she could help him best.

Caitlin was a surgeon, a mistress of decisive action. Her surgical forte was saving damaged hearts. Damaged hearts. Not broken ones. Not shattered ones. But now the surgeon must find a way to piece the estranged twin's heart back together, if only briefly, just long enough.

In the operating room Dr. Taylor could simply put the heart on bypass. Was there an emotional equivalent to that medical detour? If so, she had to find it. Had to. Would.

But there was something she must do first.

Quiet. Dying. Caitlin had been that way once. And she had been helped, rescued, by a wise and sympathetic girl. That girl was a physician now, board-certified to offer the kind of sage and soothing advice that had always come so naturally to her.

Dying was not Amanda's specialty. Survival was. With Amanda's gentle guidance her patients made bold conquests of fear, courageous triumphs over even the most daunting obstacles.

Well, survival was precisely what Patrick needed. Amanda was what he needed. Indeed, Caitlin mused, there wasn't a human being alive who wouldn't benefit from the empathetic counsel of Dr. Amanda Prentice.

Patrick had granted Caitlin permission to speak with Stephen, to learn the details of his aplasia down to the electron micrographs of his barren marrow. Admittedly, eventually, everyone at the hospital would know. Such secrets were impossible to keep.

For the moment, however, it was an intensely private matter . . . and Patrick was an intensely private man . . . and what right did Caitlin have to share the confidential revelations with Westwood's preeminent psychiatrist?

None. Dr. Caitlin Taylor was, in fact, expressly prohibited from such a disclosure.

It was then that Caitlin looked from the telephone on her nightstand to the porthole above her bed. Something had compelled her to do so. Something, or some*one*.

Look, Caitie. Look—and *see*.

And Caitlin did see. The sapphire sky. The azure ocean. The misty band of cobalt where the heavens caressed the sea. She saw the brilliant shades of blue, and more. She saw the magic.

Oh, Mother, you were right. The rules change out here. The old mandates, so important ashore, are easily forgotten, effortlessly dismissed.

A smile touched Caitlin's lips as she gazed at the vast blue magic. *So sue me, Patrick.*

With that, she dialed.

Amanda was free, between patients, and once told by her secretary who the caller was came on the line with a lilting tease. "You had better be on the *QE2*."

"Don't worry, Amanda. I'm precisely where I'm supposed to be. Can't you tell? I'm calling ship-to-shore by way of a satellite that's who knows where."

Outer, *outer* space, Caitlin decided as she awaited Amanda's reply.

"I *can* tell. Are you all right, Caitlin?"

"Yes. Well. Not really. I have a favor to ask." Caitlin did not pause for Amanda's response. But she heard it—

Anything, Caitlin, you know that—just as her own words were reaching LA. "I need you to see Patrick Falconer. I know I've been wanting the two of you to meet. I only wish I'd been more insistent."

The delay, this time, was even longer.

"Actually, Caitlin, Patrick and I have met."

"You have? That makes this easier, then—not that anything about this is easy. Patrick needs you, Amanda."

"Needs me?" Amanda echoed softly as her thoughts screamed. *You're wrong, Caitlin. Patrick Falconer most definitely does not need me.*

"He's just been diagnosed with aplastic anemia. It's primary, but some sort of intrinsic hypersensitivity is making his counts impossible to support. A marrow donor will be found." *I will find him.* "In the meantime Patrick needs to talk. And who better than you?"

"You, Caitlin."

"No, not me. Not from the middle of the ocean with these awkward delays. Amanda? You sound so reluctant. Why?"

Because I'm permitting my fears to win. And I can't permit such a victory—not now, not when Patrick may need the one thing, the only thing, I can truly offer him.

"Amanda?"

"Of course I'll see him, Caitlin. Of course I will."

"Thank you." *And I will find Jesse Falconer, estranged twin and author of erotic thrillers, the man known to his legions of fans by the Gothic nom de plume Graydon Slake.*

SEVEN

*T*rapped. Caged.

Was this the way Jesse had felt? This restless fury. This desperate wish to be free.

For Jesse the torment had lasted years. Four years, three months, and eight days to be precise. And for Patrick it had been mere hours. Endless hours.

Jesse Falconer's cage had been a prison cell. Cold, stark, steel, stone. A relentless imprisonment from which there had been no authentic hope of escape. One might try, an effort fraught with great risk—and with the guarantee of more years behind bars if it failed.

And what of Patrick's cage? The room that now imprisoned the golden twin was luxurious, one of Westwood Memorial's best. And if Patrick wished to escape, he could, whenever he chose, an effortless getaway, yet fraught with its own measure of danger.

What a fragile creature he had become. The slightest stumble, the most trivial cut, might provoke a lethal bleed. *All bleeding stops.* It was a grim maxim known to all doctors: Dead patients cease to bleed.

I have to get out of here. There it was. All that mattered. The refrain thundered so loudly within his skull
that the meager assembly of platelets left to guard the
vascular borders of his brain might be fatally dislodged
by the sheer vibrations of the thunderous noise. Jarred
from their valiant yet tenuous grip, the floodwaters—the
*blood*waters—would be dammed no more . . . and in a
matter of moments Patrick Falconer would drown.

As he had been meant to drown years before.

I have to get out of here—now.

It was so easy. He wore hospital pajamas, not a con-
vict's garb, and across a short expanse of heather green
carpet was the spacious closet that housed his clothes.

Easy. Effortless. If one ignored the dizziness. It was
worse now, the consequence of blood lost by design,
withdrawn for the vast battery of diagnostic tests, and lost
through happenstance, the consequence of the inability to
stem even the slightest bleed. Massive bruises adorned
his arms, gravestones of venipunctures, and the entirety
of his right hip, where the biopsy had been performed,
was an angry gathering of blue-black blood.

As he retrieved his clothes Patrick resolutely ignored
the dizziness; and with similar resolve he avoided catching even a glimpse of himself in the room's full-length
mirror.

Patrick saw his hands, however. The once-steady surgeon's fingers trembled, *trembled,* as he extricated himself from his pajama top.

Had Jesse's fingers been like this on the day of his release? Ghostly white and shaking in anticipation of freedom—at last.

Freedom. The word itself caused a dizzying swirl. Dr.
Patrick Falconer might be fleeing this most posh of cells.

But his imprisonment would be traveling with him. His barren marrow would be making the journey; as would those intrepid yet woefully inadequate platelets; as would his red cells, their numbers diminishing with each passing day, blissfully oblivious to the consequences of their demise.

Each red blood cell that succumbed to old age—a natural, peaceful death—virtually assured that there would be no such peaceful end for Patrick. He was not going to die of natural causes.

His death might be mercifully quick, the drowning of his brain in a rush of blood. But should his platelets manage to stave off a lethal flood, his cells would suffocate. The least critical organs would die first, a triage system over which he had no control. His heart and brain would be the last to go, the organs for which all others were sacrificed.

Patrick would be alert, aware, until the very end. He would know the racing of his heart, its pace ever-quickening as it struggled to circulate the ever-diminishing blood; and he would feel the suffocation of his liver, the starvation of his spleen; and he would hear, perhaps, the agonal screams of his kidneys as they died.

Patrick was leaving his plush prison. But he was not escaping to freedom.

And what of Jesse? Had there been freedom when his time was served, his debt to society paid in full? Or for Jesse, too, had the rest of his life merely signaled the beginning of his death?

Jesse. Every minute of his twin's incarceration had imprisoned Patrick as well. Even as he had hated Jesse, tried to hate Jesse, Patrick had been haunted by images of a small, stark cell.

Jesse had always been so wild; a savage—yet majestic—beast who would not be broken. Jesse had not been broken in prison. Of that Patrick had no doubt. Jesse Falconer had spent those caged years in churning, restless rage.

Had there been other emotions as well? Regret? Remorse? Had the twin with whom there had once been such a special bond, a knowing without words, sensed the torment Patrick felt?

And did Jesse feel Patrick's imprisonment now? Did the healthy cells in Jesse's marrow sense the death of their twin's? Would Jesse know when Patrick died, the precise moment when his heart ceased to beat? Would Jesse *care*?

Or, at long last, would Jesse finally be free?

Since his diagnosis Patrick's racing heart had pulsed frantic commands to his floating brain, urgent pleas to ask Jesse, perhaps the only viable donor on earth, to donate his marrow. Patrick had finally acceded to the frenzied demands—but only in his dreams.

Yes, Jesse had replied in those glorious dreams. Of course I will give you my marrow, all of it, Patrick, if that's what you need. You're my brother, my twin. I love—

The dream became a nightmare. They were sailing. Jesse responded to his request for marrow with dark laughter and an astonished glare. Then Patrick was in the water, and Jesse stopped laughing and simply stared, mesmerized, *satisfied,* as Patrick began to drown.

Then the nightmare became even worse—because Patrick did not drown after all. He was saved. *She* saved him. And for a few moments he was dreaming again. But her affection was for Jesse, not for him. Her fingers glittered with diamonds, gifts from Jesse. Patrick was blinded by their fire.

We want you to live, she told him. That's why Jesse is going to share his marrow with you. But that's all he's going to share. You can't have me, Patrick. I belong to Jesse.

The nightmare did not fade even in the bright light of a Southern California day, *this* Southern California day, as he was making his escape.

It was then that Patrick saw his reflection in the hospital-room mirror. His fleeting glimpse became lingering as a macabre fascination compelled him to stare.

The image, his image, was a stunning study in contrasts. His skin was deathly white, the color—the colorlessness—of ice stretched thin over a fathomless lake. His eyes were the blue of that lake. Bright, clear, bitterly cold.

Then there was his beard, so pathetically defiant, flourishing even as he died. The robust growth of near black hair, so dark against the ghostly white, was quite young, just a few days old—as old and as new as the revelation that his platelets were in such limited supply that even a nick from shaving might provoke an excessive bleed.

Patrick's gaze drifted to his torso, fully exposed, the pajama top discarded. His arms offered silent testimony . . . to what? To war, he supposed. He might have been a soldier bruised from battle, an ancient combat in which the only weapons were muscled flesh and valiant will.

He *was* a soldier. But in a different war. A modern conflict between life and death. Physicians were the generals in that fierce clash. Mortality was the enemy. And the pa-

tient was the foot soldier, and more: either the victim or
the spoils.

Patrick had been a general once, and now he was a soldier. But as with the lush beard, his torso offered evidence that his diagnosis was quite new. His muscles
appeared warrior strong, lean, and hard; an illusion of
health, of life, that was hauntingly false.

Hauntingly. Like the ghost he was? No. He was not a
ghost. His dark blue eyes grew even colder as the image
in the mirror revealed its true self: a cadaver ready for autopsy and so weak that even now it was yearning to lie on
its final bed, the stainless-steel gurney that shone in the
morgue.

Find Jesse. Ask Jesse.

The silent commands, desperate pleas from cells already suffocating from lack of air, whirled his brain and
blurred the vision in his icy eyes.

Find Jesse? Plead with his twin to save his life?

The myriad cells within Patrick's dying body were
gasping—just as Patrick had gasped, was *meant* to gasp,
on that bright blue summer day.

Patrick's vision cleared then, a brilliant clarity, as he
beheld anew the carcass in the mirror. His brain no longer
whirled. And the truth was crystal clear.

Ask Jesse?

No. He would die first.

He would die.

It took a moment for the sound to register, to penetrate
the oppressive mantle of his thoughts. It was a knock so
tentative that Patrick wondered if he had imagined it.

It could have been Death coming to take him away.
But surely Death would be more assertive even than the
doctors and nurses who came to his door. Their knocks—

crisp, staccato raps—gave fair if short warning that the meager privacy he enjoyed was about to be invaded.

Ready or not. Here we come.

As a physician, and now as a patient, Patrick knew the intrusions were necessary. But they were invasions nonetheless.

The door should have been opening.

But it was not.

Whoever stood in the hallway outside his room was asking his permission to enter, was offering him a rare shred of control. If he remained silent, the uncertain visitor would undoubtedly go away.

So whose voice said, "Come in"?

Patrick knew the answer the moment she obeyed his command. It was the voice of a demon, a fiend who had found a home in the desolate emptiness of his marrow.

The diabolical tormentor wanted Patrick to suffer even more; to ache in ways that had nothing to do with suffocating cells; to hunger for something more essential to life than mere molecules of oxygen.

For here she was standing before him.

The copper-haired angel of his nightmares.

The lavender-eyed woman of his dreams.

We want you to live, she had told him in those dreams. But you can't have me, Patrick. I belong to Jesse.

It was a metaphor, of course, imagery crafted by the marrow-dwelling fiend.

Amanda Prentice did not belong to Jesse.

She did not even know Jesse.

"Hello, Amanda," Patrick greeted, welcoming her—and the torment, the aching, the wanting.

"Hello. Oh, you're . . ."

"Dressing." In a fluid motion Patrick retrieved his shirt and concealed his naked torso. "But decent."

"You're leaving?"

"Yes. You heard about the aplasia."

"Caitlin told me. She would have called you herself, from the ship, but the satellite delays make it quite awkward—"

"More awkward than this, Amanda?"

"This doesn't have to be awkward," Amanda murmured even as the truth taunted. How can this be anything *but* awkward? Because it must be, came her silent reply. For him. I must make it possible, for him, to speak of his fear. "We could just . . . talk."

Her soft words evoked within him a stunning response: fury, unexpected and powerful, a white-hot rush of rage unlike anything Patrick had ever known. His empty marrow was filled with it, molten with it.

Patrick's marrow blazed. But his voice was ice. "Patient to physician, you mean, Amanda? Dying trauma surgeon to sympathetic psychiatrist?"

"You're angry."

"Yes," he admitted quietly, battling the rage, fighting to keep its monstrous heat from searing her. "But that's usual, isn't it? It's been a while but my memory's pretty good. As I recall Dr. Kübler-Ross defines five stages of death and dying. Anger is definitely one, as are, in no particular order, denial, isolation, depression, bargaining—with a shred of hope woven throughout. Is that right? Am I remembering correctly?"

"Yes." *Correctly. Impeccably.* "But Patrick . . ."

"Just because I'm familiar with the issues I'm hardly an expert? I agree. I even concede that, given time is of the essence, professional guidance might be prudent—to get me to the acceptance stage before it's too late. But I've made a decision—which, as the patient in question, I believe is my prerogative to do. I'm going to spend some time with this anger." *I don't want to, but I must. This bone-deep fury is not me . . . and yet it is—this new, raging, dying me.* "In fact I may just wallow in anger until the bitter end. It's a naked emotion—one which, I imagine, is best left for me to explore alone. Unless . . ."

"Unless?"

Unless you'd like to get naked with me, metaphorically speaking. We could take turns exposing raw and explicit emotions—psychological strip poker, if you will.

The thought was cruel, a taunt that went far beyond mockery of her chosen career. Patrick had seen Amanda's reaction to his naked torso: fear, as marrow-deep as his rage.

What monster had been awakened within him?

"Unless nothing. I want you to leave, Amanda." *Right now, while I still have some control over the malevolent demon haunting my bones. It wants its freedom, Amanda. It wants to demonstrate its own surefire shortcut to the acceptance stage of death. The technique is quite simple. I merely say something so cruel that you can have only one possible reply: I accept that you're dying, Patrick. And I'm glad of it. I was so wrong about you.*

Was the demon truly so altruistic? Concerned only for her?

Or did it want to hurt her, to punish her, for coming into Patrick's life so late . . . too late?

"Patrick, please let—"

"Go away, Dr. Prentice. Please. Go. Away."

Amanda obeyed. Eventually. Without another word. Before turning away, her lavender-blue eyes shimmered—at him. *For* him. *This isn't you, Patrick. I know it's not.*

Then who is it? Patrick wondered as the door closed quietly—yet thunderously—behind her . . . like the quiet thunder one knew in prison. The clanging steel that locked in despair.

Patrick had his answer then: the identity of the demon who was so willfully cruel.

It made macabre sense, he supposed. As death neared some evil buried deep within would assert itself at last, would prove in no uncertain terms their kinship. Their twinship.

So who was the monster that evoked such molten fury in his marrow? Such glacial cruelty in his veins?

Jesse, of course.

Jesse.

EIGHT

LIBRARY
QUARTERDECK, PORTSIDE
QUEEN ELIZABETH 2
TUESDAY, APRIL TWENTY-THIRD

"*M*ay I help you?" the librarian queried.

"Yes, thank you. I was wondering if you carry novels by Graydon Slake? I can't seem to find any on the shelves."

Caitlin had checked all the bookshelves in the glass-walled library above the sea, including those labeled German, Spanish, and French. She was in search of Graydon Slake's New York publisher. Even a translation, she reasoned, might include such data on the copyright page.

Once the corporate name was hers she would place another ship-to-shore call. Perhaps several. Convincing a publishing house to disclose the phone number of one of its bestselling, and most hidden, authors might take a few tries—especially since Caitlin had to be extremely discreet about what she herself disclosed.

But she would get the number. Unlisted phone numbers were de rigueur among the celebrities—and those who imagined themselves to be—who dwelled amid the palms and plumeria of LA. There were legitimate times when

Dr. Caitlin Taylor needed those exclusive listings: when a relative's consent was necessary to enable her to operate on an unconscious loved one . . . or when heroic interventions were too late and she was left with the somber task of notifying a family member of a death.

Of necessity Caitlin had become quite proficient at persuading the phone company, answering services, private security firms, and even the LAPD to break the rules.

Rules did not apply in matters of life and death.

Just as they did not apply at sea.

"We do carry his novels," the librarian affirmed. "If there are none on the shelves, I'm afraid they're all checked out. Which isn't surprising. He's extremely popular. And even though it may be excessively optimistic to imagine we'll get our carton in Bermuda I've begun the wait list for *Blue Moon*, just in case."

"*Blue Moon*?"

"His new hardcover."

"Oh. Do you happen to know who his publisher is?"

"Not offhand, but I can easily find out." She turned to her desktop computer and spoke as she typed. "Do you want one of his English-language publishers? American or British?"

"Yes, please. American, if you have that."

The librarian frowned. "In fact, I don't. It looks as if all our copies are published in the UK. But our video library does carry *The Snow Lion*, and as there are so few children aboard this week maybe one of the cassettes will still be on the shelf."

The librarian led the way to the video alcove, a short journey past a hand-carved crystal globe.

"Ah-ha." She smiled with triumph as she removed the

one remaining cassette. "There might be something in the credits, don't you suppose? A reference to the book—and hence the publisher—on which the film was based."

"Yes," Caitlin murmured, stunned but elated by the apparent revelation that Graydon Slake had authored the best-selling children's story that had become a block-buster film. "Graydon Slake wrote *The Snow Lion*?"

"A bit shocking, isn't it? His thrillers are, well, hardly suitable for children. And *The Snow Lion* is—oh, but surely you've seen it."

"No, actually, I haven't."

"Then you have a treat in store. Truly. I was going to suggest that we just fast-forward to the credits on our library VCR, and we certainly can do that. I don't mean to be foisting this on you, to urge you to spend time in your stateroom watching a movie when there's so much else to do."

"I'd like to see the movie. I've actually been intending to see it for quite some time." *Since that day, three years ago tomorrow, when I received that frantic phone call. . . .*

*W*hen the brakes failed the bus careened off an embankment and plunged into a ravine. Amazingly most of the kids walked away unscathed. We thought *he* was going to be fine, but he's really gone down the tubes."

"In what way?" Caitlin asked calmly, hoping to soothe the obvious distress she heard.

The voice belonged to a pathology resident who was moonlighting in a small hospital thirty minutes away. The hospital was perfectly good—but it was ill-equipped, as was he, to deal with trauma. Which was fine. That was why there were designated trauma centers like Westwood Memorial.

"Well," the resident replied. "The problem's his heart, which is why I'm calling you. He has obvious chest injuries. Cracked ribs. Maybe a sternal fracture. And now his pressure's dropped, his respiratory rate has doubled, and his X ray shows a water-bottle silhouette."

"So he's tamponading."

"It looks that way."

"Has anyone needled the effusion?"

"No one here is really comfortable doing a pericardiocentesis, especially in a child. Besides, at the moment he's stable. But we think he needs to be explored. Is that something you can do, Dr. Taylor? Would be willing to do?"

"You're sure it's safe to transport him? If not I can talk you—or someone else—through a pericardiocentesis."

"It's safe. For now. Can I tell the staff you'll accept him?"

The story was flaky. Caitlin had absolutely no doubt, however, that the patient was in trouble and the referring physician was in way over his head.

"Yes. I'll accept him."

"*Great.*" The young doctor's relief hummed into the phone. "I'll arrange for the transfer right away. Can you hang on a minute, though? Dr. Johnstone, the hospital's chief of staff, wants to tell you a little about the family."

With that the resident was gone, although Caitlin heard his voice still, his buoyant announcement to the rest of the team caring for the critically ill patient in the sleepy little ER. "They'll take him! Westwood Memorial. Dr. Taylor. Yes, *really.*"

As Caitlin waited for the chief of staff she worried about her new patient, wished him godspeed. She spent no time anticipating the impending admonitions about the little boy's family. Such advance warnings could range from the precarious health of a parent to the observation that one or both guardians were intoxicated to the fact that calls to malpractice attorneys had already been made.

It was something ominous, Caitlin realized, even before Dr. Johnstone spoke. She heard the apprehension simply from the way he cleared his throat.

"We're so *appreciative* of your willingness to care for little Timmy," he began. "He's Timmy Asquith, Dr. Taylor. Robert's son and Timothy's grandson."

"Robert? Timothy?"

"Robert *Asquith*. Timothy *Asquith*."

"I'm sorry. Those names mean nothing to me."

"Really? Then I'm even more glad we called you."

Meaning, Caitlin decided, that her fingers wouldn't be trembling as she operated.

Robert and Timothy Asquith must be surgeons. Caring for colleagues' families was always a little difficult, and operating on other surgeons' children could be a nightmare, especially if the surgically savvy relatives insisted on scrubbing in. Well, Caitlin could be insistent as well. She could get very tough when her patients' best interests were at stake.

She would politely but firmly inform Drs. Robert and Timothy Asquith that they were to wait in the waiting room. Like everyone else. No matter who they were.

But who were they? Admittedly she'd been in Los Angeles for less than a year, and was far from familiar with all its physicians. But Caitlin knew of the famous—or infamous—ones, those whose reputations preceded them. The chief of staff's tone suggested that the Asquiths enjoyed no small amount of fame.

"They're surgeons?"

"What? *No.* They're Gemstone Pictures, Gemstone Records, Global News. Robert is one of the most powerful men in Hollywood. His father, Timothy, holds that title on a larger scale, like maybe the planet."

So? Caitlin thought. Who *cares*?

"Timmy's parents, Robert and Faye, have been extremely nice," Dr. Johnstone hurriedly assured. "As reasonable as is possible given what's happened to their son. The problem, Dr. Taylor, may be Timothy. You don't achieve his level of success without being a little bit demanding."

"Is he making demands now?"

"Well . . . yes. He and his wife are en route from London, but he's been communicating from his private jet. He informed me politely, but in no uncertain terms, that we were to find for his grandson the best heart surgeon in LA. Which, Dr. Taylor, I believe we have."

Caitlin wondered how many other "best" heart surgeons had been approached before her, how many had simply pleaded an inability to squeeze Timmy Asquith into their busy schedules. Because of his powerful grandfather. Because of what Timothy Asquith might do if his grandson died.

The consensus reached at Westwood Memorial before their new patient even arrived was that it would be best if whatever was going to happen was a *fait accompli* by the time Timothy Asquith's private plane landed at LAX—especially if the media mogul's grandson was destined to die.

Caitlin was not party to the consensus-defining discussions. Her decision was guided solely by what was best for the breathless, cyanotic, hypotensive little boy. Within moments of seeing her supposedly stable patient she had a needle in his chest and was draining the pool of blood that was tamponading his heart.

Hours later Timmy was ready for the OR—as ready as he would ever be. Caitlin had just told his parents of her plan to operate, and was assuring Faye and Robert that of course they could spend a few more minutes with their son, when Timothy and Lillith Asquith arrived.

"May we see him, too?"

The voice was male, British, upper-crust—and demanding? Not at all. Timothy Asquith wore his wealth and power the way the authentically wealthy and powerful do—without flaunting it, without needing to. And as introductions were being made Caitlin decided that the patriarch's emotions were authentic as well; authentically British, that is: old school, formal, stiff upper lip.

Which didn't mean the emotions weren't there, or even that they were invisible. Although contained, Timothy Asquith's worry was immense. And desperate. And why not? Despite his enormous power and limitless wealth, he could not save Timmy's life.

Only she could.

And he doesn't want *me* to operate. Caitlin believed she saw that sentiment, too, on his grave and aristocratic face. Her response was swift, fervent, familiar—overly sensitive, perhaps, overly sensit*ized*, the consequence of years of experience. Dr. Caitlin Taylor did not conform to the usual image of a heart surgeon. She was young and she was female.

Sorry, Mr. Asquith, but there's really no option. Your

*grandson needs immediate surgery and I just may be the
only surgeon in LA willing to risk your wrath if things
don't go well. I'm it, Mr. Asquith. And I will give Timmy
everything I have to give.*

And if that wasn't enough? If little Timmy did not survive?

This is who I am. All that I am. This is my life.

"Do you have questions for me, Mr. Asquith? Because
if not, I really need to get to the operating room."

Her challenging gaze met his austere one.

"No, Dr. Taylor," the billionaire quietly replied. "I
have no questions."

Timothy Asquith had no questions, and in the operating room on that April night the talented hands of Dr.
Caitlin Taylor had the answers.

Two days later her young patient was breathless again.
The culprit this time was pure enthusiasm, not the rush of
blood into his pericardial sac.

"*The Snow Lion* is the best movie ever! Nothing *bad*
happens. No one dies, not like in *Bambi* or *Old Yeller,* and
it's an important movie, too, because you *learn* something. Do you know about white lions? Not white tigers,
Dr. Taylor, white *lions.*"

"I guess not. Will you tell me?"

"Sure! There are only about twenty of them in the entire world. *Twenty.* So you can see how much they need to
be protected. The way they become white is this: every
lion has two genes that decide color. If even *one* is for the
usual lion color—tawny, it's called—then the lion is
tawny. To be white *both* of the genes have to be white
genes. *But* two tawny lions *can* have a white baby if they
each have one white gene." Timmy shrugged, an expansive gesture remarkably unencumbered by his healing

sternal wound. "It's a little complicated, but that's how it works."

"You certainly understand it well, Timmy. And explain it well." In fact, Caitlin marveled, she had just heard from a five-year-old an entirely accurate recounting of the intricacies of autosomal recessive genetics.

"It's part of the movie."

"It sounds wonderful."

"It *is*! But Dr. Taylor, even though *The Snow Lion* is happy not sad, it might make you cry. Even my *granddad* cried. Even though he'd already read the book."

"The book?"

Timmy nodded energetically, then elaborated proudly, "I'm the one who showed it to him. I asked him to read it to me, because it was my favorite, and when he finished we talked about what a great movie it would make."

"So the movie was really your idea."

He shook his head as vigorously as he had nodded it. "No. It was Granddad's idea. My dad wasn't sure, not at all, but Granddad insisted. And it's doing really, *really* well."

Caitlin had no idea if the billionaire moviemaker cared about the extravagant success of his latest film. But she knew without question that Timothy Asquith cared about the health, the extravagant healthiness, of his beloved grandson.

"If there's ever anything I can do for you, Dr. Taylor, anything, ever, please let me know. Nothing could come close to what you have done for us, we all know that, but . . ."

"Thank you, Mr. Asquith." Robert, Faye, and Lillith called her Caitlin, and she in turn called them by their given names. But she and the mogul were Mr. Asquith and Dr. Taylor. Caitlin couldn't imagine it any other way. "I'm just happy that it turned out so well. I don't need anything more than that."

But surely there was something the hospital could use? Timothy Asquith posed the provocative question to Westwood Memorial's medical director.

Well, the medical director conceded, OR equipment was always nice. Westwood prided itself on being state-of-the-art. But every year, every few months it seemed, there was some new improved gadget or other.

Timothy Asquith was not interested in purchasing merely a gadget or two. He would, he decided, donate an entire wing devoted to hearts.

The Asquith Wing, the medical director suggested when he could finally breathe. Or the Gemstone Pavilion, if he preferred; or the Timmy Asquith Heart Center; or—

Timothy Asquith's preference was that the donation remain anonymous, with no allusions whatsoever to himself, his family, or his empire. Caitlin, too, refused recognition of any kind, no engravings on bronze plaques, much less chiselings into white granite walls.

Timothy Asquith's thank-you would be known, simply, as the Heart Institute . . . and it would be, simply, the most sophisticated facility on the planet for the care and preservation of human hearts.

The Asquiths returned to their Los Angeles and London homes. The crisis passed. But their legacy lingered. Caitlin's approval was considered essential for every incarnation of the Heart Institute blueprints, and she received a lovely Christmas card from Robert and Faye. The Yuletide greeting included a cheery note—yet another "heartfelt" thank-you, and the happy announcement that another Asquith, a baby brother to Timmy, was due on New Year's Day.

A month later, in mid-January, a phone call came to her office while she was scrubbed. It wasn't surprising, of course, that Lillith Asquith would be in LA. Assuming the newest Asquith grandson had been born close to his due date, he would be two weeks old, ample reason to lure a devoted grandmother from London.

What was surprising was that Lillith was calling her.

"Was there a message?" Caitlin asked.

"A long one," her secretary confirmed. "In essence she wants to see you. I have no idea why. She's incredibly polite, isn't she? And with that wonderful accent. I felt I was speaking to royalty. Anyway, at first she said she wanted to take you to breakfast or lunch or dinner or tea. *Whatever.* Then she virtually retracted all the invitations, as if they were too pushy."

That was Lillith, Caitlin mused. A ladylike reluctance to appear presumptuous in the least. Lillith Asquith *was* a lady. Indeed, should the duchess of Kent ever tire of her Wimbledon duties—her gracious thank-yous to every ball girl and ball boy followed by the trophy presentation to the Ladies Champion—Lillith could easily take her place.

Physically, visually, Lillith complemented her husband perfectly: her sublime grace, his austere elegance. But Lillith was far more than decorative. It was her inner strength, her regal dignity, that made her Timothy Asquith's ideal match—that, and the obvious affection they shared.

Caitlin heard the strength, and the dignity, when she returned Lillith's phone call. But she heard urgency as well—and she saw it that evening when they met.

Lillith Asquith looked weary, fragile, *ill.*

"It's so nice of you to have agreed to meet with me, Caitlin, even though you're on call."

"I'm *delighted* to, Lillith. I'm only sorry that we couldn't have made it a bit more, well, *away* from the hospital." At least, at this time of night, the cafeteria was virtually empty. "Is something wrong, Lillith? The baby?"

"No. He's perfect, and Faye and Robert and Timmy are all fine. As is Timothy. I'm afraid it's me, Caitlin. I'm the one with the problem."

Caitlin was not surprised by the revelation. But she was stunned by the apology in Lillith's voice. "Can you tell me?"

"Yes, which will make you one of the first to know. Ahead, even, of Timothy. He knows something is wrong. I was ill in December, when we were in Hong Kong, and on our return to London my physician found something quite unrelated to my Hong Kong flu. But it was Christmastime, and the baby was due, and we were so looking forward to our trip here once he was born. I told Timothy everything was fine. I'm quite sure he didn't believe me. After all these years we know each other so well. But he hasn't pushed. He's just been waiting for me to tell him the truth."

"What is the truth?"

"Cancer. Of my left breast."

"Oh, Lillith."

"I gather that there's hope, these days, for cancer?"

"Yes, *absolutely.* But Lillith, the sooner you begin treatment the better the prognosis." *Be selfish, Lillith Asquith! Do not put off caring for yourself even one more day.* "I know the baby's just been born, but you need to tell your family *now.*"

"I will tell them—at least Timothy—very soon, the moment I have everything arranged. I've decided I'd like my care to be in the U.S."

"Here? At WMH? If so, we have an oncologist, Stephen Sheridan, who is wonderful."

"I'm sure he is," Lillith replied, gracious still, gracious always. "Actually, I was thinking somewhere on the East Coast might be best."

Best, Caitlin echoed silently. Meaning easiest for all concerned—far away from the gossip that would inevitably result if her illness became known; and far away, too, from the grandchildren who might be disturbed by images of their disease-ravaged grandmother.

Caitlin suggested Sloan-Kettering, a proposal that was efficiently implemented by a phone call from Stephen Sheridan to a colleague at the renowned cancer institute—and which had worked out very well.

As of ten days before Caitlin's planned departure for her cruise aboard the *Queen Elizabeth 2*, a cheery call from Lillith reported that she was fine, healthy, disease-free still after more than two years.

On the Friday night before the cruise, however, a message, left hours earlier, awaited Caitlin's return from the OR.

Robert Asquith wants you to call—tonight or tomorrow. (I told him you were leaving Sunday for your cruise). He says it's nothing medical.

It was eleven P.M., a bit late to call. But Robert had inherited graciousness from his parents—which meant that "nothing medical" might be a polite lie, so that she wouldn't worry should they fail to connect.

Robert's voice, awake and relaxed, instantly allayed Caitlin's fears.

"I was calling to impose," he explained. "To ask yet another favor for the Asquiths."

Caitlin smiled. "Ask away."

"Okay. Are you familiar with the term *script doctor*?"

"No. Something Hollywood, I imagine."

"Very Hollywood. A script doctor is the screenwriter who rescues—cures, if you will—an ailing script. What Dad and I need, however, is a true script doctor. Two of them, actually, a heart surgeon and a psychiatrist. The screenplay is in its final draft, and we think it's terrific. We just want to be certain that the medical aspects are entirely correct. We'll pay you, of course."

"That's *not* necessary."

"Actually, it is. Gemstone is signatory to the Screenwriters Guild. So we must pay you and pay you well."

"Well. Whatever. In any event, I'd be happy to read the script. Would you like me to find the psychiatrist as well?"

"I'd love it, if it's easy."

"Very easy."

"Great. Thank you. This is going to be a sensational film, Caitlin. That sounds immodest, but it's not. I'm merely the expeditor. *Thief* is Dad's brainchild, just as *The Snow Lion* was."

"*Thief*?"

"*Of Hearts*. It's a great title, isn't it? And it's perfect for a film that blends the best of *Basic Instinct* and *Silence of the Lambs*."

Caitlin had not seen either blockbuster film. But she had an inkling of the erotic themes and ghastly violence.

"Will *Thief of Hearts* be so . . . brutal?" So *sexual?*

"It's going to be stylish. The violence, not to mention the sex, will be *im*plicit rather than *ex*plicit. We think it's more compelling that way, more evocative. Oh, and for the record, the heart surgeon *is* a woman, but she's *not* a murderess. In fact she's the heroine of the piece."

If there's ever anything I can do for you, Dr. Taylor, anything—ever . . .

As Caitlin descended the carpeted staircase to Two Deck, *The Snow Lion* video in her hand, she heard the echoes of the offer. Made in utmost sincerity, it had been reiterated more than once—most recently when she'd called from her office in the Heart Institute to thank him yet again for the extraordinary gift.

Timothy Asquith had dismissed as trivial his offering of stone and steel and had repeated his belief that he would never be able to truly repay her—to intervene, as she had, in a matter of life and death.

But now you can, Mr. Asquith. Now you can.

Caitlin had forgotten about the captain's reception. Her memory was gently, and elegantly, jarred by the engraved invitation slipped under her stateroom door. It was already six o'clock sea time, and many hours later in London. Too late, she decided, to call Timothy Asquith tonight. And *The Snow Lion* would be here upon her return, to be viewed in the middle of the night, a powerful antidote to the marauders of her dreams.

So I guess I'm going to the reception.

It would be, she imagined, quite grand. Tuxedoed men and sequined women, smiling, dancing, drinking champagne . . . the sort of enchanted evening in which one might see a stranger across a crowded room.

It was not going to happen. Not to her. But for Margaret, for Maggie, she would go.

NINE

*P*atrick frowned at the listing for Dr. Amanda Prentice in WMH's Medical Staff Directory. Her home phone was provided, as he had hoped it would be, but her address in the Palisades was listed as well. The directory was confidential. Once in print, however, even the most classified information might fall into the wrong hands. Such a security lapse was of little concern to a physician like Patrick. Trauma surgeons were rare targets of obsession.

But Amanda was a psychiatrist. Was she so fearless? So careless? Or was she merely so confident of her ability to soothe even the most deranged mind?

There were, of course, alternate explanations for Amanda's apparent lack of caution. Her Palisades home might be a fortress, rendering impossible an assault by even the most determined madman. There might be an elaborate security system, further embellished by a watchdog or two. And in true Hollywood style Amanda Prentice might even employ a bodyguard.

I guess I'll find out. Patrick's frown deepened. Was he really going to drive to her home? Just scant hours after leaving the hospital against medical advice? Yes. He was. Because this was not the way it was going to end.

Not with anger. Not with cruelty.

Not the way what was going to end? His *relationship* with Amanda? Counting the disgraceful episode in his hospital room Patrick had seen her exactly three times. Three unforgettable times, Patrick amended as his skeletal hand reached for his keys.

Three unforgettable times. Beginning three weeks ago, on that Tuesday night, just ten days after he'd arrived in LA. . . .

*I*t was almost midnight on that Tuesday. Patrick was on his way home. There was one final stop, the same last stop he made in every hospital in which he'd ever worked—the emergency room.

"Anything cooking?"

Patrick's query was posed to Trish, the graveyard-shift charge nurse.

"Not a thing," she replied. "We're quiet—from a trauma standpoint, that is."

"Okay. I'm out of here, then. Oh, Trish, I was wondering, is there a place to shop nearby? Something that would be open now?"

Trish gazed flirtatiously at the gorgeous new trauma chief. "Grocery shopping, Dr. Falconer?"

"Yes. I—"

"Just discovered there's a kitchen in your condo?"

Patrick smiled. "Something like that."

"*Men,*" Trish teased. "This answer is yes, there is a place. *The* place, as a matter of fact. It's called Ariel's and it's open twenty-four hours a day. And what's more, Patrick, it's conveniently located just three blocks west of here, pretty much in a straight line between the hospital and Brentwood."

Meaning the route Patrick took every day. "It's probably such a hole in the wall I didn't notice."

"Probably."

Ariel's was massive, of course, and memorable. Indeed, Patrick had noticed the aquamarine glass structure the first time he drove by. But had he been compelled to render a diagnosis, he would have guessed it was a museum of modern art.

The impression of gallery not grocery persisted even at close range. The scale was grand, the lighting bright yet soft, the blond floors crafted of polished hardwood. A potpourri of scents greeted visitors to Ariel's, the perfume of just-cut roses, the aroma of freshly brewed coffee, the buttery intoxication of newly baked croissants. And music, not Muzak, drifted from on high. On this night, Tchaikovsky filled the air.

Ariel's was a feast for the senses—including the literary, if such allusions appealed. Patrick had wondered, during the short drive, about the identity of Ariel. To him Ariel evoked Shakespeare, the airy spirit of *The Tempest.*

It was the Bard's Ariel, Patrick realized. The directory in the foyer spotlighted Prospero's Pantry, the in-store café that featured pastries, espresso, and the telltale "tempest in a teapot."

The literary allusions were limited to Ariel and Prospero, and possibly the aquamarine glass. There were no shipwrecks in sight; nor was a Calaban's Candies, a Miranda's Marzipan, or a Trinculo's Trinkets to be found.

Ariel and Prospero, encased in sea-green glass. A tribute to Shakespeare as light and airy as the light and airy spirit itself.

Ariel's boasted clientele from Malibu to Laguna Niguel. At midnight on this Tuesday, however, the majority of patrons hailed from Westwood Memorial, refugees from the just-completed evening shift. Most still wore their hospital garb, which is why Patrick recognized them. Only a few did he actually know, much less could address by name.

But Patrick's fellow shoppers knew him. The most recent issue of the medical center's monthly newsletter had carried as its feature article *him*. And on the off chance that anyone missed the article, a condensed version— with a not-so-condensed photograph—adorned the hospital's myriad kiosks and bulletin boards.

Like an FBI most-wanted poster.

Dr. Patrick Falconer *was* most wanted and most welcome. The campaign to lure him from Manhattan to Memorial had been aggressive, gracious, dazzling—and so determined that Patrick had been certain his very determined friend and surrogate little sister had been a key player in the plan. But Caitlin denied any involvement at all. She had merely been delighted—as was he—that the concerted effort had finally paid off. Patrick was happy to be at Memorial, and in LA. Nonetheless, he was privately counting the days until the hospital's next newsletter appeared and his posters were supplanted by fresher tidings.

Now, as he strolled the shining wooden aisles at

Ariel's, Patrick felt the impact of the front-page article and omnipresent posters. He was wearing neither white coat nor surgical scrubs, and his pager, clipped to his belt, was concealed beneath his blazer.

But he was recognized.

None of Patrick's coworkers had, apparently, permitted their larders of coffee to fall as perilously low as his. The aisle containing coffee—and comparably vast selections of cocoa and tea—was almost empty.

A lone woman stood at the far end, in the section devoted to teas. She stood absolutely still, staring at a shelf, focused and intent. Trying, Patrick decided, to choose among Darjeeling, Earl Grey, English Breakfast, and Ceylon. A gift, perhaps, for a friend.

Perhaps; and yet, as Patrick followed her stare, it seemed that her concentration was focused not on the teas but on their price.

She did not look like a woman who would be concerned about cost. Her periwinkle blue suit was the handiwork of a talented designer, and swirls of gold adorned her ears, and there was more gold at her throat.

Her right hand, the only one Patrick could see, was bare. The left, concealed behind her slender silhouette, might be bejewelled or barren, but it was not empty. The hidden hand held an environmentally friendly shopping bag, crafted of heavy canvas and embroidered in aquamarine thread *Ariel's*.

The woman in periwinkle was staring, and so was he, captivated, bewitched, by her aura. Invisible, yet somehow shimmering, the ethereal mist sent a message that was at once intense and fragile, vulnerable yet courageous. And did the mesmerizing haze wreathe an angel?

As Patrick focused, at last, on the physical shell, he discovered a reality as intriguing as the otherworldly halo itself.

Her hair was red, and sable, and gold.

Auburn, Patrick supposed. No, he amended decisively, *autumn*. That was a better word, the right word, for copper caressed by a harvest moon, for mahogany ablaze with the colors of fall.

The style itself was surprisingly severe, as if such bondage was necessary to contain the exuberant coppery flames. Pulled away from her face and twisted in single rope, the autumnal bounty was knotted atop her head, a crown that added to her height.

She was tall, even without her crown, or the high, high heels she wore. Quite obviously she chose to enhance her natural height; and she wore that height with pride, her carriage straight, her posture model perfect.

She probably is a model, Patrick mused. Someone I should know. Or maybe she's an actress.

But surely an actress would let her glorious hair fall free, its gilded fire luxuriantly revealed.

Patrick was in LA, home to a galaxy of stars—a universe unto itself in which legions of paparazzi made their fortunes by catching celebrities off guard, bedraggled, denim-clad, makeup free; fully as *un*glamorous as everyday folks.

There were obvious ways to avoid such unwanted photographs. One could remain hidden from even the most powerful of telephoto lenses. Or one could dress flawlessly even at midnight, even when one made a late-night journey to Ariel's in search of tea.

But this angel would rather remain hidden. The

thought came from nowhere. Powerful and confident—even though it made no sense.

A woman who yearned for privacy did not dress with such impeccable style. Nor did she so fully expose her face.

Patrick had yet to truly see that face. He saw only the silhouette, the shadowy cameo beneath the heavy copper crown.

Look at me. Don't hide from me.

It wasn't going to happen. Her concentration was too intense.

Except that now she was moving, her lips were moving, a soundless whisper spoken to the shelf of tea; and her head shook ever so slightly, a gentle *no*; and her right hand, slender and bare, touched the pricing label on the tea-laden shelf.

In another moment she would select her tea and vanish.

Look at me.

Patrick saw in slow motion her reply to the silent call of his heart. And in that magnificent moment Patrick watched his life pass before him, a kaleidoscope of images in which his inconsequential past—and all its pain—vanished without memory.

There was no past. There was only this twirl of sheer grace performed atop the highest of heels. Her hair glittered as she twirled, moonlight dancing amid the flames, and at last, at last, he saw her eyes. They were lavender-blue, as bright and clear as a harvest sky, and luminous, aglow with wonder, and now her lovely lips were beginning to part as if to whisper a joyous hello.

The world changed without warning, the kaleidoscope harshly twisted. Her eyes darkened, their autumnal brilliance stolen by winter shadows, a theft of sunshine, of bounty, of hope, and in the clouded gray Patrick saw something that looked very much like fear.

Fear.

"Dr. Falconer? Is that you?"

Politeness compelled Patrick to turn toward the voice, to smile, to speak.

"Hello, Jan."

"Hello," the X-ray tech replied, so pleased he remembered her name. "Isn't this a terrific place?"

"Yes," Patrick murmured, distracted. "Terrific."

A place of enchantment, he thought as he sent a silent command to the autumnal angel with the fearful wintry eyes. *Don't leave.*

Patrick believed she had obeyed. Even as he exchanged pleasantries with Jan, he listened for the click of heels on the polished wooden floor—and heard only silence.

But she was gone, *gone.* She had floated away, like Cinderella at the stroke of midnight, but with one monumental difference.

There was no glass slipper.

There was only the memory of wonder . . . and of fear.

The memory lingered, haunted, beckoned, and during the ensuing week, on the rare occasions his schedule would allow, he had returned to Ariel's in the hope of seeing her again. But to no avail.

Perhaps she only shopped at midnight on Tuesdays. If so, he would be there. Tonight. Soon.

As always, Patrick swung through the ER on the way out.

"*There* you are," Trish greeted.

Patrick glanced at his pager. There was no indication

of an unanswered call. "Have you been trying to reach me?"

"No. It's just that Dr. Prentice has been waiting to see you."

Dr. Prentice. The name rang a distant bell. But Patrick was focused on the present. Had he actually forgotten an appointment with a colleague? Was he that distracted? He *was* distracted, a preoccupation that extended far beyond the demands of his new job. There was his pallor, a nagging worry he was choosing to ignore; and there was *her*. "Had I arranged to meet him here?"

"No," Trish conceded. "And he's a she, Doctor. They make women physicians these days." Normally her sassiness would have teased a smile from him. But not tonight. "Anyway, I told her you always drop by on your way out, and since your chief resident had already been by, I expected you at any moment. That was a while ago."

"A while?"

"Almost two hours."

"Why the hell didn't you page me, Trish?"

"Amanda asked me not to. She said she didn't mind waiting."

"Where is she?"

"In the staff lounge."

The short walk was made even shorter by the briskness of his strides, a gait fueled by pure annoyance. How passive-aggressive could one get, waiting for someone who didn't know she was waiting?

Well, he could be passive-aggressive, too. With flawless politeness he would explain to Dr. Amanda Prentice that he really couldn't talk to her now, that he was already running late—

Dr. Amanda Prentice. The distant bell rang loud and clear. She was Caitlin's friend, the woman Caitlin had been wanting him to meet.

She's a psychiatrist, Caitlin? No thank you.

I'm not matchmaking, Patrick! You don't need anyone's help in that department and Amanda . . . well, you just need to meet her, that's all. She's very special.

Well, now he was going to meet Caitlin's very special, very passive-aggressive friend. Sorry, Caitie, but I don't like her already.

But Patrick did like her already. Passive-aggressive? No, just a physician who imagined that he was with a patient and didn't want to intrude. In fact, Patrick had been in the hospital's library, doing a computer search, harnessing his restlessness until it was time to begin his midnight search for *her.*

But now she was found. *She* had found *him.* It had hardly been a search. Even if the copper-haired psychiatrist had missed the monthly newsletter and the most-wanted posters displayed everywhere, she had undoubtedly heard Jan greet him by name—and Dr. Falconer was a name that Amanda Prentice would recognize thanks to Caitlin's campaign that they meet.

She had known all along who he was.

She was facing away from him, toward the staff bulletin board and its rainbow-bright assortment of messages.

"Amanda."

The impact of his voice was immediate. Her slender frame stiffened, and she drew a breath, and her resigned twirl spoke volumes. I don't want to be here. But I *have* to be.

Then her gaze met his, resolute and wary.

"Hello, Patrick."

"At last we meet."

"Yes. That night at Ariel's, I . . ." She faltered, unable or unwilling to explain why she had fled.

Or why she wanted to flee now. She was going to flee, he realized, and soon—for at the most inconsequential level her mission was complete: Caitlin had wanted them to meet, and they had. And now she wanted to flee, would flee . . . except that he was blocking her only route for escape.

Patrick would not trap her. Would not. He stepped away from the doorway, enabling her flight without narrowing the distance between them. She was free to go. With exquisite gentleness his blue eyes told her how much he wished she would stay.

"What were you doing that night?" he asked.

Trying to breathe, trying to speak, trying to walk toward you instead of away. But I couldn't.

And I can't now. "Doing?"

"You seemed to be studying the prices of the tea. Are they vastly inflated?"

"No." Her slender shoulders lifted in a graceful shrug. "It's just that the unit prices were wrong."

Talk to me, Amanda. About anything, even unit prices, whatever they are. "Educate me, Amanda. What's a unit price?"

"You know, on the labels on the shelves? In addition to the item price, the cost is broken down into price per ounce, per pound, or, in the case of tea, per hundred teabags."

"I didn't know that." *Men,* Trish would have teased, and in another setting, with another woman, Patrick might have offered the tease himself. But the fact that

Amanda was a woman—and he was a man—already heated the air, a truth so compelling, so volatile and so fearsome, it needed no further emphasis. "I guess I've just assumed it's always cheaper to buy the largest size. Since unit prices are provided, however, and savvy shoppers know to pay attention to them, it makes me believe that's not so."

"Often it is, but not invariably."

So you always check the unit price, he mused. And confirm the calculation? In your head? And when it's incorrect do you notify the store manager so that other shoppers won't be misled?

Patrick knew the answers. Yes to all.

And what of the answers to those other questions, the ones that danced and shimmered in the heated air? Do you feel the enchantment, Amanda? Do you feel *us?*

The shimmering moment ended abruptly, as a breathless Trish appeared.

"Amanda! Thank God you're still here."

"What is it, Trish?"

"We need you in Trauma Room One—*now*."

Patrick accompanied her. A psychotic patient triaged to a trauma room could be violent, or injured, or both.

The journey was short, swift, silent. Adrenaline sang in their veins as they cleared their minds. Such uncluttering was essential. In moments they would be required to focus wholly on whatever lay ahead—carnage, madness, a gruesome blend of each. Drs. Prentice and Falconer would need to suppress their shock, their horror, and concentrate solely on what must be done.

There was carnage but no madness. A pregnant patient, not a psychotic one. She was in the ER, in Trauma Room One, because she was delivering so emergently—and so traumatically—that even a swift transfer to Labor and Delivery posed too great a risk.

It was safer for the obstetrics team to race down, which the chief resident in OB had done; far safer for the crash delivery to happen here. Except that there was nothing safe about this crash delivery, neither for mother nor child. The baby was presenting feetfirst, the most dangerous way to enter the world.

"Footling breech," Trish told Amanda.

Amanda nodded. Her intelligent sky-blue gaze didn't leave the patient even as her slender fingers were slipping into latex with the practiced efficiency of a surgeon—and the grace of a lady donning white gloves for an afternoon tea.

A lady of leisure.

A married lady.

Patrick saw the glittering band of diamonds as Amanda slid her left hand into its designated glove.

He should have known. Caitlin had so much as told him. I'm not matchmaking, she had said. You don't need any help in that department, and Amanda, well . . .

Well. Amanda was married. Unhappily? Perhaps. Probably. But married nonetheless. *Wife* could now be added to the eclectic list of words that described Amanda Prentice. Wife. Angel. Psychiatrist. Obstetrician.

Warrior. Here, in this trauma room so very far from where white-gloved ladies sipped their afternoon tea, Amanda was in charge. And in control. She might have been conflicted personally, a wife attracted to a man who was not her husband, a beautiful woman who wished only to hide. Professionally, however, there was not a shred of uncertainty. There was only competence, and calm.

"Susan will get here as soon as she can," Trish was saying. "But it may be a while. She's scrubbed on a previa in L and D."

"Where's anesthesia?"

"You want to section her?"

"I may have to, Trish. I'd like to have anesthesia here."

"So would I," Trish said quietly. "And I'm trying, Amanda. There's a code in the RICU, and an emergency hip, and the previa in L and D. I've called for backup, but—"

"Okay." Amanda moved decisively to her patient.

The OB resident, drenched in blood and white with worry, gratefully relinquished his spot in front of the bleeding birth canal—the venue of life that had become a waterway of death.

It was, Patrick knew, far too late to turn the baby. Death would be a certainty for this half-born infant if one attempted to return it to its mother's womb.

The die was cast, and now began the life-and-death balancing act between haste and care. Time was of the essence. The uterus was clamping down, expelling its contents, telling the baby it was time to be born. For a baby born headfirst the powerful uterine muscles were welcome allies. But for an infant whose head was destined to arrive last the muscles might contract around the tiny neck, strangling in their zeal to expedite birth.

The baby needed to be delivered urgently. And delicately. An injudicious pull, an overly eager tug, could irreparably harm the infant's fragile internal organs.

Slowly yet swiftly, decisively yet gently, which was precisely what Amanda was doing.

Her eyes were closed, her mahogany lashes unflickering. She was going by feel, permitting her experienced hands to see into the shadows—

Quite suddenly the lashes flew open, as if the images within the lidded darkness were even worse than the carnage before her. Patrick saw her eyes, the luminous lavender ablaze with fury.

Fury. Why? Was she enraged that despite her efforts, everyone's efforts, the tiny life was destined to die? Anger at the certain triumph of death was something Patrick understood. All health-care providers did. Man's helplessness against the merciless whims of fate evoked anger and frustration within them all.

But fury? Rage? Amanda's reaction seemed extreme. And yet this was a case of extreme unfairness. Death was mocking, gloating, swaggering its ultimate power— killing before life even began, a chilling frost that froze forever the tiny bud.

But this contrary little life entered the world crying, not dying.

Or maybe she was singing, an aria that proclaimed her as a force to be reckoned with, as remarkable as the woman who had saved her life.

Angel, wife, psychiatrist, obstetrician—and warrior. Amanda was a general now, issuing a quiet command to her foot soldier. The resident, once frantically worried, was bedazzled—and grateful.

Amanda cloaked her command in the form of a question. "Why don't you take over?"

But it was a command. Her final one. For with that the general departed the battlefield, without uttering a single syllable to the mother whose life she had saved as surely as if she had liberated a country held hostage by the most evil of regimes.

Amanda shed her armor as she went. In a fluid movement she stripped gown, gloves, and mask, depositing the bloodied bundle in a hamper beside the trauma-room door.

She moved gracefully, as always, but she was weighted, laden with fury, an avenging angel still.

Patrick followed her. Not that it was any of his concern. Not that *she* was any of his concern.

Except that she was. Right or wrong.

And this was right. If nothing else he was acting by proxy for Caitlin, who, he imagined, most assuredly would have accompanied Amanda under similar circumstances.

"Amanda?"

She spun, startled, confused, "Patrick . . ."

"Tell me what's wrong," he urged, hoping to catch her enough off guard that she would do just that. Amanda was off guard. But she seemed far more likely to flee than to speak. "Here's a wild guess, Amanda. You have some training in OB."

Patrick had hoped for a flicker of a smile. It didn't happen. Her eyes were cloudy. Her face was grim. Only her copper crown shimmered still.

"My previous career."

"Which for some reason you no longer practice."

Which I can't practice. I became too obsessed, you see, too out of control. She was out of control now. She knew it and could have clamped down on it. But Amanda permitted her abandoned obsession to speak, to implore, "What's going to happen to that baby girl? What chance does she have?"

"*Every* chance, Amanda, thanks to you." Patrick knew Amanda wasn't searching for accolades. Indeed his praise caused even greater distress—as if she hadn't done enough . . . as if despite her intervention the baby had died. "She's a healthy, perfect baby, Amanda. Not to mention spirited and feisty. She'll do great. Thanks to you her entire life is ahead of her."

"Some life."

"What are you talking about?"

"No matter what the politicians say, in this country, in this town, *at this hospital,* excellent prenatal care is available no matter who you are or how much money you have. It's a crime, Patrick—it's child abuse—for that little girl's mother not to have sought medical care. If she had the breech presentation would have been discovered, and if not correctable in utero an elective section would have been done. There would have been no danger to the baby. None at all."

"And you think for that little girl the true danger is just beginning?"

"*Yes.*" The danger was beginning for Amanda as well. Patrick was gazing at her with concern, not alarm. His dark blue eyes were blind to what she truly was: crazed, rabid, foaming at the mouth. *But I am rabid on this subject, Patrick. Truly pathologic. And I must tell you more, until you are convinced.* "Do you know what I wanted to do when I held that little girl?"

"You wanted to never let her go."

"Yes," she whispered. *Don't you see how crazy that is?*

But Patrick Falconer was not seeing her madness. "I feel the same way when a child is injured because of being improperly restrained within a car, or when a toddler wanders into the street or falls into a swimming pool. It seems that to truly help, I should do a whole lot more than operate."

"But you've never seriously considered kidnapping a patient."

"Considered it? Who knows? I have, however, intervened—something that's far easier to do in trauma than in OB. I've always had clear-cut proof of injury, of neglect." Patrick frowned. "Not that my interventions have always resulted in the outcomes I'd hoped."

"The children have been returned to their abusive families."

"Yes. I'm not as big a believer in the sanctity of blood as our courts seem to be." A faint but infinitely gentle smile touched his lips. "You can only do so much, Amanda. *We* can only do so much."

"Given the constraints of the law."

"And the limits of our own emotions—and sanity."

But when it comes to babies, Patrick, my emotions are boundless. And as for sanity . . .

In truth something—emotion, sanity, a deep instinct for preservation of self—had constrained her. Eventually, when she began to teeter too near the edge, she had quit OB and turned to psychiatry instead, the specialty for which she had both a natural aptitude and an acquired gift.

"Amanda?"

She had overcome so many fears. Overcome? Not really. But she could keep them at bay . . . as long as her *life* was in control.

Which it was not, not now, not with this man.

This *man.* "I really should go."

"Can I drive you home?"

"Oh! No." *No.* "Thank you."

But may I hold you, Amanda? May I comfort you?

No, Patrick reminded himself. *No.*

Patrick Falconer did not pursue women who were already involved, much less married. That was the *other* twin.

"I wonder if your husband should come get you."

"My . . . oh, no. He's out of the country until early May. He travels a lot." Amanda managed a smile. "I'm *fine*, Patrick."

"You're shivering."

She had known she was trembling deep within. But her quivering was visible—and explicable. Her once-daffodil suit was crimson with blood. "I guess I'll find a fresh pair of scrubs before driving home. I'd better go do that now."

"Okay. It was nice to have met you. At last."

"Yes. Well . . . good night, Patrick."

"Good night, Amanda."

Good-bye.

It should have ended there.

But Amanda had come to his hospital room, to help him, and he had been cruel.

And now?

Now they would see each other one final time.

I'm sorry, Amanda. That wasn't really me. Or perhaps it was. Perhaps such darkness has always dwelled within me, and when I'm trapped, when I'm dying, I become my twin. But even death is no excuse. Nothing is.

Patrick would see her one last time, and apologize to her, and then . . .

Good-bye, Amanda.

Adieu.

TEN

*T*he springtime sun shone brightly in his eyes, glaring, glowering, taunting.

What is the point of this journey? the fiery star demanded. To make Amanda care? So that she will truly mourn your death? Truly suffer?

How cruel that would be, if it weren't so foolish.

You are dying. In fact, the sun sneered—and seared—you are virtually dead. Indeed this misguided mission may be the coup de grâce.

The sun was blinding him as if to prove its point. All it would take was the slamming of brakes. Such a jolt, just the jolt itself, would prove too much for his meager band of platelets. Blood would flow freely into his kidneys and his brain, a lethal scarlet flood.

You'd better stop, the sun admonished. Stop, slowly now, and scribble a note to her just in case. *I'm sorry, Amanda. Good-bye.*

Patrick did not stop. He glowered back at the taunting sun, and drove through the blindness, and eventually was rewarded with a curve in the road, away from the glare and shaded by an arcade of palms.

He was almost there. The numerals on the passing houses signaled that he was very close.

Very close, and still there was no fortress in sight. There was only a pale pink cottage, a lovers' bungalow nestled in a bougainvillea bouquet.

No Dobermans bounded out to greet him, nor did a massive bodyguard saunter his way. And as for Amanda's possibly ferocious husband? He was away, she had told him, until early May.

Amanda's home could not have been more exposed, more penetrable—at least visible—to probing eyes. The curtains were open, permitting a ready view inside.

Remotely reassuring was the silver-and-blue decal propped against a window pane, a warning that there were alarms in the residence and a security service was on the case. The decal, propped but not yet adhered, suggested that the security system had been recently installed.

Amanda, however, was not safely installed. She was outside, on the ocean side. Patrick saw her burnished copper hair glinting in the sun, vying with the setting star for sheer brilliance.

Vying, Patrick mused, and winning.

A cobblestone pathway led around the house, a fragrant journey of roses and jasmine.

She was on the grass, sitting cross-legged, staring down at whatever lay in her lap.

"Hi," he said softly, not wanting to startle her—but startling her nonetheless.

In a surprised but graceful motion, Amanda turned and stood. The book that had been lying on her lap fell to earth, while the more treasured occupant, a tiny ball of gray fluff, remained clutched to her chest.

"*Patrick.*"

"Hi," he repeated gently.

She was so delicate, so fearful, so transformed. Gone was the harsh copper crown. Her hair flowed free, a curling river of fire. And no designer would lay claim to the grass-length dress she wore. Shapeless, voluminous, the dark purple creation was abloom with bright blue flowers. And as for the feet that spent the workdays perched atop the highest of heels? They were quite bare.

Patrick's initial assessment, made at midnight at Ariel's, had been correct. She was an actress. Amanda Prentice, fashion-plate psychiatrist, was merely a role she chose to play. This was the real Amanda. Unbound hair, unbound feet, her figure wholly disguised, concealed completely beneath the billowing folds of the tentlike dress.

At work—onstage—the actress-physician wore a little makeup, subtly applied. Here she wore none.

And here, Patrick thought, she was even more beautiful, without the artifice, without the glitter, *without the band of diamonds*.

As Patrick stared at the ringless hands that cradled the kitten his dark blue eyes glittered with the white-hot intensity of a thousand suns.

"You're not married, are you?"

"Why are you here?"

"Are you?"

"No. I—"

"Have you ever been married?" he pressed, not needing the answer, knowing it already. If the diamond eternity ring was a precious symbol of a husband who had died, Amanda would wear it always. But the wedding band was a prop, like her designer clothes and tightly constrained hair and the heels that made her so very tall.

"No. I haven't." She met his glittering gaze. "I wear the ring because of my patients."

"To keep the men at bay? To thwart any awkward patient-doctor crushes?"

"Yes."

It was a partial truth. Amanda wore the ring for her female patients as well. They found comfort in believing that the psychiatrist who offered such sage advice knew whereof she spoke—that Amanda was the mistress of her own fears and quite capable of existing on the planet as a woman in all ways.

In truth, as a wholly viable woman, Amanda Prentice was an impostor. Her diamonds were real and quite flawless. But she was not. Yet the dazzling ring, and the faux assurances that came with it, did help her patients. And there was nothing false about her competence. She knew all the right words, all the right techniques, the full arsenal at one's disposal in the war against fear.

"And to thwart those awkward doctor-doctor crushes as well?"

His voice was gentle. But his face, ashen from blood loss, was as unyielding as marble.

"Patrick, no. I'm *sorry*."

Patrick heard her apology, and he saw her despair.

"That's my line," he said softly. "I came here to apologize."

"But that's not necessary! I understand."

"My behavior, despicable as it was, may have been understandable. But there's still no excuse for it. That's not the real me, Amanda. At least I hope like hell it isn't."

"It isn't." But, she thought, this *is* the real me, a woman who feels safest, happiest, in a baggy dress. It wasn't always so baggy, Patrick. There was a time when—

"Who's this?" Patrick gestured to the fluffy gray creature curled against the bright blue flowers of Amanda's billowy dress. Patrick was only modestly interested in the kitten. But he hoped very much to divert Amanda from the sudden sadness of her thoughts.

The diversion worked. As she looked down at the kitten autumnal silk veiled her face—but from behind the gilded red curtain Patrick sensed her smile.

"This is Smoky," she said. "We were watching the sunset."

"And reading?" Patrick glanced at the book that had spilled onto the grass. He didn't instantly recognize the cover art. He had not yet bought his copy. But the familiar title, scripted in cobalt and gold, glowed in the champagne rays of the April sun. "*Blue Moon.*"

As Amanda looked up from the smoky gray kitten the coppery curtain fell away. "Yes. *Blue Moon.*"

"Have you read his other books?" *Are you a fan of Graydon Slake? Are you mesmerized by the dark twin's sophisticated eroticism? His savage violence?*

"Yes. I've read his other books." All of them, more than once. There were passages she had to read, was *compelled* to read. Graydon Slake wrote about intimacies she would never know—about women who touched men willingly, fearlessly . . . and men who received such caresses as priceless gifts.

"You don't find his novels disturbing?"

"No." *I find them comforting.* "The triumph of good over evil, I suppose."

"How is *Blue Moon*?"

"The first paragraph is riveting. That's as far as Smoky and I have gotten. Having him on my lap makes for slow going."

"Smoky's not an avid reader?"

"No. Although he finds sleeping on the pages quite satisfactory. Don't you, little Smoke?"

"You two are good friends."

Amanda tilted her head in thoughtful reply. "We're getting there. He's only been with me a short while."

Two weeks, to be exact—since that night, Patrick, when you watched me deliver that baby girl, and then listened as I told you of my madness. Listened, and comforted, and cared. In another moment, Patrick, I might have reached to touch you. Willingly. And fearlessly?

No. Never.

The sky had wept that night, a torrent of tears that soaked her cotton scrubs. Was that why she was shivering? From the chill of raindrops on her skin? And was it truly raining inside the car, a warm heat that blurred her eyes?

She had driven in a blur, but only a few blocks, to Ariel's. She would not return to the aisle of tea, as if a shrine, would not stand, soaked and dripping, remembering. She would remain inside her car instead, until all storms had passed, the tempests without and within.

KITTEN NEEDS HOME. Amanda saw the words written in block print on a small sealed cardboard box. Was there really a tiny creature cowering inside, frightened of the darkness and confused by the hammering rain? Was the abandoned baby unable to escape, yet clawing for freedom nonetheless?

Amanda heard no clawing as she neared, heard no sound at all. But she found the kitten huddled within, a portrait of sheer terror. Amanda knew such terror. The monsters of darkness. The mysterious noises that echoed like thunder. The futility of escape even if one clawed.

Amanda had huddled once, silent and trembling—and waiting, as this kitten had been waiting, to be rescued . . .

"Smoky looks very happy to me," Patrick said. *Happy to be with you.* "The roaring I hear *is* purring, isn't it?"

"It is." Amanda stroked the small gray head. The kitten was awake now, fully alert, its aquamarine eyes surveying Patrick with fabled feline curiosity. "I think he wants you to hold him."

"Is that what you want, Smoky?" *Why on earth would you want to leave Amanda?*

Patrick did not question aloud the impending transfer of the gray kitten. This was the way that he and Amanda were going to touch.

In fact, their flesh did not actually caress, not even with the feathery brush of a whispered kiss. Patrick felt Amanda's warmth, however, as his hands held Smoky precisely where hers had been.

Perhaps Smoky did not want to abandon the sanctuary of Amanda after all, even if transferred to a comparably gentle embrace; or perhaps when the kitten felt Patrick's fingers he sensed a grasp that was more corpse than human; or maybe Smoky was just being a kitten, fully energized from a sunset nap and ready for a romp.

Whatever the reason Smoky began to wiggle and squirm. No more imprisonment, the furry body proclaimed.

Patrick had no intention of subjecting the baby creature to unwilling constraint. Neither, however, was he going to permit a leap from his chest to the grass. As he lowered the squirming ball of fluff Smoky's tiny claws, perhaps anticipating the fall Patrick would never let him make, dug reflexively into Patrick's skin.

They were the tiniest of nicks. Amanda had similar ones, all kitten owners did, pinpricks of no consequence whatsoever—unless one's platelets had abandoned him.

"Oh, Patrick. I'm so sorry."

"It's not your fault. Or Smoky's fault." *And that's my line, Amanda. I'm sorry that I'm dying—and that you aren't married after all—and that there will never be a chance to find out about us.*

The blood spilled, not a massive hemorrhage—how could it be from such tiny pricks?—but a reminder nonetheless, crimson sands in an hourglass that was rapidly running out of time.

Amanda started to reach for his bleeding hand, but stopped, her own pale hands suspended in midair, then falling to her sides. "You need a bandage. I'm sure I have something inside."

"No. It's okay." *Okay?* It was hardly okay on any count. "I'd better go."

Good-bye, Amanda.

Adieu.

ELEVEN

*T*hey glided like skaters over a frozen pond, tuxedoed men and begowned women dancing to a live—and also tuxedoed—orchestra. This was ballroom dancing at its best, in one of the most grand ballrooms on earth. Or sea.

Champagne flowed, or martinis if one preferred, and treasure troves of plump strawberries filled countless silver bowls.

The party was in full swing when Caitlin arrived. Her hair was swept up, Amanda-style, and she wore emerald satin embroidered with roses. Margaret's false but priceless beads encircled her neck and expensive—but valueless—clusters of real pearls adorned her ears.

In this grand ballroom on the sea Caitlin Taylor drew admiring stares. But she felt distinctly out of place. She would, she decided, spend the evening doing precisely what Patrick had commanded—observing, so that she could report back to him the most minute detail. She found a perfect vantage point, a solitary gold-brocade chair in a secluded corner.

Caitlin's solitude was not absolute. A vigilant champagne steward found her, more than once, as if she was his special responsibility, as if it was vitally important to keep the woman in the shadows amply supplied with crystal flutes of Perrier-Jouët.

For someone who rarely—never—drank, a little champagne went a long way; and when that someone had been deprived of meaningful sleep by the nocturnal hauntings of ghosts and ghouls the effect of the golden bubbly was even more dramatic . . . and surprisingly welcome.

The Queens Room blurred. Its dancers became rainbows in motion, rainbows at twilight, dancing rainbows in a lilac mist. As the iridescent dancers floated by Caitlin's thoughts floated as well—to a gentle, misty, pastel past.

She saw her mother, the most shimmering rainbow of all, dancing, floating, in the arms of the man she loved. Caitlin saw him, too. Him. Michael. Maggie's Michael: strong, dark, dashing. And wonderful. And honorable. A man who loved deeply and forever—not the bloodthirsty phantom of her dreams.

He will never be that ghoul again, Caitlin vowed, hoping it was true, wanting it to be. He will only and always be Maggie's fairy-tale prince.

Eventually her thoughts drifted to a more recent night of romance, and of champagne—the Valentine's night when she learned the secret of the other Falconer twin. . . .

It was February, Boston's snowiest in decades. Caitlin was halfway through her second year of surgical residency, and halfway through as well the clinic rotation that her fellow residents viewed as a sheer gift, an eminently civilized month of working days only, weekdays only.

The fourth-year resident assigned to supervise Caitlin in clinic was *who else?* Patrick Falconer. He was gorgeous. And wealthy. Neither of which mattered to her. What mattered was his surgical competence, which was stunning, and his unwavering commitment to the patients in his care.

For the past eighteen months Caitlin and Patrick had been teamed together often. The coincidence of schedules was thrilling for Caitlin. Patrick was the best of the best. And if Patrick minded being assigned to supervise the unidimensional—yet academically exceptional—junior resident, he never let it show. He didn't absent himself during the calms between surgical storms, didn't say *Page me, Caitlin* then disappear to find someone more engaging with whom to share the inevitable lulls. He remained nearby, accompanying her to the library, where both would read, or to the cafeteria, for ever more coffee—and conversation, as if she were interesting after all.

Maybe Patrick just felt safe with her. Caitlin was not about to pry into the personal life of the man who seemed as private as she.

Caitlin didn't pry. But she did notice. She saw the worry that stirred beneath the steady calm of his dark blue eyes; and there were late-night phone calls that left him distracted and tense; and finally, recently Patrick's solid-gold wedding band simply disappeared.

Patrick seemed less troubled after that. Relaxed. Relieved.

But on this Friday in February Patrick Falconer was not relaxed at all. He looked . . . angry.

"I need a favor, Caitlin. I want you to see a patient with me."

"Sure, Patrick. Of course."

It was the sort of request she made—of him—all the time. *Would you examine a belly for me, Patrick? I think I feel a spleen tip, but I'm not sure.* And although it never failed to astound her, Patrick solicited her input as well. *I think there's rebound tenderness, Caitlin. But it's a soft call. See what you think.* He would smile, obviously amused that she was so surprised.

Patrick was not smiling now. His eyes were darker than Caitlin had ever seen them, and the powerful muscles of his throat were tense, and his voice was taut—yet oddly apologetic.

"Is it complicated?" she asked.

"Very."

"What's . . . ?"

"The chief complaint? Actually she claims to have two, a breast mass and pelvic pain. I don't need you as a consultant though, Caitlin. I need you as a chaperon."

Without further clarification Patrick led the way to the examining room. Once there he made the usual introductions.

"This is Dr. Caitlin Taylor, Gabrielle. Caitlin, this is Gabrielle St. John."

But there was nothing usual about the situation, or about Gabrielle St. John. She was stunningly beautiful, indisputably infuriated, and essentially naked. Gabrielle remedied the nakedness by closing the patient gown she wore. But nothing, not even fury, could alter her beauty, and it was abundantly clear that she had no intention of modulating her rage.

"What is she doing here, Patrick?"

"Dr. Taylor is going to assist me with the physical exam."

"Assist, Patrick? Since when do you need assistance in examining *me*?"

Caitlin knew this enraged beauty was not Patrick's estranged wife. But was she the reason, perhaps, he no longer wore his wedding band? If so, if Gabrielle St. John had caused his marriage to falter, Patrick's relationship with Gabrielle had faltered as well.

"I don't want her here, Patrick."

"She stays, Gabrielle, or there's no exam."

"This is *malpractice*. I'm desperately worried that I'm ill, that I have *cancer*, and you are refusing to help me. I wonder what the chief of surgery would think of such treatment."

"He'd think it was terrific. If I discover anything even the least bit troubling, Dr. Taylor will repeat the exam, thus providing an immediate second opinion. You couldn't ask for better care."

"*Even the least bit troubling?* You don't think you're going to find anything, do you, Patrick? You don't think there's anything wrong with me."

"I didn't say that, Gabrielle. I would never say that."

"You're delusional, Patrick! You think I'm interested in you, don't you? That I *want* you? That's crazy, Patrick. Really *crazy*."

With the decisive pronouncement Gabrielle turned to Caitlin. When she spoke her tone was one of patrician tolerance.

"I am engaged to be married, Dr. Taylor." Gabrielle embellished by offering for Caitlin's inspection her perfectly manicured left hand, which sported a perfectly magnificent diamond. "His name is Kyle Fairfax. You've heard of him, of course. Everyone knows Boston's brilliant DA. This fall Kyle will be running for the U.S. Senate. I want to be there, to help him in any way I can. But I don't want to distract him with concerns about my health. I love him far too much. The state needs him, Dr. Taylor. The *country* needs him. And if I discover that I'm ill, well . . ."

It was a speech of courage, of selfless sacrifice for the greater good. The future Mrs. Fairfax would make a sensational senator's wife, not to mention a positively exemplary first lady. Caitlin was equally certain that Gabrielle St. John was not ill, and that Gabrielle knew it.

"I came here to be *reassured,* Dr. Taylor—or to be told the bitter truth by someone I believed I could trust." As Gabrielle's gaze returned to Patrick the tolerance disappeared. "You owe me this, Patrick! You owe me *much more.* But you're no better than *him,* are you? You're just as cruel as—"

"Enough, Gabrielle. Now why don't you tell Dr. Taylor what you told me about the lump you believe you've found."

"You *bastard.* Get out of here! You, too, Dr. Taylor. I'm far too upset to be examined now. Just wait until Kyle hears what happened. This hospital receives taxpayer money, which makes my abusive treatment an unconscionable violation of the public trust."

There had been times when Patrick served as a chaperon for her. In the emergency ward, when Caitlin was evaluating an intoxicated male, he would stand nearby, a silent yet formidable sentry, defusing a potentially volatile situation with merely his presence.

Had Caitlin now returned the favor in kind? Had her mere presence defused the fury, modulated the rage?

Hardly. But she *had* preempted what Gabrielle so clearly wanted: Patrick's hands on her naked flesh. Indeed by conjuring an imaginary breast mass and phantom pelvic pain Gabrielle had designated the intimacy of his touch.

Caitlin had just borne witness to astonishing boldness. What Gabrielle had done was misguided, inappropriate. But there was such confidence to it, the certainty that despite their obviously troubled past, not to mention her own engagement, Patrick would want to touch her still.

Had Gabrielle wanted his touch—or simply his torment? Gabrielle had definitely succeeded in tormenting him; although, perhaps, it had not been the precise form of frustration she desired.

Who was she?

Caitlin doubted she would ever know. As she and Patrick walked away from the exam room he was silent, remote, furious still.

Caitlin hated Patrick's fury. The physician within her envisioned its consequences on the arteries of his heart, the vessels in his brain, the lining of his stomach.

With astonishing boldness of her own she intervened. "Are you ready for my second opinion, Dr. Falconer? I concur with your diagnosis completely—a very complicated case indeed."

Patrick stopped, turned. And did his famous smile carve its sexy slash into the rock-hard lines of his face? No. If anything Patrick looked more serious, more severe.

"Do you have plans for this evening, Caitlin?"

For this February fourteenth? Of course she did. The moon would be full on this Valentine's night, and even from behind the blanket of snow clouds the heavenly orb would exert its gravitational effects, inducing lunacy even from those normally quite sane. No one knew quite what to expect when romance and the full moon were conjoined. But there was little doubt that Cupid and the moon would conspire to wreak havoc.

Caitlin had planned to spend this Valentine's night in the Emergency Ward. She wouldn't take the best cases, wouldn't deprive her colleagues of the chance to learn. She would just spend the night suturing. Happily.

"Caitlin?"

"No. I don't have plans."

"Good. Come drinking with me."

"Drinking?"

"Yes. Let me guess. You don't drink much—ever? Well, neither do I. But I'm planning to do some serious drinking tonight. And I'd like you to come with me."

"To drive . . . ?"

Now, at last, Caitlin was treated to Patrick Falconer's sexy smile. "No. To drink. No one's going to be driving."

Patrick led the way, on foot, from Mass General to the trendy harborside pub. The route he selected took them past a bookstore on Chatham, where he paused briefly before the window display of the week's bestsellers. Patrick scanned the titles swiftly, a virtually impassive appraisal he didn't choose to explain, then resumed their journey to the pub.

The snowy night called out for hot buttered rum. Or, what Patrick had envisioned when he'd made the impulsive suggestion, bourbon, neat, lots of it. But when the time came he ordered a bottle of Dom Pérignon—a request their cocktail waitress greeted with a frown.

"You're celebrating, right?"

"Sure," Patrick said. "Why not?"

"I mean celebrating something other than Valentine's Day. You *are* brother and sister, aren't you?"

It happened all the time, the assumption that they were sibs. There was, Caitlin supposed, a slight resemblance. Both had dark hair and blue eyes, and both were serious and intense. But if anyone really looked closely . . .

"Sure," Patrick replied calmly. "Why not?"

Patrick's reply eloquently communicated two messages to the curious cocktail waitress: that he and Caitlin were *not* related, and that it was none of her business anyway. The waitress vanished, to find a chilled bottle of the expensive champagne, leaving in her wake an embarrassed Caitlin and a reflective Patrick.

"I'll do the honors," he said when the waitress returned. His smile forgave everything. "Thank you."

Patrick poured the honey-colored bubbly with typical expertise, his surgeon's hands steady and strong, and presented to Caitlin a brimming crystal flute.

"It wouldn't be the end of the world, would it?" he asked. "I've always wanted a little sister. And who better than you?"

He was serious, and absolutely sober. The happiness Caitlin felt blended with something else, a deep, quiet, mysterious joy—as if this amazing invitation from this remarkable man was meant to be.

"Caitlin? I don't want to step on any toes. If you already have a big brother . . ."

"I don't." *And who better than you?*

"So?" Patrick tilted his flute of golden bubbles toward hers. "Shall we?"

"Yes," she whispered as crystal touched crystal. "We shall."

Patrick wanted to know all about his baby sister.

As they drank champagne and watched snow fall on Boston Harbor Caitlin told him about Maggie. It seemed important that Patrick know about her lovely mother, and even more important, an aching impossible wish, that Maggie know about him.

"Did she know you were going to become a doctor?"

"A Ph.D., not an MD."

"A researcher?"

Caitlin nodded, then looked away, to the snow-caressed waves where tea had spilled before blood. Before freedom.

She didn't want to see Patrick's reaction. A researcher, Caitlin? A basic scientist? That would have been an ideal career choice for you. Test tubes, microscopes, Petri dishes—with no requirement whatsoever for scintillating conversation.

Even if those were Patrick's thoughts, and even if Caitlin had been staring into his dark blue eyes, she would not have seen them. Patrick Falconer was far too polite to let such unkind musings show.

And, Caitlin realized, he was far too nice to even think such mean-spirited thoughts. The taunting queries were *her* uncertainties, *her* paranoia . . . not his. Patrick had, after all, just invited her to become his sister.

"He's my twin."

Caitlin turned from the snow-crested waves. "Who, Patrick?"

Patrick smiled. "You tell me."

"Graydon Slake."

"Graydon Slake," Patrick confirmed. "Was it so obvious?"

"Not really." In fact it had been quite subtle, a faint glow in the indigo depths when his gaze had fallen upon

Quicksand, the bestseller by Graydon Slake, on display in the bookstore on Chatham. "I thought he was you."

"You thought I'd been writing bestselling novels in my spare time? God, you're supportive."

That's what little sisters are supposed to be, isn't it? Admiring of their older brothers? Believing them capable of the most superhuman feats? "You *could* do it."

"No, Caitlin. I couldn't. But Jesse can."

Jesse. How long had it been since he had spoken his twin's name? Years. *Years.* But now he was telling Caitlin, wanting to.

"We're fraternal twins. Jesse's fifteen minutes older. We haven't spoken since we were nineteen."

"Because of Gabrielle?" The notion of Gabrielle St. John causing a civil war between twins came easily. Brother against brother, a spiritual fight to the death.

"Gabrielle was the coup de grâce. But Jesse and I had been virtual strangers for four years before that. Maybe we'd always been strangers."

"But you didn't think so."

"No. I thought we were best friends. It turned out I was wrong."

"Are you sure, Patrick?"

"Positive."

"But what about now? You're both older and—"

"There's no going back."

"You make it sound as if he's dead, and he's obviously very much alive. You're both very much alive."

"But we're dead to each other. This is our secret, Caitlin. It has to be."

"Of course, Patrick! I would never tell anyone, *ever.* But—"

"But nothing, Dr. Taylor. There's no going back. My relationship with my brother ended a long time ago."

It was over, the relationship between the Falconer twins *and* Patrick and Caitlin's discussion of same. They never spoke of it again, not that night, not ever. But Caitlin wondered about Jesse, and an estrangement so bitter it had no hope of being healed.

Gabrielle had been the coup de grâce. But, Patrick had said, the alienation started four years before. The Falconer brothers would have been fifteen then, boys becoming men. Perhaps for the first time they were compared in ways in which one twin—superstar Patrick—had the distinct advantage.

The arena would not, of course, have been academic. Quite obviously, both Falconer twins were extremely bright. But Jesse probably looked like a quiz kid, bespectacled and awkward, and at an age when social skills and athletic prowess were paramount he could not hope to compete.

Perhaps Jesse never even tried to compete. Perhaps he simply withdrew into his bookish shell—until age nineteen, when he was lured by a magnet he was powerless to resist: the stunning Gabrielle . . . who was in love, of course, with the dazzling twin.

You owe me, Patrick! Gabrielle had proclaimed.

Why? Had Patrick forsaken Gabrielle in the hope that once he was out of the picture she might be attracted to Jesse? Had Patrick tried to reconcile with his brother by making an offering of love?

Love didn't work that way. It seemed unlikely that even a nineteen-year-old version of Patrick would have imagined that it did. But in his desperation to reconcile with Jesse maybe Patrick had been willing to try anything.

Did Gabrielle mock Jesse's infatuation? Of course she did. Her fury toward Patrick would have translated into punishment for both twins.

And how did meek, lovesick, awkward Jesse respond to Gabrielle's contempt? By lashing out with the unexpected fierceness of a gentle animal gravely wounded.

You're no better than *him*, Gabrielle had raged. You're just as cruel as—

Jesse.

"*M*ore champagne, Miss?"

"Oh," Caitlin murmured as she found her bearings. The ever-vigilant champagne steward. Floating rainbows, floating memories, aboard the *QE2*. "No, thank you. In fact, I need to go."

The steward smiled politely, knowingly, as if quite certain that his special charge had an assignation, a romantic rendezvous, perhaps, beneath the moon.

What Caitlin had was an assignment, not an assignation; a rendezvous *with* the moon, not beneath it; with Jesse Falconer, the moon twin.

Jesse was moon to Patrick's sun. It was a conclusion Caitlin had reached long ago. Whatever brilliance Jesse possessed was merely reflected light from his dazzling twin. She would spend this night with *The Snow Lion* in hope of learning how best to approach the brother who had always been so eclipsed.

Caitlin would offer the shadow twin a chance to shine

more brightly than all the stars. He needed only to give a
bit of himself, a sprinkling of moondust from his marrow.

Would Jesse seize the chance?

Or was his heart as cold, as black, as the far side of the
moon?

TWELVE

FIFTEEN NAUTICAL MILES NORTHWEST OF BERMUDA

WEDNESDAY, APRIL TWENTY-FOURTH

"*T*his is Dr. Caitlin Taylor calling for Mr. Asquith."

"Dr. Taylor?" Timothy Asquith's secretary echoed with alarm. "Is there a problem? An emergency?"

"No, not at all." At least not one involving the Asquith dynasty. "This is a personal call. I have a favor to ask."

"Oh, well, I'm afraid Mr. Asquith is in a meeting. May I have him return your call?"

"Actually, it's going to be easier for me to call back. Could we set up a phone appointment? Today, if possible. I only need a minute or two of his time."

"Yes. Certainly. Will you hold?"

"Of course." Caitlin was holding the phone, and she was holding her breath. She needed to speak with Jesse Falconer *soon*, while she was still so confident that she could convince him to help his twin, could convince him of *anything*. Was such a notion sheer folly? Had her sleep-deprived mind finally gone totally off the deep end?

She hadn't slept, hadn't even tried. Despite the sleeplessness, however, she felt peace not torment, energy not fatigue. She *had* gone off the deep end . . . right into the deep blue sea . . . its fathomless magic, its infinite power, its intrepid rules of the heart.

Caitlin had planned to call Patrick's twin from shore, where, she reasoned, the connection would be far superior to the delayed offerings aboard ship. Bermuda was a financial epicenter of the British Empire. Its bankers would not allocate their billion-dollar transmissions to the hissing vagaries of outermost space.

Her reasoning was clearly correct. Already communications from the ship seemed to have fallen under the dominion of the systems ashore. The link to London was so flawless in fact that Caitlin decided to speak to the embittered twin while still at sea, afloat on the liquid magic— assuming she could get his phone number before they docked.

Assuming? Caitlin exhaled at last. She would get the phone number. If Caitlin Taylor could convince Jesse Falconer to part with a pint of his marrow, and she could, then convincing even the most territorial of secretaries to part with a confidential phone number was mere child's play.

"Dr. Taylor. A favor? At long last?"

"Oh! Mr. Asquith. Thank you so much for taking my call."

"You're quite welcome. And whatever the favor consider it done. You can give me the specifics after I wish you happy birthday."

"I can't believe . . ." *you knew.* But of course he knew. That night, when it was clear that Timmy was going to survive, an ICU nurse told Faye Asquith that for any health-care professional, but especially for Caitlin, there was no better way to spend one's birthday than saving a patient's life. Faye knew, as did Robert and Lillith. So, naturally, Timothy Asquith knew as well. But . . .

"Can't believe what?"

"That you would remember."

"The date on which you saved my grandson's life? How could I ever forget?"

"Well . . ."

The shrug in her voice reached London loud and clear. "I don't mean to embarrass you, Dr. Taylor. But you know how grateful I am. We all are, and always will be. So the favor, whatever it may be, is trivial—and granted."

"I need to speak with Graydon Slake."

"You've read *Thief* already? I shouldn't have thought the final draft had even arrived."

Thief? *Of Hearts*? Gemstone's future blockbuster had been written by Graydon Slake? Yes. Apparently. *Yes*.

"No, I haven't read it yet. But I do need to speak with him. I'm afraid I can't tell you why."

"Well, then," the billionaire replied, "I guess I shan't ask. He has two numbers—phone and fax. I'll have Estelle give you both. If the phone isn't answered in four rings, his answering service picks up. The operators always know where he is."

"I wonder why."

"I've wondered, too. Perhaps he chooses such immediate contact with the outside world because his home is so remote."

Caitlin imagined a place as bitterly cold as the dark side of the moon. An iceberg in the north Atlantic. A glacier in the Bering Sea. "Where does he live?"

A chuckle, soft but distinct, preceded the answer. "I've made it sound grim, haven't I? And it's not grim in the least. In fact, it's paradise. He lives on Maui, in an isolated but spectacular part of the island."

"You've been there?"

"Yes. Lillith and Robert and I traveled there to discuss *Thief of Hearts*."

And now, Caitlin mused, *I* need to travel there, to discuss saving a heart, not stealing one.

Her decision to speak with Jesse Falconer face-to-face was impulsive, and foolhardy. What of the magical confidence of the sea?

It will travel with me.

And even if the azure magic remained behind, she could still convince Jesse to save Patrick's life. *The Snow Lion* was a celebration of endangered species. To the man who was its author she merely needed to say, Your twin is endangered, on the very verge of extinction. You must help him. You *must*.

"Do you happen to know if he's in Maui now?"

"I know that he is—and will be—until the screenplay for *Thief* is signed off on by all concerned."

"I should go there then, to speak to him in person."

"This is important to you."

"Yes it is. Very. Will you give me his address?"

"With one stipulation, a promise really. You must agree to be extremely careful."

Careful? Of Jesse Falconer? Were the ancient wounds so raw that the injured beast lashed out still? "Careful?"

"The road to his home is quite treacherous, a narrow ribbon of twists and turns with sheer cliffs on either side. It should be navigated only in the light of day, preferably by someone who knows it well. In fact, why don't you meet him at Kapalua and let him drive the rest of the way? That's what we did—at his suggestion—so he certainly won't mind. If you're uncomfortable proposing that yourself, I'll be happy to suggest it when I let him know you're coming."

"No. Thank you. I will be careful. I promise. And it would be best—essential actually—that he know nothing about my visit in advance."

"I really feel I should tell him."

Timothy Asquith's voice conveyed centuries of politeness, a chivalry dating back to the age of knights. It also held a contemporary note, the definitiveness of a man who ruled an empire and was unaccustomed to being defied.

Caitlin responded with silence. But in the void, his oft-repeated promise fairly hummed. *If there's ever anything you need, Dr. Taylor. Anything, ever.*

Once a knight, always a gentleman, and this gentleman-knight had made a solemn pledge.

With what sounded almost like a smile, Timothy Asquith said, "All right, Dr. Taylor. Not a word."

"Thank you."

We're even now, Mr. Asquith. Your imaginary debt to me is paid in full. Life and death for life and death.

And both times on my birthday.

By the time the *QE2* snuggled against King's Wharf on Ireland Island Caitlin was ready to disembark. Her final phone call, to book flights from Bermuda to Maui, had been made, and she had showered, dressed, and packed.

Her Bermuda clothes became her Maui clothes, informal, tropical, and easily folded into the smaller of her two cases. The larger suitcase harbored her more glamorous attire, and would remain closed, an inconvenient appendage, until her return to LA.

Caitlin wrote a note, and left a substantial tip, for her

steward Paul. An emergency had arisen, she explained—nothing sinister, merely urgent—and she thanked him for making her time on board so enjoyable. Then Caitlin left stateroom 2063.

From the radio room she retrieved the fax sent by Estelle—Graydon Slake's unlisted phone numbers and detailed instructions to his Maui home—then settled her account with the ship's cashier. Her bill for "incidentals" was impressive. Many, many minutes of ship-to-shore phone calls—at $12.50 per minute—added up, and there were presents, too, for Amanda and Patrick.

Amanda and Patrick. One of the shortest calls had been with Amanda *after* Amanda's meeting with Patrick. Amanda's recounting was perfunctory and vague. The meeting was fine, she insisted. *Fine.*

Caitlin's final stop was the doctor's consulting room on Two Deck.

"I'm a surgeon," she told the physician on call. "And I'm about to disembark. I know it's unusual to leave midcruise, but an emergency has arisen. Here's my bill, as well as the wallet copy of my medical license."

The ship's doctor examined both documents. "What can I do for you, Dr. Taylor?"

"A friend—a fellow physician—needs a marrow transplant. A potential donor has been identified. But he may be a reluctant donor, which is why I'm planning to fly to his home in the hope of convincing him. What I'd like to do—at least be prepared to do—is draw his blood then and there. He's a bit of a recluse, and his home is somewhat remote. I might be able to convince him to drive to the nearest hospital, but . . ."

"You may have done enough convincing by then?" the doctor suggested with a smile.

"Yes. So what I need, what I was hoping I could get from you, is some blood-drawing equipment." Caitlin halted abruptly, as the doctor's smile became a decided frown. She offered her arms, palms up and bare, an expanse of alabaster skin unmarred by the tiniest puncture, much less by telltale tracks. "I'm not a drug user, I promise. What I've told you is true, but if you like we could call Dr. Stephen Sheridan in LA."

"I really don't have you pegged as a drug user, Dr. Taylor. I'm just trying to decide what supplies I can spare. Basically, except for Vacutainer sheaths, I have plenty of everything—tubes, needles, alcohol wipes, an entire drawer of tourniquets. So if you can make do with a good old-fashioned syringe . . ."

"I absolutely can."

"Then we're set. I'll show you the cabinet where everything's stored and let you help yourself."

"And you'll let me pay, I hope."

The doctor's response was wry. "Assuming, Dr. Taylor, that we—Cunard, that is—make any profit at all on ship-to-shore phone calls, I think we can offer you a few needles and syringes as parting gifts."

Twenty minutes later Caitlin stood on the gleaming marigold cobblestones of King's Wharf and bade adieu to the daughter ship. She was taking a little of the sea's magic with her. For Patrick. But most of the indigo splendor would remain here, where it belonged—with Maggie and Michael.

You are dancing with him, Mother. I saw you. You are a shimmering rainbow . . . and you will dance with your Michael forever.

Then Maggie's daughter was on her way to New York, where she made her flight to Honolulu with time to spare, enough time to purchase a copy of Graydon Slake's *Blue Moon.*

Caitlin opened the book as soon as the DC-10 lost touch with the tarmac . . . and then she lost touch with everything but the astonishing words—and the remarkable feelings they evoked.

THIRTEEN

MAUI
WEDNESDAY, APRIL TWENTY-FOURTH

*C*aitlin did not stop reading, could not—not for food, not for sleep, not even when the flight became so bumpy that most passengers abandoned their books, clutched their armrests, and gritted their teeth.

Blue Moon was dark. Sensual. Erotic. Dangerous.

And written by a man who could not possibly compete with his dazzling twin? An awkward and perhaps physically unattractive man *with an extraordinary imagination?*

Was it truly possible to imagine such passion? Before reading the lyrical prose Caitlin's reply would have been an emphatic *no.*

But now she felt the passion, its longing, its hunger, its need. Jesse Falconer made her feel it, made her *want* it.

Jesse Falconer? No. The moon twin was not the sorcerer of ecstasy. Graydon Slake was.

Graydon Slake, the alter ego of the shadow twin, the illusory author who created the most spectacular fiction of all: the fantasy of love.

Graydon Slake might beg to differ with her romantic assessment of his work. His thrillers were breathless journeys into the intimate recesses of murderous minds—and breathtaking journeys, as well, into the intimacies of sex.

Sex, not love.

Never once, not in the six hundred pages of *Blue Moon*, did *love* appear. Not in the lyrical prose and most assuredly neither in the stylish repartée between hero and heroine whilst in pursuit of the killer, nor in the provocative words they whispered in bed.

There was a definite edge to Graydon Slake's "hero," the ex-cop who understood so well—too well?—the desires of murderers. He was dangerous, and he could be cruel. In fact, the line between the hero of *Blue Moon* and its diabolical villain was fine indeed.

That gossamer thread was there, however. Without the slightest hesitation the hero had been willing to forfeit his own life to save the woman he "loved."

As Caitlin read the words of Graydon Slake—every word, more than once, during the tumultuous flight to Honolulu—she thought about the Falconer twin she did not know.

Long ago she had decided that Jesse was moon to Patrick's sun. He possessed not a kilowatt of his own dazzle and was both physically uninspired and socially inept. Passion smoldered within the moon twin, of course, passion for his writing . . . and for the snow lions of the world.

Jesse Falconer's passion was quiet yet fierce, serious and intense; identical, in fact, to Caitlin's own passion for saving endangered hearts. Indeed the *un*dazzling twin was far more like her than Patrick ever would be.

But now Caitlin had read *Blue Moon*. Maybe, *maybe*,

the novel afforded further proof of how similar she and Jesse were: irrevocably solitary creatures who were nonetheless achingly capable of imagining the wonders of love.

But it was also possible that her assessment of the dark twin was *all wrong*.

Well, she would find out. Tonight.

Caitlin's storm-delayed Aloha Airlines flight from Honolulu finally reached Maui in the late afternoon. Already the tropical tempest had imposed an early twilight on the Valley Isle. Already the Honoapiilani Highway had become a treacherous ribbon of black satin.

I will be careful, Caitlin had vowed to Timothy Asquith. It was a promise which implicitly precluded the notion of making the drive after dark. Arguably, for Caitlin, the cliffside trek would always be fraught with risk. She rarely drove. Her apartment on Barrington was directly across from the hospital and Ariel's was just three blocks away. A bone-dry street at high noon felt somewhat foreign to her, and if one factored into the equation for disaster her recent lack of sleep . . .

Her mission *could* be put off until morning. Realistically, she—accompanied by Jesse Falconer's blood— would not be boarding a plane for the mainland until tomorrow. But she had come this far, and it seemed important that she complete her journey tonight—while it was still her birthday and when the heavens had become the sea, pouring sheets of liquid magic onto earth.

She would arrive at the mountaintop hideaway a little frazzled perhaps. More than a little. Weary and raw. But she would arrive.

Even though her hands were threatening to spasm from their death grip on the steering wheel and her eyes stung from peering through walls of rain—already, and she had yet to reach Kaanapali. Twilight lay far behind, and her destination lay far ahead. Beyond Kaanapali. Beyond Kapalua. Beyond Pineapple Hill.

She was virtually alone on the rain-slick roadways, making it safer for all concerned, and streetlights glowed overhead, illuminating her journey into liquid blackness . . . until, that is, she made the turnoff onto the private road to Jesse Falconer's home.

Apparently the reclusive author chose not to provide his nighttime visitors with any insight into the perilousness of their winding ascent—or the precariousness with which they teetered on the edge of eternity.

Visitors? One did not live in a place like this if one wanted visitors.

Well, Jesse Falconer, I am coming to visit, and I'm almost there. At any moment this tortuous road will become a driveway and there will be lights. Won't there be?

Yes. Surely. Unless . . .

The mind that had been deprived of sleep by the haunting rampages of ghosts and ghouls began to conjure disturbing images of Jesse Falconer's "home." A medieval castle, perhaps, complete with chilling drafts and dank dungeons. Or, for the man with a passion for murder, something quite Frankensteinesque, a turreted monstrosity most suited to the Bavarian Alps. It was even possible the murder maven's tastes ran to the truly macabre, a home for Count Dracula himself, a Transylvanian bungalow with coffins in every room.

Surely Timothy Asquith would have alerted her to such architectural eccentricities. But Gemstone Pictures' CEO had arrived here during the brightness of a Hawaiian day. Even the most Gothic of castles would seem enchanting in such a benevolent light. Timothy Asquith would have no way of knowing the dramatic transformation induced by nightfall, not to mention a ferocious storm; a transformation as profound, perhaps, as the one Jesse Falconer underwent every time he became Graydon Slake.

Was the famous author writing now? Was he crafting the most black of terror—and the most stormy of passion—in this fierce and unrelenting darkness?

Darkness? What darkness?

Suddenly, stunningly, the world changed. Brightened. Glowed.

Glared. It was daylight now, the full luminescence of a tropical sun, a blinding brilliance made all the more intense by the prism effect of the falling rain. The golden floodlights illuminated the rain-kissed stone on which she drove. It was slate, an entire teal green driveway of it, and spiked green steel fenced the perimeter of the drive— a lofty barrier, unmistakably foreboding.

The spear-sharp barricade lay before her as well, a massive gate suspended from pillars of slate. An intercom adorned the driver's side pillar, modern technology embedded in stone. Was there a camera lens, too, zooming in on her face? Was Jesse Falconer studying her image, faultlessly clear despite the rain, thanks to the powerful wattage of the penetrating lights?

Yes, Caitlin thought. He is staring at me.

She felt the invisible appraisal, intense—and disapproving. The dark twin was noticing the dark circles beneath her eyes, and the harrowed tautness of her skin, and the bloodless hands that clutched the steering wheel.

Would he take pity on the orphan of the storm, permitting her to venture farther with no questions asked? Or would she need to compel her fingers to uncurl, if such motion were possible, then lower the window and plead her case to the intercom framed in stone?

The answer came quickly. Apparently Jesse's interest was piqued. Or maybe a face-to-face inquisition appealed to him more. In the dungeon. Where intruders were tortured until they confessed all.

Whatever the reason the spiked iron opened, a somber parting, and a silent one; and yet as she saw the gate close behind her, Caitlin sensed an ominous clang, like the barred doors of a jail cell slamming shut.

Her heart began to pound, a primal reflex of pure fear—even though there was nothing fearsome in what she saw. The world had changed again, gentled. The glaring floodlights had been dimmed, replaced by a golden mist that drifted from lampposts amidst an ocean of fluttering palms. The slate gentled, too, becoming a river of teal that meandered through gardens abloom with every hue and blossom of the tropics.

And Jesse Falconer's house? Caitlin saw it at last, as she rounded the final bend of the river of slate. It was not a medieval castle. Neither was it the secluded citadel of a scientific madman nor the night black dwelling of a vampire prince.

The sprawling white structure most resembled a lustrous strand of pearls nestled amid a rainbow of flowers.

Caitlin stopped the car at the foot of a flight of teal green stairs, the final ascent to the pearly home. She compelled her fingers to uncurl, an unfurling that precipitated a burst of tingling pain—and a clumsiness the surgeon had rarely experienced. Sheer will enabled her to turn off the ignition, set the brake, douse the headlights, unfasten her seat belt, and open the door.

Then she was outside, standing in the rain, her every

muscle trembling in relief, and release, from its isometric clench. Trembling, yet paralyzed.

Or was it mesmerized, transfixed by the apparition at the top of the stairs? It was as if the rain had parted, as if he had made it part, for Caitlin saw him quite clearly—as clearly, that is, as a shadow could be seen.

He was a faceless silhouette. But his shape spoke volumes. Jesse Falconer was physically quite whole, distinctly unmaimed. Lean, elegant, powerful, commanding.

But perhaps there were scars on his shadowed face— the ravaged face of the moon—disfigurements so grotesque that no woman would want him even in the blackest veil of night. Caitlin would know. Soon. For he was emerging from the darkness.

The lamplight fell first on his hair. Like hers, it was the color of midnight. Thick, lustrous, shining. Then the golden beams illuminated his face, revealing it, exposing it.

There were no scars. There were only hard planes and harsh angles, classic features carved in stone. Quite flawless, quite breathtaking, quite—

All of a sudden, through the parted curtain of rain, Caitlin wondered if she saw scars after all, deep slashes carved in the heart with knives of pure pain. The moment passed swiftly, the vicious wounds merely a mirage, false shadows on this night of authentic ones, and Caitlin saw the real Jesse Falconer once again.

Meek. Socially inept. Physically unattractive. Those were the words by which she had decided the moon twin would best be described. Such safe words, such comforting images. They were shattered now, splintered like fine crystal on a river of slate.

And the words that took their place? They came on a

gust of wind, a force of nature that seemed—like the rain—completely in his command.

Dark, the wind hissed. Sensual, it howled. Erotic, it mocked. Dangerous, it warned.

The gusting wind swirled with the same adjectives that Caitlin had assigned to Graydon Slake's thrillers of passion and murder. And as for the extraordinary imagination she had given him? Quite possibly Jesse had no imagination at all. The lyrical passages of intimacy had merely to be recalled from his own vast array of erotic interludes.

Lyrical passages of intimacy? You mean *sex*. Pure and simple. At least *simple* for Jesse Falconer, for whom such uninhibited sensuality was surely as instinctive *and as necessary* as breathing.

The man who stood before her wrote bestselling novels; and he had at his command the wind and the rain; and for light entertainment he enjoyed watching unwelcome visitors attempt to reach his home in the pitch-blackness of night.

But all these enterprises were trivial diversions, amusing ways to pass the time when Jesse Falconer wasn't where he belonged—in bed, making love.

Caitlin was in the presence of an alarmingly sexual creature. He was moving toward her now, a powerful gait of predatory grace, and at last she saw his eyes. They blazed with a dark green fire, a glittering inferno that sent both warning and promise. Like a Graydon Slake hero this man was dangerous, and he could be cruel. He was separated from sheer villainy by the most slender of threads.

The stealthy prowl halted a short yet generous distance

from her, not crowding her, not invading her space—at least not physically.

Jesse Falconer did not smile. But he did speak. And his words, low and deep, felt oddly protective.

"Let's get you out of the rain."

He was as drenched as she. But he supplied her with all the towels she needed before attending to the dampness of his own hair and face.

"So," he began at last, "who are you?"

"Don't you know?"

"Should I?"

He had seemed so unsurprised to see her that Caitlin had assumed he had been forewarned after all, that Timothy Asquith hadn't kept his promise of silence any more than she had kept her promise to be careful.

"Didn't Timothy Asquith tell you I was coming?"

"Not a word. And the last time we talked was about two hours ago."

"Well, I asked him not to tell you."

"And he agreed? That doesn't sound like Timothy. The two of you must be very close."

"What? Oh, no. Not really. I know his wife fairly well, and his son and—"

"Okay. Somehow you managed to convince him to conceal from me the fact that you were coming. The question is, Why?"

Because I wanted to catch you by surprise. I wanted to be certain that, once warned, you didn't flee rather than confront the bitter memories of your past.

What a foolish notion—one that rivaled the image of him as unattractive and meek. This man, this predator, would never be caught by surprise. Nor would he flee. Not ever. Not from anything.

Because I wanted to offer you the chance to become the sun, to be as dazzling as your twin, to save an endangered heart.

But Jesse was not the moon. He had his own light, his own heat. True, the fires within were quite different from Patrick's glittering gold. Dark. Fierce. Dangerous. Yet dazzling nonetheless.

And as for neediness? That was the most fanciful notion of all. Jesse Falconer had not been waiting for Caitlin to offer him the chance to help his twin.

Jesse needed nothing from Caitlin. Nothing. What needs he had—well, he could have whomever he wanted whenever he wanted her. Perhaps there was someone here now, a woman with whom Jesse shared sophisticated passion and stylish repartée. Perhaps she was in his bed, impatient and restless.

As was he. Caitlin saw his restlessness, and the immense power of his control. The restlessness was coiled tight. But like his sexuality, it smoldered.

"Why?" he repeated, his voice dangerously soft.

This was a man to whom one could not lie. At least Caitlin couldn't. Jesse would see the lie, and the blazing green fires would sear her soul.

Because I need your blood. The prospect of getting Jesse Falconer's blood suddenly seemed beyond daunting. It seemed impossible.

The magical confidence of the sea was gone, drowned by the storm that was part of him. Caitlin needed time to recover *and* to prepare an entirely new script, an alternative approach to this man who was so very far from the kindred spirit she had envisioned.

She temporized. But she did not lie. "Timothy asked me to read your screenplay." *And I will, when I return to*

LA, as soon as I've finished giving Stephen Sheridan samples of your blood.

"And you came here to discuss it with me? In the middle of the night? Despite a raging storm? This sounds serious."

His green eyes glittered, amused—and not the least bit troubled by her apparently *major* concerns with the script he'd written for *Thief of Hearts.*

Jesse Falconer was amused. But he was not fooled. And now there was a slight but ominous change, and Caitlin saw his amusement for what it truly was: contempt.

"Yes," she asserted. "It is serious." *Your twin is dying and I am going to convince you to save him.*

The magic of the sea was returning, or perhaps it was the power of her own passion for endangered hearts. *Saving hearts is what I do, who I am, all that I am.*

Caitlin's surging wave of confidence was preempted by a sudden chill. The raindrops that had evaded her hurried toweling had apparently made a beeline for her bones, where they had promptly turned to ice.

"You need to shower and change before we talk."

Caitlin answered through teeth that threatened to chatter. "Yes."

"And sleep? Can our discussion wait until morning?"

It was a gift from him to her, an overnight reprieve during which she could regroup. "That would be fine. What time?"

"Whenever you wake up."

"Should I call you then? Before I leave?"

"Leave where?"

"Kapalua. I'll get a room at the hotel there."

It was faint, just the trace of a flicker, but Caitlin convinced herself it was real. Surprise, in the man who could not be surprised. And now his gaze seemed even more intense, as if appraising her anew—as if her willingness to descend the treacherous road despite her quivering fatigue made him question some judgment he had made about her.

"Not a chance," he told her. "You'll spend the night here, in the guest wing where Timothy and Lillian stayed."

Lil*lith*, Caitlin amended silently. "Thank you."

Her faintly blue-tinged lips offered a smile—which was not returned. The flicker of surprise, and the possibility of a more positive reassessment of her, were long gone.

"I have one final question," he said to his shivering guest.

"Yes?"

"Do you have a name?"

FOURTEEN

MAUI

THURSDAY, APRIL TWENTY-FIFTH

*S*he slept so well, awakening rested and refreshed just before dawn. The sky was black velvet, embroidered with silver stars. The storm had passed, as had its figments and phantoms. The tropical tempest had conspired with her fatigue to make Jesse Falconer more fearsome than he truly was. His most alarming aspects would soften with the light of day, and Caitlin's sunlit image would improve as well.

She had arrived weary and only became worse—soggy and shivering. Today she would be the portrait of competency. The heart surgeon had neither her white coat nor her scrubs. It was possible however—absent pouring rain and howling wind—to appear crisp and efficient in an ivory-and-indigo dress.

Jesse had not given his shivering guest a tour of his home. But the layout was straightforward. Two wings stretched from the central marble foyer, one for the master, one for his guests. The entire structure was gently curved, the graceful arc of a crescent moon, its inner curve a continuous wall of glass which afforded a vista of the secluded courtyard and the sea beyond.

Last night, from the foyer, Caitlin had glimpsed the initial portion of the master wing: the living room, spacious and grand, and a dining area wreathed in mirrors. The kitchen presumably came next, then an office, perhaps, and eventually the master—master's—bedroom.

Whatever the configuration Jesse's bedroom was far away from where she had slept, at the other tip of the moon. Without fear of awakening him Caitlin showered and shampooed before venturing from her room.

Venturing? Exploring . . . searching for clues to who Jesse Falconer truly was—the man, not the shadowy figment of a ferocious storm. It was an investigation fueled by noble purpose, to ensure the success of her mission for Patrick.

Even before leaving her suite Caitlin knew that Jesse had impeccable taste—and a reverence for nature. The decor of his home was at once elegant and understated, designed to complement not eclipse the natural beauty that abounded without.

The guest wing consisted of three bedroom suites and a library. An eclectic selection of books was provided for the reading pleasure of Jesse's guests and there was a reference library as well. All manner of subjects could be found, from ancient civilization to contemporary law. The medical section was especially comprehensive. It made sense, Caitlin supposed, for a man who wrote about murder to be familiar with all the ways in which human beings could die.

One corner of the library, a bright and cheery alcove, was devoted to the novels of Graydon Slake. His thrillers, eighteen in all, were arranged in order of publication. For each title a variety of editions were on display—hardcover, paperback, and foreign translations from Chinese to Greek. And for the three Graydon Slake novels that had made it to the silver screen bound copies of the screenplays were shelved as well.

Graydon Slake's first book, *Stargazer,* commanded the entire top shelf. Published first in paperback, *Stargazer* had subsequently enjoyed a hardcover release. And, Caitlin decided as she stared overhead, stargazing herself, it appeared as if the original manuscript had been preserved.

Except, she realized, the neatly typed label read *Hell Hath No Fury.* The author's original title for *Stargazer,* perhaps, or maybe a first, never-published effort. If so, *Hell Hath No Fury* was of more than historical interest. Any publisher would be delighted to publish the bestselling author's long-lost work.

Maybe, Caitlin mused, *Hell Hath No Fury* was not a novel at all. Maybe it was a catalog of spurned lovers.

Whatever, the black notebook was inaccessible—unless, that is, she used a rattan chair as a stepping stool. Which she might have done, on the grounds that she was learning as much as possible about Jesse, but the heavy chair would have to be dragged, an endeavor that would leave telltale marks on the thick mauve carpet.

Besides, there was more to be learned right here, just below eye level, on the shelf devoted to the endangered creatures of earth. Myriad copies of *The Snow Lion* lined the shelf, as did videos of the film. The focal point, however, was a small version of the king of beasts, the title character himself, appearing at once regal and cuddly.

When Timmy Asquith had arrived at Westwood

Memorial Hospital, hypotensive and blue and gasping, he had been clutching this snowy lion's identical twin. Perhaps the stuffed animal in this Maui alcove was a gift from Timmy to the author of his favorite book. Perhaps she and Jesse shared an acquaintance with that bright little boy.

If, in fact, the fluffy lion was a gift, it was a treasured one, displayed more prominently than all the bestselling books. Indeed the entire alcove seemed a shrine to emotion, not success; to sentiment, not arrogance; a memorial that had been carefully tended—once.

A quick scan of three nearby—and unopened—boxes provided insight into when the tending had ceased, at least the point by which it was definitely gone: sixteen months ago January. That date was stenciled on one of the boxes, and additional stenciling on each disclosed what was inside—hardcover and paperback editions of *Wind Chime*, and the hardcover of *Blue Moon*.

They were complimentary copies, Caitlin supposed, from the publisher. Books for the author to give to his family and friends. Boxes of books that had never been opened.

This place of sentiment and celebration was *not* Jesse's handiwork. Of that, she had no doubt. So who had lived here once and vanished sixteen months ago? A wife seemed improbable. Too domesticated. A live-in lover, then? Caitlin had imagined for Jesse a never-ending series of lovers—overnight visitors, not permanent residents in his home.

The alcove did not truly undermine that image. The careful arranging of the works of Graydon Slake, and the sentimental display of the snowy white lion, could have been accomplished in a single day—a rainy-day project undertaken by a live-in hopeful.

Yet the alcove felt sad, lonely, cold. Like the frigid ashes of a once-cheery fire.

Did home and hearth matter to the moon twin? Was it possible that the man who seemed so complete, so contained and controlled, lived with aching emptiness deep inside? Could the phantom scars she had seen, that mirage of night and shadows, been real after all?

Maybe Jesse Falconer actually missed his long-lost brother. The thought seemed abundantly hopeful. But a chill passed through her nonetheless. What if the reunion of the Falconer twins came just in time for Jesse to watch Patrick die? What if Jesse tried *and failed* to save his brother? What then?

That's not going to happen, Caitlin told herself. It was an assertion that needed more than a silent vow. It needed action, beginning with a hasty retreat from the alcove.

The once-bright place seemed shadowy now, a frozen tomb, a gravestone of forgotten warmth.

Caitlin found light and hope in the living room.

Dawn had arrived and with it the promise of golden heat. At the moment the promise was pink, a pastel glow at the very edges of the heavens, lacy ruffles beneath a dove-colored gown.

And for the first time since arriving on the Valley Isle, Caitlin saw the sea. It lay beyond the courtyard and far below, a depthless pool of indigo magic.

She wanted to get closer to the magic, to watch in that vast reflecting pond the splendor of pink lace overtaking the sky. And she would. In the distance was a beckoning silhouette, a gazebo perched at cliff's edge, the ideal spot from which to watch the sun rise over the sea.

The lure of the sea compelled her forward, a journey that was magical in itself, an enchantment of flowers and ponds woven throughout with bridges and walkways of slate.

As she drew near the beckoning silhouette Caitlin was forced to redefine the structure: bungalow, not gazebo, a home for overnight visitors, perhaps, when all the guest-wing suites were filled.

Were those suites ever filled? Did Jesse have a circle of friends for whom he hosted gala weekends at his clifftop estate? It was not hard to envision him in the role of host, elegant and cool. But the image of gala weekends, à la Gatsby, stalled in Caitlin's mind, along with the notion of a group of friends.

Private parties seemed more Jesse Falconer's style. One guest only. In his bed.

With the exception of the necessary structural frame-work the bungalow was completely glass—which meant that if one stood in precisely the right spot one could watch the sun rise both through the glass and *on* it. The real thing and its mirror-image twin.

The glass itself was unique, faceted, shimmering; an immense diamond that captured light and created fire.

That was happening even now. Some glassy facet, or an infinity of them, had seized a nascent ray of dawn, a shaft so pale it was invisible to the human eye. Amplified, magnified, the tiny sunbeam filled the entire bungalow, a golden green luminescence that seemed to come from within.

There was, of course, another—and positively Gothic—explanation for the luminous glow: kryptonite, a gigantic meteor of it, an incandescent emerald sparkling brightly within its diamond home.

The smile that touched Caitlin's lips as she imagined something so fanciful faded abruptly when she saw the true cause of the glow. Not the sun. Not a glowing rock from another galaxy. And far from Gothic. Just the prop of a modern-day writer—a computer screen, alive and aglow.

The author was at work.

Was this an inviolate moment? Was Jesse Falconer's muse so moody, his creativity so precarious, that the slightest intrusion might irrevocably shatter some poetic turn of phrase?

Did this Falconer possess an artist's temperament, a surgeon's temperament? Would he hurl his computer across the room with as little provocation as the occasional surgeon flung his scalpel onto the floor?

Patrick Falconer, the virtuoso surgeon, never succumbed to such fits of pique, neither within the OR nor without.

And the dark twin?

We'll talk when you wake up, Jesse had said. Well, she was awake, and so was he, and the pink ruffles were everywhere, lacy tufts of hope, and where the indigo waves welcomed the bright pink light the sea rippled a satiny mauve.

There could be no more ideal time to reveal her true mission. She would get Jesse's assent, and the requisite samples of his blood, and long before the tropical sun began to glare she would be on her way to LA.

A final bridge lay between the spot where she stood and the glass wall on which she would tap. Before making those last decisive steps Caitlin paused to inhale the full measure, the full magic, of the fragrant morning air.

Only then did she notice the wrought-iron fence. Tall and spiked and snuggled against the glassy walls its forest green coloring was designed as camouflage, an artful blending with the foliage into which it dived.

But there was nothing natural about the knife-sharp spikes, and its tight proximity to the bungalow suggested purpose, as if there was some menace that needed to be kept out—or in.

The bungalow did not truly interrupt the continuity of the barricade, a weak link crafted of glass not steel. Beyond the glass loomed an imposing gate. It was open now, while the author was at work, so that the view would not be obstructed in any way.

One would be particularly loath to impede *this* view, Caitlin realized as she beheld the vista beyond the glass. The terrain was a tableau of contrasts, at once lush and stark, the ravages of a primeval volcano wreathed by the luxuriance of a living forest.

It was a moonscape, dazzling in its own way. The moon's way. Serene yet powerful. Majestic yet menacing. Sensual yet hard. Dark and dangerous.

Like the man.

Caitlin drew a final breath, a gulp of dawn and gardenias and sea. Then she crossed the arched slate bridge over the pond of koi and caught her first glimpse of the bungalow's interior. She had expected impeccable elegance. But the decor was as stark, as spartan and austere, as the moonscape.

As the man.

The furnishings included a desk, a chair, and the bare essentials of a modern-day office—computer, printer, phone, fax. There were no creature comforts to be seen, no steaming mug of Kona's finest, no svelte bottle of vintage Scotch.

There was nothing else. Just him. His silhouette. Motionless yet powerful, intent on the task of creating another world with his bare hands.

Was he in the mind of a murderer? Or was he in bed?

Caitlin hoped that she was intruding on murder not passion. Murder felt safer.

But no matter what, she was going to tell Jesse Falconer the truth—right now.

She planned a light yet confident tap on the glass. But that decisive rap was halted, her hand poised in midair, as she caught sight of the other silhouette in the barren room.

The new shape lay on the floor beside Jesse, white and bulky, not dark and spare. A comforter filled with down? A fleecy cocoon for the rare nights in paradise when the air was cool?

Jesse Falconer had no need of heat. It blazed within. And Caitlin could not envision him huddled beneath a blanket. Huddled anywhere. Ever.

Besides, this white shadow was a live thing, and now it was in motion, moving toward her with exquisite stealth and startling grace—especially for a creature so large.

Only a scant number of white lions roamed the planet. The snowy beasts were desperately endangered, vanishingly rare. Unlike humans, who were everywhere.

At this moment, however, this particular king of beasts was endangered no more.

Only she was.

The lion's predatory gaze—appraising and calm—told Caitlin of her own jeopardy in no uncertain terms. The stealthy prowl had ceased for the moment, replaced by an even more ominous stillness. That the powerful creature could leap through the glass as if it were tissue paper was not in doubt. Neither was the certainty that such a lethal leap was precisely his intent. He was putting her on notice, punishing her with fear in advance of the kill.

Once beyond the gossamer veil of glass, and with an instinct as old as time, the lion would ravage her throat in a single bite, the most delicate of nibbles for his savage jaws. A similar ancient instinct compelled the hand that had been poised to make its light and confident knock to find her throat . . . as if her trembling fingers could offer any protection at all for that most vulnerable flesh.

But Caitlin's throat already *was* protected. A single strand of costume pearls, a gift of love from a mother, encircled her neck—and for several moments the precious beads seemed a magical shield.

Then the lion moved anew, a leisurely motion, the opening of massive jaws with all the innocence of a yawn.

Caitlin's survival instincts were not deceived, and the illusion that she was somehow protected was torn asunder by the reflexive jerk of her own hand. The "pearls"— the glass beads lacquered white and strung all as one—spilled onto the slate. Some lay at her feet, bright white against green stone, and others, like tears of farewell, splashed into the crystal-clear pond of koi.

Caitlin was only vaguely aware of the fate of the treasured gift. Later, if there was a later, her heart would mourn its loss.

There was sound now; not leisurely, not lazy, just primitive and raw—thunder from the beginning of time . . . a thunderous roar that caused a lightning-quick response within the bungalow.

Jesse Falconer might have been lost in a realm of fictional terror, of fantasy carnage, but he made the shift from fantasy to reality in a racing heartbeat.

And that reality? A male lion defending his domain.

Suddenly there were two beasts within the perishable walls of glass, two creatures of fearsome power and extraordinary grace. And was the man reaching for a gun? The semiautomatic fully armed with bullets—or tranquilizers—which lay at all times beside him on the desk?

He was not. There was no such weapon, no sleek silhouette she had failed to see.

Was the human beast reaching for the lion's neck, then? For the massive collar hidden beneath the fleecy mane from which dangled a reassuringly domesticated selection of stainless-steel tags—his rabies vaccination; and if such licensing was required in Hawaii, some indication that local officials knew he was here; and, of course, the bone-shaped tag: *Hi. My name is Snowy. If you're reading this I'm lost, so please call* . . .

Jesse Falconer's answering service was suddenly explained. His round-the-clock availability was for the lion, the lethal beast who was surely wearing a collar—and was, perhaps, even tethered by a chain.

But there was no collar, no tethering chain.

Because they aren't necessary, a bold voice proclaimed. Just a simple command—"Sit and stay"—will do. In a moment Jesse will issue that command.

In a moment . . . after he and the lion finished enjoying her fear. *Savoring* it. The beast-author would plunge his hands into the snowy coat then, ruffling the glossy fleece, a reassuring caress that said he was a good guard lion, the best, but that the presumptuous woman who had so brazenly invaded the privacy of their lair did not need to be destroyed.

Then the dark and beastly Falconer twin would look at her, his green-fire eyes mocking and amused.

Don't worry, he would say. His roar is bigger than his bite.

Then he would slide open the glass wall and invite her to extend her trembling hand to the docile lion. And during that pawshake he would show her that his pet lion had no claws.

It was an infuriating—yet wonderful—scenario. But a fantasy one.

Jesse Falconer was not issuing commands or ruffling fur or looking at her with glinting amusement. His gaze, intense and intent, was focused entirely on the lion, and when Jesse moved it was not to touch but to position himself between the determined predator and his perishable prey.

And was the lion deceived by this human shield? Did he forget about the intruder he could no longer see?

No. He roared still.

It was not a questioning roar, beast to master, seeking consent. But maybe, just maybe, its fierceness was diminishing ever so slightly.

If Jesse was speaking to the lion, the human roar was too low for Caitlin to hear and was offered with utter stillness.

Seconds passed. Minutes. An eternity during which Caitlin became convinced that there was a definite decrescendo to the lion's roar.

But such a precarious decrescendo, she warned herself.

At any moment the roar could return and the beast, weary of this game, would simply attack, simply devour, simply destroy.

Finally, finally, Caitlin heard a human voice—a growl in itself, low and controlled.

"Walk to the house, Caitlin. Walk, don't run. Don't answer me. Just do it."

FIFTEEN

MAUI

THURSDAY, APRIL TWENTY-FIFTH

$\mathcal{C}$aitlin followed his command, fleeing slowly to the sanctuary of the crescent moon. Her heartbeat thundered in her brain, a sound so loud it seemed impossible that she could hear anything else.

But she did hear other sounds, amazing ones: the birdsong that greeted the dawn, the splashing of the courtyard fountain, the rustling of palm fronds like the fluttering of a thousand fans.

Caitlin heard the thunder of her pulse, and the tranquility of the awakening day, and she strained to hear even more: the near soundlessness of mammoth paws loping on slate.

That eager, lethal approach would not, she realized, be the first sound. Nor would the shattering of glass as the lion sailed through the bungalow's gossamer veil.

She would hear first the scream of a man, his final utterance on earth, as his throat was torn from his neck.

Jesse Falconer *would* scream, wouldn't he? Was it possible not to?

Caitlin had watched death, witnessed it. Patients did not scream as they died. At least not aloud. But when it came to violent death surely some innate protest was offered by all living creatures, a primal cry that pleaded for life.

On this morning in paradise Caitlin heard only birdsong, and palm fronds, and the splashing of crystal-clear water.

When she reached the safety of the house she turned toward the bungalow. The standoff continued. The two beasts were motionless statues, one ebony, one white, both limned in gold.

Finally, *finally,* the lion turned away, a leisurely saunter of dignity and grace, conceding nothing, certainly not defeat, as he strolled through the open door to the moonscape beyond.

Only then did the night black statue begin to move.

There had been no defeat in the graceful gait of the king of beasts. And the human beast? His gait was graceful but weighted. Exhausted from the ordeal, perhaps, *or weighted with fury.*

Jesse Falconer's first task was to close the massive spiked-steel gate, an act which transformed the bungalow from prism to prison. Then within that prison cell, and somehow weighted even more, he went through the motions of an author finished for the day. He saved the words he had been writing, removed from the computer a small blue disk, shut off the entire system, and turned toward the house.

Toward her.

Caitlin felt a moment of relief as Jesse left the bungalow, relieved that he was vacating the suddenly oppressive place. Her relief was short-lived, however, for now he was journeying toward her, a voyage that faltered slightly at its very outset because of her, as his frowning gaze fell on a cluster of false pearls scattered on teal green slate.

In the novels of Graydon Slake, at least in *Blue Moon,* the line between hero and villain had been distinct but real—a slight yet monumental separation between the man who would forfeit his life to save the woman he loved and the man who murdered for sheer pleasure.

Graydon Slake's cruel-yet-noble hero would willingly position himself between the massive jaws of a lion and the fragile throat of a woman. And even with that act behind him, the fictional hero would remain heroic still.

He would not cross the fine line to villainy. Would not, as he strode from the bungalow to the house, look as if he was about to kill, wanted to.

Caitlin saw Jesse's fury with dazzling clarity. As he followed the meandering slate pathways through the gardenia-fragrant courtyard sunlight caressed his face, illuminating the darkness of his rage.

The door through which Caitlin had entered the living room was open. For him. Moments earlier, as she had watched his weighted silhouette in the bungalow-turned-prison, she had even considered rushing out to meet him.

But as Jesse drew closer Caitlin felt herself backing away—an instinctive retreat of self-preservation . . . an instinct which, she realized, had not surfaced from its primitive depths during her moments of peril with the lion.

This was more perilous.

Then he was standing in the doorway, blocking every ray of light, the moon eclipsing the sun.

What folly to have decided this man was merely a nighttime mirage, a figment of the storm, a phantom of her own fatigue. What fantasy to have imagined he would be softened by daylight.

"I'm *sorry*," she whispered to the faceless fury that banished the sun.

Caitlin had no idea what to expect. With the exception of an occasionally petulant surgeon—which was, in essence, the temper tantrum of a small child—she had no personal experience with angry men. Some shouted, she supposed. And swore. And some even hit.

This man would do none of those things—any more than he would scream in agony as his throat was being torn from his neck. Jesse Falconer would remain calm, urbane, utterly civilized as he verbally ripped her to shreds.

The shadow's voice *was* calm. "It wasn't really your fault, was it?"

"Yes it was."

"You looked so tired." Jesse spoke quietly, almost to himself. "I expected you to sleep until much later. I shouldn't have let him in."

With the stunning words he entered the room, unshadowing his face and unmasking the true target of his fury.

She was the intruder, yet Jesse was angry with himself for placing her in jeopardy—her and the lion. He felt protective of both, responsible for both.

"Yes, you should have."

"Well. It's over. Are you all right?"

"Yes. Thank you. I'm fine."

"Good."

The beast exhaled, a decidedly human gesture, an honest admission of his fear and of his relief. Relief pulsed through Caitlin as well. It was over, all of it, the threat from the lion and the worry that she had irrevocably enraged Patrick's twin.

With the relief came euphoria, a giddiness which Caitlin knew to be a predictable aftermath of an adrenaline surge. She had witnessed such post-traumatic gaiety many times. A patient with a free-flowing cut would present to the ER frightened and apprehensive. Once the local anesthetic had been injected, along with an infusion of soothing words, relief would replace fear, and as the sutures were being placed the patient would become positively loquacious.

Did adrenaline, once spent, convert to champagne? If so, it was a biochemical pathway yet to be described. But Caitlin was definitely feeling its effects, as soaring heat rushed to every vein.

Caitlin couldn't tell if Jesse, too, was feeling this effervescent rush, this exuberant warmth. She knew only the heat of his appraising gaze. It blazed with searing green fire, brilliant yet dark—and utterly demanding.

Jesse Falconer wanted something from her. The truth, perhaps.

I will tell you the truth. Soon. But even this soaring giddiness doesn't give me the courage to speak directly to the fire.

On a snowy night in Boston Caitlin had learned of secrets and champagne. This was a different time, a different place, a different twin. But on this day in paradise secrets would be revealed, and as she turned from Jesse's commanding gaze Caitlin saw snow.

The lion stood on a rise on the moonscape. The wind ruffled his mane and his coat glowed pink beneath the newborn sky.

"He's so beautiful," she whispered.

"Yes, he is."

"He doesn't have a name, does he?"

"No. He's not a pet, Caitlin. He's not *my* lion. He's not anyone's lion."

"But you are definitely *his* human. And he's very lucky. You take good care of him."

"I protect him, that's all. I provide a place where he's safe. He takes care of himself."

His voice was quiet, but Caitlin heard the fierceness. Jesse had assumed the solemn responsibility of protecting the snow lion. It was a willing commitment, one that was both necessary—and dangerous.

The king of beasts did not stand a chance against a hunter's rifle. And although it seemed unimaginable that anyone would choose to hurt, much less murder, the spectacular animal, the snowy coat now tinted pink by the tropical dawn was worth a fortune. There were those who would pay handsomely to have such pristine white-ness adorn a palace floor, or cape a king, or cloak a princess.

"But you *are* friends," Caitlin insisted. "Roommates." *Moonmates.*

"Hardly."

The voice behind her held a faint hint of amusement, as if Jesse might actually be enjoying the repartée.

Emboldened, she persevered. "He helps you write. Okay, he *watches* you."

"He lets me wander in his forest. I let him come inside my bungalow."

He has a relationship with the lion, Caitlin thought. A remarkable one. But for some reason he refuses to acknowledge it.

If her own relationship with Jesse was more established, more secure, she might have asked him why.

Your own relationship with Jesse Falconer? the voice of reason queried. You mean the euphoric relief that's flowing in your veins because you weren't mauled by a lion?

The adrenaline was long gone, and not a drop of champagne bubbled within. But her euphoria crescendoed still, an intoxication attributable solely to him.

"You're just not about to anthropomorphize the lion, are you?"

"No." His voice smiled. "But apparently you are."

"Yes." *Yes,* as long as you seem amused. "Does he have a girlfriend?"

"A girlfriend? You mean a lover, Caitlin?"

"Yes, but that's not the right word, is it?" Not right, perhaps, but extraordinary when uttered by this man . . . this expert.

"I think you're searching for *mate.*"

"No," she breathed, barely. "I'm anthropomorphizing, remember?"

"Ah. Well. You must mean his fiancée then, the lioness of his dreams."

"There's a fiancée? A future Mrs. Lion?"

"Yes. But you already know that, don't you, Caitlin? Isn't that the reason you're here? To find out when she's scheduled to arrive so that you can have them both?"

"*What?*"

Her question quivered. And why not? On this tropical

morning in paradise everything had turned to ice. His voice. Her heart.

But not his eyes. Caitlin saw the fire—the inferno—as she turned from the dawn to him.

"What?" she repeated, even colder now, chilled by the glacial flames.

"You heard me."

"I *told* you who I am."

"But we know that's a lie, don't we? You haven't seen the screenplay, much less read it. Robert Asquith won't even receive it until today. And there isn't a chance in hell that Timothy would have given you my address without checking with me first, and the wife with whom you claim to have a friendship is Lillith not Lillian."

"I *know*." *But it seemed as though you were reassessing me, and I wanted nothing to interfere with what might have been a more favorable appraisal.* "It just seemed . . . unnecessary . . . to correct you."

"How considerate. But the fact remains, Caitlin. You're not as advertised."

"Do you truly believe I'm here because of the lion?" *To hurt him? To kill him? Because I must have his snowy fur against my skin?* "If that's true, you were taking quite a risk in the bungalow. I might have come up behind you with a high-powered rifle—"

"Except that you don't have one. At least not in the suitcase that's in the house. And as for the other one, well, it's locked in the trunk of the car to which I have the keys."

How polite it had seemed, how chivalrous, for Jesse to venture back into the storm to retrieve her bag. Caitlin had been in the guest room at the time, making certain—at his gracious suggestion—that the room was amply stocked with every amenity she might possibly need.

Had Jesse truly gone through her luggage? If so, it was a swift and expert search. Nothing had been disturbed.

"You searched my luggage?" *You know all about me?*

Even as she was feeling horror at the intimacy of the invasion, Caitlin found herself wishing Jesse had searched the larger suitcase, too—the one filled with flowing satin and glittering lamé. A search limited to the smaller one would have disclosed undergarments that were utilitarian at best, not to mention an utter absence of the lotions and creams that a more sophisticated . . . what was she *thinking?*

Jesse Falconer had been looking for the high-powered rifle of a killer, not the silken lingerie of a high-powered woman.

"I didn't have to search. Without revealing the specifics suffice it to say that there are detectors at various locations on the property."

Without revealing the specifics—as if he honestly viewed her as either assassin or spy. He'd probably decided the former was more likely, hit woman not Mata Hari. No one would have sent her to charm secrets from him. Not if they knew anything about him. Or her.

Caitlin was disappointed, not angry, that Jesse believed her capable of slaughtering his lion. She had after all arrived unannounced, and she had explained her presence with what he had known from the outset was a lie. Jesse had done what was necessary to protect the endangered creature against a human predator.

He could not permit her to return to Kapalua for the night, to share with her compatriots what she had learned about his home, and his solemn commitment to the snowy beast mandated that he make certain her luggage contained no weapons of any kind.

Caitlin was not a welcome guest in his moon-shaped home. She was the enemy. Indeed, at the moment, she was a prisoner of war.

And the amusement she had heard in Jesse's voice, as if he were actually enjoying the repartée? It was merely a ruse, a ploy to seduce her into feeling so safe that she might make an error. All the while, no doubt, he had been cringing at her feeble attempts at cleverness, the silliness of *roommates* and *girlfriend* and—

"Why didn't you just let the lion kill me?"

"That's really not my style. Besides, there was the possibility you weren't here because of the lion at all. You might have been a crazed, albeit rather enterprising, fan."

Which I am. A fan, definitely crazed.

"Were you planning to imprison me, Caitlin? To tie me up until I wrote what you wanted me to write? Sorry, but bondage has never been my thing. Is it yours?"

The moon twin was mocking her now, and as Caitlin felt his piercing contempt she recalled that day in Boston. Gabrielle St. John had wanted intimacy, and when Patrick had refused Gabrielle had raged, You're just as cruel as—

"So, Caitlin, are you a woman who lusts after coats made from carcasses of white lions?"

"*No.*"

"No?" Jesse echoed, his harshness relenting slightly, yet dramatically, as if some part of him wanted to believe she was not so vain. "So you're a reader."

"I told you who I am—the heart surgeon who's going

to read *Thief of Hearts*. I never actually said that I *had* read it."

"Nor did you mention the part about being a heart surgeon."

"Well, I suppose I thought that was implied. We both know a psychiatrist will be reading the screenplay, too. I guess I didn't imagine you'd think that was me. I suppose I don't fit your image of a heart surgeon, either."

Oh but you do. You're my imagination come to life— and so much more.

Jesse would never have created the vision that had appeared on his doorstep in the midst of a storm. She was a fiction not to be believed, impossibly lovely despite the sogginess of the night. Raindrops had spilled from her black-velvet hair, but they were tropical diamonds, shimmering and bright. And her eyes, the color of the sea, had glowed with sheer courage. The tempest had made transparent her cotton dress, and even though his gaze had never left her rain-damp face, her near nakedness had embarrassed her, an enchanting modesty. But she had stood her ground.

She was Venus rising from the sea—intrepid, defiant, delicate, tough. And he was not a man who could be bewitched. But for many intoxicating moments the storm-drenched temptress had seduced him.

Then the lies had begun.

And now the lovely seductress was telling him that the lies made her neither murderess nor fan. She was a heart surgeon, she said, a quiet confession made with an uncertain shrug even as her chin lifted a defiant notch.

Jesse felt the enchantment beginning anew. And stopped it. Cold.

"Why are you here, Caitlin? Tell me."

There was no oxygen in the breath she took. There was only his heat. His fire. "To ask you to save your brother's life."

Jesse went absolutely still. Like the snow lion. Powerful. Predatory. Lethal.

"Patrick is dying. He has aplastic anemia, which means—"

"I know what it means. He needs a transplant?"

"Urgently."

"Did Patrick send you?"

"No. He has no idea I'm here."

"But he must have told you about me."

"Yes. Years ago, when we were in training together in Boston."

"What did he tell you?"

"That you were . . . estranged."

"Estranged," Jesse echoed, his expression, like his powerful body, as impassive as stone. "Did he happen to mention why?"

"No."

"You wouldn't be here if he had."

"Yes, I would be."

Yes you would, Jesse realized as he gazed at her. The tropical diamonds had vanished with the storm, but her raven black hair shimmered still, and her sea blue eyes were bright with determination and resolve. *You would be here, no matter what, for Patrick. To save Patrick.* "Are you lovers, Caitlin?"

"What?"

"Are you and Patrick lovers?"

Moments before *lovers* had drifted from Jesse's lips

like a whispered kiss. Now it was a jagged-edged knife, sheathed in violence.

"No."

"Have you ever been?"

"No."

"Did Patrick tell you about *me,* Caitlin? Or only about Graydon Slake?"

"He told me about both of you. He knew that you'd become a writer. In fact, he was very interested in your—"

"Did he tell you my name?"

"Yes," Caitlin replied to the man who resisted the notion of a relationship with the lion. Such resistance clearly extended to his twin as well. Jesse did not want to hear that Patrick had followed his career, had cared about it, about *him.* "Jesse."

Jesse. The name revealed by the golden twin caused something very dark, very deep, very private within the shadowed one.

Caitlin looked away, to the world outside. Dawn was a pale pink memory, and the pink-and-snow lion, too, was gone. The sky was cobalt, as was the sea, and the tropical sun burned harsh and bright.

Caitlin gazed at the glaring world until she sensed Jesse move—sensed, not heard, for his stealthy footfalls made no sound. Caitlin felt him move, felt the chill as his fiery heat moved away.

Jesse stood before the granite fireplace, stone confronting stone, an ancient warrior surveying the ravages of his once-beloved homeland. A similar image had come to her recently, as she and Patrick awaited the pirouettes of a pale green ballerina on a computer screen.

They did not look alike, these Falconer men. But their

essence was identical, engraved with integrity, pride, pain. And when at last the granite warrior spoke his voice, hoarse and hopeful, was like Patrick's had been.

"What do you need, Caitlin?"

"For the moment, just a sample of your blood. I can draw that here, now. Tomorrow or the next day, I— Patrick—will need your marrow. The donation could be done in Honolulu, I suppose. But it would be ideal if you could come to LA."

"Patrick's in LA?"

"He moved there about a month ago."

Jesse's frown told her that Patrick was not the only brother who kept tabs on his twin. Quite clearly Jesse expected Patrick to be in New York, and in the scheme of brothers estranged for decades a month lapse was trivial. Still it seemed to trouble Jesse that he hadn't known.

"He's chief of trauma surgery at Westwood Memorial Hospital."

"Westwood Memorial."

Jesse's quiet echo held rawness—it sounded like pain—as if the name of the hospital conjured some ancient anguished ghost. The ghost of the moon twin, perhaps, aching anew as it learned of the sun's latest triumph?

No. Caitlin's thought was decisive. Jesse lived in no man's shadow, and never had. Even though he was a shadow—shadow, and stone, with dark fires deep within. She saw proof of those fires now as Jesse's green eyes found her, held her, controlled her.

"Patrick can't ever know that I was the donor."

"But—"

"I mean it, Caitlin. If Patrick even suspects the truth, the transplant will never happen."

Meaning Jesse would rescind his willingness to save his brother's life? Or would the lifesaving procedure fall apart because of Patrick? Patrick had denied to Stephen Sheridan the existence of a sibling, much less a twin. Would Patrick refuse Jesse's tissue if he knew?

Whatever the reason Jesse's words were a warning and a promise: If Patrick discovered the truth the transplant would not happen . . . and Patrick would die.

Caitlin would have to tell Stephen. But Stephen would agree to the charade, the lie, to save his patient's life. "All right. Patrick will never know."

"Good. So, Caitlin, have you done many bone-marrow biopsies?"

"Me? Well, some. As a resident. They do hurt, but—" Caitlin stopped abruptly.

The discomfort that he, as a marrow donor, could reasonably anticipate did not seem to concern Jesse Falconer in the least. *Pleasure* might be of some interest to the sensuous shadow—yes, always—but pain simply could not matter less.

Now Jesse was smiling a wicked, sexy, dangerous smile.

"I want you to harvest my marrow."

"Harvest," Caitlin echoed his use of the correct medical term. "You know something about marrow transplantation."

"I've done some reading on the subject."

"Then you must know that I can't harvest your marrow."

"On the contrary, Doctor. I know that you can. You just told me you've done biopsies in the past."

"But this is different."

"Not really, Caitlin. It's just more. More time, more tissue."

More time *spent in bone,* Caitlin silently embellished. And more tissue, dozens of samples, instead of just one.

The procedure was performed under anesthesia. The donor was asleep, oblivious, numb. Upon awakening, however, some discomfort was inevitable—the degree of which was directly related to the damage done to bone.

When harvested by an expert such damage was minimal. An expert like Stephen Sheridan knew precisely how much bone to destroy, and Stephen's practiced hands would be rock-steady as he plumbed the depths to salvage sample after sample of the precious cells.

Even if Caitlin acceded to Jesse's request Stephen would be there, guiding her as she twisted the needle ever deeper into bone. *But . . .* but there was no point in arguing pain with the man who didn't care about pain.

So what did Jesse care about? Punishment? Was there fury beneath his wicked, sexy smile? Did he want her to suffer for forcing him to give this gift of life?

I've hardly forced him.

Jesse hadn't hesitated. Yet he seemed weighted by the decision he had made.

"Why do you want me to harvest the marrow?"

"Because then you'll be my doctor. And you'll be prohibited by patient-physician confidentiality from revealing to Patrick anything about me."

"I won't reveal anything to him anyway."

"But this will make it easier, won't it? This way you won't have to lie. I think we've already established that you're not the world's most accomplished liar." A smile, not so wicked now, softened the granite of his face. "That's a compliment, Dr. Taylor."

"So you're doing this for me?" *By cloaking what lies I'll have to tell in the solemn mantle of the Hippocratic Oath?*

Jesse's smile faded.

"I'm doing it for all of us, Caitlin," he said quietly. "So, Doctor, why don't you draw my blood?"

SIXTEEN

MAUI
THURSDAY, APRIL TWENTY-FIFTH

esse arched an eloquent eyebrow at the fistful of rubber-stopped tubes that Caitlin set on the dining-room table as she readied to draw his blood.

"I thought I might as well draw all the donor blood-work," she explained. "That way, as soon as Stephen confirms the match, we can proceed right to transplantation."

"When will Stephen know about the match?"

"I'm not sure. I know he'll start working on it the instant he receives the blood. Which means, I should think, that he'll know a lot by tomorrow afternoon. I suppose it's even possible that the transplant could be done tomorrow night."

"Assuming there is a match."

"There *will* be. It may not be HLA-identical, although it might be. No matter what it will be far better than an unrelated donor ever could be."

"Unless I am an unrelated donor."

"You're Patrick's brother."

"I wonder." *I have always wondered.* "There's no physical resemblance, as I'm sure you've observed."

Yes, she thought. But there's that *essence,* Jesse, that proud nobility, that warrior strength.

Caitlin couldn't quite tell Jesse that she believed he shared a noble essence with his twin. She could only draw his blood and leave it to science to determine the truth.

Science was so advanced these days, the technology so modern, that the ancient art of medicine—bedside diagnoses of such imponderables as essence, and even of health—was rapidly becoming obsolete.

But there was nothing obsolete about the ancient *science* of anatomy. There would be no need, this time, to rely on the ultramodern imprimatur of DNA.

"You *are* Patrick's brother, Jesse." Caitlin looked up from muscled flesh to granite shadows. "Your brachial vein proves it."

"What do you mean?"

"Well." Caitlin touched the ropelike vessel she intended to pierce. "Actually, it's a tributary of the vein—this one here—that's so unusual. Patrick has this same bifurcation. It's an anomaly I'd never seen before drawing Patrick's blood. And now for the second time in a week I'm seeing it again."

Jesse said nothing. He merely stared at the vein. Caitlin's finger pointed still, resting lightly on his heated skin.

She felt his heat, and his heart. It pulsed in the artery adjacent to the vein—strong beats, powerful beats, emotional beats.

Patrick is my brother, the heartbeats seemed to say—as

if for all these years, all these decades, Jesse had truly harbored doubts.

Caitlin looked at his face, and saw only stone. The emotion was imprisoned in his heart. Or so she believed.

When Jesse spoke at last Caitlin heard the ragged edges in his voice.

"There are some arrangements I need to make before I can leave for LA."

"Okay," she replied, wanting *him* to be okay.

Jesse Falconer would be okay, of course. He merely needed a little solitude for his emotions, a little privacy for his thoughts. Caitlin would give him both as soon as she had drawn his blood.

And in the meantime . . . she heard a voice, teasing yet so confident, as if it couldn't matter less if this sensual, sophisticated man diagnosed her as silly beyond all hope.

"Arrangements for the future Mrs. Lion?"

Jesse smiled slightly, gratefully. "Among other things. In any event, Caitlin, I'll put you and the blood on the first available flight and I'll follow a few hours later."

Putting Caitlin and his blood on the plane did not afford Jesse the solitude he needed.

But he would have it no other way.

They took her rental car, which he would return later, and Jesse drove.

He's such a careful driver, Caitlin thought. Such a *good* driver.

Jesse didn't drive slowly, or with excessive caution, or with any indecision at all. He merely drove competently.

Was his care a consequence of his precious cargo? The blood tubes for his brother? *Her?* Or was he merely ever-mindful of the lion who relied upon him for survival itself?

He's being careful for all of us, she decided. He's protecting us all.

As Jesse drove, retracing her storm-tossed journey of the previous night, Caitlin saw the Valley Isle in all its sunlit glory.

"Are there whales?" she asked as she gazed at turquoise water dappled gold.

"There might be a few stragglers, but for the most part they've already headed north. March is really the best time to see them. It's a spectacular sight, Caitlin. Well worth a future trip to Maui . . ."

Jesse was quite capable, Caitlin discovered, of driving decisively yet protectively all the while providing color commentary about his island home. He told her about Maui, god of the sun, and Haleakala, the island's volcano, and he explained the sun god's relationship to Pele, goddess of fire.

Caitlin did not want the drive to end, or to talk of anything but the legends of the tropics. But as they neared the airport, because she had to, she asked, "How do you like Michael Lyons?"

The question came out of the blue, a non sequitur that might have surprised a man who could be surprised. But as if the name was merely that of a minor—and heretofore unfamiliar—Polynesian deity, Jesse replied, "I don't believe I know Michael Lyons."

"Your *nom de hospital*. If Patrick can't know you're the donor then everything—beginning with this bloodwork—needs to be labeled with another name."

Jesse smiled. "Okay. Michael Lyons is fine. Who's Michael?"

Caitlin shrugged. "Just a name."

"You're really not any good at it, you know."

"Good at what?"

"Lying."

She had never told anyone his name. Not Amanda. Not Patrick. But now . . .

"Michael is my father. Rumor has it he's quite wonderful, although we've never met."

"You're serious."

"We've already established that I can't lie."

"No bitterness, Caitlin? No resentment at all?"

She hesitated, testing the vow she had made on the night of dancing rainbows. And she felt . . . peace. Peace with Maggie's Michael. Peace at last.

"No resentment. None at all." Caitlin might have lingered in the feeling, the quiet joy, but already there were signs triaging airport traffic to check-in, parking, or baggage claim. "While we're on the subject of falsehoods, Jesse, Patrick believes I'm on vacation and won't be back until Saturday afternoon. If I'm in the OR tomorrow night, especially if I'm harvesting a marrow, he might find out."

"The transplant's not going to happen tomorrow, Caitlin. Stephen has to look at a biopsy specimen he takes from me, to determine the volume of marrow to be harvested, and I imagine that prior to transplantation he'll also want to give Patrick some of my blood. No matter when the harvesting occurs, however, you won't be in the OR."

"Meaning you've decided to let Stephen harvest the marrow."

Jesse slowed the car to a gentle stop in front of airport check-in, turned to her, and smiled. "Meaning no OR."

Meaning no anesthesia. Why not? she wondered. Because the lion refused to be put to sleep, to willingly surrender such control? If so, the anesthesia could be spinal, not general—except that the man who would not entrust his breathing to someone else was unlikely to agree to paralysis, however temporary, of his powerful limbs.

No matter how painful the option.

"The harvesting has to be done under sterile conditions."

"Just like a marrow biopsy, which does not require an operating room. Any treatment room will do, Caitlin. The hematology clinic undoubtedly has several, all of which would be deserted on either Friday night or Saturday morning. Wouldn't they?"

"Yes," she replied reluctantly. "They would be."

"You really don't want to harvest the marrow, do you?"

To bore a hole in your pelvis and withdraw syringe after syringe of marrow without anesthesia? "No, I really don't."

"Okay."

"*Okay?*"

"Sure. Stephen will probably need an assistant, though."

"Well, that's fine. I'll be there."

Caitlin was not the world's most accomplished liar. But as Jesse exited the car, to unload her luggage and open her door, she enjoyed a triumphant thought. I'm learning, Jesse Falconer, and I'm *succeeding*.

Jesse had not so much as arched a raven black eyebrow when she asserted that she would be happy to assist. The truth, however, was that Caitlin would not be there. Stephen would never permit the harvesting of marrow without anesthesia . . . which meant that the procedure would take place in the operating room with another assistant . . . while Caitlin remained sequestered in her apartment reading whatever Graydon Slake novels she could find during her hour layover in Honolulu.

SEVENTEEN

BEHAVIORAL SCIENCE CENTER
SEATTLE, WASHINGTON
TWENTY-NINE YEARS AGO

"*H*e's a thief." It was a simple statement of fact. For Stuart Falconer, however, the utterance was not simple at all. The "he" to whom Stuart referred was Jesse, his nine-year-old son. But "my son is a thief" would have been impossible. And in truth neither Stuart nor Rosemary Falconer any longer thought of Jesse as their son.

"A thief," the renowned child psychologist echoed with reassuring calm. The calm was acquired from years of dealing with anxious parents, but the reassurance was quite authentic. A nine-year-old boy who stole did not, in itself, evoke great alarm. If theft was the only concern of these parents, they needn't have traveled all the way from their posh Connecticut home to consult with him, an expert on bad seeds. "Please tell me when the behavior started and what Jesse steals."

"It started years ago," Rosemary stated, without revealing what she truly believed: that Jesse had *always* been a thief. It was a life of crime that began in the womb, when Jesse stole from Patrick the nutrients essential to life.

Such a confession would sound emotional, Rosemary knew, *irrational*; as would her description of Jesse as an infant—silent, aloof, as if disdainful of the heroic measures that were being lavished on his malnourished twin; as would her fantasy that there had been one of those unthinkable hospital mix-ups and Jesse belonged to someone else.

The mix-up scenario *was* a fantasy, for while Patrick was fighting for his life in the neonatal ICU, Jesse had been the only newborn in the hospital's nursery. And yet how else could one explain Jesse's presence in the Falconer home?

Stuart Falconer had been born to great wealth. And Rosemary, née Williamson, was *the* heiress of Montclair. And for many generations on both sides the blood had been impeccably blue. But Jesse . . . his dark green eyes glittered with wildness, and his long black hair would not be tamed; and he was left-handed, a gracelessness that shouted heathen not aristocrat. And Jesse's behavior— well, it was simply not the way that Falconers or Williamsons behaved. Ever.

But Jesse was theirs—their thief . . . and worse?

"At first, he just stole from us," Rosemary elaborated. "Keys, money, mementos, jewels. Now he finds it more amusing to embarrass us by stealing from local merchants."

"Amusing?" the psychologist queried.

"It's a *game,* one of many, expressly designed to taunt us. He's never even been caught. The items he stole from us would magically reappear, precisely where they were supposed to be, and when he steals from the local merchants he returns with the stolen item, claiming he simply forgot to pay."

"Couldn't that be true?"

"No. It couldn't." Rosemary's tone was as imperious, as patrician, as was she. "A nine-year-old cannot buy cigarettes, alcohol, or magazines such as *Playboy.*"

"What happens when you confront him?"

"He shrugs it off," Stuart replied. "As if to say, why are we bothering him? But, Doctor, we're not here because Jesse's a thief. We know it and have accepted it. We're here because of Patrick. We're worried that Jesse might hurt him."

"Has Jesse ever hurt Patrick?"

"No."

"Has there been violence of any kind? Against property? Or animals?"

"Not against animals." Rosemary's voice became hushed. "But there *has* been a fire."

"Tell me about it."

"It was three years ago." Stuart frowned. "It wasn't until recently, when we read an article in the *New York Times,* that we realized how significant that was—that it predicts children who grow up to kill."

"*Only* when it's part of a constellation of behaviors," the psychologist clarified. "Please give me the details of the fire Jesse set."

"It was small, quickly doused, but he set it in Patrick's room. He even convinced Patrick to accept the blame."

"Fascination with fire is very common, and very normal, especially for bright, inquisitive boys. Patrick might have—"

"Patrick would *never* do something like that. He took the blame because Jesse asked him to. Patrick always does what Jesse asks. He defends him, admires him, no matter what Jesse has done."

"And yet for some reason you're concerned that Jesse might harm Patrick."

"For *some* reason, Doctor? Jesse is a thief, and he sets fires, and he's arrogant, insolent, with no regard whatsoever for the rules. He obviously has no conscience, no sense of right or wrong. That's the definition of a sociopath, isn't it? Of a *psychopath?*"

"Yes, but—"

"The point is, Doctor, if there's a chance that Jesse might harm Patrick, any chance at all, we need to know *now,* so we can send Jesse—separate them—before it's too late."

Stuart's words sounded like a command, they were a command, to which the psychologist offered a measured reply. "*Any* chance is a tall order, Mr. Falconer. Doctors never say never. After I evaluate the boys, however, I will give you my best—and most forthright—opinion."

The psychologist's evaluation began with a one-on-one session with Jesse. The boy looked him straight in the eye and said almost nothing. Jesse was not particularly verbal with adults—with anyone, for that matter, except Patrick. With his twin Jesse was eloquent and imaginative, a gifted storyteller even as a child.

Jesse could not have told his own story, however, even to Patrick. Jesse knew only its ending, not how it came to be. He had no memory of the parental love that had been lavished on his frail brother and withheld from him. But long before he could walk, or speak, or form coherent thoughts, Jesse's young heart sensed the truth: There was something terribly wrong with him . . . something that made him unworthy, undeserving, of love.

Jesse's first conscious memory confirmed that aching truth. He and Patrick were toddlers. He was holding his brother, loving him—too tightly, apparently, for suddenly his parents were rushing toward him. You *bad* boy, they scolded as they pried Patrick free of his loving grasp. Don't you hold him—*don't you touch him!*—ever again. You'll *hurt* him.

He *was* bad, and wholly undeserving of love, for if he had hurt Patrick . . . the remembered terror of that moment lived in the darkness that was Jesse, the depthless ebony sea that separated him from everyone else, even his twin. It was a restless sea, churning and searching and lonely. And it was destructive, too, and greedy—for from the restless black depths came impulses that compelled him to behave in ways that made the sea ever more vast—and his isolation from others ever wider, ever deeper, ever more dark.

Jesse told the psychologist nothing, offered no insight at all. The doctor saw answers, however, in Jesse's wounded majesty, his defiant pride; answers which were confirmed when he observed the twin boys separately and together. Alone Jesse Falconer was a caged creature, pacing, watchful, worried. But when he was reunited with his twin there was desperate relief and heart-wrenching joy.

"Jesse is unusual," the psychologist told Jesse's parents when his assessment was complete. "In fact, he's more shepherd than child. He feels responsible for Patrick, a solemn guardianship—"

"But *we* are Patrick's guardians. He doesn't need Jesse's protection. He has *us*."

"Yes, of course he does, and I'm not implying that Jesse needs to have assumed the role that he has. But

Jesse has assumed that role, and as a result you have nothing to fear." The doctor's opinion was far more categorical than he had promised, or than any of his colleagues would have reasonably advised. But he had never felt more certain. "I can't imagine Jesse ever hurting Patrick. Indeed, my concern would be for Jesse's well-being, not Patrick's."

"*Jesse's?*" Rosemary was stunned. She considered the heathen indestructible.

"If Patrick were ever in danger, I have no doubt that Jesse would go to any length to protect him. Any length. And if anything ever happened to Patrick, well, I'm not certain that Jesse would survive."

The psychologist strongly advised against separating the brothers, and since there were obviously "issues" regarding Jesse, he recommended ongoing family therapy as well. Stuart and Rosemary were not interested in counseling sessions with their incorrigible son. "Therapy" was as foreign to a Falconer as was "thief." Patrick's safety was all that mattered, and on that count they felt reassured.

The visit with the psychologist had an immediate— and positive—effect. Nine-year-old Jesse stole no more. Montclair's boy thief did not, however, grow into a model teenager. Quite the contrary. Jesse smoked. Jesse drank. And he had sex.

The boy—who had never truly been a boy—could not care less about girls his own age. But their older sisters appealed. It was with those older girls, frequently from within the Falconers' social circle, that Jesse had his "relationships"—the short-lived liaisons based solely on sex.

To the impeccably bred adults of Montclair the fact of

such intimacy, such wanton *lust,* was unspeakably distasteful—an unpleasantness that was eclipsed only by the discussion of same. The parents of the inexplicably bewitched daughters did, however, find solace in one shockingly explicit detail: the rogue Falconer was not about to father a child. Montclair's bad boy, so reckless in so many ways, was compulsively responsible when it came to *that.* Jesse's girlfriends knew why, of course: Jesse's freedom mattered to him most of all.

His freedom—and his twin. All the clichés applied. Jesse and Patrick were as different as night and day, as good and evil. And yet the Falconer twins presented a portrait of harmony, of steadfast loyalty and unwavering pride. It was a portrait that remained intact even as the canvas widened—even as over time the brothers became more separate and distinct.

There was a limit, of course, to how far the canvas could be stretched without tearing—a limit that was reached, and surpassed, during that fateful July when the twins were fifteen. . . .

The lake was man-made, carved from granite at the behest, and expense, of Rosemary's great-grandfather. Graydon Williamson named his custom-made lake Enterprise. But the townspeople of Montclair preferred another name, Graydon's Lake, in honor of the man who commissioned the picturesque summertime escape. The cool clear waters were treasure enough, but Graydon provided snowy beaches as well, powdery softness imported from the tropics.

Graydon's—and hence Rosemary's—lakeside mansion stood on the southern shore surrounded by other summer homes, a compound of the affluent town's very most elite. Tennis courts abounded, as did hammocks, rose gardens, and swimming pools. The adults congregated at poolside while their offspring, the heirs and heiresses of Montclair, flocked to the lake by day and partied on the beaches at night.

Jesse planned only a brief appearance at the beach party on that momentous July 3. He would stay just long enough to hook up with Beth, the Vassar sophomore he had been with the night before. Beth was talking with friends when Jesse arrived, so he grabbed a beer, not his first of the evening, and withdrew into the shadows to drink.

Jesse stared at the hand that brought the beer to his lips. Glared at it. It was his left hand, and it held with graceful ease both the beer bottle and his cigarette. How he had loathed that hand once. How he had struggled to deny its dominion.

Jesse had succeeded in that denial, as much as a seven-year-old could. He told no one of his plan, not even his twin, and after endless months of self-imposed discipline, when his printing was as good as it could be, when *he* was as good as he could be, Jesse presented his parents with a Christmas gift—a short story, his very best, painstakingly transcribed with his right hand.

Jesse's Yuletide offering garnered no parental praise. Of the imaginative story about a magical dragon Rosemary critiqued, It's . . . *strange,* isn't it? Hardly suitable for *Christmas.* And, Jesse, the punctuation isn't *correct.* And of his handwriting Stuart admonished, You really must practice, Jesse. Poor penmanship is a significant handicap. Perhaps you should try copying Patrick's.

But I'm *not* Patrick! Jesse's aching heart cried. And I

have tried. I would be like Patrick if I could. But I can't. This is who I am. Who *I* am. All that I am.

The Christmas Eve fiasco was hardly the most dramatic scene in the saga of Jesse and his parents. But its memory was evergreen, ever painful, a razor-sharp blade that pierced deep despite the beer he had consumed. Alcohol usually worked, usually helped. And if not there was always the carnal intoxication of sex.

Jesse took a final swig, emptying the bottle, and gazed beyond the shadows to Beth. He caught her eye—she had been watching for his signal—and mouthed his command, "Let's go."

Beth obeyed at once, and as she and Jesse walked toward her fire red Corvette she promptly complied with another request: the car keys from her purse so that he could drive.

"Jesse."

The voice was hushed, urgent, familiar. Jesse turned toward his twin with the slow-motion menace of a predator on the verge of attack. "Patrick."

The Falconer twins had uttered only two words. But the tone of those words, and the body language that embellished them, brought an astonished halt to all other conversation on the snow-white sand. There was no harmony now, only conflict, only crisis.

Everyone had known of the growing separateness of the brothers—Jesse's isolation, his aloneness, even as his golden twin's popularity soared. Until this stunning moment, however, no one realized the emotions that lay—smoldering and seething—in the space between them.

Now those churning emotions, that private history, were hidden no more. With his hushed "Jesse" Patrick was telling—no, he was *warning*—his brother not to drive; an admonition that had nothing to do with their age, not quite sixteen, and everything to do with the alcohol in Jesse's blood.

And the response of the sexy, sultry, sullen twin to Patrick's brotherly concern? Jesse's dark green eyes glittered with fury—chilling fury, savage and raw.

Patrick seemed surprised by the immenseness—and the fierceness—of his brother's anger. But he stood his ground. "I can't let you drive."

"Oh?" Jesse mocked. "Sorry, Patrick, but you really don't have a choice."

"I mean it, Jesse."

"No, Patrick. *I* mean it. Leave it alone. Leave *me* alone." Jesse's ice green eyes didn't leave his twin as he spoke to his date, his lover, for the evening. "Grab a six-pack, will you, Beth? For the road. And open a bottle for me. Driving fast makes me thirsty."

Patrick's own anger flared then—hot and bright where Jesse's was dark and cold—but just as fierce. "Go to hell, Jesse."

"Don't worry, Patrick. I plan to. So, Beth, shall we go?"

Beth had not, in fact, gotten more beer. It wasn't defiance, merely paralysis. She was as riveted as everyone else. Riveted, and standing so close to the brothers that she felt the violence.

Now Jesse was speaking to her, and now Beth heard—everyone heard—her murmured reply. "Maybe I should drive."

Jesse's smile was sexy, wicked, mean. "Yeah. Maybe you should."

In a fluid motion of grace and rage Jesse dropped the

car keys into her hand and began to traverse the snowy sand. His path took him through the circle of teenagers, who hastily parted as he neared, and past the picnic table laden with chips and beer. Without breaking stride Jesse scooped up two six-packs, one in each hand, his right hand agile still after its harsh training eight years before.

Then Jesse Falconer disappeared into the woods.

*T*here was a place, in those woods, a pine-scented hideaway where twin boys had once shared secrets and dreams, and where the gifted storyteller had told his brother of magical places far away.

It was to that long-forsaken sanctuary the twins eventually journeyed on this night of such anger; and where, eventually, they whispered in the darkness, "I'm sorry."

The *sorry*, spoken in a quiet duet, encompassed events far beyond this evening, to all the arguments of the past year. The twins alone knew of those arguments, or of their cause, although Rosemary and Stuart would have been thrilled had they known. The beloved son had taken a stand against the hated one; an impassioned stand for them and against Jesse. Jesse provoked them intentionally, Patrick contended, and with just a little effort on Jesse's part, just a little, the Falconers could be a happy, loving family.

I'm sorry, Jesse. I had no idea—until this evening— how much my criticism had hurt you. You just shrugged it off, as if you didn't care. But you did care, didn't you? You felt betrayed, feel betrayed. I know that now, and I'm so terribly sorry.

I'm sorry, Patrick, but you expect too much of me. You always have—believing me to be far better than I am. I have tried to please them—God, how I've tried—but I can't. I can't. And for a very long time the trying, only to disappoint, has hurt more than any punishment ever could. And now I've disappointed you.

The unspoken words floated in the darkness, embraced by the fragrance of pines and the desperate wishes of aching hearts. Only when an owl screeched overhead did Patrick speak again.

"I didn't mean for it to be so public. But I just couldn't let you drive." *I saw such hopelessness, Jesse, such despair. I couldn't let you drive, not with all that pain. Even if you hadn't been drinking, I would have stopped you.* "What were you thinking about, Jesse? Just before you decided to leave?"

About being not good enough, never good enough. But I can't tell you that, Patrick, or even that my anger was because of that—not because of you. I can't shatter whatever belief you may have in me still.

"Nothing, Patrick. Nothing important. But I've been thinking about what you've said. I'm going to try again. With them." *Again—and again and again—no matter how much it hurts.*

"I've been thinking, too, Jesse. About you—and them. They aren't good parents, at least not for you."

"What?" It was an astonished whisper of hope. Was Patrick really taking his side against their parents—the parents whom Patrick loved and who adored him, cherished him, in return? Maybe, maybe, and something deep inside warned Jesse not to question, not to push. *Patrick has faith in you. Still. Don't destroy it with the truth. Don't tell him about the darkness, the loneliness, the unworthiness*—but something more powerful, perhaps an impulse from that destructive ebony sea, compelled Jesse to confess. "I'm . . . different, Patrick."

"You're you, and they're the parents. They should have adjusted, understood, and they haven't. I don't think they ever will."

It doesn't matter, Jesse's heart sang. "I'm going to try anyway, Patrick."

I will try even harder, Patrick, even better, and it won't hurt so much, nothing will ever hurt so much again. . . .

The weather on the following day, that Fourth of July, was flawless. The summer breeze caressed the snowy shores with the delicacy of a lady's fan even as the blue waters were churned to near frenzy by a renegade wind. Graydon Williamson had spent a fortune fashioning this sailor's paradise, where one could sail even on days that scarcely breathed. The granite cliffs had been carved just so, to imprison even the slightest breeze and then to amplify it by creating an endless ricochet against the unyielding stone.

Graydon's great-great-grandsons were expert yachtsmen, and when they sailed together they took turns at the helm. On this flawless day of reconciliation—of joy, of peace—Jesse took the first watch. He needed on this day to defy the restless wind, to conquer its power and control its fury.

"Jess! Let's trade."

Patrick stood as he spoke, unaware that Jesse had decided to come about, had already initiated the sailboat's abrupt change in course. The about-face should have been a graceful pirouette. It would have been had not the boom, propelled by the fierce yet balmy wind, struck Patrick in the head.

Jesse's response was instant, reflexive, the reaction of a sailor—and of a brother. He surrendered his grasp of both rudder and mainsheet, becalming the sloop as he freed his hands for his twin, *who backed away* as Jesse reached for him.

"Patrick?" Jesse implored. Blood streamed from Patrick's temple, and his expression was dazed and fearful—as if the savage blow had erased all remembrance of reconciliation and resurrected in its place the memory of their fight. "Patrick!"

Patrick took another step backward, a retreat which spilled him into the wind-battered waves of Graydon's Lake. Jesse dived in immediately in desperate pursuit. Then Patrick was fighting him, fighting *him*. The brothers struggled above the waves and below, a gasping battle that ended cataclysmically when Patrick's muscles—so purposeful until that moment—began moving in an entirely different way. The jerking was rhythmic and powerful. But it lacked purpose, and it came with neither Patrick's knowledge nor his consent.

Years later, when Jesse Falconer became a self-taught expert on all things medical, he would know that it was the concussive blow that had rendered his brother combative and confused, and a postconcussive seizure, the brain's electrical outrage at the assault of the boom, that had caused the rhythmic jerking.

Then, on that day at the lake, Jesse knew only terror. And helplessness. And prayer.

It seemed an eternity, those watery moments as Jesse struggled to keep Patrick's head above the waves, to calm Patrick's violent quaking with his love. But the seizure would not be subdued, and during that eternity Jesse began to feel the endless torment that would be his—the knowledge that the only human being he had ever loved was going to die and it was all his fault.

He should have told Patrick that he was about to come about. It was a cardinal rule of sailing, to which, always before, Jesse had adhered; even though, always before, it had not been necessary—for they had sensed each other's movements without words.

But on this day Jesse had not sensed that Patrick was about to stand; nor had Patrick sensed Jesse's impending change in course . . . and on this day, when they were close again, when there was peace again, Jesse's throat had been filled with such emotion, such relief, that he had remained silent.

Patrick's seizure subsided just as the flotilla of expensive speedboats roared near. But the motionlessness that replaced the rhythmic shaking filled Jesse with even greater fear. Patrick was unconscious; and his lips were as blue as the deepest portion of the granite lake; and his breathing was labored, rasping, watery.

Postictal, Jesse would know years later. But now . . .

"I'm sorry," he whispered as Patrick's body was pulled into the most fleet of the assembled boats. "Patrick! I'm *sorry.*"

Jesse's apology was heard by the same teenagers who had witnessed last night's drama on the beach; the heirs and heiresses who had concluded, after the brothers left, that if looks could kill Patrick Falconer would be dead. Now the drama had reached its cataclysmic finale. No one saw the swing of the boom just as Patrick stood. But they heard the ghastly sound as the boom cracked against his skull, and they saw the horrific pantomime that followed: Patrick's stumble into the waves as he tried to elude Jesse's murderous grasp and the watery battle during which Jesse tried to drown his twin.

Stuart and Rosemary were among the last to know. Their dearest friends, Lenore and Dominick St. John, disclosed the devastating news. Neither Lenore nor Dominick had actually witnessed the scene. They had been playing mixed doubles at the time. But their daughter Gabrielle had been among the myriad who had seen it all. And she had heard Jesse's confession, his whispered apology to his dying twin.

"*You* tried to murder your brother." Jesse's parents never confronted their son with those accusatory words.

No one did.

No one dared.

Besides, such a confrontation was not necessary.

Jesse wore his guilt like a mantle of chains, a heaviness so immense he struggled to stand, his chest bound so tightly he could barely breathe. Some viewed Jesse's obvious remorse as a hopeful sign. Maybe rehabilitation was possible after all. But such optimism was not shared by those who ventured close enough to see Jesse's eyes— the torment that verged on rage, the fury that verged on madness.

Maybe his torment was guilt. But maybe it was something else: fury that his murderous plan had failed.

Jesse was forbidden from visiting his twin in the ICU, and long before Patrick came home Jesse had been sent to Brookfield.

"Brookfield?" Patrick echoed the familiar name, the

familiar threat—the boarding school to which Jesse would be banished if he didn't behave. "Why?"

"You know why, darling."

"Because of the argument we had? That was my fault, not Jesse's, and it was nothing. *Nothing*."

"But it led to something, Patrick."

Yes, he thought. To reconciliation. To peace. To a perfect day on the lake. Then blackness. Emptiness. "What happened? Tell me. *Please*."

They really had no choice. If Patrick didn't hear it from them, he would simply hear it—less gently, less lovingly—from someone else.

Everyone else.

So gently, lovingly, Rosemary and Stuart told their son that the brother he loved so much had tried to kill him. The thief had relapsed and this time Jesse had almost stolen the greatest treasure of all.

That treasure, that most beloved son, railed against the revelations about his twin. "That's not *true*."

"But it is, darling. We're so sorry, Patrick. We know how much you loved him."

"*Loved?* He's not dead. Don't make him sound *dead*." *The love isn't dead. I love Jesse. Even though he wanted me to die.* Was it possible? He had not known, until that night on the beach, the depth of Jesse's fury at his betrayal. *Maybe I don't know Jesse at all. Maybe . . . no.* "I don't believe Jesse did what you're saying. I *don't*." *I can't.*

"That's because of you, Patrick, of who you are. You're so good, so generous, and Jesse, well, he's always been different. *Difficult*. You know that's true."

"It's just that you never understood him, never even *tried*."

"We have tried, son," Stuart said. "And we do understand him. We always have. From the very beginning we worried that he was . . . disturbed. The experts told us we were wrong, and we accepted what they said because we wanted to believe that Jesse was normal."

"But now we know the truth," Rosemary embellished. "And now Jesse's getting the help he needs."

"I want to talk to him."

"You can't. There can be no communication of any kind." Rosemary hesitated only an instant before altering the truth that Patrick might not heed—"For *your* sake"—to the lie he would. "For *his* sake, Patrick. For Jesse."

𝒯he Falconers might have placed their criminal son in the jurisdiction of the juvenile courts. But where was the proof that graduates of that system emerged as law-abiding adults? The corrective measures the Falconers chose to inflict on their delinquent son were far more harsh— the most severe money could buy. The exclusive military academy near Colorado Springs was designed specifically for boys like Jesse, wayward sons of wealth. And Brookfield's administrators promised results. Wild spirits would be broken. Defiance would be disciplined into oblivion. Guaranteed.

Except for the fact that Brookfield's educational offerings were truly exceptional, the academy was more prison than school. Indeed, in the event of future recidivism, the young criminals would do quite well in jail. The deprivation would not shock them, nor would the confinement, nor would the lack of contact with the outside world.

Unlike prisoners of the state, however, Brookfield's pupils had no rights at all. Thus, if their parents so chose, their tenure at Brookfield could be far worse than jail. The Falconers elected such a program for their son. He was not even permitted the accused's single phone call. And, Stuart instructed, no letters were to be sent—or received—ever. Further, in the spirit of prison not school, Jesse was to be incarcerated year-round. Thanksgiving. Christmas. Easter. Summer.

Brookfield's summertime curriculum was physical not academic, a concession to the families whose sons spent those months at home, so they would not be academically disadvantaged when it came to applying for the Ivy League colleges to which so many of the academy's graduates were bound.

Brookfield's summertime regime was beyond boot camp. It was survival itself, a rigorous, desolate, solitary time in the Colorado Rockies, a place so remote that escape was impossible, but supervised nonetheless. As unacceptable as an escape would be, the death of a student would be monumentally worse—the loss of that pupil's extravagant tuition, not to mention potential adverse outcomes should wrongful-death claims be filed.

Most boys pleaded for rescue after only a week.

Jesse never pleaded at all.

And he lasted the entire summer.

It was two years before Jesse returned to Montclair. It was time, Brookfield's officials—and counselors—told Rosemary and Stuart. Their seventeen-year-old son was ready to be resocialized. And, something the administrators didn't say, they were ready to be rid of Jesse, at least for the summer.

Jesse Falconer was making a mockery of every promise the school had ever made. Despite their best efforts, he showed absolutely no sign of being broken. Indeed, with each passing day and despite sadistic and humiliating punishment, he grew only stronger, more disdainful, more defiant.

Brookfield's counselors expressed authentic confidence that Jesse would not kill anyone on his sojourn home. He was neither that foolish, nor that out of control. Not foolish in the least, and in absolute control—always.

Virtually everyone in Montclair awaited Jesse's return with some combination of eagerness, apprehension, and fear. In the case of Gabrielle St. John, however, the eagerness was undiluted: she and the sexy, lethal Falconer were going to become lovers.

It was a decision Gabrielle had made that night on the beach—an astonishing decision, for until that fateful summer night she had made a study of ignoring Jesse. She wanted the golden twin, not his dissolute brother.

But on that night Gabrielle had seen—had felt—Jesse Falconer's glittering green gaze. Admittedly, Jesse had been staring through her, not at her, but his searing gaze touched her nonetheless, touched her everywhere, an invisible caress that evoked sensations so delicious that—that what? She would permit him to kiss her, to touch her, to want her? The notion of Jesse wanting her, only to be thwarted, would have been most appealing . . . had it not been for those delicious sensations.

She *would* permit Jesse to touch her, she decided. Not for his pleasure, but for *hers*. It hadn't happened, of course. Even as Gabrielle was reaching the stunning decision the confrontation between the brothers occurred, and the next day the tarnished twin tried to murder his brother, and now, two years later, Jesse was coming home.

No one, especially not Jesse's parents, believed that Jesse would be rehabilitated. No one? Well, possibly Patrick did. No one knew what Patrick thought, believed, felt. He never talked about his twin, or that day at Graydon's Lake, not to anyone, ever. But Gabrielle knew all about the fears of Stuart and Rosemary Falconer as they awaited the return of their wicked son.

"Jesse will be staying in the gardener's cottage," Gabrielle heard, *over*heard, her mother say. "And he won't be given the mansion's security code, at least not the correct one. They don't want him sneaking in at night."

"And murdering them in their sleep?" Dominick St. John demanded. "Execution style? If there's any thought that Jesse might do something like that, any thought, Lenore, I don't want him in town, much less next door. The gardener's cottage is closer to *us* than to *them*. I'm going to call Stuart right now."

"*No*. Please, Dom. No one believes that Jesse's still dangerous. They're just being careful, that's all. Protective of Patrick. I mean, what would you have them do? Put Jesse in his old room next to Patrick's?"

"You haven't agreed to any family get-togethers, have you, Lenore? Picnics at the lake? On the Fourth of July? Let me be very clear about this. I *do not* want my daughter anywhere near Jesse Falconer."

"*Our* daughter, Dom. And neither do I. And she won't be. And as for the lake, well, Rosemary and Stuart have already decided that if Jesse wants to spend time there he can spend it alone. In fact, that's what they're hoping, that he'll want to be at the lake, and they can remain in town, and never the twain—or should I say twins?—shall meet. Nor will Gabby and Jesse. She can't stand him. Remember?"

You're right, Mother. I can't stand Jesse Falconer. But that doesn't mean I'm going to stay away from him. I want to know how it feels to be touched by that violence, that heat.

Gabrielle was ready for Jesse. Her virginity was a thing of the past, a recent divestiture, cast off during spring break in Cancún with a boy—a *man*—who was a sophomore at SMU. And now, on the eve of the return of the murderous twin, Gabrielle stood at her bedroom window and gazed through lace curtains toward the gardener's cottage where Jesse would live, and where they would meet.

No one would know—except perhaps eventually Patrick. Or perhaps not. She would have to decide when the time came. The time of Patrick and Gabrielle *would* come, assuming Patrick ever *snapped out of it.* Granted, it wasn't every day that one's brother tried to murder him. It made sense, Gabrielle supposed, that Patrick might not be so carefree after that, at least for a while.

But for two years?

It wasn't that Patrick wore his heart on his shirtsleeve. There was no moping from Patrick Falconer, no attempt to garner sympathy, no drama at all. And he was as brilliant as ever, and only became more gorgeous with each passing day. But the once-gregarious twin was infuriatingly distant and remote.

Well, Gabrielle mused, maybe seeing his twin again would shock Patrick back into reality. No matter what *she* would see Jesse; and she would discover just what sort of deliciously decadent, and hopefully shocking, reality Montclair's bad boy had to offer.

*I*t was a reunion the brothers had anticipated for two years . . . and for that first glorious moment their twin hearts beat as one, a harmony of power and of speed.

Their hearts galloped toward peace, toward wholeness. At last.

Patrick believed he saw apology—and shame.

And Jesse believed he saw forgiveness—and love.

And for that racing moment both felt the oneness. Both treasured it, were healed by it, *almost*.

Remembrance intervened with a vengeance.

Patrick did not doubt the apology he saw in Jesse's dark green eyes. But all hope of reconciliation was dashed as Patrick recalled what Jesse was apologizing for. *I'm sorry I tried to kill you, Patrick. I'm sorry for despising you so much that I wanted you dead . . . and for pretending that you were loved when in fact you were loathed.*

Jesse saw Patrick's expression and realized the truth. Patrick had not forgiven the recklessness that nearly cost him his life. How could he? Jesse would never forgive himself.

Jesse remained in Montclair for less than a month— long enough for the citizens of Montclair to conclude that he had added intimacy with drugs to his long list of sensual sins. The conclusion was correct. But all the illicit substances on earth could not deaden Jesse's pain as he stood on the snowy sands of Graydon's Lake and watched his twin sail with friends—people Patrick trusted.

A month was long enough, too long, for Jesse. He left at midnight on the Fourth of July.

The townspeople of Montclair believed that he would never return. But he did, two years later, and with a splash more memorable than the flailing struggle between brothers in the wind-churned waves of Graydon's Lake. . . .

How hopeful he was. Jesse Falconer. Hopeful. He had spent the past two years doing everything in his power to make himself worthy of forgiveness. His final year at Brookfield had been a stunning success. The academy's premier survivalist became its premier student as well. And this past year, in college, he had enrolled in the most rigorous courses and earned all A's.

Jesse had forsaken alcohol, cigarettes, drugs; and he had met someone, a young woman, estranged from her family yet yearning—as was he—to be reconciled. Go home, Jesse told her, and make it right. And Lindsay echoed, Make it right, Jesse—with Patrick, if no one else.

Jesse knew what he would say to his twin, had rehearsed the words a thousand times. Forgive me, Patrick. Please? It was a foolish mistake, a boy's mistake. I'm no longer that reckless boy. I'm going to be a doctor, Patrick, a surgeon. I will ask my patients to trust me with their lives, and I will be worthy of that trust.

Can you trust me, Patrick? Will you? Trust me. Believe in me. Love—

The knock on the cottage door was decisive and eager. *Eager.* It would be Patrick, sensing he was home, sensing the words Jesse planned to speak and wanting those words as much as Jesse.

Jesse's heart soared, a stratospheric flight of hope— which crashed to earth when he opened the door.

"Gabrielle."

"Greetings." Ignoring Jesse's obvious displeasure Gabrielle breezed into the cottage she had known during that month of wanton intimacy, with Jesse, two summers before. Now as then the cottage was memorable—because of him. Jesse's midnight black hair was shower-damp, his muscled torso was hard *and nude.* Jesse had matured just as Patrick had, more compellingly male with each passing day.

"What do you want, Gabrielle?"

"Good heavens, Jesse Falconer, you're being awfully surly. That's really not the way to treat your future sister-in-law."

"My *what?*"

"You heard me." Gabrielle smiled prettily. "Patrick is in love with me."

"I find that very hard to believe."

"Well, *believe* it." Patrick had not, actually, said the words. Far from it. But at long last she and Patrick were an item. Patrick had simply needed to get away from Montclair. He was at Princeton now, and she was at Smith, and since March they had spent several spectacular weekends in New York. "Patrick is a fabulous lover. Considerate. *Giving.* It's really quite amazing that brothers, *twins,* can be so different. Not that I'm complaining about us, Jesse."

"There was never an *us,* Gabrielle. We just—"

"Made love," she interjected swiftly, preempting what she knew would be the four-letter vulgarity for what they had done. On reflection Gabrielle wasn't certain why she hadn't wanted to hear the word. Jesse had used it often enough during that month, and it sounded incredibly erotic when he did. And *it,* not making love, was the most precise description of what they had done, what she had *loved.*

"Call it what you like, Gabrielle. It was meaningless."

She knew that, and more. Jesse's passion for her was, and always had been, laced with contempt.

"But it was magnificent. Admit it, Jesse. We were good together. And we would have gotten even better if you hadn't left. Hadn't *fled,*" she embellished, goading him, wanting the danger that made *it* with him so exciting.

"Time for you to go, Gabrielle."

Who was this new Jesse? This man who refused to be provoked? Where was the smoldering rage that fueled such wild, thrilling sex?

"Actually, Jesse, I have nowhere to go, not for thirty minutes, at which point my parents and I are expected for dinner at your house. We can arrive together. And in the meantime, well, thirty minutes is plenty of time, isn't it?"

Gabrielle placed provocative hands on his naked chest—a gesture which evoked an immediate response, the curling of his powerful fingers around her slender wrists. Gabrielle felt what she had known that summer, and what she wanted now, the controlled violence that promised cold, *hot* sex.

"Come on, Killer," she purred. "For old times' sake. Patrick and I aren't officially engaged. Yet."

Gabrielle's heart raced as she felt his steel-and-velvet grip tighten around her tingling flesh.

"What did you say?"

"That our engagement isn't—"

"What did you call me?"

A thrilling frisson of fear trembled through her. Jesse Falconer was definitely provoked. But had she gone too far? "I called you *Killer,* of course. True, it's not entirely accurate. I could call you *Attempted*—or *Failed*—*Killer* if you'd prefer, if the technicality bothers you."

"Tell me why you called me that, Gabrielle."

"You're hurting me."

"Tell me."

"You *know* why, dammit!"

"Tell me."

"Because of that day at the lake. Everyone *saw,* Jesse. I can't believe you don't know that. Did you think just because you were sent to Brookfield—not to jail—that you'd gotten away with it?"

"What did everyone see, Gabrielle?"

"That you tried to kill Patrick. Let *go* of me!"

Jesse released her roughly, and the fury on his face made her want him anew. Her forearms bore bruises from the force with which he had imprisoned her. But Gabrielle liked the bruises, just as she liked the danger in his voice.

"Is that what Patrick believes?"

"It's what *everyone* believes, what everyone *knows.*"

"Including Patrick?"

"Patrick most of all," Gabrielle lied. Patrick had never broken his silence about that day at the lake. And, as

Gabrielle had learned from her parents, Patrick had total amnesia for those watery moments of terror. But to Patrick's angry, sexy twin, she said, "He was *there*, remember?"

It was an accident, Patrick! Do you really believe I tried to kill you? Why? What reason could I have to destroy the only person I ever loved?

Gabrielle saw Jesse's torment, a tempest so mesmerizing that for many moments she could only stare.

"Make love to me, Killer," she implored at last. *Touch me with that fury, that longing, that pain.* "I don't care what you've done, Jesse. I only care about what you do to me."

Gabrielle touched him again, returning her perfectly manicured hands to his perfectly muscled chest. She felt ice this time, and fire.

"Get out of here, Gabrielle."

"You don't mean that," she whispered as her fingers began a seductive journey to his throat, to the pulse that pounded with rage, and with lust? "Come on, Jesse."

"*Now*, Gabrielle."

The fury became hers; fury at his rejection, at his contempt—at his making her want him and not caring about her at all.

"Sure, Killer," she hissed as her fingers became claws, scratching him, tearing his flesh without mercy.

Jesse did not flinch, did not move.

He might have been a statue of stone had it not been for the tears of blood that began to flow as Gabrielle left; flowed freely from the deep scratches on his naked chest.

But they were such trivial tears, such an inconsequential flood compared to the crimson torrent that wept inside as the devastating truth screamed: *Patrick believes I tried to kill him, believes it, believes it . . .*

"Help me, please! *Help!*"

The authentic scream came as a reprieve to the keening wails of his heart.

Jesse ran toward the sound.

Toward Gabrielle.

She stood in the white brick driveway of his parents' home. And she was not alone. She was surrounded, encircled, by a wall of love. His parents. Her parents. His brother.

Her dress was tattered, and dirt smudged her shoulders and neck, and her forearms bore the dark purple gravestones of his imprisoning grasp. Her beautiful face was damp with tears, and white with fear *of him.*

"Don't let him touch me again! *Please.*"

"Gabby, darling," Lenore St. John whispered to her distraught daughter. "What are you saying?"

Gabrielle's reply came in sobs, each gasping word the plunge of a jagged-edged knife, vicious stabs that slashed to ribbons his brave dreams and foolish hopes. And as she uttered those devastating words Gabrielle clung to Patrick with fingernails filled with Jesse's clotted blood and shredded flesh.

"Jesse . . . tried . . . to . . . *rape* . . . me."

That's a lie! Jesse wanted to scream the words aloud. But his heart had ceased to beat. It was frozen, a fist of ice within his chest, a glacial hardening that was mirrored by the expressions that greeted him. Gabrielle's bruises and his own bloodied torso spoke volumes to those who formed the circle of love. With chilling clarity Jesse saw what his blood and her bruises told them about him.

Rapist. *Killer.*

Jesse remained frozen even when Dominick St. John lunged at him, pummeling him with blows he did not feel. There could be no more pain.

Or so Jesse thought. Until he looked at his twin.

Believe in me, Patrick. Trust me. Love me.

Patrick returned Jesse's stare. But Jesse could not even begin to read his brother's thoughts. Patrick wouldn't let him.

Still, Jesse imagined those thoughts.

Love you, Jesse? Trust you? Believe in you?

Yes, Patrick! Yes!

No, Jesse. Never.

Please, Patrick—

I said no, Killer.

🙰tuart Falconer wanted his son in prison, a sentiment shared by all of Montclair. There was no question of a fair trial. The verdict had already been rendered. There was no point, Jesse's court-appointed lawyer counseled, in pleading anything but guilty as charged.

The issue of a plea *bargain* never came up. Just the opposite. Everyone wanted Jesse Falconer put away for as long as permissible given the crime. Unfortunately, the actual crime was simple assault. If only Jesse had raped, had begun to rape . . . still, with creative lawyering a substantial sentence was handed down.

Jesse Falconer was being sent away—again. This time, however, before being banished from Montclair, Jesse saw his twin. Jesse had no say in the matter. He was locked in a cell from which there was no escape. It was to that tiny prison that Patrick came.

"Tell me, Jesse."

Tell you what, Patrick? Why? Or if?

If Patrick had a response to his brother's silent entreaty, Jesse couldn't see it. His own vision was hopelessly blurred. With anger. With betrayal. With pain. "What is it you'd like to know?"

Patrick stared into eyes that were colder, darker, than the ones that had glared their fury that night on the beach. "Everything," he said quietly. "I want to know everything."

Jesse responded like the psychopath they believed him to be, without conscience, without remorse. And why not? He was a condemned man. There was nothing more to lose. "The episode in the sailboat was an impulse. A *lark*." He shrugged with chilling nonchalance. "It seemed a good idea at the time. And as for Gabrielle . . . well, we're twins, aren't we, Patrick? Doesn't that mean we're supposed to share?"

EIGHTEEN

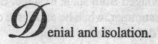enial and isolation.

Anger.

Bargaining.

Depression.

Acceptance.

With threads of hope woven in between.

Those were the stages of death and dying described by Dr. Elisabeth Kübler-Ross. Patrick had known them intimately long before he studied Kübler-Ross in medical school. He had, after all, lived through the demise of an integral part of himself, his relationship with his twin.

The five stages did not necessarily occur in order, nor was it essential to have successfully navigated one before moving on to the next. Indeed, most typically, the stages existed simultaneously, as they had for Patrick in the aftermath of that Fourth of July at Graydon's Lake.

Even as he had been in *denial,* refusing to accept the fact that Jesse had tried to kill him, Patrick had felt the *isolation* of that truth. His fatal disease, the plague of being hated so much that his own brother wanted him dead, segregated him from everyone else. And even as he was feeling *anger* at Jesse's betrayal, he experienced bouts of near-docile *depression* and despair.

And throughout it all Patrick had *bargained* without shame.

Tell me what I did wrong, Jesse! Tell me what I did to make you hate me so. I'll change, Jesse, I promise. Then we can be brothers again. Can't we?

For the four years between that day at Graydon's Lake and the summer evening when Gabrielle appeared bruised and screaming on the white-brick drive Patrick ping-ponged from stage to stage. Even during that seventeenth summer, when he and Jesse did not speak, he clung to the delicate thread of hope.

But the thread was irreparably severed that day in Jesse's cell. And without hope blocking the door to darkness, Patrick moved to the final stage.

Acceptance.

Patrick Falconer's soul had died once before, a huge chunk of it lost forever. Now his physical being was dying, decaying at an astonishing rate.

This time, as Patrick lived anew the passages of Dr. Kübler-Ross, hope was far less defiant. And of necessity, to keep pace with his precipitous decline, each stage was accelerated, an urgent rush to the serene acceptance of his fate.

But there was something new this time, something poignant and sweet. It was nostalgia, Patrick supposed. Nostalgia without melancholy, remembrance without bitterness, forgiveness with gladness.

The memories that came to him were as clear, as pure, as the crystal blue waters of Graydon's Lake.

Graydon's Lake. Graydon Slake. Was Jesse's *nom de*

plume the ultimate taunt? Or was it remembrance, too, nostalgia for better times? Happier times. Loving times.

Until that Fourth of July Patrick's memories of his twin had been loving ones. Though not always happy ones. He had worried about Jesse, the shadowed places deep within that Jesse kept hidden even from him.

Patrick had not believed, never believed, that those secret places contained evil—until he was compelled to do so by Jesse's own words: The episode in the sailboat was an impulse. A *lark*. It seemed a good idea at the time.

The words pierced him now, sharp but oddly sweet, attenuated by the floating nostalgia he felt. Patrick had never smoked marijuana. That was the other twin. But he wondered if this was the way marijuana made one feel: floating yet exquisitely aware. This was perhaps the reason marijuana was advocated for dying patients, the blunting of pain so that this poignant nostalgia could be leisurely enjoyed.

It was the leisure that was so striking. His body was racing toward death. Yet in this floating realm of remembrance, Patrick felt no urgency at all. A single moment stretched like taffy, elongated forever, a sweetness to be infinitely savored.

Now, on the balcony of his Brentwood home, his senses were spectacularly heightened. Patrick felt each ray of the springtime sun, every caress of the satiny breeze. Separately, and then as one, he inhaled the perfumes of jasmine, plumeria, and rose. And Mozart was here, an invited guest.

Patrick had not been smoking marijuana, nor had Stephen Sheridan given him the ingestible form of THC. This was a natural high. Natural? Well, yes, if one viewed as natural brain cells so starved for oxygen that they floated to a stage of death and dying that had yet to be described.

A new sound, a trilling telephone, wove into the symphony of Mozart and birdsong. Far from the staccato noise he had known for his thirty-eight years of health, this once-strident intrusion was a never-ending hum.

Patrick's phone was nearby. But he made no move to answer it. His machine would do that for him, after four rings, a thousand floating thoughts from now.

The caller might be his secretary, phoning to share with him today's list of well-wishers, the people to whom, at Patrick's request, she asserted that Patrick was "doing very well."

Or it might be Caitlin, not calling ship-to-shore but from mere blocks away, having broken her promise and cut short her cruise. But Caitlin did not break promises. And in any case she was due back tomorrow.

Patrick would see her then. His mind would be floating, but hers would not. Caitlin would see quite clearly the ravages that had occurred in such a short space of time. She would want to conceal her anguish. Her horror. But it would be impossible to do so.

The second ring seemed to wail, as if in mourning for Caitlin, a howl that was mercifully yet harshly silenced by the third. It came swiftly, real time not floating time, but then it stretched, sweetened and deepened, into the loving voice of a brother. Let me help you, Patrick. I want to. I love—

"Jesse," Patrick whispered as he moved toward the phone. Hope, so meek until this moment, accompanied him. Defiant and bold it blocked the dark doorway to acceptance even as it chided, Pride, that most expensive of

luxuries. You should have reached out to Jesse long ago.
"Hello?"

"Hello, Patrick. It's Stephen."

Patrick's brain cells went on alert, floating no more,
standing at attention as they met their fate. Stephen had
come by the condo this morning to draw Patrick's blood.
It was, Patrick had thought at the time, a wholly unnecessary confirmation of what they both already knew.

His counts were not coming back. Stephen merely had
to look at him to know. And Patrick felt the truth, was living it, as with each passing day he became more floating,
more weak.

"I have good news," Stephen was saying.

"Really? I would have bet that every count was lower,
especially my crit."

"They were. It was. Eighteen. But, Patrick, we have a
donor."

Patrick knew that the national marrow registry had
been searched and had come up as empty as his marrow.
Yet he whispered, hope whispered, "How, Stephen?"

"I faxed your immunologic profile to a long list of
blood banks. Amazingly, the one that responded is
nearby, in San Diego. They recognized the profile right
away. The donor needed blood a few years ago and, not
surprisingly, they were unable to find a match. Needless
to say the man survived, and when he was contacted
about donating his marrow he didn't hesitate. He's in admissions even as we speak."

"When . . . ?"

"Tomorrow morning. But I want you here tonight."

"I'm on my way."

"No, Patrick. *I'm* on *my* way. You're not driving."

"All right," Patrick said quietly. "Thank you, Stephen.

And please thank him. Or should I do that? Is it usual for donor and recipient to meet?"

"It's variable. Typically the reunion comes later . . . after."

When the transplant is an unqualified success, Patrick realized. When the recipient is alive and well. "Okay. Well, for now will you thank him for me?"

"Sure, Patrick. Will do."

"*You*'re a natural-born liar, Stephen Sheridan," Caitlin said as soon as the receiver was replaced in its cradle.

It was her telephone, her living room, the sixth-floor apartment where she had been sequestered for the past twenty-four hours and to which Stephen had come to synchronize their stories.

Their lies.

Now the all-important falsehood had been told to Patrick, and in response to her praise the chief of hematology merely sighed. "No, Caitlin, I am not. Did you pick up on the fact that he was asking about thanking the donor in person?"

"Patrick is a polite, gracious man. Anyway, you dodged that bullet beautifully."

"Well. The end justifies the means. At least that's what I keep telling myself."

"It does. What about tomorrow, Stephen? You were able to talk our donor into anesthesia, weren't you?"

Our donor. The possessive was presumptuous, and wrong. Stephen was Jesse's doctor. At her request, her insistence, Caitlin was off the case. Still, somehow, she'd imagined she would hear from Jesse. He—Michael

Lyons—was at the Château on Barrington, just two blocks away; and she had given him both her apartment address and home phone.

But Jesse hadn't called. Why would he? She wasn't his doctor, merely a crazed fan, one of legions of such admirers.

"No, Caitlin. I wasn't able to talk him into anesthesia."

"*No?*"

"He absolutely refuses."

"Did you ask him why?"

"Sure." Stephen's expression was as wry as Jesse's had been. "He said he's not a big believer in altering reality with drugs."

"But did you explain to him about this particular reality? That harvesting a marrow without anesthesia is . . ." Caitlin faltered, unable to find precisely the right word.

"Jesse's very well aware of what the procedure entails. And as you said, Caitlin, the end justifies the means. I told Jesse we'd meet him at nine tomorrow morning in Heme Clinic. You will be there, won't you?"

She wanted to see Jesse again—what crazed fan wouldn't?—but she did not want to see him in pain. "Is he going to hypnotize himself or something?"

"I'm not sure how he's going to handle it. But my guess is that he will. Handle it, that is."

Caitlin nodded. *Of course he will.*

"So Caitlin, nine o'clock?"

"Nine o'clock."

NINETEEN

*B*arbaric. That was the word that had eluded her last night, the perfect word to describe the boring into bone followed by the repeated removal of marrow without anesthesia.

Even with anesthesia the piercing of bone was a somewhat primitive process. The instrument was a trocar, a euphemism for a mammoth needle which sliced through skin before its descent into bone, and the drilling procedure itself was fueled not by modern electronic gadgetry but by the muscled might of an upright man.

In this instance the upright man was Dr. Stephen Sheridan. With brute strength he twisted—and twisted—until the knife-sharp trocar created a hole in the pelvic bone of his supine patient.

The boring was barbaric enough. It was the removal of marrow, however, that truly caused pain. Each aspirate severed an enclave of nerves, each torn cell of which shrieked in protest.

Today, from Jesse Falconer, Stephen was going to harvest nearly a pint of marrow, an enterprise necessitating thirty aspirates, each severing more nerves, all of which would scream and keep screaming . . .

Caitlin clutched in her hand a vial of morphine. Soon, she hoped, Jesse would permit her to inject into his veins a substantial dose of the potent narcotic. The morphine wouldn't alter the reality he was experiencing. Nothing short of anesthesia would. The morphine would merely smooth the sharpest corners, muffle the most piercing cries.

Despite Jesse's purist stance on drugs—at least on anesthetic agents—the administration of pain meds was in Caitlin's mind a primary reason she was here. There would be additional duties as well, ones that would commence as soon as all the marrow had been harvested.

Stephen would leave immediately to take the beaker to the lab for filtration prior to infusion. She would remain with Jesse to apply pressure to the biopsy site until the bleeding ceased; and to monitor his vital signs; and while the opiate was still on board to convince him to spend at least the next twenty-four hours in the hospital bed that was being held for Mr. Michael Lyons.

Those were to be Dr. Caitlin Taylor's tasks on this Saturday morning. So far, however, twelve aspirations into the grueling process, all she had done was watch . . . and listen to the ever more shrill sounds of her own screaming nerves.

Arguably certain aspects of Caitlin's own field of endeavor might meet the criteria for barbaric. There was the cutting through sternae with electric saws, followed by the prying open of rib cages with chest retractors.

Then came the invasion of the heart itself.

There had been a time, when barbarism ruled the planet, that human hearts were carved in sacrifice to the gods. A primitive, savage, uncivilized time.

So why did the relatively tame process of harvesting a bone marrow make Dr. Caitlin Taylor feel so squeamish? Because she was watching, not doing. Even the most seasoned surgeon was susceptible to queasiness when compelled to look at mangled flesh—to look, not to touch, not to help.

Don't just stand there, do something. How Caitlin wished she could. Jesse had offered her the chance to be a true participant: the harvester, the torturess. But Caitlin had declined—which left the torture to Stephen.

Stephen hated doing this without anesthesia. Caitlin could see how much. But he was doing it, expertly, efficiently. And silently. He didn't warn Jesse in advance of each aspirate; offered no warning, no apology, at all.

Stephen Sheridan simply did what was necessary.

And what of the patient? Was he suffering?

If so Jesse Falconer was an Oscar-caliber actor. Indeed he looked like a Hollywood celebrity in the midst of a massage. The principal difference lay in the texture of the towels. The coverings that draped Jesse's body were fashioned from sterile cotton not plush velour.

Jesse's muscled flesh enjoyed modesty, although not total occlusion. His powerful shoulders were exposed, as were his sinewy calves and the flank muscles that encased the iliac crest, the site at which the barbaric act was taking place.

Caitlin's right hand clutched the morphine vial, a clench tight enough to shatter glass, and the palm of the left ached as if embedded with such glassy shards. Her fingernails, clipped surgeon short, were tiny scalpels carving deep. By contrast, the hands of the writer of passion—hands which undoubtedly created real-life passion for numberless women—lay flat on the treatment table. Jesse's forehead rested on those relaxed hands, and his eyelids were closed, smooth and unflickering as if in dreamless sleep.

But the muscles of his jaw were taut.

Was he counting as she was?

Twelve aspirates so far. Eighteen more to go.

"Why don't you harvest the other hip as well?"

Jesse Falconer's voice was absolutely calm, the movie mogul casually suggesting to his masseur that the muscles of his other hip needed a little more work.

"What, Jesse?"

"While you're at it, Stephen, why don't you take enough for a second transplant? In case he needs it."

Stephen looked at Caitlin with absolute astonishment. She in turn was absolutely astonished, and infinitely impressed, by the evenness with which Stephen replied. "That's not a good idea, Jesse. Well, all right, it is, but not now. You're going to feel the effects of this marrow donation, especially given the amount of blood I took from you last night."

Stephen's patient was lying down, not even halfway through a surgical procedure for which he should have been anesthetized. Jesse did not move as he spoke, could not move without jeopardizing the sterile field.

But it was as if he were standing, a commanding presence, looking Stephen straight in the eye.

"I feel fine, Stephen."

"Believe me, Jesse, you won't. The volume loss is going

to catch up with you, not to mention the drop in hematocrit—"

"To what, Stephen? The high thirties? That's a far cry from eighteen."

"Yes, but Patrick's crit didn't drop to eighteen overnight. His body had time to adjust. I'm not bleeding you, or anyone, down to a hematocrit of eighteen. Besides," Stephen reminded him, "as a result of last night's transfusions Patrick's crit is no longer eighteen."

"He may need more transfusions."

It was true, and they all knew it. The time from transplantation to engraftment was variable; typically a matter of weeks. In the interval, if Patrick's hematocrit became precarious once again, he would need additional units of Jesse's blood.

"He may," Stephen concurred.

"In which case you'll call me." It was amazing that a man who was lying down, and with a massive needle impaled in his bone, could issue an order. But that is precisely what Jesse did.

Stephen smiled slightly in reply. "You know I will."

Stephen's smile faded as he returned to the task at hand, the withdrawal of more marrow, more fragments of bone, more brutalized pieces of screaming nerves.

No more words were exchanged during the remainder of the procedure, and finally, finally, it was over.

As soon as Stephen removed the trocar from Jesse's hip, Caitlin's gloved fingers began applying pressure to the site. Stephen vanished moments later, leaving Caitlin and Jesse alone in the treatment room—alone, and silent, but touching.

She touching *him*. The treatment room was not large to begin with, and it became infinitely small, impossibly intimate, as Caitlin applied pressure to his wounded, bleeding flesh.

"There," she murmured at last as—removing the small square of sterile gauze—she confirmed that the biopsy site no longer bled. She placed a Band-Aid over the wound, and the intimacy came to an end. "I'm going to take the biopsy tray to the autoclave. It's just down the hall. Are you all right?"

"I'm fine."

"Okay. Good. I'll be back in a few minutes." *Just as soon as I warm some blankets for you.*

It was a trick that every health-care professional knew, especially those who had worked in emergency rooms in the dead of winter. Standard-issue hospital blankets were pitiful things, neither fleecy nor plush. When heated within an autoclave, however, even the most utilitarian coverings could adopt the illusion of coziness, of hominess, cocoons of warmth for the sick, the scared, the cold.

Jesse Falconer was neither sick nor scared. And if skin temperature was any indication he was far from cold.

But Caitlin knew she was going to fail in her attempt to convince Jesse to be admitted to the hospital—which meant he would be spending the next few hours in the far-from-homey treatment room, lying on the far-from-cozy table, resting, clotting . . .

"What are you doing?" she gasped on her return.

Her arms embraced a bountiful stack of heated blankets, a situation promptly remedied by depositing the warm bulk onto the treatment table. And why not? The table was quite vacant, having been abandoned by its patient.

In another moment she might have rushed to him, the doctor dashing to a patient in peril. But this particular patient did not seem in jeopardy of any sort.

"Getting dressed," he replied.

"You can't."

"It seems, Doctor, that I can. In fact"—Jesse embellished as he buckled his belt—"I have. Perhaps I misunderstood. I could have sworn I heard you say *there,* after which you left the room to give me privacy in which to dress."

"The *there* meant that I'd compressed the wound site long enough to prevent further bleeding, *assuming* you kept lying down. Like for *hours*. The area needs time to truly clot. And . . ."

"And?"

Caitlin had been about to mention pain, the sheer discomfort of standing on what amounted to a fresh fracture in the pelvic bone. But arguing pain with Jesse Falconer was a futile endeavor. "Didn't Stephen tell you that?"

"Yes. He did. But I'm a terrific clotter, and I have a plane to catch."

"A plane?"

"I thought I'd head back to Maui. You remember the future Mrs. Lion."

"She's arriving today?"

"No. But soon."

"You really should spend today in bed."

His green eyes glittered. "That's a very appealing proposition, Doctor. But I'm afraid I have commitments elsewhere." *I'm committed to being alone. I must be.* "So, Caitlin, I'm out of here."

"You're walking to the hotel?"

"It's just across the street."

"Maybe I should walk with you."

Jesse smiled. "To make sure I don't exsanguinate en route? That's a gracious offer, Doctor. But an unnecessary one. I do have a question before I go."

"Yes?"

"Do you know Dr. Frank Farrell?"

"He's one of my partners. Why?"

"Research. I've read a few of the articles he's written. They seem scholarly and careful to me—but of course I'm not a doctor."

"Well, Frank's terrific, both surgically and academically. You should feel completely comfortable using anything he's written in one of your books."

Caitlin might have added that Frank's specialty was pediatric hearts. But the treatment room had contracted anew. And as calm as Jesse seemed, as casual and as cool, she sensed his restlessness, its power, its heat.

"That's good to know. Thanks." His shrug was deceptive in its leisure. "So, Caitlin, I'm gone."

Jesse was gone, and moments later so was she. Caitlin stood on the sky bridge, a glassy structure four flights above earth, her gaze riveted on the double doors through which Jesse would necessarily exit the clinics building. If he did not appear soon, in the next thirty seconds, she would race to find him, and he would be lying in a pool of blood, two pools, one from his wounded hip and the other from where his head struck concrete as he fell.

Was thirty seconds too long? The number had been superstitiously chosen—the precise number of times that Stephen had severed nerves and torn cells.

Thirty, no more, no less.

Jesse appeared in twelve, a night black lion, sleek, graceful, powerful. And not staggering. Even to her well-trained eye, and despite her detailed knowledge of the damage that had been done, Caitlin could not detect even the slightest limp.

Wild animals could not show weakness of any kind, especially not the king of the forest. As if wary of some invisible predator, this human beast concealed all traces of his cracked bone and screaming nerves.

Jesse's gait was so normal that Caitlin found herself expecting to see even more: a whisper of buoyancy, a soupçon of joy. Undiluted elation would be premature. But Patrick's vigorous acceptance of Jesse's transfused blood boded extremely well for the fate of the soon-to-be-transplanted marrow.

Jesse knew that his twin's prognosis was excellent. Yet the silhouette four flights below seemed weighted by the heaviest of mantles, a cloak so immense that his powerful limbs fairly trudged through the misting air—as if the storm promised by area forecasters had already arrived.

Wait, Jesse. Don't go!

She almost started after him, almost heeded the impulse that so brazenly bypassed her brain. The scientist's brain, however, was not so easily circumvented. Before so much as a step, reason intervened with a vengeance.

Just because you've read his books and have been casting yourself as heroine to his heroes does not mean that you *are*. Can you imagine his response if you went racing after him? His dark green eyes would glitter with astonishment.

But they glittered when he confessed—so meaningfully, so *intimately*—that the idea of spending the day in bed definitely appealed.

That was a *joke*. He was *mocking* you. You cannot begin to read Jesse Falconer. And, fortunately, you're not going to have to try. He is gone.

He *wants* to be gone.

*H*ad she remained aboard the *QE2*, Caitlin would have disembarked this morning in New York; and depending on how efficiently the disembarkation process went, she might have caught the nine A.M. nonstop from La Guardia; which meant that assuming an on-time arrival at LAX, she could reasonably appear in Patrick's hospital room at one o'clock.

Which is precisely what she did.

"Caitlin."

"Hi."

"You're back early."

"No. Right on time. I breezed through Customs and caught the first available flight. I wasn't about to miss this." Caitlin gestured to the dark red blood that was infusing into his pale white arm.

Except for the waiting for engraftment, marrow transplantation was—for the recipient—remarkably easy: in essence little more than a transfusion. *Except for the waiting*. We waited too long! Caitlin's thought cried. Patrick was gaunt, skeletal, more dead than alive. Even the rich dark blood of the dark, dark twin could not save him now.

But the corpse did not seem to understand his plight. His ravaged face was smiling.

"So, Caitlin, how was your cruise?"

"What? Oh, it was great. I know why people become addicted." Caitlin waved a dismissive hand and somehow managed a smile of her own. "But enough about me, Patrick. How are *you*?"

"At the moment, Caitlin, appearances notwithstanding I'm terrific. This transplant was a rather monumental surprise."

"A wonderful surprise."

"Yes. I'm very hopeful."

"Me too. Stephen, too." She tilted her head and teased, "I really love the beard, Patrick."

"It's gone as soon as the infusion is finished. My platelets—*his* platelets—are sufficient to stave off any bleeding from a shaving mishap."

Good, Caitlin thought. At the moment the beard seemed the only part of Patrick that was truly alive, as if a renegade rush of testosterone had insisted upon a final fling before death. Without the beard he might look less stark, less dead.

The thought was slightly hopeful, yet still unacceptably grim, and as Caitlin sought refuge from the gloom, she remembered the bag clutched in her hand. How could she forget it? Her palm still throbbed from the cropped fingernails that had buried themselves deep.

Purchased at Harrods on One Deck, the bag celebrated the marriage of the London landmark and the grand monarch of the sea. "Harrods" and "QE2," emblazoned in gold, floated on bright azure amid life buoys and Union Jacks.

"I come bearing gifts," Caitlin said. "A little *QE2* memorabilia."

"Thank you."

"You're so polite, Patrick! I think it's arguable that you haven't been sitting here wishing for either a *QE2* mug or a *QE2* key chain."

"Sure I have."

"Well," Caitlin said as she withdrew a round, plaid, tin container. "Here's something you *can* use, beginning right now—extremely high-calorie shortbread cookies from Harrods."

Patrick's skeletal hand accepted the red-and-green tin. "Thank you."

"You're *welcome*." With a shake of her head Caitlin declined his offer of a cookie before sampling one himself. "So, Patrick, are you going to sue me?"

"Sue you?"

"For telling Amanda." *It was a small betrayal, Patrick, a minor breech. Guess who else I told?*

"No, it was fine that you told her."

Fine. That was the word Amanda had used. Fine; a bland little word capable of layers of mystery. And mystery, Caitlin realized, was precisely what she had heard from Amanda even ship-to-shore . . . and it was mystery that she was hearing now from Patrick.

"Does Amanda know about your transplant?"

"I don't know. Probably not. You're my first visitor. It won't be long, however, before the entire hospital knows."

"So may I tell her?"

"Sure."

Sure—it sounded like fine—a noncommittal word laced with meaning.

But Patrick's sure seemed laced with something else, something that sounded very much like *hope*.

TWENTY

"*D*r. Taylor." The page operator's voice held authentic fondness. "Welcome back."

"Thank you, Darla."

"You're not officially back, are you, Doctor? Our schedule says you're gone until Monday."

Darla did not protect every doctor. But in the estimation of Westwood's page operator corps, Caitlin Taylor worked too hard—an assessment that would have been confirmed had Caitlin revealed that at this very moment she was in her office checking messages and mail.

Mail? Just that one document. That one screenplay.

Thief of Hearts had not yet arrived. It wasn't a major tragedy, of course. Caitlin was officially home from her cruise, sequestered no more. She could roam from bookstore to bookstore if she liked, scavenging until she found copies of every Graydon Slake novel ever written.

There were eighteen such books, not counting *The Snow Lion*. Caitlin had read four of his erotic thrillers so far, and she had seen the film version of his children's book.

Scavenging for the collected works of Graydon Slake seems a bit excessive, doesn't it? the taunting voice of reason, such a reasonable voice, wanted to know. Jesse Falconer is gone.

"I'm not officially back, Darla. But if you need me—"

"I'll find you!"

"Good. Please do. Speaking of finding, I'm trying to track down Dr. Prentice." There had been no answer at Amanda's home, and even though Caitlin's copy of the psychiatry on-call schedule indicated that Amanda was off, such schedules were subject to change. If Amanda was with a patient Caitlin did not want to intrude with a page. "Is she in the house? Do you know?"

"Yes. She is. She's with a patient on Seven West. Shall I put you through?"

"No. Thank you. I'll just drop by."

Seven West was Westwood Memorial's locked ward, home to patients judged to be a danger to themselves or to others—suicidal, homicidal, or merely so psychotic that they needed to be watched.

On occasion Caitlin was asked to do a consultation on Seven West. A psychotic patient, even a homicidal one, was as susceptible to heart disease as anyone else. Caitlin always approached her Seven West consultations with a sense of dread.

It wasn't fear of the patients, but merely of their plight—being locked up, imprisoned . . . like when a spiked green gate closed across a glassy bungalow, jailing the man within and casting ominous shadows on the moonscape beyond.

Jesse Falconer is gone. In fact, reason asserted, he was never really here. *Not for you.*

The door that separated Seven West and its residents from the rest of the medical center was thick, metal, and impenetrable—unless admitted by the staff within. A wire-meshed window enabled on-duty personnel to screen potential visitors.

Caitlin was recognized on sight and buzzed right in.

"Hello, Dr. Taylor. Are we expecting you?"

"No. I'm looking for Dr. Prentice. Is she in the midst of—"

Caitlin's unfinished question was answered by a sound that every physician knew: a quaking gurney, shaken by a patient's rage.

"Yes, she is," the ward clerk said. "He's a college kid, supposedly an above-average student and extremely straitlaced. At the moment, however, our straitlaced student is positively wild. There's alcohol on his breath, but there's obviously more than that going on. PCP probably, at least. Can you believe it's called Angel Dust? What kind of angel would sprinkle that poison on anyone?"

Caitlin had no answer, but she found herself envisioning another angel, her friend, the compassionate woman who was ministering to the psychotic young man. Psychotic patients, especially male ones, posed a significant threat to women. Even a patient who seemed completely out of touch was often *in* touch with his own views of life; and if that worldview included rage toward women, any woman who came within his delusional sphere could be in jeopardy.

"He is restrained, isn't he?"

"You bet. Five-point. Well, actually nine."

"Nine?"

"Double restraints on his arms and legs."

"Has he been medicated?"

The ward clerk nodded. "They managed to hold him down long enough to give him something IM—a little something. Dr. Prentice is being cautious with meds. She has to be, given the unknowns about what he's taken. The on-call resident is here, too, but I'm not sure that Dr. Prentice will want to be pulled away, at least not yet. Unless . . . is it an emergency?"

"No. Not at all. In fact it's good news. May I just leave her a note?"

"Of course."

Caitlin wrote:

Amanda, in case you haven't heard, a donor's been found for Patrick. The marrow, an incredible match, is being infused even as I write. Needless to say I'm back, and will be at home. So if ever you shake free, and are in the mood to talk, please drop by!

A donor's been found. Caitlin hoped Amanda wouldn't ask for specifics. Over the years there had been sins of omission, truths too painful to share, but from the beginning of their friendship there had never been lies. . . .

"*I*'m Amanda Prentice, and for those of you who don't know me, I'm president of Future Aesculapians, something I believe we all hope to become, *true* Aesculapians, that is. Anyway, as you know, it's med-school application time, and once the applications are processed the interviews will begin. Whether or not it should be, the admissions interview is important, even critical, and therefore definitely worth practicing. A number of us have spoken to students who've gone before us—successfully, I might add. They've told us the type of questions that are asked, and have also offered helpful hints. Neither the questions nor the hints are surprising, but there's no harm in being prepared. Which brings me to the reason I'm here, to invite anyone who's interested to come to our practice sessions. *Anyone,* even if you don't belong to FA. Even if you would rather *die* than belong!"

Amanda's light-hearted remark caused a ripple of uneasy—yet relieved—laughter in the lecture hall. Not every UCLA premedical student belonged to the premedical society. For some just being in class with other premeds was pressure enough. Extracurricular activities with those classmates would have been too much, especially given the number one item discussed at society meetings: how to get into medical school.

Everyone agreed that there was no foolproof formula. But theories abounded. Volunteer work at hospitals was a must, some students—and advisors—maintained; as was, some insisted, basic-science research.

Admission committees were looking for Renaissance types, others contended, well-rounded human beings who would epitomize the *art* of medicine. Therefore—such advocates asserted—philosophy, English lit, and world history needed to be woven into schedules already laden with physics, math, and biochem.

Never admit to watching television, most admonished. Devote spare time to writing sonnets instead.

There were as many theories as there were applicants. Some students enjoyed the dialogue. Others found the rampant speculation anxiety-provoking in the extreme.

Caitlin did not belong to Future Aesculapians. She had chosen the path to medical school that made sense to her: earn top grades in all classes and set the curve on the MCAT exam.

To date, in the fall of her third—and hopefully final— collegiate year, Caitlin had done just that. Her application to UCLA School of Medicine was already complete, and she would be accepted after only three years, and . . . but what if she didn't get in? What if top grades weren't enough?

Caitlin recognized the girl who was issuing the all-inclusive invitation to practice the interviews. She had noticed Amanda Prentice, marveled at her. Amanda radiated confidence. Despite her size. In fact, as if she were a giant sun, everyone wanted to bask in Amanda's warmth, Amanda's brilliance, Amanda's glow.

Now came an invitation so generous, so heartfelt, it seemed as if Amanda truly wanted everyone in the lecture hall to be admitted to the medical school of their choice.

"The practice sessions will begin Monday and run for the next six nights. Please sign up in advance so we can reserve enough classrooms. Please do not, however, sign up for *every* night." Amanda's smile glowed. "If you feel your session didn't go well and you want more practice— fine, you can easily add on another night. But nobody, I mean nobody, needs six nights!"

Caitlin signed up for Saturday. At the time, her name was seventh on the list. But the combination of social lives—which some premed students actually had—and the anxiety shared by all had compelled even those on the Saturday list to come earlier in the week.

Which meant Caitlin alone appeared in the designated classroom. Caitlin . . . and the girl who cast such warmth and hope.

"I guess it's just us," Amanda said.

"Oh! Well, if you'd rather cancel. I mean . . ."

"No, let's practice. I think I'll forgo my little opening speech, though, if that's okay. It's intended more to settle nerves than to impart knowledge, and you don't seem nervous at all."

Caitlin was not nervous, not for this practice interview, not for the real thing. She was going to become a doctor. A surgeon. It was who she was.

"Are you ready to begin?" Amanda asked.

"Sure."

"Okay. Well, let's see, I think I'll start with the easy question first, the obvious one." Amanda paused as if to shift the scene from two college coeds, dateless on a Saturday night, to the more solemn setting of a medical school interview. "Please tell me, Miss Taylor, why do you want to be a doctor?"

Because, because, because . . . a beloved image filled Caitlin's reeling mind. Hello, Caitie-love, the lovely vision was saying, her beautiful eyes bright with wonder, as always, when she saw her daughter, every time she greeted her anew. Good morning, Caitie-love. How was school, Caitie-love? Dinner's ready, Caitie-love.

"Caitlin? What's wrong? Can you tell me?"

Caitlin frowned at the voice, so different from Maggie's, yet gentle and worried. She responded at last, with a shake of her head.

Surely Amanda would leave. Surely Caitlin's obvious distress—the anguish of an absolute stranger—would drive her away.

But Amanda did not budge. She merely waited, serene yet determined . . . until Caitlin confessed.

"Because I'm going to save my mother."

"But that's a *good* reason, Caitlin. A wonderful reason."

"No, it's *not.*"

"It's not? Why not?"

"Because she's . . . dead."

But Maggie had not been dead, not until that moment, not in Caitlin's heart. She had been alive all this time, and she had been waiting *so patiently* in the operating room at UCLA . . . waiting for her heart-surgeon daughter to save her. *Hello, Caitie-love.* I'm so glad you're here. I knew you would come, my Caitie. I *knew.*

But Margaret Taylor was not waiting.

She had never been waiting.

She had already died.

Already *died.*

It began that night, this most important friendship. They were girls becoming women; women becoming doctors. But there was another bond, essential and deep. Both Caitlin and Amanda were motherless daughters.

Neither, until their friendship, had acknowledged the irretrievable loss, much less grieved it. Together they grieved.

And together they learned the truth known to every daughter who had lost her mother: that no matter the age, or how conflicted the relationship had been, the wound never truly healed. Even decades after the loss, and from a place too deep for tears, came the desperate, piercing cries.

Where are you, Mother?

I miss you *so much.*

Come back, Mom. *Mom?*

Please.

TWENTY-ONE

*E*xcept for the fact that reading Graydon Slake was a wholly inappropriate and amazingly foolish endeavor, there could not have been a more suitable night to read a book entitled *Come in from the Rain*. The misting air had become a full-fledged storm, a tempest from the Pacific. Indeed, perhaps the same black clouds that had spilled their soggy tears on the Valley Isle were weeping here . . . as they had wept that night in paradise when Jesse Falconer had invited both would-be assassin and snow-white lion to come in from the rain.

Stop thinking about him, Caitlin commanded even as she clutched his book, a grasp as ferocious as the one with which she had clutched the steering wheel on that journey through darkness to light—to glistening green slate . . . and glittering green eyes.

Caitlin's command was, of course, entirely futile—especially since Jesse had chosen as the title for his book one of her favorite songs. Was it one of his favorites, too? Probably. He certainly took every opportunity to reprise the lyrics of love, even as he catapulted the heroine's daughter into ever-crescendoing peril. Caitlin wanted to help the girl named Risa. But the fictional child was in the hands of Graydon Slake—Jesse's hands, the shepherd's hands.

Jesse will protect her.

Even so, as she read his words, Caitlin's fingers became restive, the surgeon needing to do more than clutch. Don't just stand there, do something. She had long since pulled the rubber band from her nape, freeing her entire mane of hair, and her surgeon's fingers had gone to work on the fallen strands, twisting, twirling, knotting, braiding, yet never entirely relinquishing their grasp of the book.

The doorbell sounded, melodic yet startling.

As Caitlin rose to greet her visitor, surprise was replaced by welcome. It was eleven o'clock, eight hours since she'd left the note on Seven West—eight hours which, for Amanda, had undoubtedly been grueling.

Still, Amanda was dropping by, as Caitlin had hoped she would, choosing to wind down, to decompress. . . .

But Caitlin's nighttime visitor was not Amanda. And the favorite love song, with its celebration of homecoming amid a rain storm, danced and twirled.

A man like Jesse Falconer, *home*? To *her*?

The thought was preposterous. Yet there it was, pirouetting with exquisite joy in the humid night air.

And there *he* was, raindrops spilling from his coal black hair, his eyes searching, intense.

And there *she* was, in her tattered flannel bathrobe, her black hair as tangled as his, not by the tempest outside but the storm within—the gale-force suspense created by the gifted pen of Graydon Slake.

With a wordless gesture, she invited Jesse Falconer into her home.

Come in from the Rain.

"Thank you," he said.

"You're welcome. Let me get a towel for your hair."

"I'm all right, Caitlin."

"Oh," she murmured, disappointed—then alarmed. Was she trying to re-create that evening in paradise, when Jesse had given her towels for her rain-damp hair and invited her to spend the night?

Jesse Falconer had believed he was harboring an assassin—or a spy—and his crescent-moon home had an entire guest wing for nighttime intruders such as she. And if Caitlin returned the favor? She would be harboring a man, no more, no *less,* and she had only one bedroom, one bed, to offer him.

"You're not in Maui," she said. *We're* not in Maui.

"I've decided to stay here for a while."

Despite the dangers. There were most definitely dangers in LA. But Jesse never ran from danger, so long as the risk was merely for himself. And when his presence jeopardized the safety—or the happiness—of those he loved? Jesse left, as he would leave this time, and from the Maui moonscape, the white lion at his side, he would turn his heart, his soul, back into stone.

Jesse knew the dangers and their cause—that most bewitching of all mistresses: hope. It was hope that had seduced him to Montclair that final disastrous time. Now the temptress was enticing him anew, a seduction abetted by the haziness of his own brain. His blood loss created a misty blur, a fog so dense it altered remembrance and softened truth.

Patrick had welcomed Jesse's blood, Jesse's marrow,

as if welcoming *him*. And hope had spent much of the day urging Jesse to go to his twin. Jesse had resisted that temptation, as well as another perilous pursuit: the house in Bel Air. Just drive by, hope goaded; just for a fleeting glimpse, enough to assure yourself that she is strong enough to survive her impending ordeal.

But hope had triumphed when it came to the intrepid heart surgeon. Caitlin had arrived in Maui in the midst of a storm, oblivious to all danger, wedded only to her mission. This morning *he* had been her mission. She had warmed blankets for his comfort, and her cheeks had heated, had glowed, at the notion of spending the day in bed . . . with him.

An invisible trocar had pierced him then, its knife-sharp blade plumbing uncharted depths and finding an aching, a wanting, he had never known.

The trocar was twisting anew, as he gazed at her, this woman, this surgeon. She was both, an utterly bewitching blend of flushed cheeks and intelligent concern.

"How are you feeling?" she asked.

The trocar plunged deeper, but Jesse Falconer smiled. "Let's just say I have a certain awareness that a small chunk of pelvic bone is missing and that I'm a few pints low on blood."

"Ah-ha," Caitlin replied, as if discovering that the beast was human after all, and not the least bit disappointed with that truth. "You spent the day resting?"

"I did. Just as you advised. So much so that now I'm restless."

"And therefore taking late-night walks in the rain? You really should be in bed."

"You keep saying that, Doctor. Suggesting it. Maybe that's the reason I'm so restless."

Restless for me, Jesse? Wanting to be with me?

Jesse believed he saw those questions—that temptation, that peril—in her shimmering sea blue eyes.

"I have something for you, Caitlin." *My darkness, my restlessness, this piercing ache I cannot permit myself to name.* "I'd arranged to have it delivered to your office on Monday. But since it was ready, and since I wasn't leaving after all, I decided to deliver it myself."

It came in a paper sack adorned with rainbows and engraved with the words *Castille Jewelers, Beverly Hills.* The Castille boutique aboard ship was where Michael had purchased the flawless rope of pearls, and Castille in Beverly Hills was where Maggie had sold for a fortune that long, perfect strand—a fortune that enabled Maggie's fluttering heart to survive the birth of her baby girl.

That baby girl's heart was fluttering now as she withdrew the necklace from the rainbows. Her beloved strand of lacquered glass. *Sometime* in Maui—between driving Caitlin to the Kahalui airport and his own departure a few hours after that—Jesse Falconer had salvaged the drowned and scattered beads. And sometime in LA—between biopsies and bloodlettings at WMH—he had convinced the Castille jewelers on Rodeo Drive to string the glass beads as if they were the most priceless of pearls, with tiny knots in between.

"They aren't real," Caitlin murmured to the treasured—but valueless—necklace. "I'm sure they told you that." She looked up from the false yet precious beads to the gemstone green of his eyes. "I'm sure you didn't have to be told."

"What I didn't have to be told, Caitlin, was how important they were to you."

"Yes. They were. They *are*." Caitlin looked down

again. She had to. She was reading so much, too much, in his glittering gaze. "They were my mother's. Thank you."

Her suspense-tangled hair veiled her face, a blackness as dark and dense as the shadows of his heart. Slowly, gently, Jesse wove his lean fingers into the glossy silk, parting the veil, compelling her to meet his eyes once again.

"You're welcome." He wanted to kiss her, to hold her, to further tangle her lustrous hair. Instead he withdrew his touch, an abandonment that was greeted with disappointment—and uncertainty . . . as if she truly did not know how much he wanted her. Jesse caressed Caitlin still, with his eyes, his voice, his words. "I would very much like to spend time, with you, in bed. A lot of time, Caitlin, and any time. Tonight, if you like."

"But . . . you're injured."

"Don't make excuses for me, Caitlin. Don't make excuses at all. Just say no. Or, even easier, just don't say yes. The invitation stands—a candlelight dinner followed by whatever you want. It's your call, Caitlin. Your choice." *It has to be your choice, Caitlin. I cannot choose this peril for you.*

But we don't know each other, Jesse! It was an excuse, which he had forbidden. And it was also a lie. And as Jesse Falconer had correctly pointed out, Caitlin was not the world's most accomplished liar.

She and Jesse *did* know each other. At least she knew him: lion, shepherd, shadow, stone.

And what did Jesse know of her? That her favorite bathrobe was tattered flannel, and that she cared, as he did, about his twin, and that her passion, like his, was saving endangered hearts. But he must imagine something else, some magnificent fiction: that she was as savvy as his heroines, and as soft as Maggie.

"Think about it, Caitlin," he was saying. "Be certain. Okay?"

"Yes. Okay."

He smiled, a caress of exquisite intimacy and extraordinary promise. "Well. Good night."

"Good night."

With that Jesse Falconer returned to the storm. Caitlin permitted him to.

In paradise Jesse had not allowed Caitlin to venture back into the tempest—because of the lion. But here, in LA, Caitlin permitted her lion to leave. She had to—for Jesse was right. She needed to be very certain, to weigh carefully the temptation she felt with the consequences that might ensue . . . the immeasurable endangerment to her own fluttering heart.

TWENTY-TWO

*E*very muscle ached, her arms, her legs, her throat, her chest—as if she, not her patient, had been fighting the restraints. As if *she* had been bound.

Amanda's soul ached as well. She hated the confinement she had imposed on him; even though it had been for his own good, to protect him from harm while the drugs raged within.

There had been a time in Amanda's life when she had been so tightly bound. One could never argue, however, that for her the bondage had been good—not good at all, but definitely monumental. Those moments of imprisoned terror had irrevocably altered Amanda's life, bestowing it with direction and purpose.

Because of that terror Amanda became a psychiatrist. And on this day, for hours on end, she stood beside her patient, aching for his torment, enduring his rage. Despite his drug-induced psychosis, he sensed his bondage and rebelled against it. The fear of imprisonment was so primal that it asserted itself even in the midst of madness—as did its mirror-image twin, the impulse to be free.

Amanda's college-student patient was now sound asleep, the consequence of the sedatives she had judiciously administered and the fact that the "recreational" drugs which had caused such chaos had largely relinquished their frenzied grip. By morning he would be groggy, exhausted, but in all likelihood otherwise back to normal. Free of bondage. Free of terror.

And, come morning, Amanda would be bound still, held captive by ancient fears and engaged as always in a battle from which she would never emerge victorious—but could, with constant vigilance, preserve forever a wary truce.

"Oh, Dr. Prentice. Wait a sec." Seven West's night clerk stopped Amanda just as she was leaving the locked ward.

"Yes?" she asked wearily.

"I have a note for you from Dr. Taylor. She left it hours ago, at the beginning of evening shift. It was passed on to me when I came on duty."

"Oh. Thank you." Good, she embellished as she left Seven West. Caitlin was back. Patrick would no longer be alone. Caitlin would be there, talking to him, helping him.

Patrick. Patrick. He was with her, in her thoughts and in her heart, every second of every day. Every night. There had been times, since his sunset visit to her home, when Amanda had been compelled to imprison herself. Her bondage had been forged of sheer will, a viselike restraint. The confinement was essential, for what if she confessed to him both the impossible truth and the unutterable lie?

I've never felt this way, Patrick. I never believed I could. That was the impossible truth. And the unutterable lie? You will survive, Patrick, and then you and I . . .

Patrick would survive. He had to. But there was no *then*, no *you and I*. That was the lie.

Patrick must survive, would survive, was going to. As she read Caitlin's note Amanda embraced that joyous truth.

She clutched the note, a life buoy in a raging sea, and the long limbs that should have been restrained, had been, began moving of their own accord, walking free of their bondage.

$\mathscr{P}$atrick's footsteps slowed as he neared his hospital room, halting entirely before she realized he was there. She stood in the hallway outside his room, directly in front of the door. But, Patrick decided, she was not going to knock. Nor was she going to enter his room, his bedroom, unannounced—not ever perhaps and most assuredly not in the middle of the night.

So what was Amanda doing here?

She was touching, *touching*. Her slender fingers traced the neatly stenciled lettering—Falconer, P.—in the nameplate on the door. Her caress was delicate, thoughtful, as it had been when she touched the item prices at Ariel's.

She's a toucher, Patrick mused. She touches labels on grocery shelves, and nameplates on hospital doors, and fluffy kittens the color of smoke.

Amanda caressed inanimate objects and innocent creatures. But what about human beings? Men? *Him?* She had almost touched him, at sunset, when his palm bled from the tiny pricks of kitten claws.

Almost . . . and perhaps she would have had he truly needed her touch, had he been dying before her eyes. But Patrick had only been dying slowly then, and Amanda's hands had stalled, as if blocked by an invisible—yet monumental—shield.

I am no longer dying, Amanda, and this is a monumental day.

It was as if already the donor cells were engrafting in his marrow, as if he could feel them making a home deep within his bones. It was an illusion, of course, a fantasy of robust health created by the transfusions he had received last night.

And yet the illusion had crescendoed throughout the day, beginning with the marrow infusion and soaring far beyond. Finally, two hours ago, Patrick had felt so well, so infused with health, that he had dressed, as if a patient no more, and roamed the night-darkened halls.

At first his roaming had been purposeful, a search for his donor. That most generous man was somewhere here, asleep in a hospital bed, convalescing from the donation he had made. Or maybe he was awake, kept awake, by the deep ache in his pelvic bone.

Either way Patrick would know when he neared the man's room. The cells within his veins would sense their twin's, and he would feel that bonding, that longing.

But Patrick felt nothing, nothing—except his own gratitude. Eventually his purposeful prowl became a leisurely wandering. He saw the medical center as never before, taffy stretched forever, and as he wandered the dimly lit halls, he vowed to revere the magnificent moments of life as he had learned to savor the nostalgic moments of death.

Patrick might have spent the entire storm-ravaged night wandering the shadowed hallways, marveling at the dance of raindrops on glass.

But suddenly restless anew he had returned to his room.

Now he knew why.

Amanda had come to touch the inanimate label that bore his name, and then to leave, to drive through the torrential downpour to her Palisades home and the smoky kitten that awaited her there.

You can't leave, Amanda. Not now. Not yet.

"Hi."

"Oh! *Patrick.*"

"Hello, Amanda."

"Caitlin left me a note."

"Did she mention that I look like a skeleton?"

"No. I, you . . ."

"Do. Look like a skeleton. At least I'm no longer a bearded one. And soon, hopefully, the skeletal motif itself will be merely a memory."

"The transplantation went well?"

"Very well. Effortless for me. An act of extreme generosity on the part of the donor."

"I'm sure that he was happy to do it."

Happy, Patrick echoed in silence. Are *you* happy, Amanda? "Can you stay for a while?"

"Oh, I . . ." She cast an uneasy glance at the door.

"Come with me, Amanda. I've found the perfect spot from which to enjoy the rain. Come with me and tell me about your day."

The perfect place was the Drawing Room, so named

by those for whom it had been designed. Located on the eighth floor of the Heart Institute the Drawing Room was an oasis of tranquility and elegance—a world far away from the chaos and tragedy that could at times be overwhelming.

The Drawing Room might have come from Manderley—a lone survivor of Mrs. Danvers's vengeful blaze—or from its real-life twin, a baronial manor perched atop the rugged cliffs of the Cornish coast.

Westwood Memorial Hospital boasted unique waiting areas for its patients and their families, spaces that had been created to feel as if the occupants were in the privacy of their own homes. But the Drawing Room was for staff not patients, a sanctuary for the healthcare providers who were also away from home. Before the Drawing Room, the spaces allocated to staff had been distinctly institutional, brightly lighted areas where one could chat, drink coffee, but not truly decompress.

On this Saturday, after midnight, the Drawing Room was empty, and lightless—save for the night-lights of Los Angeles spun through the dainty prisms of the falling rain.

Patrick followed Amanda to the wall of windows.

"Beautiful," she murmured.

"Yes. Beautiful." Patrick spoke to her rainbowed reflection, frowning as he caught sight of his own. She was a Titian angel. He was a Shakespearean ghost. "Caitlin must have left you the note hours ago."

"She did, although I just got it. I was with a patient on Seven West."

"He or she must be better now."

"Yes. He is." And *she*?

"You sound uncertain, Amanda."

No, she thought, suddenly decisive. I am not uncertain at all. This is something I must do, I *must,* so that Patrick will understand how impossible this is.

"I'm certain about him. But there's another patient who has been worrying me. She's a she, a physician in fact. Superficially she seems quite . . . normal. But it's an illusion. In truth she's precarious, teetering on the edge. As long as she stays precisely where she is, she'll be all right. She's done well, overcome so much. She needs to be content with that."

"But she's not content?"

"Yes, she is." *She was.* "Still, sometimes she wonders about taking that next step. And she can't. She *can't.*"

"You sound very sure, Amanda."

"I am. Very. I wonder, Patrick, could I tell you about her?"

"Of course." *Tell me about the woman physician who has accomplished so much yet still has such fear. Tell me about you.*

Patrick knew that Amanda was the patient. Amanda *wanted* him to know. But she needed the pretense, and the distance—physicians discussing a patient with dispassionate calm.

Could he truly be dispassionate? "Tell me about her, Amanda. Tell me everything."

Amanda nodded, then turned from the splashing drops of color toward the shadowed room. Her copper hair shone in the gloom, a beacon which he followed.

Patrick wanted to see her as they talked. If, however, she needed shadows for her darkest secrets, then so be it. But, as if wanting brightness to glare upon the truths she was about to reveal, Amanda moved to the massive stone fireplace and flipped the switch, filling the hearth with light and heat.

A cozy couch had been placed before the fireplace. Amanda forsook such comfort. She selected a straight-backed wooden chair instead—a period piece, stylish but austere—and faced the flames as if facing a firing squad.

Patrick found a comparably spartan chair and positioned it as close, and as far, as two physicians would sit while discussing a case.

"Her name is Sherry." Amanda's voice belonged to a concerned—yet analytical—MD. "She has another name now, but she'll always be Sherry. She was born in Las Vegas. Her mother, Brandy, was a showgirl. 'Brandy and Sherry,' her mother loved to say, 'the two most intoxicating girls on the Strip.' Sherry's father was unknown to both of them. The pregnancy was undoubtedly a mistake, although Brandy never confessed as much to Sherry. Brandy *accepted* her daughter, a part of her life that Brandy never thought to question. But Brandy wasn't ready to be a mother, even though she was twenty-four when Sherry was born."

"Twenty-four," Patrick echoed. "Sherry was probably about that age during her internship." *During that rigorous year in which Sherry—Amanda—delivered new lives, saved tiny infants, even contrary ones who entered the world feetfirst.*

"Sherry *was* twenty-four as an intern," Amanda murmured. "That makes them sound very different, doesn't it? It makes Sherry sound brighter, more capable, than Brandy. But that's really not the case. Brandy was terribly bright, and savvy, worldly. And yet she was oddly out of touch. She viewed Sherry as a child's toy, a doll that could be plumped between pillows when Brandy wasn't in the mood to play. Sherry was left alone at a startlingly young age. What harm could a doll get into? What maintenance could she possibly require?"

"Love, Amanda." *Love . . .* Amanda.

She heard the tenderness, and for a breathtaking moment her lavender eyes brightened, glowed, as if a long-forgotten ember in her heart had suddenly sparked to life. But it was a tiny ember, a faint flame.

"I believe that Brandy did love Sherry, in her own out-of-touch way. But Brandy didn't begin to understand Sherry's fears."

"Sherry's fears?"

"Fears and worries. Sherry had so many. The first she remembers was her terror of heights. Their apartment was on the eighth floor, with windows Sherry could easily reach and which were often left open. Do you know what many acrophobics fear most? Jumping, *choosing* to jump. The impulse is curiosity, not a wish to die. Can I fly? they wonder. Am I truly mortal? What would happen *if*? The urge is powerful, compelling, and frightening—especially for a three-year-old."

"She was *three*? And she remembers?"

"Vividly. That same year they moved to another apartment, on the tenth floor this time, and with a balcony. Sherry never told Brandy of her fear that she would jump. She could not at that age put such anxiety into words. Instead she told her mother she was afraid she'd fall."

"And Brandy's response?" Patrick asked, dreading it, enraged by it . . . and then surprised by it.

"*Sympathy*, but not empathy. Brandy had no fear of heights—no fears at all. Still, she took her daughter's fright seriously. She had locks installed and made certain they were secure whenever she left Sherry alone. Sherry's acrophobia was contained, locked away, but the fear of imprisonment promptly took its place. Sherry knew that she was trapped, without the possibility of escape, a circumstance made more fearsome at night."

"Brandy left Sherry alone at night?"

"Las Vegas showgirls don't have much choice about the hours they work. At least they didn't then. Nor did they make much money. One night—it was almost dawn—Brandy returned to discover that Sherry had fallen asleep with the lights on. It was a waste of money they simply could not afford. Brandy didn't get angry with Sherry. She *never* got angry. She merely explained their financial situation and forbade Sherry from turning on any lights, ever. Sherry complied, of course. As a result she spent many hours alone in a darkness populated by all manner of monsters."

"Brandy was the monster."

"No, Patrick. She wasn't. She just didn't know any better. She had no idea how fragile Sherry was."

"That's not child abuse?"

"No."

"*No?*"

"Brandy was neglectful, negligent. But she was never cruel. And even though she didn't understand Sherry's fears, she listened to them, tried to *remedy* them."

Patrick did not agree with Amanda's charitable assessment of her mother. But Brandy didn't matter. Sherry did.

Amanda did.

"What did Sherry do all alone in the darkness?" *Was she cold, too, and starving?* "What did she think about?"

"She didn't think. She counted. It was her version, I suppose, a child's version of counting sheep. Sherry saw numbers, not fleecy creatures, but the images were bright, lovely, comforting. Each numeral was unique in color and shape. Alone and in combination they glittered like the Las Vegas strip. The numeral one was the color of rubies, and for a *one* it was remarkably ornate. *Two* shone—and twinkled—emerald, and *three* was both silver and gold, and . . . well, you get the idea. In combination the effect was quite dazzling, brighter and more sparkling the higher she counted. As Sherry grew older she realized that some of the colors clashed. But she never made changes."

Of course she didn't, Patrick thought. The numerals were her friends, each with its own personality, make-believe images that helped her combat the phantoms of darkness.

"Every night Sherry would begin with *one,* and she would count until she fell asleep. She counted slowly, at a carefully measured pace, but even so she remembers some astonishingly high numbers. Eventually she went beyond simple counting. She gave herself math problems—a useless talent . . . and ultimately a disastrous one."

Useless, Amanda? Hardly. It was that rare mathematical talent, that frightened girl's survival instinct, that placed the woman Sherry became at Ariel's, at midnight, calculating the item prices for tea.

"Disastrous?" Patrick echoed, not wanting more sadness for her, but sensing—knowing—that there was much, much more.

"Brandy had boyfriends. They came and went, an ever-changing landscape. Most of Brandy's men were on their best behavior, far more interested in Brandy than she was in them. As I said, Brandy was savvy, worldly, and realistic about men—until Royce. She was infatuated with him, and quite blind to his considerable flaws. Royce was mean, even when sober. He called himself a 'professional' gambler, although *compulsive* was more apt. Like all gambling addicts he fantasized about devising *the* system. When he wasn't at the casino, he was at Brandy's, dealing hands to himself—and, if Sherry happened to be around, making her deal to him.

"Blackjack was the game with which Royce was going to break the casino's bank. One day, when Sherry was dealing to him, her up card was eight and he had twelve. Conventional wisdom advises the player to take a hit, which is what Royce signaled to do—to which Sherry shook her head. Royce ignored her, of course. The card busted his hand, and would have busted hers. How did she *know*? he demanded. Was she *cheating*?"

"She wasn't cheating," Patrick said quietly. "She was merely counting. And calculating the odds?"

"Counting, yes. And at a subconscious level, I suppose, calculating as well. It was automatic for her, reflexive. Not surprisingly Sherry suddenly became Royce's surefire technique. She was thirteen and physically precocious, already in full possession of Brandy's showgirl figure and height. For some time, in fact, Royce had been making lewd comments about Sherry's womanly shape. The remarks mortified Sherry and had they been made by any man other than Royce, Brandy would have thrown him out.

"But Brandy was infatuated, so much so that she endorsed Royce's plan to dress Sherry in Brandy's sexiest dress, and make up her young face—after which they would go to the casino and win a fortune. The plan was perfect, foolproof, until Sherry flatly refused. It was against the law, she said. Dishonest. She was eight years shy of Nevada's legal gambling age. It was even possible, she argued, that if she was caught, Brandy might lose her job. Sherry stood her ground. So Royce insisted that she teach him her technique."

"Which she couldn't do."

"No. She couldn't. Sherry had no gimmicks, no tricks. She simply recalled every card that was played. It was neither talent nor gift, merely a consequence of her fears. Royce was furious, *livid.* He took every penny he had—and all of Brandy's money, too—and went to the casino. When he returned, having lost everything, he was drunk, in a rage. Sherry was awakened by the argument that ensued and rushed into her mother's bedroom. It was all right, Brandy told her. Sherry just needed to return to her room and go to sleep. Sherry obeyed, although sleep was impossible. She lay in the darkness, listening to their anger, praying for peace. Her prayers were answered, or so she thought, when at last there was silence."

There was silence then, and silence now—except for the soft hisses of flames and the faint splattering of raindrops upon glass . . . and except for that other sound, heard only by him, the keening wail of her lonely heart.

"But there wasn't peace, was there? Not for Sherry?"

"No. Not for Sherry." Amanda's slender body stiffened, as if steeling herself for what she would say, must say. When she spoke her voice was flat, empty, and so detached that it seemed separated from life itself. "Royce came to her, and for the first time in all those years of darkness Sherry saw her bedroom ablaze with light. Royce wanted the brightness. He wanted Sherry to see him, to see everything. Sherry recognized Royce's madness, knew it at once, although she had never seen psychosis before. It was all her fault, Royce raged. If she hadn't defied him, they all would have been rich and happy. As it was, because of her, he had been obliged to hit her mother. Sherry was responsible for the injuries Brandy had already suffered. And, Royce warned, Sherry would be entirely to blame if Brandy died, if Royce was *compelled* to kill her—which he would if Sherry didn't do everything he asked *and to his satisfaction.* Sherry might have refused to teach him *her* tricks, Royce taunted. But he would generously teach her his—every conceivable way to please a man."

It seemed impossible that Amanda's voice could become more devoid of life. But it did.

"Sherry's education went on forever. She still remembers the numbers to which she counted. She counted that night, counted not calculated. It was a regression, perhaps, or maybe her mind was merely otherwise engaged—attentive to what she was being made to do and consumed with worry about Brandy. Sherry knew how badly injured her mother must be. She believed absolutely that had Brandy been able to intervene, she would have done so.

"Finally only one sex act remained, the most usual one of all. Sherry would not have resisted the rape. At Royce's instruction—and warning—she had offered no resistance at all, and had remained totally mute. But for some reason he decided to tie her to the bed, his own version of four-point restraints. And when he finished raping her, Royce left her that way, still bound, still exposed."

No more, Patrick pleaded. It was a gentle plea—for Amanda—even as a ferocious rage pulsed within. He wanted to murder Royce. He *would.*

"Royce dressed, lit a cigarette, and with a smile that Sherry will never forget announced that he would be right back—with Brandy."

"But he never returned," Patrick said, amazed by the calmness of his voice. *Where is he, Amanda? Tell me. Please.* "And Brandy was already dead."

"Yes," Amanda whispered, no longer flat, no longer dead, but still without hope. She was Sherry now, a daughter now, not the skilled psychiatrist Sherry had become. "Brandy was dead. She had been dead all along. But Royce *did* return with her as promised."

"Oh, no." Oh, *no.*

Amanda and Sherry, doctor and daughter, described what Sherry saw—a clinical description that trembled with emotion.

"Brandy's beautiful face was white, ashen from death, and blotched with bruises from Royce's savage blows. Her eyes were open, and Brandy, who had never been frightened in life, seemed frightened in death, *beyond* death.

"Royce put Brandy on the bed beside Sherry, with one of Brandy's arms on Sherry's naked chest. That arm, so cold, so weighted, became the fifth point of Sherry's restraints. As Royce positioned Brandy he talked about other poses, intimate ones, and he bemoaned the fact that Brandy died before mother and daughter could put on a showgirl show for him. That was the second to last thing Royce said to Sherry. His parting shot was a word of advice. Never believe anything a man tells you, he said, especially when that man wants your body."

You can trust me, Amanda. You can believe me.

No she can't, Patrick's own violence, his own *violence,* screamed in reply. How can Amanda trust any man, ever?

"Royce turned off the lights as he left. Sherry saw Brandy's eyes still, despite the blackness, and as she whispered words of love she believed she saw Brandy's terror disappear. Eventually Sherry's voice became hoarse, choked with grief . . . and smoke."

"Royce set the apartment on fire." How *clinical* he sounded, as if emotionally immune to any and all horrors. But Patrick was far from immune. Each successive atrocity evoked ever more fury deep within, molten silver that coursed through every vein. "Didn't he?"

"Yes. He did." Amanda's voice was as matter-of-fact as his. "When Sherry realized what Royce had done she felt relief, *relief*—and for the first time in her memory an utter absence of fear. There should have been pain. She was significantly burned. But all she remembers is the brilliant glow that haloed Brandy's face . . . and her own feeling of peace. Then, quite suddenly, she wanted to be free of her restraints. Even now Sherry isn't certain what prompted the impulse. Maybe she wanted to wrap her arms around Brandy, so they could die together in a loving embrace. Or maybe Sherry wanted to carry Brandy to the balcony, then to leap, to fly . . ."

"Or, maybe, Sherry wanted to live."

Patrick wasn't certain that Amanda had heard him. She was in that burning room, seeing her mother's face—and trying yet again to understand Sherry's urgent need to be free.

But Amanda had heard. She answered with a slight shake of her head, the same delicate yet decisive gesture that Patrick had seen at Ariel's—and which Royce had seen when Sherry had dealt to him that fateful hand.

"Sherry was tightly bound, especially her wrists. In her struggle to be free she tore her own flesh. The scars are still there, and if seen could easily be mistaken for a suicide attempt."

But those scars are never seen, Patrick realized. The clothes Amanda Prentice wore always had long sleeves. On this night the silken cuffs of a heather green blouse concealed entirely the vestiges of severed silken flesh.

"Are there other scars?" *Trivial obstacles, Amanda, easily overcome.*

"A few. For the most part the skin grafts were virtually seamless. And Sherry was rescued before her lungs suffered irreparable damage from the smoke."

So there are only those most important scars, Patrick thought. Those monumental scars, invisible to the naked eye . . . but not to the naked heart. "Sherry was rescued? It sounds as if she rescued herself."

Amanda frowned at the flames, and her head, more glittering than fire, tilted thoughtfully—and briefly. Straightening anew she repeated emphatically, "Sherry was rescued. The apartment had no alarms, but a neighbor saw the smoke. Sherry had freed herself from the restraints by the time the firemen arrived, but she was still in her bedroom on the bed, holding Brandy."

"And Royce?" *Where is he, Amanda? Tell me.*

"Royce died that night, after leading the police on a high-speed chase. Thankfully, no one else was hurt."

Except you, my lovely Amanda. Except you.

"Sherry spent the next three months in a hospital. No one knew what Royce had done to her, sexually. They knew, however, that he had murdered Brandy and left Sherry to perish in the flames. In addition to her medical care Sherry met regularly with a psychiatrist. She felt safe in the hospital, truly safe for the first time in her life."

Feel safe in my arms, Amanda, for the rest of your life . . . and mine. I am going to live, I will live, so that I may keep you safe.

Patrick wanted to speak the impassioned words. But it was far too soon. The future of his transplant was a wish, a hope . . . and on this stormy night it was Amanda's wish that, as physicians, they discuss her "case"—the story of Sherry, the ravaged girl who dedicated her adult life to comforting others.

"The safety Sherry felt in the hospital must have influenced her decision to become a physician."

"Yes."

"A psychiatrist?"

"Eventually . . . yes," Amanda hesitated, as if debating whether to jump ahead in the story. Finally, decisively, she resumed precisely where she had left off, the conscientious physician including all pertinent aspects of her patient's medical history. "Since Sherry had no relatives, she became a ward of the state. Upon discharge from the hospital she was assigned to a foster home. Her foster father saw what Royce had seen, her sexual precociousness. And because of Royce Sherry's foster father saw even more—that Sherry was a victim already . . . which made victimizing her again all the easier. For a while Sherry let him abuse her. That's classic, of course. The sexually abused girl believes she is loved only for her body. Her self-esteem thus demolished, she becomes promiscuous, perpetuating her own destruction in a desperate search for love.

"For Sherry, however, being touched was so horrific that she rebelled against the molestation. Her fear actually became empowering. Not only did she confront her foster father, she blackmailed him—two hundred dollars to buy her silence. Otherwise, she told him, she would report him to the police. I'm not certain if the man felt threatened, or merely titillated by the idea of paying Sherry for sex. Perhaps the latter, because when he gave her the money he called her 'his little whore.' Sherry used the money to do precisely what Royce had wanted her to do. She put on makeup, dressed provocatively, and went to the casino."

"And she won."

"And won and won and won. It was *so* easy, and she hated it *so* much. If only she had agreed to Royce's plan . . . In any event, within hours she'd made enough money to leave Las Vegas and to live on her own for a very long time. Before leaving Sherry reported her foster father to the police. She gave the officer two hundred dollars, to be returned to her abuser upon his arrest, and agreed to testify at his trial.

"Sherry moved to Los Angeles and found a basement apartment near UCLA. The landlord believed she was in college and eventually that was true. In fact, Sherry lived in that basement all the way through medical school. Anyway, that first summer, before enrolling at Santa Monica High, Sherry changed both her appearance and her name. She gained weight, a lot of it. Like promiscuity, eating disorders are classic sequelae of sexual abuse. I don't like the word *disorder*. It seems wrong for a behavior—be it eating or starving—that's really just a desperate attempt to impose order on chaos . . . to control, in some way, the massive emotional disarray. At the time Sherry had no insight into why she gained the weight. She knew only that she was compelled to eat. It's a primal instinct, I suppose, a survival strategy that exists beneath cognition. Sherry constructed for herself a thick coat of armor."

"She was rescuing herself." Again, Patrick amended. First from the flames, then from her foster father . . . then from all men. *But I would hold you so gently.*

"What? Oh, yes. I guess so." Amanda shrugged, a delicate gesture of thin shoulders and fragile bones. "It was necessary for Sherry to gain a great deal of weight to prevent the attention that came her way. She had inherited Brandy's height and shape and carriage, and even at thirty to forty pounds overweight she drew stares, *leers*.

"At her heaviest, a weight she maintained for almost thirteen years, Sherry weighed a hundred pounds more than she weighs now. She was truly an imposing presence, especially in high school. In addition to her weight, she towered over her classmates, both female and male. Sherry might have been a figure of contempt, of teasing and taunting, but she felt so safe in her armor, so fearless and confident that she was actually admired. Boys and girls alike flocked to her for advice. They decided that she was wise—and, I guess, Sherry's experience did impart a wisdom beyond her years. In retrospect the counsel she offered her teenaged peers *was* quite sage. She told them to be kind to others and to themselves . . . to love themselves."

"Good advice, timeless advice."

"Yes, and popular advice as well. Counseling the teenagers of Santa Monica High to give themselves a break—not to torment themselves for minor failures— made Sherry not only the school oracle but everybody's teddy bear. Everybody's friend."

"Did Sherry's classmates ever notice that she was their friend, but they weren't hers?"

"No," she said softly. "But that was *fine,* the way Sherry wanted it. She didn't want to tell anyone about herself."

"And she wasn't truly a teddy bear, was she? She didn't want to be cuddled."

"No. She didn't. And she wasn't. No one ever touched her, and she never touched them."

"But no one noticed."

"No one noticed."

High school was one thing. But Sherry was a doctor now.

"Sherry is a physician," Patrick said quietly. "Is touching a problem for her?"

"*Being* touched is the most difficult." After a moment, and presenting her patient's history with utmost accuracy, she clarified, "In fact, for Sherry, being touched is impossible. Touching, however, *choosing* to touch, is something she can do, *has* to do."

"Even touching men?"

"Yes . . . as long as she views them as patients. As long as she's their doctor, not Sherry."

"You said that she's a psychiatrist?"

"Yes, now she is. Psychiatry was the specialty she had

planned all along. But she took a brief detour into obstetrics. She couldn't resist. From the moment she delivered her first baby she was hooked. She still can't explain the attraction."

"She can't?" *Wasn't it obvious?* "Wasn't it a wish to have children of her own? To love them as she should have been loved?"

"That's the logical explanation. But that isn't it."

"You're sure?"

"Very. Sherry is relentlessly analytical. She wants to understand why she is who she is, and as fearful as she is of some things—so many things—she's positively fearless when it comes to examining herself. Still, her attraction to OB remains a mystery to her. A dangerous mystery at that."

"Dangerous?"

"Sherry sensed the risk from the start. She wanted to deliver babies so much, *too* much. It was a desperate desire, and one which ultimately proved quite harmful to her. She became obsessive about the babies she delivered, far too protective of them."

"Can you really be too protective of a newborn?"

"When that newborn isn't yours, yes. Absolutely."

"She wanted to take babies from mothers who wouldn't cherish them and cherish them herself." *It's not a crime, Amanda. It's a gentle, generous, loving wish.*

"No. Sherry doesn't want to be mother. She can't be."

"But she would be a wonderful mother."

"She *can't* be." She was a russet-haired Joan of Arc, standing before the searing flames, willing to die rather than recant her beliefs. "Her intention was to keep the babies only until loving homes could be found. Sherry never actually kidnapped an infant, of course. And you know why? Because it came to her one day: If Brandy had been her patient, she would have wanted to take Sherry away."

"Which would have been for the best."

"Would it? Who knows? Never once has Sherry wished for a mother other than Brandy. Never *once*. So what gave Sherry the right to make judgments about other mothers and other daughters?" Without so much as a pause, Amanda answered her own question. "Nothing gave her that right. *Nothing*."

"Which is why Sherry quit OB."

"Yes, because despite her insight she still felt obsessively protective of other women's infants. And there was something else, the mysterious—and dangerous—attraction itself. Sherry could not solve that mystery, but it gnawed at her, diminished her. Finally, to protect herself, Sherry had to quit, *had to*."

"And is she happy now? In psychiatry?" *Are you happy, Amanda?*

"Psychiatry is where Sherry belongs, helping others conquer their fears. She helps newborns, too, by sponsoring support groups for their parents. So yes, she is happy, content."

"Does she take her own advice? Does she love herself?"

The fragile shoulders, weighted yet brave, rose and fell. "She's proud of herself."

"As she should be." *I'm so very proud of her.* "You said she's considering taking another step?"

"Not really. Sherry knows she's gone as far as she can go. The fears are with her still. She confronts them constantly. She must. It's the only way she can keep them at bay."

"How does she confront them?"

"Oh. Well . . . she lies awake in the darkness and summons the monsters that terrified her as a girl. She feels the ancient panic, makes herself feel it, then forces calm."

"By counting?"

"No. She doesn't permit herself to count anymore. There are times when she wants to, when it's too painful to think, to feel, but she always blocks the impulse."

"Maybe she shouldn't block it. Maybe Sherry should take the advice she gave her high-school classmates and give herself a break. It sounds to me as if Sherry demands too much of herself, too much perfection."

Amanda hesitated, stunned. "She's hardly perfect, Patrick. I just told you she's in a constant battle with her fears, that she must make herself face the invisible monsters of darkness, and the beckoning temptation of heights, and the memories of fire—"

"Oh, Amanda."

She looked from the blaze to him, drawn by the emotion of his voice—and confused by it. Her glance was bewildered, and fleeting. In moments she returned to the flames . . . and the sentence he had interrupted.

"And, of course, she lost her hundred-pound cloak of armor. It was a health decision on two counts, physical and mental. She was a young woman massively overweight. And the studies were clear: Thin people live longer. By permitting herself to be overweight she was permitting Royce to be in control—and ultimately to kill her. She's slender now, and she looks so much like Brandy."

A reluctant showgirl, Patrick thought. But a determined one. She would not let Royce win, neither by forcing her to die, nor to hide. She had abandoned her luxuriant cloak of armor, an exposure of sheer courage, her stunning beauty fully revealed. Her only defenses now, against the leering assaults of men, were her high, high heels and the diamond wedding band she wore.

"Oh!" It was a soft cry of surprise, as if she was awakening from a trance . . . or as if, like a psychiatrist in the movies, she suddenly realized her patient's session was through. "It's stopped raining. I really should go. Smoky's been on his own for hours."

Smoky . . . a living creature Amanda could joyfully touch. Was the motherless baby a permanent fixture in Amanda's life—or like the babies she had longed to kidnap was she merely offering Smoky temporary shelter until she could find for him a better home?

There could be no better home, Patrick thought, recalling images of the kitten in Amanda's arms, snuggled against her purple dress, the billowy vestige of the time when she felt safe.

Smoky might be home alone on this stormy night. But Patrick had no doubt that the lights in Amanda's Palisades home were aglow, and there was warmth, and food, and the companionship of the TV. And there was that alarm system, recently installed. Should the bungalow catch fire in Amanda's absence, firefighters would be summoned and Smoky would be safe.

Once a little girl named Sherry had huddled in darkness, alone, afraid, counting. And now a smoke gray kitten lived with Sherry . . .

"What does Smoky do when he's on his own?"

A smile touched Amanda's face. "He sleeps, which is a euphemism for recharging his batteries. I think I can anticipate quite a bit of frolicking on my return. I've been away so long that his batteries will be fully charged."

Despite her own fatigue Amanda would play with Smoky, frolic with him, until he crashed. *And you wouldn't be a good mother, lovely Amanda? My precious Sherry?*

"I'll walk you to your car."

"Oh, Patrick, that's not necessary."

"But let me, Amanda. My batteries, too, are fully charged."

They walked to the doctors' parking lot, the living ghost, the dying angel. The sky wept no more, and the heavens glittered as if freshly washed, sweet and bright and crystal-clear.

Patrick wanted to hold her, to provide sanctuary within his gentle arms. But touching was difficult, she had told him; and being touched was impossible. Even a most gentle sanctuary would feel like a prison to her.

He held the car door instead. Before closing it, before tucking her in for the night, he asked, "Will you have dinner with me?"

She looked up, bewildered.

Her confusion might have been because of him—the delusional ghost who, just hours after receiving a marrow transplantation, was already speaking as if the future was his. But Patrick doubted that was the case.

Still, with an easy smile, he clarified, "A celebration dinner, Amanda. Sometime after the donor marrow officially engrafts." *Two weeks, Amanda, maybe three.* Or maybe never. "If it engrafts."

"It *will* engraft. I *know* it will. But Patrick . . ."

"I heard every word you said, Amanda," he said softly.

"Every word. And the question remains, Will you have a celebration dinner with me?"

You may have heard every word, Patrick. But you did not understand. I can't. We can't. There can never be a you and me, because there is no me. I'm a frothy creature, spun from my fears, as perishable as cotton candy.

"Amanda?"

The voice that replied sounded neither frothy nor fearful. And although Amanda knew it to be the voice of madness, as she heard it speak her entire being filled with joy.

"Yes," the voice promised. "I will celebrate with you."

TWENTY-THREE

WESTWOOD MEMORIAL HOSPITAL
FRIDAY, MAY THIRD

"*Y*our screenplay is wonderful," Caitlin told Jesse by phone, between surgeries, late Friday afternoon. "Medically, surgically, it's absolutely flawless."

"But?"

But I'm not *her*, the heroine of *Thief of Hearts*, the woman heart surgeon who's so strong, and soft, and delicate, and brave. "But nothing. It's magnificent."

"So there's no need for us to meet? Is that what you're saying, Caitlin?"

"Yes, and no. I'd like to go to dinner with you if you still—"

"Just say when," he interjected softly.

Caitlin had rehearsed the words she would speak if the invitation was still open, as Jesse had promised it would be. But the intimacy of his tone stalled her carefully practiced recitation.

When? Never, a wise voice counseled. You're *not* her.

Another voice, perhaps even wiser, urged her on. "I'm on call this weekend. So Monday?"

"Will you have slept?"

"Oh. Sure." *No*. Of course not. Even if, from the standpoint of damaged hearts, the weekend was the most quiet in memory, Caitlin's own heart would know no rest. Already every fluttering heartbeat sent the same reminder, the same promise, the same warning.

On Monday night you and Jesse Falconer will make love.

Make *love*? I'd like to spend some time, with you, in bed. That was what Jesse had said, *all* he had said, the promise, and the warning, of sex—no more . . . and no less.

"*P*atrick, it's Stephen. Are you awake?"

"At eight-thirty Monday morning, Stephen? I've been up for hours." Since dawn. He had been watching the sun rise over the City of Angels and listening to the myriad sounds that accompanied the golden aurora. Once a surgeon, always a surgeon. But Dr. Patrick Falconer was a different surgeon now, one who savored every precious moment . . . and one who might never operate again.

"Good. How are you feeling?"

Patrick hesitated. How was he feeling? Terrific. The enhanced senses that had been the gift of his impending death had turned their heightened awareness toward the hope of his impending life. And what those acute senses believed they felt was engraftment itself, the migration of the donor cells from his bloodstream to his bones.

Patrick believed he felt even more: emotion from those donor cells, *elation*, as if they cherished their new home in his marrow and wanted to nest there, to flourish there.

"I feel good, Stephen."

"Are you in the mood for a biopsy today?"

"So soon?"

"I've been looking at your most recent smear and I think I see retics. I *do* see retics. I've never seen engraftment happen this quickly, Patrick, but I honestly think it has."

So do I. It has. Already. For life. For love.

For her.

$\mathcal{H}$e was facing away, toward the fountain, where the dancing spray glittered like golden diamonds in the afternoon sun. Not that seeing his face would have been of any help. His image never appeared on the covers of his books. But he was standing at the appointed place at the appointed time.

"Mr. Slake?"

He turned from the gilded diamonds to her. "Dr. Prentice?"

"Yes. Amanda."

"And I'm Jesse."

"Hi."

"Hi." Jesse tilted his head. "I know you. At least, I've seen you before."

"You have? Then I was right. You *are* a psychiatrist."

"I'm flattered, Amanda. But I am definitely not a psychiatrist. The setting was medical, however—here, in the hospital, six years ago. Is that possible?"

"Yes," Amanda murmured. "It's possible. But you would have seen a far more substantial version."

"More substantial?"

More substantial. More confident. More *whole*. "Six years ago I was quite heavy."

She had been heavier, Jesse realized. But it was not her weight that had lingered in his memory. She had been on the obstetrics ward, speaking to a very pregnant mother-to-be. The woman had been pacing in the hallway outside L & D. Her anxious strides became a leisurely stroll when Amanda joined her, when Amanda imposed, with her mere presence, a serene and hopeful calm.

Jesse had assumed that the compassionate doctor was an obstetrician. But there were ample reasons for a psychiatrist to roam the halls of OB—not only the soothing of frayed nerves, but the grim task of consoling parents for whom the long-awaited birth ended in catastrophe not joy.

"It was you," Jesse said. "I'm sure of it. You were wearing a floor-length dress under your white coat. It was purple, I think, with tiny blue flowers—forget-me-nots, maybe? You wore your hair down, and it was long, almost to your waist. Does that sound right?"

"Yes," Amanda said—and suddenly, as if Jesse's words had transported her back to that time, she felt a surge of confidence, the kind of self-assurance she had possessed when protected by her plush cloak of armor.

It was extraordinary to feel such confidence, especially with this dark-haired stranger, this man who was so unrelentingly male, so alarmingly sexual. But who was not predatory, Amanda realized, at least not with her. He's involved with someone, she decided. Involved, in love. Or maybe he believes that *I'm* involved, in—

She had not seen Patrick in the ten days since that Drawing Room night. They were keeping separate vigils, waiting for his marrow to engraft. During the wary vigil

Amanda had been reading, *re*reading, the novels of Graydon Slake, his stories of women who touched without fright . . . and who could *be* touched without terror. Amanda found hope in his words and read them voraciously—as if by repetition, and by magic, such fearlessness might engraft into her very soul.

Now the sorcerer of hope was standing before a fountain of gilt-edged diamonds, and she felt so comfortable with him, so confident that . . .

"I have a confession to make."

"Oh?"

"Your screenplay is *perfect*. I wouldn't change a word. Arguably that's something I could have told you over the phone."

"But you didn't, because?"

"I wanted to meet you." *Needed* to meet you? "I'm a fan, you see."

"Well." Jesse smiled. "I'm a fan, too, ever since I saw you six years ago. So, Dr. Prentice, unless you have an office full of waiting patients why don't we go get coffee as planned?"

"*T*ake a look." As he spoke Stephen relinquished the chair in front of the microscope and gestured for Patrick to take his place. "Trust me, Patrick. It's worth it."

It was Patrick who had set up this monumental moment, with Stephen's blessing. As soon as the biopsy specimen was ready for review—having been meticulously sliced, mounted, and stained—the two would look at the slides together.

Now the moment was here, and even though the news

was clearly good, Patrick hesitated. There was something profound, and a little disturbing, about seeing one's tissue through the lens of a microscope . . . about viewing oneself as a collection of brightly colored cells.

Finally, reverently, Patrick gazed at the sublime work of art. It was a masterpiece without rival, an Impressionist painting that celebrated the astonishing marriage of strangers.

His bones, stained brilliant fuchsia, provided sanctuary for the pastel donations of pink and blue, and within the vibrant tableau Patrick saw proof of what had been singing in his veins. The stranger's cells were happy in their new home, healthy and thriving. Their nuclei signaled their intent to divide, to replicate, to raise their families within the fuchsia walls.

Stephen spoke into the lingering silence. "My son David was born three weeks ago, but I've already begun familiarizing myself with the words kids use these days. *Awesome* comes to mind."

"Yes," Patrick said quietly, gazing still at the multicolored passport to life, to love, to her. "Awesome."

Awesome danced in his mind as he strode to her office. His gait was light, buoyant, fueled with joy.

"Dr. Falconer!" Amanda's receptionist greeted with surprise. Marianne had never met Westwood's new trauma chief. But like everyone else she knew who he was. And, like everyone else, she knew about his aplasia, and the transplant he'd received ten days ago. Just in time, everyone said. He had been standing, quite literally, at death's door.

Now Dr. Patrick Falconer was standing at her door. He was pale and gaunt. But, Marianne thought, he is *not* dying. Just going a little crazy, perhaps, as he waited to learn his fate? Just needing a little of Dr. Prentice's serene advice?

"Did you want to see Dr. Prentice?"

"Yes. If possible. Is she in?"

"No. I'm sorry, she's not. In fact at the moment she's not even in the hospital."

"Oh?"

"She's doing something very Hollywood. She's having, *taking*, a script meeting with Graydon Slake."

*A*riel's was an easy three-block walk—unless, Jesse suggested, one happened to be wearing the highest of heels. But Amanda assured him that it was fine; that she was quite accustomed to walking long distances in high heels.

Besides, on this balmy springtime afternoon, Amanda was floating. Graydon Slake, who wrote with such authority about fearless women, gazed at her with respect, as if he believed her to be quite normal, quite whole.

Now, in a secluded booth at Prospero's Pantry, Amanda might have confessed what his writing meant to her. But she was not that bold, not yet. Instead, as they sat amid a garden of orchids and shared a pot of tea, Amanda told Jesse what else she liked about his books.

"You're not an apologist for the villain. You never try to explain—or worse, to justify—evil behavior based on some distant childhood horror."

Jesse's smile was wry. "It doesn't work to make villains sympathetic, Amanda. The reader doesn't want ambiguity when it comes to whom to root for."

"But it's more than that, isn't it? More than just a concession to commercialism? It's what you believe."

His expression became solemn. "Yes, Amanda, it is what I believe. I guess I feel that—at least as adults—we are responsible for the choices we make, no matter what might have happened when we were too young to choose. So, you're right. I'm not an apologist for my villains. I have no sympathy whatsoever for any of them. I wouldn't make a very good psychiatrist, would I?"

"I think you would. You understand the harm villains inflict on those they choose to hurt."

"Do you see the ones who've been hurt?"

"For the most part, yes."

"You must see women—and perhaps children?— who've been raped."

"Yes."

"Which means you're probably familiar with Gabrielle Fairfax."

"Certainly. But I'm a little surprised that you are. You're sure you're not a psychiatrist?"

"Positive. I'm just an author who keeps his fingers on the pulse of social consciousness. I read magazines and even watch the occasional talk show—which, along with congressional hearings, feature Ms. Fairfax from time to time." *Ms. Fairfax.* Gabrielle. And her impassioned recountings of the sexual brutality she had personally endured. Her vicious assailant had been caught—she reassured congressmen and television viewers alike— and punished. Still, out of respect for his family—who were victims, too—she declined to publicly reveal his name. "Do you think she rings true, Amanda?"

"Do you mean has she recovered too well from her own experience?"

"Yes." *That's exactly what I mean.* "She seems remarkably . . . unscathed."

"She does. *But* she wasn't actually raped, and she was in her late teens and sexually experienced when the assault occurred. Both of those circumstances could definitely attenuate the amount of trauma."

"So you do think she rings true."

Amanda shrugged. "I guess I think it doesn't matter. She's done immeasurable good, both by her willingness to talk about the issue and by the legislation that has resulted from her work."

There it was. Gabrielle St. John Fairfax, high-profile advocate of victims' rights, had helped legions of women and innocent girls. The harm Gabrielle had caused, the death of hope in one solitary man, was trivial, of no consequence at all.

Unless, of course, you happened to be that man.

TWENTY-FOUR

THE HEART INSTITUTE
MONDAY, MAY SIXTH

*C*aitlin glanced at her watch, glared at it. Three-thirty-two. A mere five minutes since last she checked. This first Monday in May was as memorable for its quietness as the weekend had been.

Caitlin's patients were stunningly stable. No new surgeries were scheduled until tomorrow. Today's mail had been virtually nonexistent. And even the advisory meeting for Air-Lift LA had been conspicuous for its absence of debate.

The world was quiet, holding its breath. In anticipation of her night of passion with Jesse?

Certainly not. In fact, just fifteen minutes ago, the real *and wondrous* reason for the breath-held calm had been revealed. The call had come from Stephen, the spectacular news that Jesse's cells had already engrafted in the bones of his twin.

The wondrous revelation had come and gone. But it had left in its wake a feeling of joy. The world was spinning anew, a euphoric merriment that had no impact whatsoever on the sluggish passage of time.

Three-thirty-*three*. Caitlin could go home. Right now. And do what? Spend a few hours getting ready for Jesse?

The phone trilled, a most welcome intrusion into her thoughts. Precisely eight minutes ago Caitlin's secretary, as bored as she, had proffered an unusual request to leave early. Of course, Caitlin had said. *Go.* So for the past eight minutes, in addition to being an idle surgeon, Caitlin had assumed the mantle of physician's secretary as well.

With relief and welcome, no matter who the caller was, Caitlin greeted, "Hello."

"Hello," the elegantly British voice replied. "Have I reached the office of Dr. Caitlin Taylor?"

"You've reached Dr. Taylor herself," Caitlin confirmed lightly, warmly. "Lillith? Is that you?"

"Yes. I didn't imagine that you'd be the one to answer."

"It's an unusual day. How *lovely* to hear from you. You sound nearby. Are you in LA?"

"I am. We are."

"Is everything all right?"

"Everything's *wonderful*, Caitlin. The entire Asquith clan is enjoying excellent health and high spirits. Robert and Timothy are positively ecstatic about the script for *Thief of Hearts*."

"As they should be. It's sensational. Have you read it?"

"Oh yes, and I absolutely agree. Well, I don't want to keep you. I was just wondering if we might get together sometime? Away from the hospital?"

Caitlin's heart ached as she remembered the last time Lillith had made such a request. "Oh, Lillith, everything *isn't* wonderful, is it? Is it the tumor? Has it recurred?"

"*No.* Everything is just fine. Truly, I'm in shamefully

good health. I just thought it would be nice for the two of us to meet in a leisurely setting, to sip tea, perhaps, while we chatted."

"That would be very nice," Caitlin agreed, worried despite the cheeriness of the elegant voice. If only Lillith had called earlier, and even now, if she happened to be at Robert and Faye's in nearby Holmby Hills . . . No, Caitlin decided. We should meet when we can talk all evening, if that's what Lillith needs. "Let's see, I'm looking at my calendar. There's always the proviso that at the last minute an emergency might come up."

"My dear, as Timmy's grandmother, Timmy's forever *grateful* grandmother, I appreciate your willingness to preempt personal plans for professional disasters."

"Well," Caitlin murmured, embarrassed—and frowning as she consulted the calendar on her desk. Starting tomorrow the surgeon would be working with a vengeance, the way she liked it best. Tomorrow was impossible. Booked solid. "How would five-thirty Wednesday be for you?"

"Lovely."

"Let's try for that, then. We could meet at Prospero's, the café at Ariel's."

"That sounds perfect."

"Oh, good. I'm looking forward to seeing you, Lillith."

"And I, you."

As soon as the conversation ended Caitlin jotted *Lillith, Prospero's* on her calendar. She had just begun to inscribe a reminder, to bring to work on Wednesday a dress suitable for high tea with an Asquith, when a shadow fell across her desk.

Caitlin looked up—to a vampire. It was an image that had been unwanted from the start, and Patrick Falconer as vampire was even less apt now. He was going to live, was living, the way human beings did—from blood replenished deep within, not drained from the necks of innocent prey.

So why did the vampire image come to her now? Because Patrick's ocean blue eyes blazed with fire—just as Michael's, fierce and haunted, had once seared her dreams.

"Patrick?"

"Jesse's the donor, isn't he?"

"Yes."

"How?"

"How did he know? I told him. How difficult was it to convince him? Not at all. He agreed in a heartbeat." Caitlin rose. "I know you view what I did as a betrayal, Patrick, and you have every right to do so. But I would do it again, *and again and again*, in the same situation. So sue me."

Surprise flickered amid the dark blue frames. But the fierceness remained. "You think I'm upset, Caitlin?"

"I . . . can't tell. You're *something*."

Yes, Patrick thought. Something. Everything. A gamut of emotions swirled within: elation that the cells had engrafted so swiftly; and torment that Amanda was with Jesse; and fury with himself for feeling such torment. Every ancient conflicted emotion about his twin had surfaced with a vengeance.

There was no conflict, however, when it came to Patrick's emotions about Caitlin. They were brilliantly clear, exquisitely pure.

"What I am, Caitlin, is deeply grateful."

"Oh," she whispered, relieved. "*Good*."

"How did you find him?"

"Through Timothy Asquith. He gave me directions to Jesse's home on Maui."

"And you went there?" Her shrug gave him his answer. "You are really amazing."

"No, Patrick, I'm not. Given a similar circumstance you would have done precisely the same thing."

Caitlin frowned at the presumptuousness of comparing herself to Patrick . . . a frown which Patrick interpreted accurately and at once.

"You really don't get it, do you, Caitlin?"

"Get what?"

"How incredible you are. How nice you are."

Nice. There it was, that bland—yet profound—little word, like sure and fine and hope and love. At this moment, embellished by his smile, *nice* far surpassed even *incredible*.

"Well," Caitlin murmured.

"Don't argue," Patrick commanded.

"Okay."

"Okay." After a moment that spanned years, a solemn and reverent reminder of their friendship, Patrick asked, "What did Jesse say?"

"He said yes," Caitlin reiterated. "*Yes*, Patrick. Just like that."

"And?"

"That he didn't want you to know he was the donor. I think he actually believed you might have refused the transplant if you knew. Is that true, Patrick? Would you have died rather than receive Jesse's help?"

"No, Caitlin. It's not true."

She hesitated, but only briefly. Emboldened by Patrick's words, by their bond, she suggested, "Maybe you should tell him that."

"Maybe I should. Do you know where he's staying?"

"At the Château. He's registered as Michael Lyons." Caitlin Taylor and Jesse Falconer were going to make love, *have sex*, tonight. But what was a little passion compared to the reunion of twins? Nothing. *Nothing*. "Do you think you might see him tonight?"

"No." Patrick's reply was quiet but emphatic. It was too soon. His emotions raged, conflicted and churning, and this was the night he would celebrate with Amanda—Amanda, who was with Jesse even now. The turbulent emotions surged anew, but his voice remained calm. "Definitely not tonight."

"*T*his is quite a place," Jesse said as he and Amanda lingered over tea amid the orchids. "Not just Prospero's Pantry, but the entire Ariel's experience."

"You've been here before?"

"Not to the café. I have, however, spent some time roaming the aisles." Restless roaming. Dangerous roaming. For days he had wandered the streets, pacing, worrying—and waiting: for news of Patrick . . . for Caitlin to call. Eventually he had strayed into Ariel's, and subsequently channeled the full force of his restlessness into a project that had been taunting him for over a year. Now, astonishingly, he was talking about that bewitching—and self-destructive—project, making it real, etching it in stone. "I was doing a little research."

"Research? For the next Graydon Slake thriller? Murder and mayhem at Ariel's?"

"Not exactly." He could still back out. He could shrug it off. But to the copper-haired psychiatrist who so obviously had tormenting secrets of her own, Jesse Falconer said, "Shall I show you, Amanda? Do you have time?"

"Yes. Show me."

Jesse led Amanda to a place she had known well— until to protect herself she had forbidden herself from venturing anywhere near.

The forbidden place was not a stories-high ledge, nor a room black as night, nor a fire ablaze with searing heat. Such locales were permissible, necessary, places she was required to visit to maintain her truce with the fears within.

The place in Ariel's was a venue of obsession, not of terror—of confusion, of conflict, of mysterious longing and aching joy: of bibs adorned with pink kittens, yellow roses, and roly-poly puppies in baby-boy blue; and meticulously calibrated shatterproof bottles; and hummingbird chimes; and barnyards, jungles, and oceans of stuffed animals.

Most agonizing were the tiny glass jars, rows and rows of them, neatly arranged by food group and infant age. Amanda had touched those little jars, *held* them, reading every word on their colorful labels and mentally preparing impeccably well-balanced meals.

For who? she would ask herself. The babies you will never have, should never have, *don't even want* because you believe so strongly it would be wrong?

As a psychiatrist Amanda had a great deal to offer—to grown-up human beings that is, creatures mature enough to learn to love themselves. She could not, however, impart that all-important gift to a child, to a *daughter*. She could not teach a precious little girl to touch, to love. And what if the infant was a son?

Amanda Prentice would never be a mother, *should not*

be. It was a life issue serenely settled. Still, the nameless ache consumed her whenever she came to this place, a longing that stole her breath and stilled her heart. And when the impostor—impossible—mother bore witness to the legitimate patrons of these shimmering aisles? Her longing became sheer pain.

"How about chicken?" an authentic mother would ask as she offered a tiny glass jar for her baby's inspection. The jar would receive an enthusiastic chubby-fingered pat, embellished with a gurgling smile. "That sounds good? Okay. Shall we try a *3*? You're getting so big, so grown-up. *Too* grown-up." Emotion would clog the mother's voice. But she would find cheer again, for her child. "How about some peas to go with the chicken? For balance? Would you like that? Yes, my little love, I thought so."

Amanda's pain was surpassed only by the piercing truth: she could plan meals, perfect ones for a newborn life . . . but never, *not ever*, could she provide the most essential nutrients of all—the ingredients that would enable confidence, fearlessness, the ability to love.

The baby section in Ariel's had always been vast, an appropriate symbol of its importance. Now, as Amanda and Jesse neared, she saw that even more space had been allocated to the store's youngest and most treasured clientele. The toy department had been significantly expanded, and there was a mini-bookstore, and the video library offered the best of Disney—and Gemstone.

An entire alcove was devoted to Graydon Slake's snowy lion. A pyramid of videos formed a massive white mountain, and myriad copies of the book papered the walls. The focal point, however, was a miniature savannah populated by an impressive pride of lions. They lounged imperiously, families of them.

Was this the research Jesse had been conducting? Making certain that his books—and subsidiary merchandise—were lavishly displayed?

Surely Graydon Slake had more than enough money and fame. And before this moment Amanda would have asserted that he cared about neither—an assertion which, she realized, would have been correct. Without so much as a glance Jesse strode past the families of felines toward the rows and rows of small glass jars.

Amanda's showgirl legs, the graceful limbs that drew lascivious stares, should have ventured no farther. This was close enough. Too close. But empowered by something she could not control, she followed him. And her eyes, blessed—and now cursed—with perfect vision, saw with excruciating clarity the changes that had occurred during her absence from this forbidden place.

The manufacture of baby food had undergone a major revolution. New companies had emerged, ones with names that promised the earth's natural bounty, and established companies offered a multitude of new, improved options. Every label emphasized nutrition, and all boasted politically correct constituents of salt and fat.

Amanda felt her hands becoming as willful, as defiant, as her legs. In another moment she would be touching the jars, caressing them, as she surveyed the ingredients that assured healthier, happier babies.

Other women's babies.

Amanda stilled her hands, clenched them, and her voice, too, was taut and clenched.

"Jesse? Why are we here?" Are you a psychiatrist after all? she wondered. A diabolical therapist who subscribes to a confrontational approach, a sinister brew of shock and pain? Have you brought me here as a harsh reminder not to dream of things I cannot have? Are you going to turn to me with a look that is both wise and cruel, a gaze that chastises me for the fantasy that I could heal myself by reading the fictional works of Graydon Slake?

No, Amanda realized, you are not.

Her Pied Piper of torment was not about to stage a psychiatric intervention amid the pride of lounging white lions and the tiny jars of low-salt pasta. Jesse was remote, staring at the jars as intently as she. He had not even heard her query, her whisper of despair.

We are twins, Amanda mused. For both of us this place that celebrates children evokes haunting pain and aching joy.

The tautness vanished from her voice as she shifted from her torment to his.

"Jesse? Why are we here?"

He heard her this time, turning from the glassy symbols of nutrition, of nurturing, to her. And he frowned, as if astonished that he was here, that *she* was here. "I'm writing a book."

"Another children's book?"

"Yes. You're familiar with *The Snow Lion*?"

"Of course. I recommend it to all the expecting parents I see. I want them to believe their babies are like the white lions of Timbavati—precious, fragile, endangered."

"Endangered?"

"Their hearts, their spirits, their souls." Her shrug was delicate, uncertain. "I'm using your lions as metaphors, Jesse. I hope you don't mind."

"Not at all," he assured quietly. "I believe it, too,

Amanda. I suppose I believe that we all are precious, and fragile—and endangered."

A companionable silence fell, one of private thoughts but shared peace. Both peace and silence ended when a nearby flock of cuckoo clocks began to chatter and cheep.

"I have to go! I have a group session beginning in twenty minutes."

"I'll walk you."

"Thank you, Jesse, but no. It's going to be a mad dash, not a leisurely stroll. This has been . . . I've really enjoyed meeting you."

"I've enjoyed it, too, Amanda. Very much."

"Thank you."

She should have left then, to begin her mad dash to the hospital. But she asked one final question, the title of his new children's book, the story for which he was conducting research in the baby-food section of Ariel's.

"Sweet Potatoes, Daddy."

Jesse's voice was soft, but the words thundered. The words . . . the answer, the *answer*, to the tormenting mystery that had eluded her so; her compulsion to practice OB, and why those years had blended such anguish with such joy.

She wanted babies, after all. Babies—and so much more.

Sweet Potatoes, Daddy.

Daddy.

There it was, the key to the mystery, the answer to the longing, the reason for the ache. She wanted to be a mother, but with one all-important proviso. Her babies would have a daddy.

Her babies would be gifts, and treasures, of love.

Sherry wanted it all. The whole magnificent package. Sherry, who was not whole. Sherry, for whom touching was difficult and being touched was impossible.

The epiphany came in a flood of comprehension and pain, and by ancient reflex she started to count. Amanda permitted the counting only until she managed her hasty farewell to Jesse—then banished the twinkling brilliance.

Amanda's return journey to the hospital wasn't a mad dash, merely a dash of madness. The high heels on which she had glided toward Ariel's became precarious spikes as she ran away. She tripped, she stumbled, beneath the blazing sun.

Amanda knew what impeded her journey. The sizzling pavement was littered with the shattered shards of a glittering dream. *Her* dream. Her fantasy of babies, of motherhood, of love.

Amanda never looked at the scattered shards beneath her feet; could not bear to see the splintered remnants of her impossible hope. She staggered, but her gaze remained straight ahead—and as she neared the hospital, the fountain came into view.

Its gilded diamonds danced no more. Instead they spilled, sodden and tarnished, like rusted tears.

"*O*h, good, you're back, and with two minutes to spare. You need to . . ." Marianne frowned. "Amanda, is something wrong? You look upset."

"I'm fine, just rushed."

"Well, I know you don't like being late, but I'm afraid you'll have to be. Dr. Falconer wants to speak with you."

"Dr. Falconer?"

"He's in his office waiting for your call. The number's on your desk. In the meantime I'll tell the folks on Seven West you'll be down shortly."

Patrick wouldn't be calling about his engraftment. It was far too soon. So why?

Amanda's fingers rested, trembling, on the telephone as she gazed outside. She saw quite clearly the pavement along which she'd stumbled. The ribbon of sidewalk was gray not glittering, as if swept clean of its scattered shards.

But the shards, perhaps, had never glittered. Like a brilliant diamond violently shattered, the splintered remnants would sparkle no more. The shards lay on the pavement, cloudy and gray, and the dancing fountain still wept rust.

Amanda dialed with fingers that no longer quivered.

Patrick answered on the first ring.

"Amanda?"

"Yes. Hi."

"Hi." Patrick's relief that she had returned was instantly replaced with new worries. Her voice was flat, empty, as barren as his marrow had been before Jesse. *Jesse*. "How was your meeting with Graydon Slake?"

"Oh. It was . . ." *monumental*. We touched on rape, and endangered hearts, and a book called *Sweet Potatoes, Daddy*. Mysteries were solved, the secrets of Sherry, her delusions of grandeur . . . and of love.

"Amanda? Did something happen?"

"What? Oh, no. How are *you*?"

"I'm fine. In fact I'd like to invite you to a celebration dinner."

"Oh, Patrick," she whispered. "A celebration? So soon?"

"So soon. Are you free tonight? I know it's last-minute."

Free? No, I'm not free, not ever. "I . . . tonight isn't good."

"Okay." His voice was calm even as his heart thundered. "Another time, then. But may I call you at home later this evening?"

"Is something wrong, Patrick?"

Yes, Amanda, something's terribly wrong—with you. "There are just some things I'd like to tell you about Graydon Slake."

"Graydon Slake?"

"He's my brother, Amanda. My twin. The donor of my new marrow. We've been estranged for decades. I'd like to—I need to—tell you why."

TWENTY-FIVE

*C*aitlin wore the pearls and a sequined cocktail dress, a shimmering frock that would have been worn aboard the *QE2* had she not decided to abandon ship. Her hair was swept up, sophisticated and sleek, but she had been tempted to give every strand its unbound freedom, as she had on that stormy night while reading *Come in from the Rain*.

Jesse had come in from the rain that night, and he had touched her, so that he might see her eyes, parting the hopelessly tangled veil that curtained her face.

Jesse Falconer is going to touch you tonight, no matter how you style your hair. He's going to touch all of you.

He wants to.

You want him to.

But will he be terribly disappointed? Will he discover a creature of ice, a womanly shape carved by the sharpest of scalpels?

No. Caitlin touched the pearls that symbolized her inheritance from Maggie and Michael, a legacy of passion and of love.

Who said *anything* about love? Not Graydon Slake, not once, in any of his novels. And Jesse Falconer had made his intentions eloquently clear: *I would like to spend some time, with you, in bed.* The proposal had been made as casually as one might suggest a game of tennis. Sex was, undoubtedly, sport for Jesse, a pleasurable exercise that kept his sensual body lean and fit.

Tonight was about chemistry, not love. Chemistry, a subject in which Caitlin Taylor had always gotten A's. This particular type of chemistry, however, had eluded the standard scientific texts.

But it was quite real. Both she and Jesse felt it, acknowledged it, and tonight they would journey to the chemistry lab to conduct elaborate experiments, all manner of scientific inquiry into the elemental properties of passion.

This was all very modern, deciding in advance to have sex, thinking about it, being certain. In this contemporary world, after all, the consequences of reckless passion could be spectacularly—and irrevocably—grim.

Leave nothing to impulse, the experts advised. Be fully prepared, wholly informed.

Caitlin might not be prepared, not really, not emotionally. But with regard to the relevant medical issues she was fully informed.

Indeed—how modern could one get?—Caitlin Taylor, heart surgeon, had actually drawn her lover's blood. The blood tests that were recommended in anticipation of sexual intimacy were also a routine part of the marrow-donor screen. And why not? What greater intimacy could there be than the nestling of one's cells within the marrow of another human's bones?

Jesse had passed all the tests with flying colors, and

tonight Caitlin and Jesse were going to spend some time together in bed. The chemistry was there. The blood tests were clean. They were both consenting adults.

It was all so modern, so sophisticated, so grown-up.

But I'm in love with him. Caitlin's fingers curled around the costume pearls that were the symbol of Maggie's love, the lacquered beads strung anew by Jesse.

Faux gems—but true love—for both mother and daughter.

Oh, Mother, it's happened, as you knew it would. I am your daughter, truly. And for me, as it was for you, it's an impossible love. Your Michael was committed elsewhere—as is Jesse. He has other women, perhaps, of course, and he is most definitely bound to his endangered lion.

But most of all, Caitlin thought, Jesse Falconer is wedded to his solitude, his privacy, his loneliness.

Caitlin frowned as *loneliness* did its somber dance in her mind. Loneliness was the wrong word, surely, for Jesse. Aloneness, she amended silently. Aloneness not loneliness.

I'm the one who's lonely.

And after this night, with Jesse, she might be even lonelier.

Then so be it. I will live this night of passion, of love, and I will treasure the memories as Maggie treasured forever her memories of Michael.

Jesse had promised candlelight. It seemed a surprising concession to romance—unless, that is, one was familiar with the works of Graydon Slake. His heroes enjoyed elaborate preludes to passion, provocative seductions that invariably took place in the most elegant locales.

But seduction was not necessary tonight. Caitlin was

already seduced, and Jesse knew it. By accepting his invitation to dinner, she had implicitly agreed to the rest, to *bed*, with him.

The promise of candlelight could be amply honored without elegance. Any of the city's many pizzerias would do, providing waxen balls encased in blood-red glass and enmeshed with white plastic webbing . . .

At six-fifty-five, and with the same precipitous decisiveness with which she had determined to abandon ship, Caitlin decided to abandon both her glittering sequins and her swept-up hair.

She would change into something more casual, less romantic, less hopeful—a freshly laundered pair of scrubs perhaps, or as a compromise a scrub dress. The casual look was safer on all counts . . . especially if Jesse left, alone, within moments after he arrived—once she told him what she must.

Her black-silk crown yielded to a single yank, an utter decimation of sophistication that coincided precisely with the doorbell's melodious chime.

He was early.

It was too late.

"Hello, Caitlin," he greeted softly.

"Hi."

"You look sensational."

"Oh! Thank you." *So do you.* He was dressed elegantly, in charcoal hues of shadow and stone. His green eyes glittered with their deep, dark fire, and his midnight black hair, ruffled slightly by the wind, framed in lustrous sensuality the planes and angles of his face. Suddenly remembering the chaotic spill from her demolished crown Caitlin murmured, "I was just . . . rethinking . . . my hair."

"It looks great."

"Well. Anyway, come in."

It was there, the magnificent chemistry. Caitlin felt it the moment she opened the door, and it was powerful still, ever more demanding, as she led him to her living room.

We are separate glass beakers, Jesse and I, and we are filled with a magical potion that exists only in this heated air, and tonight, oh how I want this night—but . . .

Jesse saw her apprehension, felt it like a blow. The wariness had not been there when she opened the door. Then there had been only wonder, only desire, only joy; and it was only Jesse's immense will, his solemn vow not to overwhelm her, that prevented him from touching her, holding her, kissing the night black smudges beneath her eyes as he tangled further her silken cloud of hair.

But suddenly, everything had changed—as if Caitlin had misgivings despite the attraction she felt . . . as if she sensed his darkness, the twilight shadows that compelled his parents to despise him and made even Patrick believe him capable of the most heinous of crimes. Maybe Caitlin knew of those crimes. Maybe sometime during this past weekend she had persuaded Patrick to tell her the truth about him.

This past weekend. For Jesse it had been an eternity, an infinite voyage across an endless desert. He had clawed his way along the burning sand, dying of thirst, dying of life, yet believing in the oasis of her.

An oasis which, apparently, was merely a mirage.

His voice was parched from his futile journey across the arid wasteland. "What is it, Caitlin?"

"It's Patrick."

He told you about me, and you believed him. Every word. Every crime. "What, Caitlin?"

His voice was savage, raw. She trembled at its fierceness. But she had no choice. "Patrick knows you're the donor. I'm *sorry*."

Once before, in paradise, Caitlin had apologized to him. She had expected fury then, rage that she had compelled him to shield her from the massive jaws of a snow-white lion.

And Caitlin expected fury now.

But now as then, she was surprised.

Jesse greeted her confession with what looked almost like relief, followed by his wry, sexy, devastating smile.

"It doesn't matter. Not anymore. It's too late."

"Too late?"

"He can't really undo it now, can he? According to Stephen my cells are already engrafting in his bones."

"Patrick doesn't *want* to undo it, Jesse. And if you believe Patrick would have refused the transplant had he known you're *wrong*."

"I'm not so sure about that, Caitlin."

"Well, *I* am. Patrick is *grateful*. In fact he wants to talk to you, to *tell* you."

"Oh?"

Everything about Jesse Falconer was calm. But Caitlin sensed the raging restlessness deep within.

"Yes, he does. He said it wouldn't be tonight. But . . . you could always find him."

"I have plans for tonight, Caitlin." Jesse's tone was dangerously soft, impossibly intimate; but Caitlin felt his fierceness still, his impatient desire *for her*. "Remember?"

"Yes," she breathed, barely. "I remember."

Jesse touched her then, her neck, her pearls, a caress that made her tremble—with desire, not with fear. The fear on this night belonged to Jesse.

He dreaded the day when he would be compelled to leave her, when the peril—for her—became too great. And if that impossible day never came, another day—so perilous for him—would take its place—the day when he told Caitlin of the crimes for which he had been punished.

Trust me. Believe in me. Love—

"Are you hungry, Caitlin? For dinner? Or are you ravenous, like I am, for you?"

"Ravenous," she whispered. "Ravenous."

It could have begun then, the touching, the loving. But Jesse saw shadows of worry. "Caitlin?"

His powerful hands rested beneath her jaw, curled with deceptive gentleness around her neck; hands that could crush, or caress. Lion . . . and shepherd.

Jesse's glittering green eyes sent a dual promise as well: to devour and to protect.

"Ravenous," she whispered again. "And daunted."

"Daunted? By . . . ?"

"You. Your experience. Your expectations."

"Well," Jesse answered softly. "I'm daunted, too. By you."

"Jesse, I'm serious. I . . ." Her words were stopped by the kiss of his thumb as it grazed with exquisite delicacy across her lips.

"So am I." Jesse waited until her sea blue eyes shimmered with comprehension—and wonder. "The only experience that matters, Caitlin, is what we experience together. Nothing else exists and never has. And as for expectations, the only way I could be disappointed is if you told me to leave right now."

"I'm not going to tell you that."

Jesse Falconer smiled. "No?"

"No."

*I*n the novels of Graydon Slake the hero and heroine spoke explicitly about sex. Their words were never dirty, never vulgar. Yet they were shocking somehow, enthralling, stirring . . . and very modern.

In the love, the loving, of Caitlin and Jesse, there were no explicit words, no modern queries, no sexy, savvy repartée. There were only names, his and hers, spoken in whispers and carried on sighs.

It was a love scene, not a sex scene, and it existed nowhere but here, on this night. It had not been written before, or lived before, or even imagined before.

Not by him.

Not by her.

Neither could have imagined such tenderness, such desire, such need.

"Jesse," she whispered. "Jesse?"

The query was soft, and ancient not modern, a woman wondering if her lover was feeling the enchantment, the astonishment, the joy.

"Caitlin," he replied, feeling it all, feeling it, too, marveling as she was marveling. Then suddenly needing closeness, needing oneness, with her, with *her*, Jesse whispered, "*Caitlin*."

"*B*ut you don't *remember* that day at Graydon's Lake."

Amanda spoke for the first time since the story of the Falconer twins had begun. She wasn't interrupting even now. The saga had ended, in Jesse's cell in Montclair, just hours before he was sent to prison; and there had been silence at the other end of the phone.

"No," Patrick replied. "I don't remember. But Jesse *admitted* it to me. That day in jail he confessed to both crimes."

"But . . ."

"But?"

But, Amanda thought, if Jesse is a rapist, if he harbors such contempt for women, I would have sensed that seething cruelty . . . wouldn't I?

For as many years as the Falconer brothers had been estranged, Amanda, too, had known estrangement. For Patrick and Jesse the severed bond had been the mysterious tie that binds all twins. For Amanda the disrupted bond was equally mystical, and magical: the wondrous, vital link between women and men.

Amanda knew that all men weren't Royce. But she had been estranged nonetheless, wary of them all, especially ones who were interested in her. Until Patrick.

He had enabled her to see goodness . . . and it was goodness that Amanda had seen, with Jesse, at Ariel's.

"But," she answered finally, "I felt safe with Jesse. *Safe.*"

Just as I always felt with Jesse, Patrick mused. Safe, protected, loved. Safe long ago, as boys . . . and safe now, *saved* now, with Jesse's cells nestling in my bones.

TWENTY-SIX

*T*hey were going to love each other all night. *Love* each other.

Neither would sleep. Neither would want to.

And nothing and no one would intrude.

Caitlin was not on call. And in the unlikely event that one of her very stable patients needed care Dr. Frank Farrell would capably intervene.

Their loving would not be disrupted by professional catastrophes, nor would personal ones interfere. Jesse's twin was doing well. And that twin, Jesse's blood brother and Caitlin's surrogate one, was all the family that either one of them had. No middle-of-the-night call would inform Caitlin of a beloved mother whose heart had burst. That tragedy had long since happened; and Caitlin's father, Maggie's Michael, was a mystery never to be solved.

The pager beeped insistently, with a pace and pitch identical to her own. But Caitlin's pager was on the nightstand, and this staccato signal came from across the room.

"It's mine."

Jesse rose from the bed as he spoke, and crossed the room in swift, graceful strides. The paging device was in a pocket of his charcoal gray slacks, the elegant trousers that had been tossed aside in their haste. Even as he retrieved it, Jesse began dressing, as a surgeon dressed, knowing from years of experience that a late-night page meant he was needed elsewhere, urgently.

Caitlin's bedroom was illuminated from without, from streetlamps floors below, luminous shafts of light that had bathed their loving in ebony and gold.

Jesse was a shadow within a shadow until he activated the pager's lighted display. Caitlin saw his worry, an eerie glow in the faint light, as strikingly pale and stark as snow.

Snow. Had there been an assault on his clifftop fortress, the sounding of alarms in paradise, the glare of lights brighter than the tropical sun? If so, perhaps a small army had been summoned, a force assigned to defend the endangered creature when Jesse wasn't there. And now an officer in that army was calling to notify Jesse of the outcome—their arrival in time to thwart the slaughter . . . or their finding, too late, of a bloodied carcass stripped of snow-white fleece.

"Jesse? Has something happened to the lion?"

"No. Phone, Caitlin?"

"Here. On the nightstand."

As Jesse walked toward the phone, toward her, Caitlin reached for her robe. She would disappear into the living room, to give him privacy for his call.

But before she could rise, Jesse's hand was at the nape of her neck, stopping her, stilling her, telling her in that silent yet eloquent gesture what he had been showing her for hours.

I need you, Caitlin.

Amid shadows limned in gold Caitlin learned a little about the real reason Jesse Falconer was available twenty-four hours a day.

The number Jesse dialed was local, seven digits, and it was answered by a man named Daniel. Jesse seemed surprised to be speaking to Daniel, as if expecting someone else, and he spoke with taut formality and crescendoing concern.

Finally he issued a command. "Let me talk to her."

When Jesse spoke again, his voice was transformed, gentle, soft, calm—despite the tension Caitlin knew he felt. She had seen the tension during his conversation with Daniel. Jesse had paced, a caged animal, a restless roaming that moved his lean silhouette from shadow to light, from concealing ebony to illuminating gold.

Now, speaking with exquisite gentleness, Jesse was absolutely still and wholly shadowed.

"Hello, Risa. Yes, sweetheart, it's really me. And guess what? I'm in LA. In fact, I'm just across the street from the hospital. Can you tell me what's wrong, honey? Why you're so afraid? No, sweetheart, it's better if *you* come *here*, to the hospital—to me. We'll talk when you get here, okay? Just the two of us. I promise. Okay, Risa? Good. I'll see you *very* soon. Now, sweetheart, let me talk to Daddy again."

When Daddy, who was Daniel, returned to the phone, Caitlin heard dark fury.

"Why the hell do you *think* she's so afraid, Daniel? She can't *breathe*. You need to come now, Daniel. *Now*."

The conversation ended just seconds after that command. And now, from the gold-tipped shadows came another command, low and fierce.

"Come with me, Caitlin. Come with me."

$\mathcal{R}$isa. It was the enchanting name of the little girl who had been in such jeopardy in Graydon Slake's *Come in from the Rain*. The novel had been published years ago—which meant that if the character had been named for someone Jesse had known then, had loved then, she would be a teenager by now. But the Risa to whom Jesse had been speaking seemed younger than that, a little girl herself.

At least that was Caitlin's guess.

It could be only a guess, for the man who knew the answer to the mystery of Risa was silent during the short walk from her apartment to WMH. And although the emergency entrance was well marked, Jesse followed Caitlin's lead, as if he wasn't seeing the signs . . . as if all that Jesse Falconer was seeing, all that he could see, was a little girl named Risa who could not breathe.

Am I leading him to tragedy? Caitlin wondered as they entered the emergency room.

The hospital was her domain, the venue—until tonight—of Caitlin Taylor's greatest passion . . . a place where, despite the most heroic efforts, not everyone, not every little girl, could be saved.

But everyone would try to save Jesse's Risa. And, Caitlin realized with relief, some of those heroic efforts would be provided by the best ER nurse Caitlin had ever known.

"Trish?"

Trish looked up from her task, the inventory of narcotics in the locked cabinet beside the EKG machines. The careful record-keeping of narcotics on hand had to be done every shift. But the fact that Trish was attending to the semi-elective paperwork now meant that the ER as a whole was quiet.

"Oh, Caitlin, hi. Do you have a patient coming in?"

"No. Actually I'm here because . . . you're expecting a girl named Risa?'"

"Frank's patient? The pediatric heart?"

Caitlin had been imagining a child with asthma, or some other acute respiratory event. She had not considered the possibility that Risa's heart was damaged. Perhaps she hadn't wanted to. A little girl whose heart was so distressed that she could scarcely breathe was a little girl who was deathly ill.

But, Caitlin realized, she should have known. Jesse had questioned her about Frank, an out-of-the-blue question asked with his famous nonchalance and under the guise of research. But Jesse's query had not been casual at all. He had been researching Risa's doctor, Risa's *heart surgeon.*

"Yes," Caitlin murmured. "Frank's patient."

"We're expecting her to go right to the Cardiac ICU. Frank is with her, as is Marty Gantz." Trish paused a beat before explaining why both the pediatric heart surgeon and pediatric cardiologist happened to be accompanying their patient to the hospital. "Frank is very close to the family, a neighbor as well as a friend, and both he and Marty have been following Risa since birth. She has a septal defect, and . . . do you already know this, Caitlin?"

"No." *I know nothing, except that Risa means everything to Jesse.* "Please tell me whatever you know."

"Well, what I know I learned about an hour ago, when Marty stopped by to pick up some meds en route to the house in Bel Air. Anyway, I suppose Risa is five or six—"

"Six." The word came softly, hoarsely, a low sound from a caged animal.

Trish looked up at the gorgeous, tormented man who stood behind Caitlin. When it became obvious that introductions would not be forthcoming, she repeated quietly, "Six. She'd been fine, healthy. The plan was to repair the defect, electively, sometime in June. Risa knew about the surgery, and seemed unfazed by it until a week ago— when she announced, with no warning whatsoever, that she wasn't going to have the operation after all. Ever. No one was terribly concerned, because Risa was well. The surgery could easily be postponed for a few months, until she was comfortable with the prospect once again. But something happened yesterday, something dramatic, although they don't know what. Risa's so terrified of coming to the hospital that no studies have been done. According to Marty, though, it's as if the defect has suddenly become larger."

"So she went into failure."

"Yes. For the past twenty-four hours, she's refused meds, insisting that she's fine. But tonight she's gone into pulmonary edema, which needs to be treated, at least controlled, until Frank can get her to the OR. I guess that's the plan, now—at last. The ambulance dispatcher just called to say they're on their way."

Trish frowned, debating what more to say in front of Caitlin's shadow . . . whoever he was . . . then decided in favor of the truth. It would be revealed soon enough, when the ambulance arrived.

"She's on oxygen, and they have a line, but I'm not

sure, the dispatcher didn't say, whether she's less afraid about coming in or . . ." *whether she no longer has a choice.*

"She's less afraid," Caitlin said. Less afraid—because of Jesse. Risa's doctors couldn't calm her fear, nor could Daniel. But Jesse could. Jesse . . . Risa's real father? Was that why there had been such strangled emotion when Jesse referred to Daniel as Daddy?

A sudden shrillness pierced her thoughts, the screech of sirens nearby.

The strident sound prompted an efficient reply within the emergency room. An assembly of nurses congregated at the main entrance, prepared to escort the new arrival into Room One, in the event that she was too precarious to go directly to the Cardiac ICU. The ER admitting clerk hovered near the telephone, poised to call the unit once the verdict was known. And an orderly raced to the bank of elevators, to hold one so that the young patient, if sufficiently stable, could be whisked to the eighth-floor ICU without delay.

Please, please, please, Caitlin prayed in those endless seconds as the ambulance attendants opened the van's rear door and prepared to unload their precious cargo. They were moving quickly, a signal at least that their small patient was still alive—

—and conscious, Caitlin realized with relief as the wheels of the collapsible gurney touched the pavement and Risa—and her two doctors—emerged.

The little girl was in a fight for her life. She sat upright. It was the only way she could breathe. She was breathing—barely, frantically, gasping breaths that required every ounce of energy she possessed and every muscle of her delicate neck and slender chest.

Her blond hair was damp, plastered to her small face, and her eyes above the misting oxygen mask were closed in desperate concentration.

"We're going right up," Frank announced to no one in particular and everyone at once. His concentration was as intense as Risa's and intent *on* Risa. "Could someone call the CICU?"

"We're already calling."

The gurney wheeled into and through the ER, a rapid journey during which neither Frank nor Marty even noticed that Caitlin was there.

Jesse followed the gurney, followed Risa, and Caitlin followed him, catching his powerful hand just before they reached the elevator, preventing him from getting in.

Jesse's face did not register surprise. There was no room for such an inconsequential emotion.

"We'll take the next elevator," Caitlin explained. "It's best to let them get her up and settled."

"We'll take the stairs."

No. Caitlin's thought came decisively. Jesse Falconer's reticulocyte count was not as robust as it should have been, not nearly as robust in fact as Patrick's. Caitlin had learned that hematologic tidbit this afternoon, during the monumental phone call in which Stephen told her that Jesse's cells were engrafting in Patrick's marrow—already. Indeed, Stephen had remarked, Jesse's cells seemed happier in Patrick than in Jesse.

Jesse's hematocrit, checked this morning, was still quite low; lower than Stephen would have anticipated at this point following his donations of marrow and blood. Stephen was not particularly concerned. Jesse *did* have reticulocytes. His hematocrit *was* coming back, just slowly.

Soon the twin brothers would have twin hematocrits. Patrick's was twenty-six and climbing swiftly, and Jesse's was too low for him to climb, swiftly, eight flights of stairs.

Or did he *want* to become as breathless as Risa? Perhaps. Or perhaps Jesse Falconer would not become breathless at all. There had been nothing in his fierce yet tender loving to suggest compromise of any kind.

Caitlin did not offer, aloud, her opposition to climbing the stairs. Such objection was preempted—and eclipsed— by the simultaneous arrival of another elevator . . . and Risa's parents.

The four of them rode up together and remained together—a reluctant, wary grouping—as Caitlin led the way to the Heart Institute's CICU. Somehow during those tense minutes of transit introductions were made, or at least happened.

The handsome, taciturn man was Daniel. Daddy. No one could doubt Daniel's love for the gravely ill little girl. But something else shadowed Daniel's worried face, something just for Jesse, an intense look of unmistakable disdain.

The beautiful woman at Daniel's side was Stephanie— Mommy—and Jesse's onetime lover? The woman he had loved and lost, along with Risa, when Stephanie chose Daniel over him? Of course she was. Quite obviously it was Stephanie, not Daniel, to whom Jesse had expected to speak when he answered the page. And Stephanie looked at Jesse precisely as an ex-lover might, with apology for the hurt she had caused.

"They can treat this," Caitlin said to all three parents as they stood outside Risa's room.

Despite the crystal-clear glass, Risa was scarcely visible behind the wall of health-care professionals surrounding her. Frank and Marty were at her bedside, as were two ICU nurses, a lab tech, and the respiratory therapist—who, from his expression, clearly believed it was time, past time, for anesthesia to intubate.

"They can make her much better," Caitlin reiterated despite her concern. *They are not going to have to intubate. Risa's breathing will respond to the meds, and she'll be able to speak to Jesse, to explain why she is so afraid.* Caitlin saw only Jesse's profile, a portrait of pain, as he strained to see beyond the wall of white coats to his beloved little girl. "You won't be able to talk to her until then, Jesse. It shouldn't be terribly long."

"She needs to know that I'm here."

It was a quiet, desperate assertion made to Caitlin but spoken to the glass.

"Okay," she said.

Jesse turned to her, reluctant to relinquish his vigil and yet needing to—needing *her*. And when he spoke, it was an entreaty, not a command. "Now, Caitlin?"

Caitlin smiled. "Yes. Right now."

With that Caitlin entered Risa's room.

"Hello, Frank," she greeted quietly.

"Caitlin. What are you doing here?"

"I'm with Jesse."

Frank frowned. "Jesse? You know him, Caitlin?"

"Yes."

"Well?"

"Very well." *No, not at all. But I'm in love with him.*

Caitlin did not know what lay in the deep, dark shadows of the man she loved. Frank Farrell, it seemed, had more insight than she. Usually unwaveringly nonjudgmental Frank clearly knew—and believed—something unfavorable about Jesse. Well, Caitlin supposed, that made perfect sense. Frank was Daniel's friend, Daniel's neighbor, and hence Jesse's enemy?

Unwavering herself, Caitlin said, "Jesse wants Risa to know that he's here, as he promised he would be, and that they will talk as soon as her breathing is improved."

"Okay." Frank did not articulate what he and Caitlin both could see, that Risa's breathing was not improving, not yet.

"Would you tell her now, Frank? I want to get Jesse away from the window. He shouldn't be watching this."

"Neither should Dan and Steph," Frank murmured, looking beyond Caitlin to his friends. "All right. I'll give Risa Jesse's message, and while you find a place for Jesse I'll escort Dan and Stephanie to the quiet room."

"Good," Caitlin agreed, realizing that Frank already knew what she had just recently learned: that the three parents did not do well together and should not—especially on this night—be compelled to share the same space.

"Oh, and Caitlin, when Jesse talks to Risa he needs to convince her to have surgery. You know that. And I know that. But will you make sure that he knows it, too?"

"I'll make sure. I think I'll take Jesse to the Drawing Room, Frank. Will you let us know the minute he can see her? Or if . . ."

"Absolutely." Frank smiled, imparting a confidence that neither of them felt.

Then he moved to Risa.

Caitlin could not hear Frank's words. But she saw the reaction to them on the small, lovely face. Risa's eyes opened—an expense of energy she could ill afford, yet had to make, in case Jesse was right there.

Her eyelids fluttered closed as Frank finished his message, but in that fluttering moment Caitlin had seen the truth. Risa's eyes were green like Jesse's, and despite their dark cloud of distress, they glimmered at the news that her father was near.

Caitlin wondered if she would be able to convince Risa's father to leave the ICU, to abandon his frantic vigil, to journey to the sanctuary that was only a few steps away.

I will convince him. I have to.

Caitlin could not, would not, permit Jesse to witness the scenarios that might unfold if the medications did not work: the laryngoscope's steel blade invading Risa's mouth . . . the further intrusion of plastic tubing into her throat . . . and the most gruesome, impossible spectacle of all—a team of doctors and nurses pumping with measured but urgent pressure on Risa's young and dying chest.

TWENTY-SEVEN

DRAWING ROOM
HEART INSTITUTE
ELEVEN-THIRTY P.M.
MONDAY, MAY SIXTH

"*W*ill you tell me about her, Jesse? Will you tell me about Risa?"

They were in the Drawing Room. She had managed that. And now, in this place illuminated only by the lights of the city, Caitlin was asking Jesse to talk about the little girl he loved so much.

Jesse answered her query with a frown.

"You don't have to tell me, Jesse, but . . ."

"I'm just trying to decide where to begin," the master storyteller murmured, as if he were truly uncertain.

"The beginning?"

"The beginning," Jesse echoed, drew a breath, and began. "Risa's mother and I met as college freshmen. We were alike in many ways, both estranged from our families, both unhappy about that estrangement. In fact, that spring we made a pact. We would spend the summer trying to reconcile with our respective relatives, and by the time we returned in fall all would be right."

"But that didn't happen," Caitlin offered as she recalled one of the few facts she knew about Jesse. The summer following his freshman year would probably have been his nineteenth—the summer of Gabrielle St. John, the beautiful woman who was the coup de grâce for the already alienated Falconer twins.

"No, it didn't happen. Not for either of us."

"Which brought you and Stephanie closer together."

"Stephanie? No, Caitlin, Stephanie is Risa's *step*-mother. Risa's mother's name was Lindsay."

Then why isn't Risa with you?

Caitlin did not pose the question. She would learn its answer as the story unfolded—assuming it did unfold. Jesse was obviously debating what to say next, trying to decide perhaps whether Gabrielle was a subchapter that needed to be included.

When Jesse spoke, his decision made, Gabrielle St. John had been omitted from the tale.

"Neither Lindsay nor I returned to college, and it was thirteen years before I heard from her again. She wrote to me, to Graydon Slake, in care of my publisher . . ."

Jesse Falconer, is that *you?* Cleverly disguised as Graydon Slake? It must be. Who else would choose such a *nom de plume?* It's a commemoration, isn't it, of the Fourth of July that changed your life?

Your life has changed again, apparently. You were going to be a surgeon. Of course, maybe you are. There's so much medicine in your books. I've even wondered if you—Graydon Slake, that is—are actually Patrick, the *good* twin. That day at Graydon's Lake was undoubtedly memorable for Patrick as well.

But you, *Jesse,* made such a point of telling me how dissimilar the two of you were. It seems improbable—

although quite a boon for the women of the planet—that both of you would be *so* sexy. So *sexual*.

It *is* you, isn't it, Jesse? I know it is. Even without the Graydon Slake clue, I would know from the sheer eroticism of your books. I have never forgotten that spring we had together. The sheer eroticism and much, much more. That spring, before *that* summer. I wanted to come back in the fall—to see you, to be with you. But I couldn't.

Needless to say my summer was a disaster. In the midst of my pathetic attempts to make things right with my parents, my grandfather died. Somehow, even though he knew he was dying, Grandfather forgot to cut me out of his will. Maybe it wasn't forgetfulness at all. Maybe he left me in, *really* in, on purpose. It's certainly possible. As you may remember the dysfunction that defined our family spanned generations.

Grandfather probably wanted to skewer my father one final time, and he definitely did. I was the principal beneficiary of The Fortune. There were no strings attached, either—no hoops for me to jump through, not even a single psychiatric test for me to take, much less to pass.

My parents weren't nearly so sanguine about my history of psychotic depression, and the ensuing legal battle was long, and ugly, and painful. The joke is that they could have had *everything*, every penny, all the millions. I would have given it to them willingly, a trivial purchase price for their love.

But they never asked me for my inheritance. They simply attacked (and lost, by the way). Mom and Pop and I haven't spoken since.

So, Jesse, that was my summer. I hope you fared better. Will you call me, Jesse Falconer? I'm the same girl you knew at nineteen—but wiser now, tougher, and even *sexier*.

Even if you're *not* Jesse, even if you're Patrick (or if, by some extraordinary coincidence, you happen to be a man named Graydon Slake), why not give me a call? We could have fun. Lots of it. I promise.

Oh *hell*, what am I saying? I need *you*, Jesse. Only you. Please? Soon?

Lindsay was living in Los Angeles, and she was more wealthy than her grandfather had ever dreamed of becoming himself. She was a venture capitalist—an *ad*venture capitalist, she liked to say. It was adventure for her, an intricate balancing act of risk and profit for which her instincts proved uncanny.

Lindsay's name appeared at the top of Hollywood's A-list, of everyone's A-list. It was because of her position on such lists that she met Daniel, at Spago, at the party following the Academy Awards. Daniel practiced entertainment law, an A-list attorney with a client list to match.

Their affair was torrid and brief—called to an abrupt halt by Daniel the day Stephanie entered his life. Lindsay was pregnant when she and Daniel broke up. Neither knew it, nor would have predicted it. Lindsay was scrupulous about birth control. Her own experiences with "family" coupled with her unforgiving insight into her own flaws had convinced her she had no business becoming a parent.

Neither, however, did Lindsay believe she had the right to terminate the pregnancy, to abort the life that had managed to assert itself despite her elaborate efforts to keep it at bay.

Lindsay had just learned of her pregnancy when she wrote her flippant—yet serious—letter to Jesse. Ten days later he was sitting in her posh condominium on Wilshire Boulevard and Lindsay was telling him about the tiny life that was growing within.

"Maybe together we could manage," Jesse said quietly, as they discussed the formidable idea of deeply flawed Lindsay raising a child.

"That would really be the blind leading the blind," she murmured in reply, not rejecting the notion. In fact, she realized, it was what she had hoped—that this man, who knew her so well, would be willing to help . . . that Jesse would be there for her baby when she couldn't be, during those times when her demons of depression demanded that she journey with them into blackness. "Wouldn't it?"

"Maybe not, Lindsay. Maybe we both know enough to avoid the most devastating mistakes."

Lindsay didn't want to tell Daniel about the baby. But Jesse insisted. Daniel had a right to know, he said. If he chose not to be involved in his child's life, then so be it.

But Daniel wanted to be involved. Daniel and Stephanie.

Lindsay refused to permit Daniel to witness her baby's birth. Not that Daniel suggested that he do so. But he and Stephanie were at Westwood Memorial when Risa was born. Married by then, Stephanie was pregnant with Risa's little sister.

It was Jesse who was in the delivery room, Jesse who was with Lindsay . . . and with Risa, holding her within moments of her birth—and loving the baby girl with a ferociousness that verged on fear.

Jesse was afraid of losing her, so fearful of the harm that might befall her as it had befallen the brother he had so fiercely loved. Despite his misgivings, Jesse Falconer was unable to let Risa go . . . to set her free.

*J*esse's retelling stalled then, in memories he would not or could not speak. His recounting had been skeletal at best, the barest of bones, an unemotional recitation of facts. But Caitlin felt the emotion, the love.

Jesse stood before a wall of glass, facing her but faceless. Behind him the city twinkled, a rainbowed galaxy of stars. Jesse was the moon in the center of that sparkling universe, a dark black moon on this twinkling spring night.

"You named her Risa," Caitlin spoke to the dark, still, silent moon.

"Lindsay did."

"But she got the name from you? From *Come in from the Rain*?"

"Yes. Risa means 'laughter'—you know that from the book."

"It's a beautiful name, one I'd never heard before. How did you know it?"

For a moment Caitlin believed she could see into the blackness, could see a wry smile on the moon's shadowed face.

"I discovered it in the same way, I imagine, that many authors find names for their characters. I went to a bookstore and bought every baby-name book I could find. The salesclerk assumed I was the expectant father."

"Which you were," Caitlin said softly. "You were choosing a name for your daughter."

"Risa is not my daughter, Caitlin."

Oh yes she is. "She lived with you, didn't she?" Caitlin already knew the answer—and even, she realized, when Risa left. The alcove in the library in Jesse's paradise home dated the departure with excruciating accuracy: sixteen months ago. Since then the alcove had fallen into disarray, as forsaken as the ice-cold ashes of a fire once aglow. "Didn't you and Lindsay and Risa live together?"

"Yes. For five years—except, of course, when Risa was in LA with Daniel. Lindsay would travel then, while Risa was away."

"Travel? Without you?" She left *you*?

"Lindsay needed time away, time to herself."

"Did you?"

"Need time away? No."

"Where did Lindsay go?"

"Various places. I received postcards from all over the world."

"Was she alone?"

"You mean was there another man, other men? My guess would be no, but I really have no idea."

"You never asked?"

"No. It wouldn't have mattered, Caitlin. It *didn't* matter. All that mattered was Risa. As far as she was concerned Lindsay and I were together—forever."

"But you cared for Lindsay, didn't you?"

"Sure. Very much. And vice versa. And if you're wondering if I was faithful to Lindsay, the answer is yes. I was thirty-two when Risa was born. Sexual variety might have been important, I might have believed it was important, when I was younger. But not then."

"But Lindsay was free to be with other men."

"Free," Jesse echoed quietly. "You know what they say about freedom, don't you?"

"No," Caitlin murmured. "What?"

Jesse Falconer's voice was as stark, as empty, as the statement he made. "It's all that's left when there's nothing left to lose."

*W*henever Risa and Lindsay were away, Jesse remained in Maui awaiting their return and fighting the fear that it would not happen.

His "girls" wouldn't willingly leave him. Jesse knew that. But he knew as well the whims of fate. He had witnessed the crash of a boom against a brother's skull . . . and he had felt, still felt, the shattering of his heart.

For five years Lindsay and Risa returned precisely when Lindsay said they would. When the shattering event finally came, it was Jesse who was away from their tropical home.

"You need to go somewhere," Lindsay told him. "For one month *s'il vous plait*."

"Because?"

"Because Risa and I have plans. Here. It's a Christmas present, Jesse, for you. The present itself requires your three-week absence and the fourth week Risa will be in LA. You *cannot* see the surprise until she's with you."

"Okay. I'll disappear."

"But you'll be in Los Angeles when Risa and I arrive?"

"You know I will."

"Good, because I'd really like you to see Frank Farrell with us."

"Lindsay?"

"Everything's *fine*, Jesse. You know how healthy Risa is. But the repair is necessary, we both know that, and it's time for you to see Frank again, not to mention Daniel. It's been five years."

Five years since that day, when Risa was only a few hours old, that all four parents learned what her heart murmur meant, and what it *might* mean. The worst possibilities had not come to pass. Risa had not needed surgery as an infant, and her growth had been right on track, and she had not suffered recurrent respiratory infections— had not suffered at all.

The elective, but necessary, septal repair would happen next year, when Risa was six.

"I'd like to be there, Lindsay. I *want* to be. But Daniel may not be happy about the idea. He's not too fond of me, as you know."

"Daniel resents the time you have with Risa, that's all."

"Are you sure that's all? Are you certain he—"

"I'm *certain*, Jesse. I'm also certain that you need to be with us when we see Frank Farrell."

With us, Lindsay had said. But when the time came she said something else.

"I'm out of here, Jesse."

"Tonight? On the eve of the surgeon's appointment you wanted us all to attend?"

"I mostly wanted you to be there. And I have to go. Tonight. Really. I have an appointment myself, a rendezvous with my demons."

Jesse knew it was true. He had spoken to her every day for the past three weeks, while she was in Maui, orchestrating his mysterious surprise, and he was in Los Angeles, writing. Jesse had heard, with each passing day, the heaviness that signaled darkness was descending, the fraying at the edges as Lindsay tried to fight it off . . . and finally the resignation as she prepared to succumb.

Jesse had suggested, almost daily, that he return to Maui. The Christmas surprise would not be spoiled. He would merely learn of it a little sooner than planned. But Lindsay had been determined to stave off her depression until Jesse's Christmas gift from her, from Risa, was ready.

And Lindsay had staved it off. But the moment Jesse met them at LAX he saw what the battle had cost her.

Now Lindsay was saying she needed to leave tonight, to journey to places she did not know with languages she could not speak. That was the way Lindsay got through her bouts of blackness. It was the only way she could. Medications didn't work. She had tried them all. Only time helped. She always chose to spend that time far away.

"I know you need to go, Lindsay. I can tell. But maybe this time you and I should both rendezvous with your demons. I'm acquainted with them, you know. We've met a few times."

"But only briefly."

"Maybe it's time for me to get to know them better, after Risa's appointment, when she's with Daniel."

Lindsay seemed so tempted. But finally, decisively, she shook her head. "No. I need to do this alone." Then she smiled, tried to. "You won't have any difficulty finding Frank's office. It's on the eighth floor of the Heart Institute, which is the wing made of rose-tinted glass. Besides which Risa knows the way."

"Okay." Jesse touched her cheek, felt its coolness, the tiny blood vessels clamped down by the restless surge of adrenaline that pulsed within. Fright or flight, the response was called. Lindsay was both. Frightened and fleeing. "Take care, Lindsay."

During his banishment from his crescent-shaped home Jesse had lived in a small room in a modest Southern California motel. He was writing and needed nothing more. In anticipation of the arrival of Risa and Lindsay, however, he had moved to a two-bedroom suite in the Château on Barrington, the upscale hotel located directly across from the hospital.

Jesse was in the living room of that suite, putting the finishing touches on *Blue Moon*, when he heard the small voice. It was two A.M.

"Jesse?"

She stood in the hallway, and her feet were bare beneath the ruffled hem of her favorite nightgown, and her hair was a cloud of golden curls.

Jesse moved to her swiftly, knelt before her, and spoke gently to her lovely, worried face. "Risa? What is it, sweetheart?"

"I'm *scared*."

"Scared, honey?" *Oh, my little love, please don't be scared, not of anything, not ever.* "Why, Risa? Do you know?"

The curls shook, and Jesse hesitated, weighing in his mind the questions he might ask against the prospect of introducing new fears. It was a delicate balance. But some questions had to be asked.

"Is it because of your appointment with Dr. Farrell?" he began, exploring the safest territory first.

Unless there had been a dramatic change during their three weeks apart Risa's answer to this question would be an emphatic *no*. She had no fears about the "gate in her heart"—the gate, not the hole. A hole in Risa's heart? Impossible. She had filled the dark, depthless holes in his.

Years before and together Jesse and Risa had abandoned the traditional image. The septal defect was a gate that permitted oxygenated blood to flow the wrong way. Eventually the enabling passageway would need to become a solid wall.

The prospect of open-heart surgery was terrifying to all parents involved. But not to Risa. Unless . . .

"Are you scared about seeing Dr. Farrell?"

"No."

It wasn't as emphatic as Jesse would have expected. But the Risa on this night was a little girl he had never seen, fearful and uncertain—yet truthful as always.

Her fear had nothing to do with the passageway in her heart. Was she afraid of seeing Daniel, then? And was this fear something Lindsay confronted before each visit—confronted yet didn't truly confront?

Was that why Lindsay was so insistent that he and Daniel see each other again, because she suspected but could not face the specter of Daniel abusing Risa? Or perhaps Stephanie was the culprit, as cruel as the wicked stepmothers in the fairy tales from which—because of Jesse—Risa had been spared.

There was no reason, he decided, for his lovely little girl to be exposed to stepmothers who plotted to kill their stepdaughters with a hunter's piercing arrow, or the prick of a thorn, or a bite from a poisoned apple.

Jesse told Risa other stories, snowy, happy, pure—tales of fleecy lions who, like all creatures on earth, should be treasured, and loved.

Had he sheltered Risa too much? Had civilization truly

reached a point where it was necessary to teach five-year-old girls to be wary of *everyone*?

"Are you afraid of Daddy?" *Daddy*. The name—legitimately Daniel's—inevitably evoked pain, and now it caused ice-cold rage. If Daniel hurt Risa, ever ... well, the man believed by all of Montclair to be entirely capable of murder would murder now, and gladly.

"Daddy?" Risa echoed with surprise, and with a frown. "No."

"Stephanie?"

Risa's confusion deepened, reassuringly, as she shook anew her cloud of curls.

"Do you know why you're scared, honey?"

"No! But I *am*!"

"I know, my love. I can tell. Maybe you had a scary dream."

Risa lifted the small shoulders beneath her flannel ruffles. "Maybe."

"Well, maybe if I tell you a story we can love the scary thoughts away. What do you think?"

She seemed uncertain, but she nodded.

"Okay. Let's try that then. What story shall I tell?"

Jesse expected a request for one of the never-published—never-even-written—adventures of the cherished white lion. The fleecy beast had myriad daring escapades, each of which, over the past two years, had been her *very favorite*.

But on this night when Risa was so inexplicably scared, his growing-up little girl regressed to a more distant time of joy.

"Sweet Potatoes, Jesse."

She curled in his arms, on the overstuffed couch beside the table where he had been working.

"Once upon a time," he began, "there was a little girl. Let's see, what was her name?"

She giggled, just a little—but as always, remembering the ritual of this storytelling as if it were yesterday, not six hundred yesterdays ago. "Risa. Her name was Risa."

"Ah, yes, that's right. Her name was Risa. And what was one of the things Risa liked to do?"

"Go to the grocery store! With Jesse."

It wasn't long before her delicate eyelids fluttered closed. Jesse might have carried her to bed, as he had so many times when a bedtime story had the desired effect. But on this night when Risa had been so afraid, he simply held her, watching her sleep . . . and seeing the worry that lingered even in dreams, the dainty furrowing of her innocent brow.

Was she fearful still? Jesse prayed not. Freedom from fear, from even knowing fear, was a gift that Lindsay and he had given her—and in fairness Daniel and Stephanie had given her such serenity as well.

"No, no, *no!*" Risa awakened frightened, and clinging to him with all her might.

The time was three-eighteen. They would never know if it was at that precise moment that Lindsay's car plummeted off the cliff. The wreckage wasn't discovered until dawn.

Lindsay had been driving north on Highway One, a scenic journey by day, but a treacherous one by night— especially on this night just days before Christmas. The fog had rolled in from the sea, an opaque shroud for Lindsay's journey to Carmel, the home that had never been a home.

Never before, not in all her travels, had Lindsay made a pilgrimage to the lush green valley that stood in such sharp contrast to the desolation of her youth. Such emotional journeys were something they had discussed: hers to Carmel, his to Montclair.

What would those places look like from their vantage point as adults? Would their homes glower at them as they always had, as if living, breathing, disapproving things?

One day Jesse and Lindsay would find out. Together. And if Lindsay was unable to see the truth of the mansion in Carmel, if all she saw, still, was a malevolent monster, Jesse would tell her what the formidable structure really was: a realtor's dream, nothing more.

And if in the blue, blue waters of Graydon's Lake Jesse could see only the drowning spirits of twins, Lindsay would tell him that the rippling waves were just like any others. And the gardener's cottage, where Gabrielle's sharp fingernails had shredded his flesh and ravaged his dreams, was merely a shack in desperate need of paint.

For some reason Lindsay had chosen to make her journey alone. And she had died.

The discovery of the crumpled wreckage of Lindsay's car, and of her crushed body within, was only the beginning of the shattering revelations . . .

"I know all about you, Jesse. I've known for years."

Daniel's quest to learn all there was to know about the man with whom his daughter was spending most of her life had commenced two years after Risa's birth. The search might have begun sooner. But Daniel felt guilty about investigating him.

He owed Jesse, and he knew it. Had it not been for Jesse he would never have known his baby girl. But it was because of that baby girl that Daniel needed to know all that he could.

Daniel's law practice gave him access to an array of private investigators. He chose the best. Within months the investigator had uncovered both the attempted fratricide at Graydon's Lake and the assault that had landed Jesse Falconer in prison—which, according to everyone with whom the investigator spoke, was precisely where he belonged. The name of the would-be rape victim had been redacted from court records, and even the most wagging of Montclair tongues refused to divulge her name.

The missing detail frustrated the compulsive investigator, but mattered not at all to Daniel. He had what he needed, and far more than he had wanted to find. Daniel had hoped to find nothing untoward about Graydon Slake and instead . . .

He immediately shared the alarming revelations with Lindsay.

"It's all nonsense."

"Nonsense?" Daniel echoed, stunned. He had expected her to leave Maui then and there, to bring Risa to LA, to find a place in Malibu, in the Colony perhaps. "Rape and murder are *nonsense*, Lindsay?"

"No one was murdered, Daniel. Neither was anyone raped."

"So that makes it okay? That he *failed*?"

"He didn't fail. Jesse doesn't fail. The accusations are bogus."

"Bogus?"

"It means false, Daniel. I'm surprised you're not familiar—"

"He told you the accusations were bogus and you believed him, no questions asked."

"Yes, he told me. But he didn't *need* to tell me. I knew.

And if you knew Jesse, you wouldn't need to be told, either."

"I'm coming to get her, Lindsay. I will not permit my daughter to spend one more night in the home of that man."

"She's *my* daughter, too, Daniel. And I promise you, if you try to take Risa away from me, she and Jesse and I will disappear. We can do that, Daniel, you *know* we can. And we will. And you will never see Risa again. Is that what you want?"

"What I want, Lindsay, is for my daughter to be safe."

"*So do I*. And she is safe, and loved, and happy."

"Will you promise me something, Lindsay?"

"Maybe."

"Never let him be alone with her."

"She never is."

She never is. The words, recounted by Daniel, pierced Jesse's soul. Had Lindsay doubted him after all?

Jesse had never tested Lindsay, had never told her the lies to see if she would leap to his defense. He had simply told her the truth.

Lindsay had accepted his claims of innocence without hesitation, and with a lilting tease: You lusted after another woman, this Gabrielle creature, within twenty-four hours of leaving me? Impossible, Jesse. *Impossible*.

Lindsay had not, in fact, doubted him. Her last will and testament, executed just weeks before her death, underscored her conviction that Jesse was neither murderer nor rapist—nor a would-be abuser of precious little girls.

The entirety of Lindsay's vast fortune was left in trust for Risa. But her daughter, the only treasure that truly mattered, was entrusted to Jesse.

Jesse was to assume Lindsay's parental rights, to share

with Daniel the custody of Risa precisely as it had been shared when Lindsay was alive.

The will was properly executed, by the most high-powered attorney money could buy. Lindsay's words and wishes were legal.

"But," Daniel told Jesse during those days of death and loss before Christmas, "they are not enforceable. In any court battle, in any court in the land, I *will* prevail. We both know that."

There's so much he isn't telling me, Caitlin realized. So many secrets he is keeping still.

Lindsay's will, and Daniel's vow to contest it, were re-counted in a single succinct sentence.

"But you fought for her, didn't you?" Caitlin asked. "Despite what Daniel said you fought to keep Risa with you."

"No. I didn't fight."

"Why not?"

"Because, Caitlin, I knew I wouldn't win."

"Why not?" she repeated, frustrated by how much she didn't know, how much Jesse wouldn't tell her. "I don't understand."

"It was best for Risa to be with Daniel and Stephanie and Holly, the little sister she loves so much."

"And what about you, Jesse?" *Did you decide it would be too burdensome to assume, by yourself, the care of a little girl? That it would infringe too much on your freedom? You know what they say about freedom, Jesse Falconer.*

Caitlin did not fire the questions at him. They were

angry, she knew; fueled by frustration at being excluded from his secrets, not by concern *for him.* And Caitlin was concerned for Jesse, this dark, dark shadow against the sparkling sky. She heard his pain, in the words he did not speak, and his love for Risa in the words he did.

"What about you, Jesse?"

"I have the lion. That was my Christmas present. The spiked fence, the security system, the lion himself. That was the surprise that was so important for Lindsay to complete before she and Risa came to LA. She wanted me to have something, *something.*"

"Oh," Caitlin whispered. "You think Lindsay knew she was going to die? You think she killed herself?"

She heard his sigh, weighted and dark.

"I think it's possible, Caitlin. There weren't any skid marks at the scene. But given the fog that's not conclusive. It may have been an accident, or suicide, and I've even wondered if Lindsay was planning simply to disappear. She would have made it look like a death."

So there would be closure, Caitlin realized. And so that her will would be read. Lindsay must have known that despite her wishes, Jesse might not get custody of Risa. Perhaps she had even known he might not fight.

So she gave him the lion. Because Lindsay knew that without something precious to protect and love Jesse Falconer might not survive.

"When was the last time you saw Risa?"

"Christmas Eve, sixteen months ago."

$\mathcal{D}$aniel wanted him to leave without saying good-bye.
Jesse refused.

Nor would he tell Risa that it was best for him, that he wanted to live alone. In a conversation during which Daniel stood nearby, Jesse bade adieu to Risa.

"I have to go now."

"Go, Jesse?"

"Back to Maui."

"Oh."

She didn't understand, nor did he want her to. Not now, not yet. Jesse wanted comprehension to come slowly, gently over time—so that when Risa finally realized he was gone forever her life would be so full that he would not be missed.

"You're going to stay here, sweetheart, with Daddy and Stephanie and Holly. If you want, you can begin school here, in January. I think that would be fun."

"You do?"

"Yes. Absolutely."

"But what about you, Jesse?"

"I don't need to go to school," he teased. After a moment, he added solemnly, "I'll be with you always, Risa. Mommy and I both will be. Mommy's in heaven, in the sky. She's watching over you, loving you always."

"Will you be in the sky, too?"

"Yes. But you know where I'll be, Risa? In the moon. You remember about the moon, don't you? It's there, all the time, even when you can't see it."

"I remember."

Jesse smiled. "Good. Now remember this, sweetheart. I'll be there, all the time, even when you can't see me."

"*B*ut you've talked to her, haven't you? Since that Christmas Eve?"

"No."

"But you knew her surgery was scheduled for June."

"Stephanie has kept me informed." Stephanie was not a wicked stepmother, after all. She was just a courageous spy behind enemy lines. "I guess Daniel knows that now. Stephanie undoubtedly revealed all when she told him how to page me."

Caitlin would have remarked how relieved Daniel must have been, how grateful that Stephanie knew how to reach the man who could convince the breathless Risa to come to the hospital. But at that moment the Drawing Room door opened, casting artificial luminescence onto the moon.

Caitlin saw Jesse's ravaged face, that dark, savage, barren place. And she saw the raw emotion in his dark green eyes as he stared into the blinding light toward the white-coated physician who hovered at its source.

"Jesse?" Frank Farrell said. "You can see her now."

TWENTY-EIGHT

*S*he was so small, so precious, so fragile.

A small, precious, fragile marionette.

Appended to her pale limbs was a web of plastic tubing, an attachment accomplished by the invasion of needles into her delicate skin. Additional translucent lines fed misted oxygen to her face while multicolored wires transmitted the electrical impulses of her racing heart to the chattering monitor above her head.

She was sitting upright still. Her breathing remained labored, although less so, and the lips that had been so very blue were a stark but reassuring beige.

The medications were working. But it was too soon for her to speak . . . wasn't it? Or was it *his* voice that Jesse Falconer was so uncertain of?

He almost withdrew, to give the medications a little more time. But Risa's eyes opened, and for him, *for him,* the cloudy green began to glow.

"Jesse."

"Hello, sweetheart."

Jesse moved to his little marionette, as close as he could get amid the webbing, and as she looked at him Risa found the breath not only to speak, but to exclaim. "You're crying. Don't *cry!*"

"I'm okay, honey. Don't worry about me." Jesse touched her small beloved face. He felt dampness, from the misting oxygen, and from the fierce battle she waged. "But what about you, Risa?"

Jesse had the answer before she could summon the strength to reply. Risa was gasping, drowning—just as Patrick almost drowned in Graydon's Lake. Now as then Jesse felt the desperate helplessness, the anguished foreboding of irrevocable loss.

No. Not this time. Not Risa. I will not let it happen.

"I'm fine," she managed at last. "Much better. If I just . . ."

Her words stopped, they had to. She could speak only as she exhaled, on that rush, and now she was inhaling again, gulping, gasping, preparing to complete her sentence. *If I just rest a while I'll be able to go home. I won't need surgery. Not ever.*

As fearsome as this breathlessness must be, as terrifying as it was to gasp, to drown, that fright was apparently trivial compared to the fear of surgery—a fear which predated her breathlessness by almost a week.

"I think I know why you're so scared, Risa. At least I know part of the reason. You're afraid to have your heart fixed, aren't you? To have the gate become a wall?"

Risa answered with a nod, her gaze riveted to his, searching, imploring, trusting.

"It's something we've known about for a long time, though, isn't it? Something we used to talk about." Had there been, for the past sixteen months, a moratorium on talking about her surgery? Had Daniel and Stephanie decided it was something best not discussed? "You weren't afraid then, were you, Risa? When we used to talk about it?"

She shook her head, but her curls, damp and weighted, did not move, did not dance. The golden spirals *had* danced that other time, when Risa sensed her mother's impending death.

Her fear on that night had been unfocused. And now?

"Sweetheart? Do you know why you're so afraid?"

She nodded, and it was weighted, too. With reluctance, Jesse decided. And with apology.

"Tell me, Risa. Whatever it is, it's okay. Truly it is. You can tell me anything."

She hesitated, or perhaps she was merely summoning the strength to speak, for at no time did her eyes leave his. Not even for a racing, fluttering heartbeat did Risa revoke her trust.

Finally, on a rush of air, she whispered, "Dr. Farrell."

Jesse suppressed his surprise. Risa had known Frank Farrell all her life, as her doctor, as her neighbor, as the father of her best friend. No wonder this fear was so hard for her to admit, the lovely little girl who was always so careful never to hurt anyone's feelings.

Now Jesse suppressed his own feelings, a white-hot rush of anger. If Frank Farrell had hurt Risa . . .

"Tell me why you're afraid of him."

"I had . . . a dream."

"About the surgery?"

She nodded, gulped, then breathed. "*And I died!*"

"Oh sweetheart," Jesse whispered, not breathing now, and dying, too. The little girl who once before—and so accurately—sensed an impending death was sensing such tragedy again. And this time the death was her own.

"It wasn't his *fault*!"

"No, of course it wasn't. But that doesn't matter, does it? Because the dream was so scary, so real."

"Mommy was there."

"Mommy," Jesse echoed softly, blocking the immense impulse to say more—to guess at Risa's words, Risa's thoughts, to spare her the monumental task of speaking. He could tell, because he knew Risa so well and loved her so much, that there were words she needed to say herself.

He waited, watching her fight, and blocking the most powerful impulse of all: to scoop her into his arms, and pull her free of this ungodly web, and run with her, and run and run . . . until they reached the kind of magical place that existed in their fairy tales.

In truth the place to which Jesse wanted to take his little girl was one that he had never shared with Risa. But Jesse knew it well. His mind had journeyed there often, from the moment the doctors first heard Risa's murmuring heart. It was a place of true magic—where just by holding Risa close her damaged heart would be exchanged with his.

"I want to be with Mommy, Jesse. I *do*."

Risa managed all the important words on one breath, a feat which she greeted with a faint frown of surprise. Her frown deepened as she realized even more, that despite the flow of words she was gasping less than before.

The medications were truly working at last, a magic in itself. If only some magic could vanquish the torment of her dream, the image of Lindsay calling to her, pleading with her to join her, she was so lonely in heaven by herself. Jesse saw that torment on Risa's lovely face. He saw, too, that there were more words she must speak—with his help.

"I know you want to be with Mommy, Risa. But . . . ?"

"But what about Daddy and Steph and Holly and *you*?"

"Oh, Risa. Mommy's with you, sweetheart. You *know* she is. She's here now, and *all* the time. But you're right, Risa-Risa. *We* need you with us." Jesse found a smile, for her, a smile that concealed everything but his love. "We really do."

"But I'm so afraid!"

"I know. But if another doctor did the surgery I wonder if all your fear might simply go away. Poof."

During their five years as father and daughter Jesse and Risa had *poofed* all manner of things, from skinned knees to broken toys.

Now, as he suggested *poofing* her fear, Jesse saw the glorious beginning of a Risa smile—until a lovely frown intervened.

"But what about Dr. Farrell?"

"It wouldn't hurt his feelings, sweetheart, *not at all*. He wants what's best for you, and he knows how powerful dreams can be, how real they can seem."

"Are you sure?"

"I'm absolutely positive. So you can poof that worry, too. And you know what else? I just happen to have a friend, who just happens to be here at this very moment, who just happens to be a heart surgeon."

"Really?"

"Really. Would you trust her, Risa, if I do?"

"You trust her, Jesse?"

With my life, with my heart . . . with this little girl who is my heart. "Yes, honey, I do. Completely and utterly."

"Then so do I!" Risa smiled at last, bright and rosy, and echoing his words, as she had always loved to do, she whispered, "Completely and utterly."

"*Y*ou're glaring, Daniel."

"I don't like having him anywhere near her."

"But she's *talking* to him," Stephanie insisted. "Maybe she's telling him why she's so frightened."

Caitlin overheard the whispered exchange. She and Frank and Marty were there, too, witnessing this critical conversation through the glass. Caitlin couldn't see Jesse's face, only Risa's. And what she saw was love for the black-haired lion. Risa's love, Risa's trust.

Was that the source of Daniel's hostility? Risa's love for Jesse? Was Daniel that jealous, that unwilling to share his daughter's heart . . . until it was absolutely necessary because that precious young heart was about to die?

Caitlin's thoughts were suspended by movement within the glassy room. The lion was standing, turning.

Her heart contracted at the emotion she saw, emotion that had been contained, she was certain, while he gazed at the small trusting face. But Jesse's emotion was hidden no more, and now he was gazing through the glass, searching, searching . . . until he found her.

Oh, Jesse Falconer, what do you want from me?

But she knew, she knew, even before he reached her and the question was posed.

"Will you do this?" he asked softly. "Will you operate on Risa?"

Jesse was not asking if she *could* do the surgery. He knew that answer. Dr. Caitlin Taylor was an expert at such delicate repairs.

He was asking her only if she *would*.

The repair of damaged hearts was Caitlin's passion, had been her only passion until him, and now Jesse was asking her twin passions to join, to entwine, to become one . . . as on this night she and Jesse had become one.

"Yes," she whispered. *I can, I will, I must.* "Of course I'll do it."

"Thank you." His intense green gaze lingered, thanking her more articulately than any words ever could. Then he turned to Frank, with quiet apology, with Risa's apology, and explained the reason for Risa's fear. "She had a dream about the surgery. You were operating, and she died. She knows the dream isn't real, but she can't shake the fear. She didn't say anything—other than her decision not to have surgery—because she didn't want to hurt your feelings."

Physicians were scientists. But they believed in miracles just like every one else. And physicians believed, too, in a miracle's evil twin. If a patient was convinced of a disastrous outcome, the premonition was taken very much to heart. With the passion of a true believer, Dr. Frank Farrell asked, "You did tell her that it wouldn't hurt my feelings, didn't you?"

"Sure. But she needs to hear that from you as well, as soon as possible."

"How about right now? I can introduce her to Caitlin at the same time."

"I'll introduce Caitlin to Risa." Jesse's quiet voice thundered with authority. "I'll introduce her when you're through."

"And in the meantime," Caitlin said, "I think I'll just scamper down the hall to my office and grab a white coat and stethoscope."

And while I'm there I'll make that all-important phone call.

TWENTY-NINE

"*I*t's Caitlin, Patrick. I need you."

"Caitlin," he murmured, shifting gears, shifting focus.

He had spent the evening saying hello to Amanda.

Hello, Amanda. We can do this. We will. Patrick had not uttered the provocative words. He had merely shown her the ways in which they were already touching: with words, with silence, with their hearts.

The conversation had begun with great wariness but ended with celebration, the promise to celebrate on Saturday night. They had spoken for hours, a reluctance to say good-bye that matched the wonder of saying hello.

Finally, just moments before, they had wished each other good night and pleasant dreams, and when the phone rang Patrick was certain that it would be Amanda, feeling as he did, both euphoric and empty—and needing to know that the euphoria was real.

But it was Caitlin who was calling. Caitlin who spoke the words which one day he hoped Amanda Prentice would speak.

"You need me, Caitlin?"

"Yes, Patrick, I do. As does a six-year-old girl. She's in failure and needs a septal repair. I've agreed to do the surgery, but I need an assistant. You."

"What about Frank? Or—"

"Frank can't do it, and I haven't asked anyone else. I'm asking you, Patrick."

"Because?"

"Because in all ways except biology the little girl, whose name is Risa, is Jesse's daughter."

"Oh, Caitlin."

"She's not your niece, Patrick, not genetically. But she *is* Jesse's daughter in the only ways that truly count."

"He's not right there, is he? He has no idea that you're making this call."

"That's right. He's not, and he doesn't, and if you say no, Patrick, if you feel this is something you can't do, I'll understand—and Jesse will never know."

"I can do it, Caitlin." *I have to.* "How soon are you planning to scrub?"

"Sometime in the next few hours, once she's as medically stable as she can be. She's being diuresed, and she *is* responding, so my guess would be between three and four. Shall I call you back?"

"Caitlin, this is me you're talking to. I'm on my way, you know that. I'll want to see her, review the cath data, take a look at her chart. The reason I asked about your OR plans is that I'm wondering if there's time for me to be transfused. I'm okay to operate, Caitlin, *more* than okay. But time permitting, and if Jesse's willing, a little more oxygen-carrying capacity couldn't hurt."

*J*esse was waiting just where Caitlin had left him, standing outside Risa's room. By himself. Frank, Marty, Daniel, and Stephanie were all within the glass walls. With Risa. But even had Jesse been there, too, he would have been excluded from the circle of love.

Alone, isolated, outcast.

Caitlin wanted to touch him, to hug him, to wrap her arms around the taut muscles of his lean waist. Embracing him with a smile instead, she greeted softly, "Hi."

"Hi." His voice was soft, grateful, in reply. "All set?"

Caitlin patted the stethoscope in her white coat pocket. "All set."

"As soon as they come out we'll go in."

"Okay." Caitlin knew it would be soon. Frank had seen her return and was already guiding the others toward the door. As the adults moved away Caitlin got a clear view of the little girl. "Her breathing's gotten *much* better just in the few minutes I've been gone."

Jesse's expression became a breathtaking vision of hope. "Yes, it has."

Risa's breathing was so much better that she greeted Jesse with an appraising gaze. Her golden head tilted in thoughtful contemplation as she studied him, a gesture which Jesse answered with a mirror-image tilt and a gentle tease.

"Yes, *mademoiselle?*"

"You look different."

"I do?" *Of course I do, Risa, without you in my life*.

The loss was irrevocably etched in his face, a change he could neither alter nor conceal. Risa saw that change, she couldn't miss it, but it was something she could not possibly articulate. She stared at him, searching and confused—until at last she found a difference she could comprehend.

"Your hair is longer!" The pronouncement came with triumph, and relief. "*That's* what it is."

Jesse smiled, relieved as well. "So is yours, munchkin."

"Yes, but mine is *supposed* to be long."

"Ah, I see." Jesse touched her cheek. It was damp still, but not nearly so cold. "Your breathing's even better, isn't it?"

Risa nodded. "But I still need surgery, don't I?"

"Yes. You do. All right?"

Risa nodded again and for the first time looked at Caitlin. "Are you going to operate on me?"

"Yes, Risa, I am—if that's all right with you."

Risa turned to Jesse.

"This is Dr. Taylor," he explained to the young—and trusting—face. "She's a terrific surgeon and everything's going to be just fine. Okay?"

"Okay," Risa whispered. Not wanting to leave Jesse's reassuring gaze, but knowing it was the polite thing to do, she looked again at Caitlin. "Okay, Dr. Taylor."

"Okay," Caitlin echoed. "Another doctor will be helping me, Risa. He's a wonderful doctor, and someone Jesse knows very well." Caitlin felt Jesse's reaction, the heat, the blow. But neither her eyes nor her smile left Risa. "He'll be here soon, so you can see for yourself how nice he is."

Risa listened politely to Caitlin's words then turned to the only critic who mattered. "Is he nice, Jesse?"

"He's very nice, Risa. As a matter of fact he's my brother."

The green eyes, so much like Jesse's and yet not his at all, grew wide with surprise. "Your *brother*?"

"My twin brother. We don't look alike though, not a bit, so you won't get the two of us confused."

"But if he's your brother, why didn't he ever visit us?"

"Well . . . lots of reasons. One of which was that he was terribly busy becoming a surgeon."

"So he could operate on me?"

"Yes, sweetheart, so he could operate on you."

At that moment a handsome male doctor strode into the room.

"Is that him?" Risa asked softly.

"No," Jesse murmured. In addition to calling Patrick, Caitlin had obviously made at least one other call. "That's Dr. Sheridan."

Dr. Stephen Sheridan might have looked very stern were he also not so nice—and not so concerned, as they all were, about the little girl. But Stephen had other concerns as well, significant ones, all of which had been sternly shared with Caitlin during what she had termed a "courtesy" call.

Medical protocol mandated such communication when one physician planned invasive procedures on patients in another doctor's care; and invasive—and disruptive—procedures were precisely what Caitlin had in mind. She was going to drain the blood from one of Stephen's patients and transfuse it into another.

Caitlin had expected reluctance from Stephen, resistance even, and she had also expected Stephen Sheridan to be at home. But Stephen had been in the hospital, on Five South, managing a patient in hemolytic crisis.

And now he was here.

"You need me, Stephen?" Jesse asked.

"Apparently I do."

"Okay." Jesse spoke to his beloved little girl. "It seems, Risa-Risa, that I have to go."

"*Go*, Jesse?"

"Just to another part of the hospital. Don't worry. I'll be around. Even if you don't see me I'll be nearby, watching over you."

"Like the moon," she murmured.

"Yes." The short word was shortened further, abruptly curtailed, by a surge of emotion. He was saying farewell—again—as he had on that Christmas Eve. Jesse knew it. But Risa did not. Risa would live, *she would live*; but he would be banished as before—and once again—from her life.

"Like the moon," Jesse repeated finally. Then, as casually as was possible, he said, "Well. I'd better go."

Caitlin would have watched Jesse's journey to the glass door had it been possible to draw her gaze from Risa's face.

Caitlin wondered, instantly yet fleetingly, if the bewildered panic she saw was the patient's sense of doom, the ominous foreboding of death. But Risa's lips—and cheeks—were rosy testaments to her ever-improving health, and her breathing remained unlabored.

And as for the slightly increased heart rate broadcast above her head? The tachycardia made perfect sense. Risa's heart was crying, Don't go, Jesse! Please. Don't leave me!

Caitlin's heart had once made such a plea, as she had watched the wounded lion walk, without a limp, into the mist. Jesse had not heard Caitlin's frantic cry. Or perhaps he'd merely ignored it.

But Jesse Falconer did not ignore the urgent pleadings of this young and desperate heart.

He turned, and smiled at Risa's lovely worried face, and whispered, "I love you, sweet potato."

Risa's panic vanished, an overcast day suddenly gloriously bright. And as she had done so many times, she echoed joyfully, "I love *you*, sweet potato!"

"*H*ow risky is this, Stephen?"

Stephen frowned slightly, not at the question—which was a logical one—but at the timing. The large-bore needle was already in Jesse's vein, and assisted by the powerful pull of gravity, Jesse's blood was already flowing into a beaker of sterile glass.

Stephen watched the rapidly filling glass as he replied.

"Twenty years ago, before AIDS, before hepatitis B, blood transfusions were given all the time, even for modest degrees of anemia. We have screening tests for AIDS and hepatitis now. But what about the next blood-borne illness, the one yet to be described?" Stephen looked from his patient's blood to the patient himself. "Anyway, the lesson has been learned and these days transfusions are given sparingly. But, Jesse, I can tell you that if this were a couple of decades ago I would be *giving* you blood, not taking it away."

"I'm not talking about the risk to me. So my hematocrit drops a few more points. So what? Maybe a little more anemia is just what my sluggish reticulocytes need. What I'm wondering about is the risk to Patrick."

Stephen should have known, probably had known, that Jesse's concern was for Patrick not for himself. But

Stephen had not wanted to introduce the theoretical worry about Patrick's transplant if Jesse hadn't already considered it.

Which, of course, he had. Jesse knew—they all knew—that the cells that had engrafted so swiftly and so robustly might be fickle still. For the moment those cells were detecting Patrick's anemia and responding with great vigor to remedy it.

It was a wondrous harmony, but a delicate one. What if, following this transfusion, the donor cells became confused, discouraged, or even annoyed? You don't need us working so hard to make you well? Fine! We'll shut off production entirely. In fact, we may just decide not to make our home here after all.

"There's a potential risk," Stephen conceded. "But it's one that Patrick willingly accepts. He says he'll take as much blood as you can spare."

For Risa, for Risa.

"In that case, Stephen, take as much as you can."

THIRTY

ARIEL'S

THREE A.M.

TUESDAY, MAY SEVENTH

*D*r. Sheridan told Jesse that
he should spend the remainder of the night lying on the
gurney in the donor room adjacent to the blood bank. Unless, Stephen suggested quietly, Jesse would like to be
wheeled to the hematology floor where he could rest in a
bed next to his twin's while Patrick received his blood.

Stephen sensed that Jesse would not choose this moment for a reunion with his twin. Jesse's focus was on
Risa, and his emotions, raw and ravaged before Stephen
took all but the most minimal reserve of blood, would become even more precarious after.

Stephen's intuition was correct. Jesse declined the invitation to be with Patrick, although he asked Stephen to
convey to his brother his immeasurable gratitude for
what Patrick was about to do.

But what Stephen Sheridan did not anticipate, would
never have anticipated, was that Jesse would utterly disregard his instruction to remain supine for the remainder of the night. Nor would Stephen have imagined, not
in a million years, that Jesse Falconer would spend the

hours of Risa's surgery standing—*standing*—before the shelves of tiny glass jars in the baby food section at Ariel's.

"Sweet potatoes, Jesse!"

It was part of the ritual of going to the grocery store. It began when she was very young, when he strolled the aisles with her in his arms, and she patted his cheeks and clapped her hands and pointed her tiny dimpled fingers at the rows of baby food.

Then, when she was very young, Jesse fed her only foods that came in small glass jars. Jesse did not trust himself, not then, as a father, and Lindsay had comparable worries about making unwitting yet monumental mistakes.

Later, when Jesse had read everything there was to read and became an expert on the nutritional requirements of little girls, he cooked for Risa—with Risa's help. The glass jars became a thing of the past—all save one. Her favorite.

A new ritual began then, when Risa and Jesse no longer shopped the baby-food aisle. As they were rolling their grocery cart toward the checkout line, Risa would gasp, and cover her mouth, her eyes twinkling above her fingertips.

"What, Risa?" Jesse would ask with mock horror. "Did we forget something?"

"Yes! Sweet potatoes, Jesse!"

And now his precious Risa, his lovely little sweet potato, was in the operating room. His blood was there, and his marrow—helping Patrick, please, helping not tainting, not shrouding with his darkness the place that needed to be so bright.

Jesse knew all there was to know about this particular

surgery. He knew how Caitlin and Patrick would open Risa's chest, and how they would keep it open; and how once they had exposed Risa's heart they would isolate it, routing her blood from its natural pump and sending it to a machine instead.

When she was on bypass, and the machine had assumed the vital tasks of a living heart, Risa's own heart would become still . . . and it was in that state of suspended animation that Caitlin would cut into the precious organ . . . and with the swiftness of the gifted seamstress she was Caitlin would transform the lethal hole into a solid wall. Without incident. *Please.*

Risa was on bypass now. Jesse knew it, felt it—for as he stood before the jars of sweet potatoes at Ariel's, his mind afloat from loss of blood, Jesse Falconer became suspended in a netherworld between life and death.

His heart, like Risa's, was alive . . . but still.

*C*aitlin thought of nothing but the task at hand, forbade herself all other thoughts. Emotion had no place here. Neither did the reminder that she was not operating on a single heart but two, Risa's and *his*. Nor could Caitlin allow herself to ache about *why* Jesse had vanished: because he was so disliked, so disdained, so contemptuously excluded from the circle of love. Nor could she wonder where her beloved pariah had gone.

Those thoughts were for later, when Risa was recovering, which she *would* be. The thought was permissible, based on science not hope—for as Caitlin touched the edges of the septal defect, searching for sites where placement of tiny stitches might be problematic, she found none, *none*.

"Healthy tissue all the way around, and her leaflets and chordae are just fine." Caitlin made the pronouncement to the small motionless heart. But she felt Patrick's relief.

"Good," he whispered. "Are you ready for the patch?"

"I'm ready."

*I*t was going well. Jesse felt it. Soon, *soon*, the suspended animation would cease, and her heart, healthy and new, would beat with joy, and she would float, as gently as he was floating, back to consciousness.

Already *his* heart was beating anew, pounding, racing, knowing—

—and then stopping.

Stopping.

Stopping dead.

"*P*atrick?" Caitlin's query was calm despite her horror.

Never say anything in the presence of a patient that you would not want the patient to hear. It was a maxim to which both Caitlin and Patrick subscribed; and which, they believed, should apply at all times—in the operating room, even under anesthesia, and in the ICU, despite neurologic parameters that defined coma . . . and even in those hushed moments just after a patient had died.

All physicians had heard anecdotes about comatose patients awakening with vivid recall of bedside discussions held during their deep—yet not oblivious—sleep. Sometimes such discussions were disturbing, and irreparable: a relative bemoaning the fact they had not pulled the plug, a physician advising the family there was no hope.

Caitlin and Patrick adhered to the maxim. Always. Even now, as their hearts screamed with despair.

The surgery had been flawless, from sewing the patch to healthy tissue, to suturing the incision in her heart, to removing her from bypass. But Risa's heart remained motionless. It had failed to respond to the usual measures, and had failed still when more aggressive techniques were tried. They weren't at the end of the line, there were even more heroic measures available, but, *but . . .*

Patrick answered Caitlin not with words but with motion. Propelled by a force that was not his, a mystical power deep within his bones, Patrick cupped the small still heart in the palm of his large gloved hand.

Then gently, and so confidently, Patrick closed his fist, enclosing Risa's entire heart. And when he opened that fist, and her heart remained motionless in his palm, he squeezed again, and again. And again.

Patrick's hand opened and closed, compressing and releasing, a measured rhythm that was so confident, so certain, that even after twelve cycles neither its pace nor its urgency increased.

Patrick's powerful yet gentle hand, fueled by the powerful yet gentle will of his twin, was going to bring Risa back to life, had to, would—

—and did. On the fifteenth compression.

Fifteen, the age the brothers had been on that fateful July Fourth at Graydon's Lake.

"*Y*es. He called." Jonathan, the OR charge nurse, frowned. "The call came less than a minute after her heart started beating again. I don't know where he was. He sounded a little breathless. He said he would call back later, to check on her recovery in the CICU. Oh, and he also said to thank both of you, and the anesthesiologist, and the nurses who scrubbed, and—well, he basically asked me to thank everyone."

No one saw Jesse Falconer, not for the entire day. But he called the unit, as he said he would, and two dozen white and pink roses were delivered to Caitlin's office with a card that read, simply, *Jesse*. And at two that afternoon he placed a call to his brother's office.

"I'm sorry, he's not here at the moment. But he *is* around," Patrick's secretary affirmed. Her voice held unmistakable fondness for Patrick despite her disapproval of his precipitous return to work. "Apparently he's back, fully recovered! At least, as of an hour ago, he was on his way to the ER to consult on a motorcycle accident. You said you're his *brother*? Maybe *you* could talk some sense into him."

Patrick walked into his office a minute later, a minute too late. He was left with only the message: Jesse had called, to thank him, again.

Caitlin believed that Jesse Falconer was somewhere nearby, as he had promised Risa he would be, a shadow within a shadow, an invisible moon in the peacock blue sky.

She called his hotel room once, then no more. Jesse would appear when the time was right, and this was the busy Tuesday she had longed for yesterday, a day when her skills as a surgeon were put to good use.

The world might have stood still, halted in reverent wonder by the happenings in Operating Room Two, the awakening of an innocent heart by a most gentle caress of love.

But there were other patients, other families, who awaited miracles, and Risa, in the able care of Marty and Frank, was doing just fine.

THIRTY-ONE

*T*he shadow appeared at ten P.M., in time to escort her home. Night had long since fallen, although the world wasn't truly dark. The streetlights of Barrington Avenue twinkled gold, and the moon glowed burnished amber.

But there he was—shadow, lion, shepherd, moon.

And there she was—a woman in love. She carried two of the long-stemmed roses he had sent her, one white, one pink. The twin roses would spend this night in her bedroom. But would he?

They walked in silence to her apartment door.

"I wanted to say good-bye."

Her hands clenched, piercing her flesh with scalpel-sharp thorns. "Good-bye, Jesse?"

"I'm returning to Maui tomorrow."

"I see," she murmured. "Will you come inside?"

Caitlin didn't know what she planned. She had no plan.

But once inside, before illuminating a single light, she freed her hands of the roses and reached for him. She felt the unshaven roughness of his cheeks, and the pounding pulse in his neck. His heartbeat was strong, powerful—and brisk from loss of blood.

"Make love to me, Jesse."

Beneath her fingers Caitlin felt his wry, sexy smile.

"I can't. I'm a little too low on blood."

"Then let me make love to you."

Jesse's smile faded, Caitlin felt it fade, and as her eyes acclimated to the darkness she saw the harshness of his face.

"No, Caitlin."

"Jesse, I—"

"This has been nice."

Nice. There it was, that four-letter word that could sound *so nice*—that could, when uttered gently, sound like those other small but magnificent words. Hope. Love. But now, spoken by him, nice sounded empty, barren, alone. Caitlin withdrew her hands from his face, from him. "Nice? You mean good sex?"

"Terrific sex."

Lion, shadow, moon, shepherd. But Jesse Falconer was not protecting her now. His dark-fire eyes glittered, but the searing green blaze was frozen beneath a glacier of ice. Why? *Why?*

Jesse saw her confusion, her *pain*, and fought the urge, the magnificent temptation, to tell her the truth. *I don't want to leave you, Caitlin. I never want to leave you. But I must, for your sake.*

He had vowed to leave when the risk—for her—became too great, when temptation was eclipsed by peril. The peril was monumental now, for his wanting of her, his need for her, threatened the very edges of his control.

Whenever Jesse had loved this fiercely—had he ever loved *this* fiercely?—fate had intervened with punishing vengeance. Fate, that merciless enemy of his heart, that whimsical force he could not control. All his love had been unable to avert the life-shattering swing of a boom, or to prevent a monstrous hole in a tiny heart, or to stay the mutiny of cells from a brother's marrow.

I have to go, Caitlin. I must leave you. And it will be easier for you if I leave with cruelty not with love.

"So, Caitlin, good-bye."

"*Wait*, Jesse. Will you tell me a few of your deep dark secrets before you go? I really feel I have a right to know."

He didn't want to tell her. But it was a selfish wish, the bewitching fantasy that she would dismiss as impossible every crime; that she would trust him, believe in him, love—

His shrug was lazy, nonchalant. "Why not? When I was fifteen I tried to murder Patrick. We were sailing at a place called Graydon's Lake. I shoved the boom into his head, and when the blow wasn't quite as lethal as I'd hoped I tried to drown him."

"I don't believe you!"

There was such temptation now, such limitless peril. His intrepid love had forgotten her bewildered pain, her astonished hurt. She was a warrior, engaged in a ferocious battle, defending him, trusting him, loving him. Joy pulsed within, warming his veins, heating his soul, threatening to melt every crystal of ice. He had to stop the magnificent heat—and he did, by stilling, stopping, the pounding of his heart.

"Don't take my word for it, Caitlin. Ask any of the citizens of Montclair. Or, even easier, ask Patrick."

"I don't *have* to ask anyone, Jesse. I *know* it's not true."

Caitlin's passion glowed in her sea blue eyes, and

Jesse's passion was frozen deep. But his battle was as ferocious, more ferocious, than hers. *Hate me, Caitlin. Despise me. It's so easy to do.*

"When I was nineteen I assaulted Patrick's girlfriend—assault with intent to rape—for which I spent the next four years in prison."

Not prison, Jesse. Not you.

"There you have it, Caitlin. The truth about Jesse." He should have left then, when his heart was so frozen it scarcely moved. But some demon of temptation—and of torment—compelled one final question. "So, do you feel raped?"

"No!" *I feel loved.*

The trocar that had pierced his heart, since the day when Stephen had pierced his bones, made its final assault. Twisting. Plunging. Daring him to survive. "Well, good. Then you agree it's been nice. Aloha, Caitlin."

With that Jesse Falconer began the short journey to her door, and his forever journey to Maui, to paradise—without her.

Caitlin felt panic, despair; emotions identical to Risa's when Jesse had started to leave with Stephen. From Caitlin's desperate heart came the same frantic cry.

Don't go, Jesse! Don't leave me, please!

Jesse had heeded the silent call of the girl he loved so much. He had turned, and smiled, and whispered, *I love you, sweet potato.*

And now amazingly Jesse was turning toward her, as if he had heard—and cared.

"Caitlin?"

"Yes?"

"About Risa." The master wordsmith, the man who wrote so lyrically about passion and violence and murder and love, paused . . . and finally shrugged. "There are no words."

Then Jesse Falconer was gone, but his final utterance lingered. Haunted.

There are no words.

But there were words, ones she should have spoken, no matter his response—no matter if his glacial eyes glinted with disdain.

I felt loved. She should have said that, and more. She should have told Jesse what had happened at dawn in Operating Room Two.

I didn't save Risa, Jesse, and neither did Patrick. You saved her, your blood, your will, your love. You, Jesse Falconer, saved that precious little girl.

There were words. And Caitlin spoke them. To Patrick, not Jesse, to the answering machine that picked up at Patrick's Brentwood home.

"It's Caitlin, Patrick. Jesse's leaving tomorrow, so if you want to talk to him, tonight's the night. Jesse told me *everything*, Patrick, what supposedly happened at the lake and the attempted rape of your girlfriend—who I assume was Gabrielle. Jesse could *not* have tried to kill you, Patrick! He *could not*. Do you really believe that he did? And as for what happened with Gabrielle, well, there's a notebook in his home, an unpublished manuscript I think, and it's entitled *Hell Hath No Fury*. Maybe Gabrielle was scorned by Jesse, *scorned* not assaulted. Don't you think that's possible? *I* certainly do, especially given her behavior in the clinic that day. I guess I sound a little impassioned, and maybe this is none of my business, but . . . well, it's too late now, isn't it? I've spoken—recorded—my piece."

Patrick was not at home. He was at the hospital, in the

CICU, waiting for his twin. Visiting hours were over, and even though families with dying loved ones were never sent away, Daniel and Stephanie had been told to go, a gentle yet firm enforcement of the rules not for the patient but her family.

Daniel and Stephanie were exhausted and exhilarated, with ample reason for each. Risa had awakened from anesthesia with a smile, despite the endotracheal tube; and without a flicker of fear, despite that alien intruder in her throat; and without the slightest grimace of pain, despite all the places where the serene landscape of her delicate flesh had been pierced.

The endotracheal tube was removed at noon. Risa smiled, and still there was neither fear nor pain. But every so often her green eyes would search, desperately, urgently, until she remembered: He's nearby, even if I can't see him. He's here, watching over me, like the moon.

Patrick watched Daniel and Stephanie leave. Indeed he bade them good night. Then he began in earnest the wait for his brother.

Jesse would come under cover of darkness and with total disregard for the rules. That was Jesse. Defiant, rebellious, wild—yet loving, protective . . .

Jesse arrived within the hour, so intent on seeing Risa that he was blind to all else. Patrick withdrew into the shadows, unseen yet seeing, and watched as his twin spoke to the sleeping angel.

"I love you, sweet potato," Jesse whispered, not wanting to awaken her, yet hoping his words would entwine themselves in her dreams.

And they were—for Risa was smiling.

"Remember this dream, my little love. Remember that I'm here, loving you, always."

Jesse touched her then, and as with his voice, his years of loving Risa had taught him how to modulate his touch, so that she would feel the comfort, the love, without awakening.

He touched her golden curls, the silken strands no longer damp with disease and fear, and gently, so gently, her rosy cheeks . . . and through the sudden mist that filled his eyes he saw her smile anew.

Then Jesse left.

He had to.

He emerged from Risa's room in a trance, his expression one of immense sadness, immeasurable loss. Patrick followed unseen. He took the stairs, eight flights down, an effortless sprint for a man whose veins were filled with dark, rich blood.

The blood in Jesse's veins was dilute, meager, pale. But that was not, Patrick decided, the reason Jesse took the elevator. His brother's selection was fate not choice. The elevator was there, its doors open, offering Jesse the only thing that mattered—the promise of swift escape.

*T*he fountain was a gift from Timothy Asquith, trivial compared to his donation of the Heart Institute but significant to the many patients and staff who never set foot in the Institute itself.

By day the fountain was illuminated—gilded—by the sun, and with nightfall, colorful floodlights created a treasure trove of jewels, an ever-changing spill of emeralds, rubies, sapphires.

The dancing spray glistened sapphire as Patrick neared the place where his brother's hasty retreat had come to an abrupt halt. It was across that blue, blue haze that the Falconer brothers spoke—at last.

"Hello, Jesse," Patrick murmured to the silhouette beyond the glistening veil.

"I suppose that's a safe distance."

Patrick heard Jesse's anger, saw it, felt it; a savage reminder of that long-ago day: the harsh assertion that when water was involved Patrick dare not get too close to his murderous twin.

Jesse had taken them to Graydon's Lake . . . which was where the Falconer twins needed to be . . . needed to begin.

"Will you tell me about that day, Jesse?"

"You tell me, Patrick."

"I can't. I don't remember."

The fountain changed, suddenly, from lustrous sapphire to shimmering green. It was not the green of Jesse Falconer's eyes. His shade was far darker. But through the curtain of emeralds Patrick saw those dark green eyes, their surprise, and their hope.

"You don't remember? I thought . . . "

"I have amnesia, Jesse, from shortly before my head was struck to when I awakened in the hospital." *So you can tell me anything and I will believe it.*

"But you know what happened. The whole town saw it. And that day, in my jail cell, I told you."

"Tell me again, Jesse," Patrick commanded through a rain of rubies as bright as the blood that had saved his life. And as Patrick saw Jesse's face the blood within soared with joy. Patrick had been prepared to accept whatever lie Jesse chose to tell. But now, but *now* . . . "And this time, Jesse, tell me the truth."

Jesse did not answer at once. Indeed it was only when

the spray was once again sapphire that words found their way from his barren heart to his parched lips.

"It was an *accident*, Patrick. You stood up to take the helm just as I was coming about. You were looking at the waves not at me. You didn't know. And *I* didn't know." After a moment, and with such harshness toward himself, Jesse repeated, "I didn't know—and I didn't forewarn you as I should have."

An accident, an *accident*! Patrick's blood heated and sang; but the joyous chorus did not obscure the anguish he heard. Jesse's anguish.

"It wasn't your fault, Jesse. *I'm* the one who broke the cardinal rule of sailing. *I'm* the one who stood without checking the boom."

Jesse didn't hear. He was aboard *Gemini* reliving those watery moments of terror.

"I tried to help you, Patrick, but you backed away. The blow had stunned you, and yet you seemed certain of your fear of me, of *me*. It was because of our argument the night before, I suppose. When you fell into the lake I followed, and we struggled. You were *fighting* me. The battle stopped when you began to seize. It was a tonic-clonic seizure, I know that now, and you were postictal— breathing in that deep, desperate, gasping way—when the rescue boats arrived. My banishment to Brookfield seemed fair punishment for what I had done, for the reck-lessness that had nearly cost you your life. I didn't know until Gabrielle told me what everyone—including you, she said—really believed."

"But I didn't believe it, Jesse. *I didn't*. Not until I heard it from you."

Jesse still wasn't listening, wasn't hearing. Perhaps he

couldn't until he had confessed to every crime. His confession resumed amid a sparkle of blood-red rubies.

"I'm responsible for the bruises on Gabrielle's arms. I grabbed her and held her, *hard*, until she explained why she called me *Killer*. Then I let her go, shoved her away, never touched her again."

"Even though she wanted you to."

"We'd been together during that month two summers before."

Jesse's voice held apology again, as it had when he explained the life-shattering swing of the boom. But the lust of seventeen-year-old Gabrielle St. John was no more Jesse's fault than was the injury to Patrick's head.

And now it was Patrick's turn for anger. "Why, Jesse? *Why?*"

"Why what?" Jesse asked, startled by the sudden fury.

"Why did you lie to me? Why did you admit to crimes you didn't commit?"

Jesse shrugged behind a galaxy of emeralds. "I was hurt, angry, betrayed. I suppose I wanted to hurt you in return, to make you ache as I ached. A selfish reason, petulant and foolish."

"I think there was another reason," Patrick countered quietly. "One so deep you didn't even know it was there. I think that you were trying to protect me, as you *always* protected me."

"Protect you, Patrick?"

"Sure. You'd given up on yourself. And why wouldn't you? You'd been abandoned by your brother, your parents, your entire town. But maybe you sensed I hadn't truly abandoned you, that I would have defended you still. Maybe you decided such loyalty was not in my best interest. You were a lost cause. To drive me away, *for my sake*, you decided to make me hate you. But it didn't work, Jesse. I hated myself instead, loathed whatever it was within me that had failed you, that had made you want me to die. I hated myself, not you . . . and I never stopped caring."

"How could you *care* about a brother who admitted he'd tried to murder you?"

See, Jesse? I was right. You were trying to protect me, trying—for my sake—to make me no longer care. But it didn't work. Patrick's smile, gentle and wry, glowed through the crimson mist.

"How could *you* care, Jesse, about a brother who accepted your confession of guilt without a whisper of protest—a twin who betrayed you in that most essential way? But you did care, didn't you?"

"Yes." Jesse's whisper was hoarse, raw, husky with hope. "*Yes.*"

Patrick wanted to go to him. His brother. His twin.

But it was too soon. They both needed more time, another cycle at least, another fortune of gemstones cast into the night.

"Do you remember that day?" Patrick asked as the air shimmered as bright, and as true, as the sapphire waters of Graydon's Lake. "Before the accident?"

Jesse answered with a frown, followed by an uncertain shake of his dark black head.

"It was a perfect day, Jesse. The wind was brisk and warm, and the sky and the lake were a brilliant blue."

"This blue," Jesse whispered, beginning to see, beginning to *see*. "This blue."

"Yes." *Come with me, Jesse. Journey with me beyond the pain.* Quietly, reverently, Patrick repeated, "It was a perfect day. But what I remember most is how happy I felt."

"Happy," Jesse echoed, as if *happy* were entirely unfamiliar, a word from a foreign language his brother was teaching him to speak. He pronounced it again, precisely as Patrick had, feeling its shape on his lips, its meaning in his soul. "Happy."

"And safe," Patrick instructed gently.

"And safe."

The Falconer twins were many long graceful strides apart.

But, already, their hearts were one.

And as the sapphire water danced with joy, and in a language that was no longer foreign to either of them, Patrick and Jesse shared an identical thought: happy, and safe, and loved.

And loved.

THIRTY-TWO

WESTWOOD
WEDNESDAY, MAY EIGHTH

*C*aitlin was halfway across
Barrington when she remembered that this was Wednesday, the day on which she would be having tea at Prospero's with Lillith. It didn't feel like Wednesday, or any other day that Caitlin Taylor had ever known. It felt only like the morning after Jesse Falconer had vanished from her life, a dark and heavy morning despite the brilliant rays of the springtime dawn.

Get a grip, Caitlin counseled herself as she did an about-face in the middle of the street. You knew this was the most likely scenario. You *knew* Jesse never promised anything more than a little time in bed.

Caitlin and Jesse had had that time in bed. In passion. Terrific sex, Jesse had quietly proclaimed. Terrific—a nice endorsement from the master . . . but a small consolation for her heart.

I don't need to be consoled, Caitlin reminded herself as she returned to her apartment to retrieve a dress suitable for tea. But maybe, despite what she told me, Lillith will need consolation. I will be there for Lillith, and for my patients, and—

Caitlin's heart raced as she ran toward the phone that had begun ringing just as she inserted her key into the lock. It would be Jesse, calling from the airport to tell her he couldn't board the flight for paradise after all, not without her.

"Hello?"

"It's only me, Caitlin."

"Patrick," she murmured. Then, with enthusiasm, she greeted, "*Hi*. I guess you got my message. Pretty presumptuous I know, but—"

"But you were right."

"You talked to him?"

"All night. In fact I just got your message. I just returned from driving him to the airport."

"So he is leaving."

"Yes, he is. Caitlin?"

"Yes?"

"You're in love with him."

"Did he tell you that?"

"No. You did."

"What can I say, Patrick?" she asked with a flippancy they both knew to be false. "Jesse's a terrific guy." *We had terrific sex*. "I mean, why wouldn't he be, given the gene pool?"

Caitlin heard Patrick sigh, and the solemnity of his voice when he spoke. "If I could wish one thing for my brother it would be you."

"Patrick . . ."

"I mean it, Caitlin."

"Thank you," she said softly, gratefully—even as she

heard, amid Patrick's unreserved endorsement of her, his unspoken reservation about *them*. "But?"

"But I'm not sure I'd wish it for you."

"Jesse is not a murderer, not a rapist. You *know* that, Patrick. Don't you?"

"Yes. I know that. But there's something very solitary about Jesse. There always has been. And there's a sadness, too, a private sorrow that can't be reached, much less cured, even with love. I know because I've tried—and will keep trying."

"You . . . the two of you . . . are close again?"

"The beginning of closeness, thanks to you."

"You'll be talking to him, then?"

"Yes, and visiting him."

"You won't tell Jesse how I feel, will you? Please? You won't tell anyone."

"No, Caitlin, I won't."

"*O*h, my dear, you look so tired. You should have canceled. We can *still* cancel, Caitlin."

Caitlin found a smile for the elegant woman who greeted her at the entrance of Prospero's Pantry.

"I'm fine, Lillith. It's been a long day, that's all. But it's over. My patients are doing well, and I've signed off to one of my partners, and my beeper's been silenced. *You*, by the way, look positively wonderful."

"I *am* wonderful, Caitlin. You didn't really believe that, did you? Despite my assurances you expected some grim hidden agenda."

"I wasn't sure."

"Well, there *isn't* one. Which means, my dear, that you

can go home this minute and go to bed. Maybe I'll escort you just to be sure."

The notion of being tucked in by Lillith Asquith, who was as British as Maggie and about the age Maggie would have been, flooded Caitlin with a wave of emotion.

Finally, if shakily, she replied, "I will go to bed early tonight, Lillith. But right now there's nothing I'd rather do than share a pot of tea with you."

"Tea," Lillith agreed. And in a tone that was marvelously, achingly, maternal, she added, "And scones."

While awaiting the tea and scones Caitlin admired the most recent photographs of Lillith's beautiful grandsons and talked about the boys' father.

"I played telephone tag with Robert today," she said. "Until our secretaries decided to intervene. According to the detailed message mine left me, Robert—and Mr. Asquith—are planning to wander around the Heart Institute tomorrow afternoon."

"They are. Robert has discussed with the medical director the possibility of filming much of *Thief of Hearts* right there. Apparently there are patient areas that aren't always fully occupied and operating rooms that aren't in use at night?"

"Yes, that's right."

"So location filming wouldn't be disruptive to your patients or their care?"

"Not at all." *It would only be disruptive to me, to my heart, if Jesse Falconer were on location, overseeing the filming of his magnificent script, making certain that his heart surgeon heroine is as soft, as feminine and as enchanting, as written.*

"Caitlin? You're frowning. Would you prefer that *Thief* not be filmed at the Institute?"

Caitlin shook her head. "My frown was because of an unrelated thought."

"It seemed related."

Caitlin was a little surprised at Lillith's persistence. But it was such gracious persistence, offered with such concern, that Caitlin heard herself admit, "Well, yes, in a way it was. I was wondering if Jesse will be on the set during the filming. I mean, Graydon Slake."

"We know his name is Jesse, Caitlin. We know all about him. Jesse believed we needed to know *everything* before permitting Gemstone Pictures to invest time and money in *The Snow Lion*."

"Everything," Caitlin echoed. "Jesse told you he was innocent?"

"He didn't have to. And believe me, if Timothy weren't absolutely certain of Jesse's innocence, he would never have let you travel—alone—to Jesse's home. In any event, in answer to your frown, I don't think Jesse will be on the set."

"But will Robert be? It would be nice to see him again."

"Oh yes, Robert will be there every day—as will Timothy."

"Really?"

"We're planning to move to LA. I suppose we already have, at least mentally. All that ties us to London is habit and history—and the fact that Global News is headquartered there. We've decided that habits can be broken, even at our age, and if Timothy and I can make the move, so can Global. It makes no sense for us to be in London when Robert and Faye and our grandsons are in LA."

"You have no other children in London?"

"No. Our entire family is right here." Lillith smiled, took a ladylike sip of tea, and spoke again only after replacing the cup in its saucer. "What about you, Caitlin? Do you have family here? Or is yours as scattered as ours has been?"

"I . . . have no family."

"Oh, Caitlin. My dear, I'm so sorry."

"It's *fine*, Lillith, really. I had a wonderful mother, and we had sixteen wonderful years together. My childhood was very happy, very secure."

"I'm glad." Lillith tilted her head, and frowned.

And Caitlin smiled. "Are you wondering about my father?"

"A presumptuous train of thought, I admit—but yes, that is what I was pondering."

"Well," Caitlin began, suddenly wanting to talk about him, about *them*, about love. She touched her pearls as she spoke. "He and my mother met aboard the *Queen Elizabeth* on a transatlantic voyage from Southampton to New York. He was married, but . . . they fell in love. That's not an *excuse*, just a reason. They both knew their love had no future, only the days and nights at sea, during which I was conceived."

"You don't sound bitter, Caitlin."

"I'm not. My father never knew about me, so I feel neither rejected nor abandoned, and he gave my mother indelibly joyous memories of love. Maybe he didn't really love her. I don't know. But she *believed* that he did. She died believing that. And for that I will be forever grateful to the mysterious Michael."

"His name was Michael?"

"Yes. At least that's what I assume. My mother never

told me his name, but my middle name is Michaela, and since he was the only man in my mother's life *ever*, well, he was Maggie's Michael."

"Maggie."

"Her name was Margaret. But he called her Maggie, *his* Maggie." Caitlin smiled. "I guess if you discount his infidelity, it's pretty romantic."

"Yes it is."

"He was a good man, my mother said. A wonderful man. She said that he, like she, knew their shipboard romance was wrong and felt great guilt about it. She predicted he would return to his wife and remain faithful to her always. I suppose that's a little far-fetched, but it's what she truly believed."

"And maybe it's true. Maybe Maggie's Michael broke his wedding vows just that once, just long enough to create you. No matter what that was a good consequence of his infidelity." Lillith smiled at Caitlin's obvious surprise. "You must know how much you mean to us, Caitlin . . . and since you have no other family you would be more than welcome to become part of ours."

"Oh, Lillith," Caitlin whispered. "Thank you."

THIRTY-THREE

PACIFIC PALISADES
THURSDAY, MAY NINTH

"*I*t's me, Amanda. Patrick."

Amanda's hand curled more tightly around the phone. "Hi."

"Hi. Are you in the midst of another call?"

"No. Smoky and I are outside, playing with whatever is so endlessly intriguing about grass."

Patrick heard the smile in her voice. "May I join the two of you? I know you're on call, but I have something to show you."

He sounded so casual, as if they saw each other every day. But they had not seen each other since that night in the Drawing Room, when Amanda confessed everything to him . . . and Patrick heard every word . . . and wanted her still.

Amanda's grand delusion had begun that night. And despite the shattering epiphany at Ariel's the delusion had managed to flourish, in her heart, in her mind, and over the phone. She and Patrick had talked Monday night, wondrous hours of hello; and Tuesday he had called from the CICU, while waiting for Jesse; and last night, until her call-waiting signaled a patient in need, Patrick had shared with her his reunion with his twin.

With each successive phone call it became ever easier to talk, ever easier to believe, ever easier to *pretend* that they were touching. Amanda clutched the phone, close and tight, and Patrick caressed her, embraced her, with his voice, his words.

But it was pretense, make-believe. Amanda knew that now, as Patrick's wish to see her evoked familiar tremors of fear. Pretense. Folly. Fantasy. Delusion.

"Amanda? May I drop by?"

"Yes." *No.* "Of course."

Of course, Patrick, because it is time for me to end these fantasies of normalcy—and of love.

Amanda was dressed in blue jeans and a cotton tee. Her coppery hair was twined in a single loose braid. She wore no makeup, no shoes, no diamond ring. This was her delusional disguise, attire suitable for a casual evening at home, but from which she could rapidly change should she be required to return to work.

As she waited for Patrick to arrive Amanda felt an almost frantic urge to dash to the house and change into her purple dress with bright blue forget-me-nots; a mad dash to rival Sherry's shard-strewn dash of madness from Ariel's. But Amanda remained where she was, sitting on the grass, watching the antics of her smoky gray kitten in the fading rays of the springtime sun.

She would hear Patrick arrive, the sound of his car, and only when she heard the car door close, only then, would she rise to greet him, to *see* him.

Amanda never heard the car door close. Perhaps it happened so gently, too quietly, for her to hear. Or maybe the thunder of her heart obliterated all else.

Quite suddenly, and without warning, a second kitten appeared on the sun gold grass. The feline visitor was smaller than Smoky, in size not in fluff, and she was bright orange—and incredibly bold.

Smoky had not yet sensed her presence, but the plucky intruder had most definitely spotted him. Indeed she was stalking him. Crouched low to the grass, the baby creature moved with the predatory stealth of all cats, a slow-motion dance of menace and grace.

In truth this small animal did not project much menace. And when Smoky saw the interloper at last, and sprang at her, the kittenish courage promptly vanished. She flew—straight up—into the balmy air, as if both bravery *and* gravity had forsaken her.

Gravity reasserted itself. But all vestiges of stealth seemed gone forever. The kitten arched her fluffy orange back—even fluffier now—and began to prance. It was an anxious dance, but not a disinterested one. With each prancing step, she grew ever more curious.

Softly, not wanting to startle her, Amanda asked, "Who are you, little one?"

"She's Smoky's friend. At least that was my hope."

"Patrick," Amanda whispered, startled herself, by his voice—and by him. He looked wonderful, healthy, *normal*. "You . . ."

"Look a little better? Less terrifying?"

Better, yes. But *far more* terrifying. Patrick had been a skeleton on that night, and she had been a gossamer shell, and in her fantasies—such foolish delusions—everything had been possible.

But now, revealed before her in golden sunlight, was the terrifying truth of Patrick Falconer. He was robustly, powerfully, devastatingly male.

I can't do this. I can't even begin to do this.

Patrick saw her fear. Aching yet smiling he gestured toward the prancing, growling kittens. "I thought it would be nice for Smoky to have a friend to play with when you weren't home. It looks as if Smoky may not agree."

Patrick made his impulse to find a friend for Smoky sound quite casual, and he concealed entirely the immense disappointment he felt. The impulse wasn't impulse at all, and it was far from casual. He had weighed the decision carefully on all its layers.

On the surface it was quite simple. It would be nice for Smoky to have a playmate. But below that surface dwelled other truths. Such companionship was nice for *all* creatures, wasn't it? Including, especially, for *them*?

And there was more, a reminder that although some fears could be conquered alone, others required a partner to be truly vanquished. Lying alone in the darkness—and summoning the phantoms of night—could be a solitary pursuit, as could standing on balconies high above earth, or inhaling the terrifying scents of fire and smoke.

But touching, loving, trusting . . .

There was nothing subtle about the deeper meanings of Patrick's gift, and despite his attempt to portray his decision as a casual one Amanda undoubtedly knew the truth. How could she not when the kitten who was to be Smoky's friend was not only the color of flames but a *she*?

Such obvious metaphors had not been Patrick's intent, but there she was, this kitten, *this* kitten, needing a home, needing love, needing him. She told him so in no uncertain terms, snagging his shirtsleeve with her tiny claws as he started to walk past her cage.

So now I have my own kitten, Patrick thought as he watched the standoff on the grass. It wasn't a troubling notion. Already he was attached to the little creature of flames, as she was to him. She had spent the afternoon on his lap, purring, sleeping, recharging her batteries. And when he and Amanda got together, which they *would*, they'd face the classic dilemma of single parents trying to find harmony between their recalcitrant teenagers.

We can do that, Amanda. We can do anything.

In unison the kittens lunged, clasping each other in a ferocious—yet paradoxical—hug. Their front paws embraced, as if each were clinging to its long-lost love, even as their hind legs kicked, and kicked, and kicked.

"I'd better separate them," Patrick murmured, disappointed at having caused discord where he had hoped to create joy.

The kittens parted before Patrick reached them, but the smoke-and-flames boxers did not return to their separate corners, their own small patches of grass. Smoky chased the intruding kitten instead, and when she was tired of being chased she spun, so abruptly that this time it was the gray fluff that lost all touch with gravity. *She* chased *him* then, and eventually they collided, embracing and hugging and kicking anew.

"Is this usual?" Patrick asked.

"I don't know. I've never had a kitten before Smoky. But most of this behavior is what Smoky does when he plays, even the kicking. He has a toy, which I think he really loves, that he hugs—and kicks—at the same time, and all the time."

"Well," Patrick said. "Maybe we should just watch them for a while."

For a long while, he amended silently as she nodded in

the burnished rays of the setting sun. The fading light gilded her autumnal hair, a halo of pure gold, and her face held the breathtaking serenity of an angel. Her fear, for the moment, was forgotten. Her lavender eyes glowed, and a soft smile touched her lips, and . . . *for a long, long while, Amanda. Perhaps forever*.

The kittens played, and the sun fell, an amber farewell that left in its wake a most spectacular gift, a sky the color of her eyes and shimmering with hope.

It was beneath that pastel sky that the kittens collapsed, finally and together. Curled as one, their tiny limbs entwined so completely, so naturally, that even though before this lavender twilight they had roamed the planet as distinct beings, it seemed as if each had been merely half of a greater—and magnificent—whole.

"It looks so easy," Amanda murmured as she beheld the portrait of peace.

What could he tell her? That touching *was* easy? It was for Patrick. Touching, kissing, entwining, joining. Such intimacies were effortless for him, and absolutely trivial compared to the intimacies of emotion. It was love that had been difficult, impossible, until Amanda.

Difficult. Impossible. For Amanda those words described touching, and being touched. And love itself? No, he thought, he *knew*. Amanda feared only the physical expression of that most intimate of all emotions; had reason to fear it . . . abundant reason to view with terror the most innocent touch.

Patrick could not tell Amanda it would be easy for her. Nor could he tell her that the physical intimacies of love were trivial compared to the emotional ones. Making love would never be trivial for Amanda—and with her, for Patrick, the physical union would be wondrous beyond words. Wondrous. Not trivial.

Never trivial again.

And if making love could not be wondrous for Amanda? If touching was impossible always?

Then so be it. *We have already touched, Amanda, in the most important ways.*

As Patrick looked from the sleeping kittens to Amanda, to tell her that nothing mattered but love, he steeled himself for her fear. But what greeted him was confidence, so bright and glittering at its surface that it precluded so much as a glimpse into the darkness beneath.

And in a voice Patrick had never heard before, Amanda said, "It *is* easy."

She reached to touch him, her hands trembling with fear even as her eyes shone with glittering confidence, artificial confidence—a luminescence as bright, and as surreal, as the twinkling lights of the Las Vegas strip.

"No, Amanda."

Her hands halted in midair, a ballerina's graceful pose, trembling still.

"No?"

"You're counting, aren't you?" *You're filling your mind with numbers so comforting that if you focus just on them you can endure anything—a blackness haunted by monsters . . . or an evening, a lifetime of evenings, in bed with me.* "Aren't you?"

"I . . ." *have to, Patrick, don't you see? It's the only way. It's not that I can't have sex. I can. I have. In fact I'm an expert. If I can just see the numbers during the moments of our life when we touch—just those moments,*

Patrick!—everything else will be fine. "Yes, I am. But Patrick, it's okay."

"*Okay*, Amanda? No, it's not okay. I'm not that kind of man. I'm not Royce, or your foster—"

"I *know* that. It's just that I can't do it any other way. I will never be able to."

Do *it*, sex, terror, humiliation, pain. *It*, not love, not making love, not being loved.

"Maybe that's true."

"It *is* true, Patrick."

His mind filled then, not with twinkling numerals but a shadowed future—Amanda's future if he persisted in insisting that one day they might touch. Such a future held for her the specter of unrelenting pressure: the belief that he was waiting, perhaps in agony, for her to be ready for him . . . and the unremitting worry that he was watching, ever vigilant, lest she begin to count.

It was a future in which Amanda would be imprisoned as surely as if she were locked in a lightless room filled with monsters, a future he would never permit her to endure.

"All right," he conceded softly. "It is true."

"So . . . ?"

Patrick smiled. "So touching won't be part of our life." *Part of our love.* "It's not an essential part, Amanda. Not to me. Not to us."

Patrick was saying they could love each other chastely, and there were no provisos to that promise. Never would he utter the solemn amendment: Of course, Amanda, I would need other women. I'm a man, after all.

Patrick would never say those words, nor would he think them, nor would he act upon them. Patrick was

willing to live his life her way—the way in which her fear
mandated she must live.

"But it's essential to me," she whispered. *We must
touch, Patrick. We must have that normalcy, that wholeness. If not, we will walk together, yet not even hand-in-
hand, into the abyss of my madness.* "Please, Patrick."

"Please what?"

"Let me . . ." *count while you kiss me, touch me, make
love to me. Let me fill my brain with such light, such
color, that I will never, not ever, mistake your passion for
the violence of Royce. Even if your desires are as powerful as*—"Let me go."

I'm not touching you, my lovely Amanda, Patrick answered silently. And I never will. Are you asking me now
to release you from the invisible caresses of my heart?

"Amanda?"

"I can't do this, Patrick. Not any of it. I *can't.*"

Patrick saw her despair, and he sensed her silent plea: I
can't do this, Patrick. Please don't make me try. I was
doing so well, Sherry was doing so well, and now . . .

Now, for her, he must say farewell.

Good-bye, Amanda. Adieu, my love.

THIRTY-FOUR

HEART INSTITUTE
WESTWOOD MEMORIAL HOSPITAL
THURSDAY, MAY NINTH

*C*aitlin sighed, then forced herself to analyze the weighted breath. Fatigue, she decided. And relief that the surgery for which she had emergently scrubbed had gone so well. And sadness, and loss, missing him so much, wishing she had meant more to him, *anything* to him.

All the Jesse Falconer emotions were there. They always would be.

Caitlin drew another breath, calculated and buoyant. She was at the foot of her secret stairway, the passageway from the Institute's operating suites to her office four floors above. For that four-flight ascent she would think only uplifting thoughts. Her patients were doing well, including the little girl who wasn't officially hers. Risa had been transferred to the ward, and soon would be going home, to Bel Air not to Maui—

Caitlin intercepted the thought, but not before a deep ache pierced her soul. Aching still, she banished the thought and focused anew on her self-imposed challenge. She filled her mind with images of other recovering patients, following which she recalled the pleasant memories of tea with Lillith at Prospero's and the prospect of many future rendezvous, a cheerful certainty given that the Asquiths were moving to LA.

Then, a natural segue, Caitlin's thoughts drifted to Robert and Timothy . . . a drift that began to skid perilously close to pain, to the author of *Thief of Hearts*, the greatest thief of all.

Caitlin managed to swerve back on course before spinning out of control. The medical director had officially hosted the Gemstone Pictures location-scouting tour. But the visit had been scheduled late enough in the day that Caitlin might join them should her schedule permit—which in fact it did. Her patients were stable, and she had signed out. For twenty minutes she had wandered with them; twenty minutes during which the attention, Robert's especially, was not on the physical plant, but on her.

Would she be available to consult during the actual filming? he wondered. To make certain that scalpels were held with the authentic blend of delicacy and strength? And that X rays were displayed correctly on viewboxes, their cardiac silhouettes appearing on the right—that is *left*—side?

Robert seemed genuinely eager to recruit her as an active participant in the film, and although less vocal, Timothy Asquith seemed to concur. Caitlin heard herself agreeing to each request. She felt so welcome, so wanted. Then her pager sounded, although she wasn't on call, and in moments she was dashing down this same stairwell to assist with a patient whose opened chest revealed pathology far more advanced than had been anticipated pre-op.

The memory of feeling so welcome propelled Caitlin

up the final flight, and as she emerged from the window-less passageway she was greeted by a sight that seemed a reward for successfully meeting the challenge of four flights of happy thoughts.

"Oh," she whispered as she beheld the lavender sky.

"It's beautiful, isn't it?"

"Oh! Mr. Asquith. I didn't realize you were here."

"I'm sorry. I didn't mean to startle you."

"No, it's fine. You're still here?" Caitlin glanced beyond him, a logical search for his son.

The corridor was empty.

"I'm the only one here," Timothy Asquith said. "Robert left a while ago. There was something I wanted to discuss just with you."

"Oh," Caitlin murmured, uttering the tiny word yet again. Like "nice," *oh* was capable of many meanings. At this moment, and quite eloquently, it conveyed her confusion—and her concern. "I'm sorry if you've been waiting for me all this time."

"I wanted to wait, and I've enjoyed the sunset."

"Oh." *Oh?* "Good. Should we go to my office, or . . ."

"Right here is fine. What I need to show you is in my briefcase."

Timothy Asquith's briefcase lay on the carpeted floor directly across from where she stood, as if he had known she would take the stairs when she finished operating.

The medical director had probably told him. Of course he had. Westwood Memorial's most politic spokesperson would have made certain that the center's most generous benefactor knew that every one of his surprise details, which included the inner stairwell, was very much appreciated. The director had undoubtedly raved about Timothy Asquith's Drawing Room as well, a legitimate rave given that the sanctuary was used, and appreciated, by the entire Heart Institute staff.

A vague yet powerful force compelled Caitlin to stay precisely where she was, bathed in misting shades of purple, rather than joining Timothy Asquith across the corridor. Perhaps it was just reluctance to appear too chummy with the austere Mr. Asquith. Yet it felt more expectant than reluctant, and so overwhelming that she was required to remain where she was, with the wall at her back, for support.

He faced her now, holding a small envelope in his hand. And maybe it was this extraordinary sunset, or maybe the monumental feelings that sang in her veins. Whatever the reason, Caitlin saw him differently. Emotionally.

There *was* emotion on his face, and in the eyes that were so dark, so blue . . . and in this ethereal light the silver in his midnight black hair sparkled like a tiny galaxy of shooting stars.

Then he spoke.

"His name wasn't Michael."

She could not speak, could not breathe, and oh how she needed that wall.

"Michael was his brother."

Caitlin knew about that brother, the one whose death changed the course of his life. She had been named for that beloved brother, not for the man Maggie had loved, not for—

"His name, Caitlin, was Timothy." Emotion clogged his throat and threatened to stall his words. But these words would not be stalled, could not be stilled. He had waited a lifetime to speak them. "Your father's name was Timothy."

Timothy. Timothy.

Timothy.

Caitlin was breathing again, light, joyous breaths of shimmering air. But still she could not speak. And there was more that he—her father, her father—needed to say.

"That night . . . I knew even before I heard your name. You looked, you *look*, so much like her."

"Like Maggie," Caitlin whispered, finding voice, finding words, not for herself . . . but for her mother.

Oh, Mother, if only you could see his expression as I whisper your name—the tenderness, the love. But you *are* seeing this, aren't you, Mother? *Mummy*? I feel you in this lavender mist. *I know you are here.*

"Maggie," he echoed, whispering the love, whispering *to* his love, as if he, too, knew she was here. Emotion threatened again. But he did not succumb to it. Would not succumb. "There you were, my daughter, my *daughter*, about to operate on your nephew."

Timmy is my nephew, and Robert is my brother. Robert, who had been so welcoming this afternoon. Robert, who had created such landsickness in Michael's—Timothy's—wife that she had forsaken their honeymoon cruise.

Caitlin was about to ask, to be certain that Robert knew, that her *brother* knew, but an echo of her own thoughts intervened. Timothy's wife. No longer was she an unknown spouse, a nameless, faceless, forsaken bride. She was . . .

"Lillith."

Pain shadowed Timothy's face. "I didn't know until last night that Lillith knew. But she had known about Maggie all these years. By chance a friend of Lillith's—an acquaintance, really—was also on the ship. She was no one I knew, and in any case Maggie and I were very discreet. At least we tried to be. Until last night I believed we had succeeded. On the rare occasions when we strolled along the open decks we stood safely apart. It was during one of those strolls, and unbeknownst to either of us, that this snapshot was taken."

Timothy Asquith looked down at the envelope in his hand. The photograph was within, but he saw its image of love nonetheless.

"Maggie and I were standing apart from each other, but all the distance in the world could not hide the way we felt. *We* couldn't hide it, it seems, even when we tried. The woman, the supposed friend, could not wait to give this incriminating picture to Lillith."

Lillith, who had kept silent about her breast cancer until the holidays were over. "Who never said a word."

Timothy answered with a slight smile, a loving smile, an acknowledgment that his gracious, patrician wife was far from a pushover.

"Lillith might have said much more than a word, indeed she *would* have, had I not returned to her a changed man. I had learned about love, and I realized that Lillith truly loved me. She always had, even when she was engaged to Michael. Over the next few months, as we anticipated the birth of our son, I fell in love with Lillith. It would not have happened, Caitlin, at least not as soon and certainly not as deeply, had it not been for Maggie. My love for your mother awakened something within me, and because of that, because of Maggie, my love for Lillith is strong, and deep, and true. Lillith has never— again—had any reason to doubt it."

It's just as you said, Mother, just as you knew it would be.

"Lillith recognized you, too, on the night of Timmy's surgery. She hadn't looked at this photograph in years, in decades, but the image of your mother remained clear in her mind. Lillith wasn't sure what to do, or what I was going to do."

And what had Timothy Asquith done? He had built the Heart Institute—for Caitlin; and he had designed a hidden stairway just for her; and a drawing room, a twin perhaps of his drawing room in England . . . a place where in another lifetime father and daughter might have spent hours of happiness before a roaring fire.

Timothy Asquith had also built a fountain. During the day, when Caitlin was at work, its sunlit spray glittered gold. But late at night, from her apartment, Caitlin saw the treasure trove of shimmering gemstones. Her favorite liquid jewel was sapphire, the deep, dark blue of the ocean where her parents had met, had danced, had loved.

But glittering symbols of sparkling blue seas were not enough for Timothy Asquith, nor was the physical transformation of the hospital that was Caitlin's home *into* a home. For home, he knew, was much, much more. Home was *family*.

And what family could Timothy give his daughter? Her surrogate brother Patrick, who had been so aggressively recruited to WMH—at Timothy's clandestine behest—and who was the authentic brother of Jesse, the gifted writer Timothy had come to know and respect— and who, Timothy knew, was tormented by his estrangement from his twin. Timothy Asquith couldn't orchestrate *reconciliation* between the Falconer twins. But he could most certainly arrange *reunion*—a chance encounter, perhaps, during Gemstone Pictures on-location filming of *Thief of Hearts*.

Fate—Patrick's aplasia—had summarily trumped the need for chance. And even had there been no Patrick Falconer, no hope of mending *that* shattered family, Timothy would have chosen Jesse to write *Thief of Hearts*—the gift to Caitlin that was a celebration of her passion, her career . . . and which would permit Timothy to see her, his daughter, again and again.

As he was seeing her, speaking to her, now.

"Lillith realized that I was never going to reveal the truth—that I couldn't without knowing in advance what if anything you knew about me. I didn't know how to go about that," he confessed, a decidedly human—and oddly helpless—confession coming from one of the most powerful men on earth. "If I invited you to tea and started asking you about your parents . . . well, that would have been quite out of character, wouldn't it? It might have confused you, troubled you."

But Lillith could make such discreet inquiries; and she had, Caitlin mused, recalling how seamlessly Lillith had directed the conversation from the Asquith family to hers. Lillith had had a hidden agenda after all.

Hidden, Caitlin realized, even from her husband.

"You didn't know about our tea, its true purpose, until after."

"No. It was only when Lillith returned from Prospero's that I learned she had known about Maggie all along. Lillith made the decision to speak to you on her own—because, Caitlin, she loves us both."

And I love Lillith, Caitlin thought. I love the gracious, lovely woman who offered to tuck me into bed, and insisted that we order scones, and invited me to become part of her family.

"Did Lillith tell you that . . ." *Maggie is dead?*

Caitlin did not finish the question, could not, because it wasn't true.

Maggie was alive, in her heart, in his heart, and in this misting lavender air Caitlin could see her, *see* her, a floating rainbow in the sky.

He's dancing with you, Mother. Then, now, always. Your Michael, your *Timothy*, is dancing with you, loving you . . . always.

It was true. Timothy Asquith was dancing. Caitlin heard the slight breathlessness as he answered her unfinished question.

"As soon as I saw you, discovered you, I learned all that I could learn . . . about both of you."

The enchanted lavender sky was yielding to darkness, to grayness, and it was from that graying twilight that Caitlin heard the full measure of emotion he had been fighting to control.

"Can you ever forgive me?"

"Forgive you?"

"For not being with you, for not taking care of you, both of you. And for not being there to love you when . . ." *she died.*

He could no more say the words than could she. But there were other words that Caitlin needed to say to this man, this father.

"You *were* there, all those years. Even before she told me about you, you were always there, in her heart, and in the way she loved me. You were always there."

"And may I be here now, Caitlin?" he asked, a quaver of love, of hope.

Yes, she thought. *Oh, yes.*

Caitlin's thoughts did not falter, nor did the wishes of her heart. But for several long, gray moments of twilight she was silent, and searching . . . for his name. They had come such a long way, Dr. Taylor and Mr. Asquith, and at last Caitlin understood why she had never called him Timothy.

He was not Timothy, never Timothy, not to her.

Was he Father, then? No. Because this man, this aristocrat steeped in generations of propriety, no longer seemed so formal or austere.

Dad, then? The name by which Robert called him? Yes. That seemed—

"Caitlin?" he repeated softly, hoarsely, fearful of the anguished meaning of the graying silence. "Caitlin? *Caitie?*"

The world changed anew, brightened, glowed. The air was silver not gray, and it shimmered with a magical light.

She would call him Dad. Someday. Tomorrow.

But on this silvery night, as the rainbowed spirits of eternal lovers danced in the shimmering air, there was only one name for this man who loved his daughter, his Caitie, so very much.

"Daddy," she whispered. "*Daddy.*"

THIRTY-FIVE

EMERGENCY ROOM
WESTWOOD MEMORIAL HOSPITAL
THURSDAY, JUNE SIXTH

*C*ode Red signaled fire. Code Blue announced cardiac arrest. Code Green heralded mass disaster.

"Code Green, Emergency Room," Darla, the page operator, proclaimed with admirable calm.

The announcement preempted all other overhead pages, and by entering a brief instruction into her computer Darla simultaneously sounded the pagers of all hospital personnel assigned to the Code Green team on this sunny June day.

Mass disasters could range from trauma—the collapse of a building, the collision of many cars—to food poisoning in an elementary school to employees overcome by unexplained fumes. As a result the Code Green announcement mandated an in-person response from representatives of every discipline. Once the reason for the potentially overwhelming influx of patients had been determined appropriate fine-tuning could be made.

Amanda and Patrick came from opposite directions,

journeys that brought them face-to-face in the final stretch of linoleum that led to the emergency room.

"Patrick."

"Hello, Amanda."

It had been almost a month since they had seen one another. But each was in the other's thoughts. Each lived with a feeling beneath cognition, a deep, piercing, relentless ache. And each imagined words they might someday say, fantasy scenarios in which there was no past, only a magical present and a glorious future.

For a moment, on the shining linoleum, Amanda and Patrick were lost in those fantasies. Was this the chance meeting of which they had dreamed? The reunion that would end forever the emptiness they felt?

No. They shared the same thought as reality intervened—the harsh reality of Amanda and Patrick, of Sherry and Patrick, and whatever disaster had compelled them here.

"Do you know what's coming in?" Amanda asked, logically, of Westwood Memorial's trauma chief.

"Yes." Patrick's expression gave fair warning of the grimness he was about to reveal. "During an assembly at a nearby junior high one of the students opened fire with a semiautomatic weapon."

"Oh, no. Not again. Not *another.*"

"Yes. Another. And it's very bad. There was significant loss of life at the scene, and there are so many living victims that the paramedics are triaging them here, UCLA, and St. John's. Even with that triage we're going to be very busy. We're already calling people in from home."

"If you need me, Patrick . . ." She was Dr. Prentice, and he was Dr. Falconer, and both were focused on the crisis at hand. But her words touched the impossible longing that dwelled within. Amanda saw the ache in his dark blue eyes.

I need you, Amanda.

"I . . ." *can't, Patrick.* "I'd be happy to scrub," Dr. Prentice said, "if you need an extra pair of hands."

"Thanks," Patrick replied as the first—of so many— sirens screeched into the balmy air. "But your hands will be full, Amanda, overwhelmed with family and friends of the injured and dead."

𝓗er name was Evie, and she was only thirteen, and she had refused the advances of a sixteen-year-old boy. Today that boy had become an assassin, and Evie had been among those specifically singled out for death.

Evie was virtually dead when she reached the emergency room. Her long auburn hair was matted with blood, and her skin was the color of ice, and her light blue eyes did not see. The only reason her slender chest rose and fell was because a paramedic provided breaths with an Ambu bag, and blood flowed within her lifeless body only because another paramedic pumped rhythmically on her pale, young chest.

"Doc?" The paramedic looked at Patrick, his expression completing the query in silence. Can we stop the code?

"Let's get her to the OR," Patrick replied.

𝓓id he ask you to get me, Trish?"

"No, Caitlin, he didn't. But it's a gunshot wound to the heart."

"Patrick is a heart surgeon, Trish. He's fully trained in hearts as well as trauma."

"Yes, I know." Trish frowned. "I just think it would be good, best, for you to scrub in. I'm sure the reason Patrick didn't ask for you was because he imagined you'd be tied up with another patient. But things are under control, aren't they?"

"Yes," Caitlin admitted. "They are."

Every teenage victim had been seen, and plans had been formulated. Five, including Evie, had gone directly to the operating room, emergent surgery being their only hope. Six others, all less critically injured, were being admitted, to be stabilized prior to surgery.

None of the teenage patients had become Caitlin's primary responsibility. Those with abdominal wounds went to the general surgeons, and those with chest—but not cardiac—trauma were in the capable hands of the thoracic team, and the one patient with head wounds, the teenage assassin himself, was being cared for by the neurosurgery chief . . . and was not expected to survive.

Caitlin had responded to the Code Green, and had helped wherever she could, lending her years of expertise to the therapeutic decisions that needed to be made. Until the revelation made by Trish in hushed tones and with obvious concern, Caitlin had not known that any of the teenagers had sustained specific injuries to the heart. She hadn't needed to know. Not if Patrick was on the case.

But it was as if Trish's concern was for Patrick, not his patient. Patrick. Caitlin's friend. Who for the past month she had scarcely seen. Just as she had neither seen nor spoken to Amanda. She'd been avoiding them.

We've been avoiding each other.

Caitlin knew that Patrick was well. Cured. But it was

awkward for her to speak with the brother of the man she loved, and who knew of that unreciprocated love, and who had undoubtedly spoken to Jesse during the past month—and who knew that Jesse never asked about her. Caitlin had seen Patrick in passing, in the OR and in the CICU. Both smiled, both waved. But his smile, she thought, seemed sad.

Caitlin had not seen Amanda, not even in passing, until this tragic day. Even now she saw her friend only from a distance, as Amanda ministered to the families of the dead and dying.

Caitlin and Amanda did not tell each other lies.

But we avoid each other, Caitlin mused, when there are truths too painful to share. *Sins of omission.* Something too painful to share is going on with all of us—with Patrick, with Amanda, with me.

Caitlin's loss was obvious: Jesse. And there was that other ache, the deep wound that *could* be healed. Dr. Caitlin Taylor vowed to heal that lingering wound. She *would*. This weekend. Then she would forget her own sadness and focus on her friends.

But if one of those troubled friends needed her now . . .

Caitlin smiled at Trish. "Maybe I'll just wander on over to the OR to see what's going on."

"Good, Caitlin. *Good.*"

It was far from good. The thirteen-year-old girl was dead. It was an outcome that all the surgical talent in the world could not have changed.

Evie's chest was open, still, when Caitlin arrived. Her young heart was broken, shattered beyond repair by the savage assault of leaden missiles. Beyond repair . . . and yet with ferocious fury Patrick had tried.

But pieces of Evie's heart were gone forever, disintegrated entirely by the brutal force. Surely Patrick had known that before he even attempted the repair.

Caitlin gazed wordlessly at the irreparable carnage, the senseless end of hope. At last she looked up, to Patrick, who had yet to acknowledge her presence. And who wouldn't acknowledge it, she realized. He doesn't even know I'm here.

Patrick was staring, too, at the shattered heart, and it was as if his own heart was in desperate need of repair, as if it, too, had been violently shattered.

Caitlin watched Patrick suture closed the pale, young, lifeless chest. He placed the sutures carefully, reverently, as if worried about hurting her even in death.

When the suturing was complete, and there was nothing else he could do for the girl, Dr. Patrick Falconer left the room. Without a word.

Caitlin saw him through the glass.

As soon as he exited the operating suite of death Patrick was approached by his chief resident. He listened attentively to the younger doctor's words, wholly focused on the next patient who might—who did—need his care. There was no time to mourn, to reflect, to grieve. The surgeon was needed again, *now*.

By the time Caitlin looked back at Evie the anesthesiologist had removed the drapes from her body, the tube from her throat, the aquamarine cap from her auburn head. And what Caitlin saw, so white—so serene in death—was a girl who looked hauntingly like Amanda.

"May I help you, Dr. Prentice?"

Amanda turned in the direction of the polite voice, a

little surprised that she would be recognized in the surgical ICU. She had on occasion seen SICU patients. But the last had been months ago, long before Dr. Patrick Falconer arrived.

The nurse who made the polite inquiry had cared for one of those rare consults.

"Actually, Laurel, I was looking for Dr. Falconer. I don't want to interrupt him if he's with a patient."

"He's not. Amazingly, knock wood, our young trauma victims are all relatively stable, tucked in for the night."

It was after midnight, the end of a day that had been an ordeal for so many, a roller coaster of hope, of despair. Evie had died, as had her assailant. But Susannah had survived, had been saved, by Patrick. Just moments after leaving Evie he had performed what everyone considered a "miracle" on Evie's blond-haired, amber-eyed sister.

Amanda had not seen Patrick, had somehow missed seeing him despite the fact that they were caring for the same families, he in the operating room, she in the quiet rooms where families waited and prayed.

At the precise moment that Patrick was speaking to Evie's family—to Susannah's family—Amanda had been in another room, a distant one, offering solace to the parents of the sixteen-year-old boy who had caused such anguish. That son had just died, a revelation that evoked yet another layer of grief—and guilt, more guilt, unspeakable guilt, for at some level the boy's parents felt relief that the son who had become a monster was no longer alive.

With Amanda's gentle and enabling encouragement the boy's parents finally articulated their guilt-laden relief, and by the time Amanda rejoined the family who had lost one daughter—and who, but for Patrick, would have lost two—Dr. Falconer had returned to the operating room. And now?

"Has he gone home, Laurel?"

"No," the SICU nurse replied. "Although he could, *should*. At the moment, however, Patrick is up on the roof, at the helicopter pad. We transferred a patient about thirty minutes ago. The rest of us came back down right away, but he's still there. It's not a place *I* choose to stay even a second longer than I have to, and I'm usually not afraid of heights."

Amanda had been on the roof, years ago, to greet a patient with eclampsia. Her focus had been on her desperately ill patient, but she had been so very aware of where she stood. More fearsome than a balcony, unobstructed by railings of any kind, the roof was rimmed merely by a low, thick wall. One step up . . . and one step down.

The roof had been there, beckoning, challenging. Someday, she had vowed, some faraway day—and in the bright light of day—she would return, and allow her panic to engulf her, then banish it.

This was not a faraway day, and this moonless night was dark and black.

But Patrick was on the roof.

"How do I get there? It's been years . . ."

"You take the middle elevator. But it won't go to the top without a key—which, now that I think about it, is in Patrick's pocket. The option is to walk up. It's just three flights. As soon as you enter the stairwell there's a second door. It's always locked, it locks automatically, but there's a keypad right beside it, so it's just a matter of punching in the code. Shall I give it to you?"

"Yes. Please."

"Okay. It's 1-1-4-7. Why don't I write it down? You'll

need it when you reach the roof as well; otherwise, you'll be trapped inside."

Trapped inside.

"No, you don't need to write it down. I'll remember." *I'm very good with numbers. My fears, you see, have made me an expert.*

*T*he heavy door locked loudly, decisively, behind her, and what lay ahead was more tunnel than stairs.

The rooftop was fifteen flights above the earth, but Amanda might never reach that lofty destination. She might forget the number that would permit her escape, and she would be in this tunnel forever, and sometime during that eternity of darkness the tunnel would catch fire, and now it was a certainty she would forget the exit code, for other numbers were filling her mind, pleading to be counted.

Too long forsaken, the numerals cherished this chance to twinkle *and to be heard*. Why attempt this perilous journey? they wondered. Have you surrendered, at last, to your fears? Have you finally decided to make that fatal step into the depthless abyss?

Don't worry, the glittering sparkles assured her. We'll be there when you fall. We'll illuminate your mind so brightly that even as you descend into darkness you'll be protected . . . until, that is, the bitter end.

Amanda had only one reply for the shimmering, querying numbers. I have to see Patrick.

The knowledge had been with her throughout this day of tragedy, when innocence had been shattered and dreams had been destroyed. Most of today's victims were thirteen, as Amanda herself had been on that day when her own life had spun irrevocably out of her control.

I have to see Patrick. It was a constant chorus, a song of surprising joy amidst the pervasive sadness. The chorus serenaded ever louder, and with ever more insistence, as day became night; and when Dr. Amanda Prentice had finally helped in all the ways she could on this devastating day, she began her search for Patrick.

Sherry began the search. At least, it was most assuredly Sherry who trembled now in the darkness, her mind ablaze with numerals—and with questions. Why? Why? Why?

Because of Patrick.

I have to see Patrick.

The chorus became a mantra, so soothing that her panic seemed to disintegrate in the shadowy air. The numbers vanished, too, or at least relocated. The passageway became quite brilliant, as if her twinkling friends had lined its narrow walls, illuminating this, her final journey.

Amid sparkling air, Amanda began the perilous ascent to dizzying heights and moonless darkness. The stairwell could have been pitch-black, or filled with dense smoke and searing flames, or with every imaginable monster of the night. It would not have mattered. She would have journeyed onward, upward, propelled by a feeling she had never known and could not name . . . a feeling more bright than an infinity of numerals, more immense than a blazing inferno, more soaring than a leap from a towering precipice.

Amanda did not forget the exit code. She knew it by heart. Her heart knew it. Unbidden, and without a falter, her fingers danced across the keypad.

Then she was on the roof, and the night wasn't nearly

as black as she'd imagined. The city glowed below, and the moonless sky twinkled with a galaxy of silver stars—starshine that was enhanced, perhaps, by the zealous glitter of displaced numerals.

Patrick was standing near the ledge, at the ledge. She would not startle him, she knew, a treacherous surprise for one who stood so close to the edge. He wouldn't hear her approaching footsteps, for she was floating, flying, and when she drew close enough to whisper, her voice would be so soft that he wouldn't be startled at all.

But Patrick turned to her before she uttered the slightest sound. Amanda saw his torment, still and dark and deep, as if he had just borne witness to a death.

"Amanda," Patrick whispered, speaking to a ghost—and to an angel. "What are you doing here?"

Here. As he'd stood at the very edge of the building, of eternity, Patrick had tried to feel her terror of heights, the overwhelming urge to leap, to fly; tried—and succeeded enough, more than enough, to be terribly worried that she was standing here now.

But there was no fear on her lovely face.

"Amanda?"

"I came to see you."

"Because?" The query was a little harsh, an edginess evoked by remembrance of the other time Dr. Amanda Prentice had come to him: when he had been a dying patient who might need her psychiatric expertise. Patrick had been dying tonight, too. But it was a trivial death compared to the young lives lost today. Had Amanda heard about his desperate attempt to save Evie? Had someone, perhaps Caitlin, suggested that she offer a little curbside—ledgeside—counseling to the tortured trauma chief? "Because, Amanda?"

I have to see Patrick. The refrain had sung within her throughout the day. But it had been there for the past month, she realized, too soft to be heard, yet unwilling to be silent. *I have to see Patrick.*

Why? Why? Why? the twinkling numerals had queried.

Amanda had not truly answered that query, could not, and then a nameless feeling had compelled her forward, upward, to him. And now, standing before him, she knew the answer at last.

It came in a whisper of joy.

"Because I need you, Patrick. Because I *love* you."

"Oh, Amanda."

"I . . ." *must touch you.*

The thought was so shocking, so wondrous, that it stole her voice. But Amanda needed no words. Her delicate hands were abundantly eloquent as they reached to touch his beloved face. There was no hesitation in their journey, not even as they passed through that invisible barrier, that once impenetrable shield.

Then she was touching Patrick, *touching* Patrick. Amanda felt the coolness, and the roughness, of his unshaven cheeks, and her fingertips gently caressed the darkness beneath his dark blue eyes.

Amanda saw those loving eyes, alight with wonder, and with worry.

Touching is difficult for Sherry, she had told him, had warned him. But being touched is impossible.

Patrick's hands were at his sides, clenched, restless, powerful, imprisoned.

"Touch me, Patrick."

"Amanda . . ."

"Please."

She watched his fists unfurl, and it seemed as if his lean, gifted fingers were trembling.

They *were* trembling. She felt the astonishing fluttering as he touched her, touched *her*, as if she were the most perishable creature on earth.

Am I so perishable? she wondered. Will even this cherishing caress, as delicate as a whispered kiss, evoke remembered terror and the brilliance of a thousand twinkling lights?

She saw those questions, that worry, in his loving blue eyes, and for several moments both were still, breath held, touching, waiting . . .

But the numerals had a new home, amid the stars in the heavens, and her mind filled only with images of him. Images of love. Amanda believed she had been flying before, but she hadn't been, not really, not until this moment. Now she flew, now she soared, over the treacherous abyss—to him.

"Hold me, Patrick. Hold me tight."

Hold me, Patrick. Kiss me, Patrick. Love me, Patrick.

Throughout the starlit night of love, of loving, Patrick heard those words, whispered on breaths of joy, and he saw them in her shimmering lavender eyes, aglow with wonder, and he felt them in her brave, willing, fearless touch.

Patrick embraced her joyous words, as he embraced his intoxicating angel, in his arms . . . and in his heart.

THIRTY-SIX

*T*he anatomic hole in Risa's heart had been repaired. But there was another hole, dark and deep. Until that invisible gap had been closed, the operation could not truly be deemed a success.

Dr. Caitlin Taylor was going to repair that languishing defect. This weekend. The operation would be both delicate and aggressive, a battle of wits and will with a formidable foe.

Caitlin possessed a most powerful weapon—the truth—a defense for which, quite obviously, her opponent had absolutely no regard.

I will prevail, Caitlin vowed. I will. I must.

She stood at her bedroom window, mesmerized by the fountain of glittering gems, drawing strength from the celebration of light and color—and from the remembered magic of the blue, blue sea. Both parents were with her, as Maggie had promised they would always be, and both would be journeying into battle with her this weekend.

Caitlin might have asked her father to actually accompany her. He would have, in a heartbeat, and arguably the sheer power—the sheer influence—of Timothy Asquith might accomplish in an instant what hours of her own persuasion could not.

But Caitlin had not asked for her father's help. It was essential that she do this on her own . . . and in the most significant ways, Timothy and Maggie would be standing right beside her.

The doorbell sounded, distant, melodic, and fifteen minutes ahead of schedule.

Her taxi had arrived, and that was fine. She was ready. She had, perhaps, been ready for this operation, waiting for it, all her life.

She opened the door decisively, then whispered her surprise. "Jesse."

"Hello, Caitlin," he greeted softly.

Too softly, too gently, too tenderly. Wariness sharpened Caitlin's voice. "You're staring."

"Sorry. It's just that you look"—*so beautiful, so hurt, so brave*—"tired. Sad."

So do you. Tired, sad, and ravaged: a man who has lost everything there is to lose. "I'm fine, Jesse."

"Well. Good. May I come in?"

No! "Of course."

He stepped inside, and she stepped away, a retreat which required stepping around her garment bag.

"You're going somewhere."

"Yes."

"Where?"

She shrugged. "Business trip."

"A short one. You're on call as of eight Sunday morning."

It was true. And she ached, how she ached, that he had bothered to check. What had he hoped for the next thirty-

six hours? More time with her in bed? A *nice* weekend of
chemistry, of passion, of terrific sex?

"It's a short trip. I'll be assisting with a difficult case."

It was almost the truth, Jesse decided. Or maybe
Caitlin was just getting better at telling lies. Maybe she
had learned that destructive talent from him.

Jesse took the plane ticket from her hand, and as he
saw her apprehension, he wondered if she had been planning to fly to Maui—if she was going to arrive at his
doorstep and issue a courageous challenge. It was more
than sex, wasn't it, Jesse? *Wasn't* it?

But Caitlin was not planning to journey *to* him but *for*
him. The red-eye to D.C. tonight, the red-eye return tomorrow. "You're going to see Gabrielle."

The statement was soft, astonished, and his eyes glittered with what looked like, looked like, love. But Caitlin
knew to mistrust her reading of the dark green flames.

She answered as a surgeon. "Yes, I am, for my patient,
for Risa. She needs to see you, Jesse, and it's just a matter of convincing Daniel of the truth. Patrick can tell him
what really happened at Graydon's Lake, and Gabrielle
can tell him what really happened that night in the cottage, and—"

"Caitlin." His voice was intimate, stunningly raw, the
same voice with which he had whispered her name on
that gold-and-ebony night when they had loved. "You're
doing this for me, too, aren't you? For me perhaps most
of all—even though I've hurt you."

"You haven't . . ." she faltered, unable to utter the lie—
and not needing to, for the doorbell chimed.

Her ride had arrived, a situation Jesse dispensed with
swiftly. "She won't be going after all," he told the cab dri-

ver as he extracted from his wallet an amount that far exceeded the fare to LAX. "Thank you for your time."

When the cabby was gone, Jesse turned once again to Caitlin, and encountered sheer defiance.

Not one tropical diamond spilled from her raven black hair. But she was the enchanting temptress who had come to him in a raging storm, Venus rising from an ocean of raindrops, her sea blue eyes glistening with courage. She had come, on that stormy night, determined to save Patrick's life.

And now she was determined to save his.

"I *am* going to see Gabrielle. If you like, we can see her together. You can tell her about *Hell Hath No Fury*, that you'll have it published if she doesn't rescind her false accusations against you."

"*Hell Hath No Fury* will never be published, nor should it be. I wrote it in prison, Caitlin, and it's a fairly graphic—and disturbing—chronicle of every fantasy I had about revenge against Gabrielle."

"All of which she deserved."

"No one deserves what I wrote. In any event, there's no point in confronting Gabrielle. She'll never recant. She can't afford to. Rape has become her *cause célèbre*, and it may just be her ticket to the White House."

"Based on a lie."

"A lie that has helped many true victims of rape. Thanks to Gabrielle the world is a little safer for women. For Risa."

"But Risa *needs* you, Jesse, and you . . ."

"Need Risa," he admitted quietly. "But my need is far greater than hers. Daniel is a loving father, and Stephanie is a wonderful mother, and it's important for Risa to be with Holly. She'll be fine."

"And what about you?"

"I'll survive." A faint yet infinitely sexy smile touched his ravaged face, and there was such harsh longing, such aching desire. "Maybe."

"Maybe?" she echoed, barely.

His smile vanished, and in the starkness, his longing—and his desire—became even more intense.

"I've missed you, Caitlin."

"I've missed you, too."

"All my life."

"Jesse . . ."

"I didn't want to leave you, never wanted to leave. But I believed it was best for you if I did. I lied about what we had, what you meant to me, because I thought it would make it easier for you. I've learned that such calculated cruelty doesn't always work. Patrick should have loathed me. Instead he blamed himself, as if the fault lay with him not with me. There's nothing wrong with Patrick . . . just as there is nothing wrong with you." A shadow of fury crossed his face; fury with himself for hurting her. "But you decided there was, didn't you? You concluded, somehow, that you weren't *enough* for me."

"You could have anyone, Jesse."

Her words evoked amazement. But from the deep green darkness began to glow a most dazzling light, a most glittering fire. "But I don't *want* anyone."

"You don't?"

"You know I don't. I want you, Caitlin. *You.* In bed, out of bed, always. I love you. *I love you.*"

Love you. Love you. Throughout the night, as an infinity of gemstones danced in the distance, Jesse showed Caitlin his love, his need, the passion that existed only and always for her. Their loving before had been limned in ebony and gold. But on this night there were no shadows, no darkness. There was only golden wonder, gilded joy.

"I would have come back sooner," Jesse whispered. "I *should* have."

Caitlin lay in his arms, so safe in the shepherd's sanctuary, the lion's lair. She felt his tautness, his fierceness, as he spoke, and swiftly, gently reassured, "You came back at just the right time."

Jesse's lips caressed her love-tangled hair. "Well, I was delayed by the arrival of Mrs. Lion."

Caitlin smiled against his chest. "She's there? And they're married already?"

"Happily married."

"Did you officiate at the ceremony?"

"No. Nor did I observe it. It's a private matter, between lion and lioness. It turns out that lions marry the first time they make love."

Caitlin looked up, and because she felt so confident, offered a gentle tease. "You would have been married a few times."

"No," Jesse countered softly, without a trace of a tease. His expression was fierce, solemn, with love. "I would have been married only once, Caitlin, only to you. I have never made love—made love—with anyone else."

THIRTY-SEVEN

"*I* was wrong," he told her on her wedding day.

Her wedding day, and his.

"Wrong, Patrick?"

"I told you there was a solitude about Jesse, a private sorrow that could never be reached. But I was wrong, Caitlin. His sadness, his aloneness, are gone . . . because of you."

"Oh! Patrick, I—"

"Don't argue with me future little sister-*in-law*," he commanded.

"Well . . ."

Patrick smiled. "*Well.*"

That conversation had begun their journey down the winding road from Jesse's clifftop estate, and now they were on their way back up, their mission accomplished.

It was a mission from which Jesse had been excluded, a prohibition that had proved no easy feat. When Patrick told Jesse that he and Caitlin and Amanda were going to run some last-minute prenuptial errands, Jesse had immediately offered to drive. He knew the twists and turns of his road, he said, and even though the morning sun was shining brightly, it would be safer with him at the wheel.

No, Patrick had countered so casually that the surprise was not revealed. Neither, however, was Jesse deterred.

It was Amanda who saved the day, deciding not to accompany Caitlin and Patrick after all, and asking her polite host to remain behind, too, for mugs of Kona coffee and a flower-by-flower tour of his garden.

Later, Amanda would reveal what a pacing, restless tour of tropical blossoms it had been, how anxious Jesse was, how he seemed to be listening for something beyond the rustling of palm fronds and the sweet songs of a thousand birds.

Patrick and Caitlin had taken Jesse's whisper-quiet car, and they knew how to electronically open his whisper-quiet security gate.

Still, Jesse heard them return.

Jesse was walking down the stairs when the car door opened . . . and then she was running up the teal green stone, and he was running down to meet her . . . and then she flew into his arms, her golden curls dancing in sunlight.

"Risa," he whispered, hugging her, too tightly, he feared. "*Risa*."

She didn't look too tightly hugged, nor did she seem fearful of losing him when he relinquished his embrace and knelt down to meet her sparkling eyes.

"*Hi*, sweet potato," she greeted. Her smile, so radiant, so Risa, wavered slightly as her bright green eyes detected a mist in his. Jesse blinked the mist away, forced it back into his overflowing heart, and the Risa radiance was fully restored. "You need a flower girl, don't you?"

"Yes, I do."

"Well, here I am!" She curtsied extravagantly, then became thoughtful. "We get to see each other again, Jesse, if you want to."

"You know I want to."

"Me too. And it's going to be easy, because you'll be in LA *a lot* with Caitlin. But . . . could there still be times when I could come here?"

"Of course," he whispered.

"And could I bring Holly?"

"Yes, as long as . . ." Jesse looked to Caitlin, to Patrick, both of whom smiled their reply.

Yes, Jesse, it's all right with Daniel. They would tell him, later, how they—Caitlin and Amanda and Patrick—had told Daniel the truth. Amanda had been prepared to offer a personal testimonial, more compelling than her professional one could ever have been: her abiding belief that Jesse was incapable of the violence against women for which he had been imprisoned. But Amanda had not needed to utter a word.

They would tell Jesse, later, how easily Daniel had been convinced, how he *wanted* to believe in the man Risa loved so much, how Daniel knew that it was best for Risa to have Jesse in her life.

Jesse was in Risa's life now, and always.

And now Risa was asking Jesse if her room existed still in his crescent-shaped home—of course it did—and now she was wondering if he would show her the snowy white lions and the orange-and-yellow koi she had known by name and . . .

Before they wandered off, hand in hand, father and daughter, Jesse looked above her golden head, and this time he made no attempt to conceal the emotion in his eyes.

Jesse Falconer gazed at the loved ones who had given him this gift, this miracle, and whispered, "Thank you."

*T*hey were married at sunset in paradise, the Falconer twins and the women they loved.

The little girl for whom *The Snow Lion* had been written carried a bountiful bouquet of gardenias and roses. And the little boy who had loved *The Snow Lion* and shown it to his grandfather carried all four wedding rings, the bands of gold engraved with promises of endless love.

Their wedding vows were witnessed by a magenta sky, and the entire Asquith clan, and Daniel and Stephanie and Holly. They were family, all of them, bonded wondrously, joyously, and forever.

The snow lions witnessed the ceremony as well, so hidden within their forest that Jesse alone knew they were there. But later that night, after midnight, as Jesse and his bride stood in the perfumed garden, the lions appeared.

Caitlin did not see them at once, so mesmerized was she by the moonlit sea, that moonlit magic, and the glass bungalow afire with starshine and moonglow.

But when she looked beyond the brilliant diamond and far above the magical sea, there the lions stood, on their moonscape, shimmering silver as moonbeams caressed their fleecy coats.

Lion and lioness. Bridegroom and bride. Husband and wife.

The *other* Mr. and Mrs. Lion, Caitlin mused as she

turned to Jesse, a soft twirl within his embracing arms . . . but a dizzying one.

"Caitlin?" he asked, worried, loving, holding her with the strong and gentle promise that he would never let her fall.

"I . . . we're . . ."

"Pregnant?"

"Yes," she whispered, dizzy anew.

This magnificent whirling, however, had nothing to do with their daughter, their Maggie, who was dancing and twirling deep within. This dizziness was caused by him, by moonlit eyes ablaze with joy.

"Oh, Caitlin. *Caitlin*."

They danced, a slow dance beneath the silvery moon, a waltz of wonder, of love . . . and a promise that with wonder, with love, their hearts, all hearts, would be endangered no more.

More
Katherine Stone!

Please turn this page
for an
excerpt from
her exciting new novel,

Island of Dreams

available in hardcover
August 2000.

*G*iselle Trouveau's Carmel Valley studio was a meadow's walk from her Carmel Valley home. The studio was the larger of the two structures. Much larger. And not merely because the artist needed space in which to gather molten glass from flaming fire and twirl it, spin it, gentle it into shape.

Giselle's studio was where she spent most of her life. Chose to. Wanted to.

Loved to.

Giselle's melting furnace could have come from Murano, where glass had been crafted for a thousand years. So too from the Venetian isle her blowpipes, her mavers, her recipes for colors pure and true. And, as Italian glassmakers had done for centuries, Giselle kept a pan of pasta water simmering on the stove.

There were no windows in Giselle's studio, or clocks, or computers, or phones, or fax—no way to discern dawn from dusk, night from day, winter from spring.

Giselle slept in her studio when she worked, and soaked her weary muscles in its bath. And when an inner chime inevitably sounded? A signal that it was time to emerge from her volcanic cocoon?

With a sense of interest, she would. Interest. But not urgency. Not on a personal level at least. Giselle was ever mindful of the tragedies that befell strangers. Mourned for them.

But no private crises would be awaiting her. She had no family. No lovers. No tight-knit circle of friends. No circle at all.

There would be no professional crises, either. There didn't exist, in her view, authentic emergencies when it came to selling art.

Whenever she had pieces to sell, Giselle simply made a local call, to the Ocean Crest Gallery, where, from the first, her creations had been welcomed as if she were an established sculptress and not an utter unknown.

Giselle sold exclusively with Ocean Crest still. Exclusively, and around the world. And as for the commissioned pieces she was asked to do? The architectural installations for homes, opera houses, palaces, hotels? She created such installations for Pierce Rourke only.

Pierce. Who'd left a phone message, she discovered when she emerged from her studio on this

February day. She'd been working for a week. It was noon, FOX News informed her. Thursday. The nineteenth.

The nineteenth. The day, the date, of destiny for her.

Of love.

Pierce's message, her only one, had been left on Saturday night, Valentine's night, at 12:22 A.M.

At 1:22 A.M. his time.

She'd told him years ago that he could call her anytime. If she wasn't home, she advised him without apology, it might be days before she checked her messages and returned his call.

There'd been many such times. A days-old, week-old message from Pierce. But never, she thought, one that had actually been left in the middle of the night.

The Carillon Square and Commons project was in its final stages, this message revealed. The Commons would be a lake, Pierce said, not a park after all.

It would be frozen, the Carillon lake, for iceskating, that gliding gaiety, year-round. There'd be a lake within the lake, an island of water at its westernmost tip. It was there, in the watery island within the sea of ice, that Pierce would place the glass fountain she would make.

He wanted violets, like the ones that bloomed on her chandelier gift to the school. And rising from the center of the bouquet, he wanted a skater. She would spin, Pierce said, and dance and twirl as she reached for the moon.

Fountain and skater both would twirl, he added. Separately and together.

Giselle listened to Pierce's message twice, confirming on the second pass her surprising impression from the first. Not only had Pierce been precise about what he wanted, but he'd sounded unyielding as well.

It wasn't that Pierce never voiced opinions about the glass installations she made to complement his designs. Of course he did. Often. Just as without the slightest hesitation, and within moments of seeing it, she'd said of his Island, *Venice*.

But from the beginning of their collaboration, the architectural art had been his and the glass art had been hers.

True, the collaboration existed only because of Pierce. The celebrated architect had called her out of the blue. His first Wind Chimes Hotel, the Denver one, was nearing completion, and he needed a chime for its lobby.

He hadn't even been thinking glass. But when his Alta Vista search for "wind+chime" found a chime of cherry blossoms on the Ocean Crest Gallery web page . . .

He would install two Giselle Trouveau wind chimes, he decided, when he saw the photograph.

A forty-foot fall of petals for the hotel, a twenty-foot one for the Towers. The individual blossoms would need to be commensurately enlarged, of course. Massive. Heavy. Huge.

No, Giselle had told him. Without telling him why. She worked alone. Had to. In her private world of glass and flames.

She'd make life-size cherry blossoms for him only. Yes, thousands upon thousands, fluttering, chiming, in every shade of pink, of rose, of orchid, of pearl.

She'd been unyielding, she'd had no choice, and the famously uncompromising architect had quite amiably acquiesced.

Over the years Pierce had pushed her to create pieces she'd never believed she could. He needed a fountain, he'd tell her, or a statue, a mural, a floor-to-ceiling sconce.

Giselle had created those sculptures—massive, heavy, huge—as if crafting an immense jigsaw puzzle, piece by tiny glassy piece, sealed as seamlessly by fire as if she'd had the help, as many glass artists did, of a strong and many-handed team.

Pierce would usually specify the category of installation he'd like her to do. Chandelier, fountain, statue, vase. But sometimes, when the project was architecturally the way he wanted it to be, he'd simply say, "Your turn, Giselle."

The Carillon project was, apparently, the way

Pierce wanted it—would be, once the lake was made. And Pierce's vision of *her* finishing touch for *his* lake of ice was magnificent.

But still . . .

Pierce answered her call on the sixth ring. Giselle had decided, as the rings went unanswered, that there was significant background noise in Denver, with Pierce, on this Thursday afternoon. The sound of creating from scratch a brand-new lake.

But when he answered, she heard only silence. The sound, knowing Pierce, of water in his already carved lake turning to ice.

"The skater's a she?" Giselle greeted. And hearing more silence, "Pierce? It's Giselle."

"I know. Sorry. I guess I'm a little distracted. The answer is yes. The skater's a she."

"And she's skating alone?

So alone, Pierce thought. As she was. His lovely skater. Twirling with grace in *her* private dream, with courage in her private hell, and reaching for the moon for as long as she could. "Yes. Alone."

Pierce was not, Giselle realized, going to insert even an "I was thinking" into his vision, *his mandate*, of what he wanted from her. Much less an "assuming you agree." And there wasn't the slightest chance of hearing "It's entirely your call."

It wasn't her call. Not entirely. *Not at all.*

"Pierce?"

"Yes?"

"What's wrong?"

"Wrong?"

"You sound . . ." *lost*. *Sad*. Lost? Sad? *Pierce*? "Something."

"I am, Giselle." The quiet confession came with a sigh. "Something."

Something personal, she realized. Private. Which, despite the artistic closeness they shared, their relationship was not. Had never been.

But this was February 19, the anniversary for her of love.

And gratitude.

"Here's *something*," she said softly. "Thank you, Pierce Rourke. I've never really said that before."

"Giselle? You've said it at least a million times, all unnecessary, and that was just in the first year."

"And you've said it, too—incredibly, unnecessarily, at least a million times."

"At which point we agreed to impose a permanent moratorium on such exchanges."

"We did. Yes. But this is a personal thank-you, Pierce. And it's long overdue. So thank you, belatedly, for putting up with me. It can't have been easy. I know. I lived with it. Me. I know very well how difficult I was. Brittle. Hostile. Wary. Tense."

"Unhappy," he said quietly.

"That's a gracious way of putting it."

"That's all I ever thought, Giselle. That you were

unhappy. Were. Past tense, as of your return-to-Venice trip. True?"

"True. My newfound happiness must have been a relief for you."

"For you."

"Yes. Definitely. Pierce? Is there anything I can do? For the 'something,' whatever it is?"

"Make me a skater, Giselle. Make her dance with joy."

KATHERINE STONE is the author of thirteen novels, including *Bed of Roses*, *Imagine Love*, *Pearl Moon*, and *Twins*. A physician who now writes full time, Katherine Stone lives with her husband, novelist Jack Chase, in the Pacific Northwest. Please visit her at her website at www.katherinestone.com.

He had never been in love—
until her . . .

He is the stunning and powerful Chase Tessier, the gray-eyed maestro who creates the poetry that is Tessier wine.

And she had never been loved at all—
until him . . .

She is Cassandra Winter, the fierce yet fragile waif who joyfully gave him her heart during an enchanted summer of newborn grapes and moonlit roses. But she left him. Cold.

And now . . .

Cassandra lies in the ICU. Ravaged. Broken. And needing Chase. Yet there is such danger on this journey to rainbows and love. For the perilous secrets of the past beckon and haunt—as does the vicious assailant who vows to destroy Cassandra still.

BED OF ROSES
(0-446-60-622-7, $6.99 U.S., $8.99 Can.)

AVAILABLE EVERYWHERE FROM WARNER BOOKS

The place is Manhattan. The time is midnight. And beneath the glittering diamond lights passion sizzles . . . and danger smolders.

HE CHASES KILLERS . . .

Lucas Hunter has stalked murderers all over the world with his sixth sense for evil. Now his quarry is the cunning madman known as "Lady Killer," the monster whose victims are always glamorous, beautiful women who were at one time intimately close to Lucas Hunter.

SHE CHASES DREAMS . . .

Galen Chandler's career is on the edge—again. Indeed, the soon-to-be ex-anchorwoman is on the verge of leaving Manhattan when the madman calls her—to use her to lure Lucas Hunter out to play.

TWO STRANGERS IN THE CITY

Theirs is an unlikely alliance, the glacial-eyed hunter and the woman-on-the-run. Theirs is an even unlikelier love. But with this killer on the loose, they are locked in a perilous game of life and death, where ice can turn to fire . . .

HOME AT LAST
(0-446-60-677-4, $6.99 U.S., $8.99 Can.)

AVAILABLE EVERYWHERE FROM WARNER BOOKS

FOR HIM, LOVE WAS A NIGHTMARE

Haunted by memories of a Christmas Eve inferno, trauma surgeon Jace Colton guards his solitude as fiercely and as passionately as he tends to the desperately ill who need his care.

FOR HER, IT IS AN AWAKENING

Julia Anne Hayley's memories are lovely, not haunting, a billowy cocoon in which she has hidden from life, from living, far too long. But now her cherished sister is gone, and at last she must dare to fly . . .

NOW THEY BOTH NEED A MIRACLE

They have six days, six nights, in London. Their time together is like a snowflake; delicate and perfect, it cannot last. Jace must leave to help the victims of a terrible war. And when tragedy strikes anew, Julia and Jace must hope for the magic that comes only on . . .

A MIDNIGHT CLEAR
(0-446-60-678-2, $6.99 U.S., $9.99 Can.)